THE SCOTLAND PROJECT

A MATHIEU JAMES THRILLER

MATTHEW FULTS

THM

Ten Hut Media
tenhutmedia.com

ISBN: 978-1-96400-720-5 (Paperback)

Always remember to forget the things that make you sad.

PROLOGUE

Late December
Wrexham, Wales

Standing in the kitchen with the phone receiver to his ear, a tall, dark man listened intently to the caller. A glass door led outside to a patio, a pane leaked soft blue light from the empty night sky. On the stove, a kettle simmered atop a blue natural gas flame. In the next room, a television glowed, throwing a white hue across an empty space.

The tall, dark man shifted his weight on his feet, still listening closely. He had missed the first call to the old-school land line in this bland home near the corner of Fenwick Drive and Bryn Grove. The impatient caller had dialed back once more, and he'd rushed in from the patio, where he'd been sucking a tobacco stick, watching the orange heat grow hotter beyond the tip of his nose, and taking in the sting of smoke and the ecstasy of nicotine.

He'd assumed it was a wrong number. No one called this phone. Few had the number.

When it rang immediately and again, his gut had told him to answer. He'd set the cigarette on the concrete patio and gone inside, pulling the receiver from the wall and placing it to his left ear. He said nothing. The voice on the other end did the talking.

"Hello, my son. This is your father. It's time to wake up. We have a new project developing in Edinburgh. I will see you soon."

Click.

The caller terminated the line. The man stood for a moment, still holding the receiver to his ear, replaying the message in his head.

The intensity of light from the television in the next room waned softer, as if it were gasping for air, before exploding in a technicolor dream, and then died softly, until the room was barely lit. Outside, a car drove past, the rumble of its tires audible on the broken asphalt.

The man put the receiver back on the wall and placed his right hand over his heart. He was calm, at peace with the message delivered. He gathered his keys from the kitchen table and headed back out to the patio. He locked the door handle before closing it from the outside and bent over to grab his cigarette, which was still alive but barely. He placed it on his lips and sucked hard, igniting the tiny tobacco engine into an afterburner, its orange glow widening, the burn accelerating, the intake both noxious and exhilarating.

It was darker now, and the man walked around the side of the house and into the street. He paused for a moment, taking in the normalcy. A man walking his dog. Windows aglow with a warm yellow tint, offering a look at lives being lived inside. A wife and mother bustling in the kitchen. Children chasing each other, their euphoric shrieks penetrating the glass, softly adding to the ambient soundtrack of the neighborhood.

In the distance, he could hear a siren wail. A train whistle pierced the air. Faintly, he could make out the distant drum beats and sing-song chants of the crowd at the local football stadium.

Snapping back to reality, the man fumbled with his keys until he found the proper one to unlock the gray panel van parked on the curb. He pulled himself inside, adjusting his hips until he sat squarely and comfortably in the seat.

He exhaled as he inserted the key, put his foot on the accelerator, and turned over the ignition. The engine sputtered and cranked itself to life as he fed it petrol by tapping his foot down a couple of times, watching the RPM meter spike and fall, spike and fall. He then reached for the light knob and pulled it toward him. Twin yellow beams lit the street in front of him. He cranked down the transmission to drive, and pulled away from his home, down the street, where a high school lay in the shadows, and a trail of exhaust followed him as water dripped from the tail pipe.

The tall, dark man calmly navigated the roads and side streets of the industrial town. He continued to work on his tobacco stick, turning to blow smoke out the cracked window as he bounced wildly in his seat, the suspension of this rig long worn by potholed pavement and cobblestone alleys.

In just under ten minutes, he was on the outskirts of town, where warehouses mixed with auto shops and lumber yards. He turned right into an alley lined with trash bins, power poles, and the silhouettes of stone and brick buildings. The tires bounced on the cobblestones as the van crawled forward. The man jiggled in his seat, then flicked the filter of his cigarette out the cracked window. He had burned it to the core, and it bounced and tumbled aimlessly, offering a single spark from a stray piece of tobacco.

Halfway down the alley, he killed the lights on the van and pulled up to a white barn door, framed by stone masonry and a single tin light that was centered overhead. The light was off, meaning the crew was inside. He put the van in Park and turned off the engine. The man leaned back in the seat, closed his eyes and put his head back, his face now pointed toward the heavens. He grimaced. Not from pain. From emotion. He let out a long sigh before placing both hands on his face, then moving them away, keeping them in front of him, as if offering a prayer.

Seconds later, he entered the building through the barn door. Inside, a television sat on a countertop, offering a football match for entertainment. Three men sat around a folding table, watching the game while they played cards. A pot of tea sat next to an ashtray. A half-eaten sandwich rested on a chipped plate. A loaded Beretta PX4 pistol lay silent; its presence said enough.

As the man made his way around the table toward the television, his eyes wandered to the back of the building. Plastic barrels. Jerry cans of petrol. Bags of fertilizer. Pallets of nitrogen. A wooden crate filled with automatic weapons, military-grade C4 explosives, and two rocket propelled grenade launchers.

Indeed, this den of iniquity was ready for evil.

He reached the television and switched it off, turning to face the three men seated at the table. Idle chatter went silent as they locked eyes on their leader.

"My brothers, the call from above has finally come. It's time for us to perform our mission and deliver glory to god."

The three men rose from the table silently, eyes locked on the man who had just changed their lives forever.

"My brothers," he continued, "go home and get your affairs in order. Martyrdom awaits. We must be prepared for battle in twenty-four hours." The tall, dark man was fidgeting with the ring on his finger as he delivered the news. He took in a deep breath and offered praise to his god. "Allahu Akbar."

The three men returned the praise in unison.

"Allahu Akbar."

1

Joshua Tree, California
Present Day

The embers glowed red and orange, matching the painted horizon to the west of his campsite. The flames licked skyward, shooting glowing bullets toward the stratus. As the smoke curled and ascended, he tilted his head back, took a sip from his cup and emptied his mind, taking in the evening light show from above.

When the stars came out in the desert, it was like a Michelangelo painting. Brilliant. Confusing. Breathtaking in its detail and grandeur.

Mathieu James came to places like this—the desert near Joshua Tree, the alpine lakes near Mammoth—when he needed to clear his mind. It was part of the beauty of living in California. Nature's diversity was a short drive from Los Angeles.

There were plenty of things wrong with California these days—the cost of housing, taxes, homelessness—but few states could alter your mind in the same way.

As a young boy, he would eagerly look forward to trips like this with his father or even his grandfather. Every young boy finds heaven on earth when his imagination is nurtured by nature. Now, as an adult, James came to places like Joshua Tree to figure shit out.

Women.

Work.

Why the Detroit Lions are suddenly good.

Here he could try to solve the world's problems—and his own.

He'd arrived at this patch of dirt the day prior, driving his slightly abused Land Rover LR4 out from L.A. The trip took about two hours, traffic included, and he came later in the day to avoid the normal crawl that is the 10 freeway.

In the back of his truck, his weekend gear was always packed and ready. Four Front Runner Cubs loaded with a tent he never used, kitchen stock, sleeping bag and a solar-powered generator. A Yeti cooler was ready to serve refreshments, and a Grayman Tactical rigid molle board was strapped to the back of the passenger seat for the purpose of keeping his toys and tools organized and at the ready.

If nothing else, Mathieu James liked things in order.

A rare tropical storm earlier in the summer had brought havoc to the desert, with rivers of rain gouging the landscape, ripping roads, and redrawing what was navigable. It was a wonder he'd found this place in the darkness. The road into camp was buckled, and deep veins carved through the landscape, shaped by the same forces of nature that make the desert so inhospitable in summer.

As the senior investigative reporter at the *International Herald Tribune*, James found himself working on a variety of stories involving global intrigue. Somali pirates and their thirst for merchant ships. South American cartels and their obsession with the American dollar (and client). Wall Street sharks and the rise and fall of capitalism. Saudi weapons dealers.

With so much happening in the world, journalists see themselves as the town crier, eager to bring eyeballs to the next grievance. James had just finished his Wall Street piece, which resulted in the heads of two major investment banks testifying before the Senate. In the end, even single individuals can manipulate markets. All they need is money and inside information.

Here, though, where that red-orange painting on the horizon was turning shades of blue, yellow, and white, James found solace.

As he sat fireside in his canvas-and-wood chair, the Yeti tumbler in his left hand felt light. On the concrete picnic table thoughtfully and artfully placed by the National Park Service, his JBL Flip4 filled the night air with the smooth southern tones of Cody Jinks. He rose and walked toward the truck to put Tito's and ice into his cup.

This is the life, he thought, as he returned to his seat, hedging a smile.

And then, in the right pocket of his climbing pants, his phone vibrated. He didn't even need to look. It was Frank Murphy, his editor at the *IHT*. He was the only one who knew which number would reach James on this night.

He reached into his pocket and pulled out his iPhone. The facial recognition avatar smiled at him, and he made a goofy, pissed-off face back. Siri wasn't playing; she delivered a "Face not recognized" message and ordered him to enter his passcode.

Annoyed, he did so, punching the screen with his index finger while holding one eye shut. The combination of a roaring fire pit and the bright LCD screen temporarily blinded him.

"Where are you?" Frank Murphy inquired.

"None of your business."

"Are you in L.A.?"

"Fuck off, Frank."

"Mathieu, we're in business. We need to talk."

"You might be in business," James replied cheekily. "But I am out of the office."

"Maybe a good idea if you get back in the office—or at least get back to the real world," Frank said.

"Why's that?" James replied.

"The Scotland Project," Murphy whispered.

James pulled his phone from his ear and looked at it.

Did he just say that?

"Shit," James said to no one.

The Scotland Project.

Time suspended his thoughts, leaving a vacuum of silence between James and his editor. Finally, he offered just this.

"I'll call you tomorrow."

James held down the buttons on both sides of the phone required to shut it down. He swiped right and pushed the devil back into his right pocket. The Bluetooth speaker offered an awkward digital squawk, indicating it was disconnected.

He tilted his head back against the top of the chair, staring at the smorgasbord of stars above. The fire crackled and snapped. Aside from that, his breathing, and the swishing of ice in his tumbler, the night was dead quiet.

"Shit," he whispered, exhaling slowly. He took another pull from his cup and closed his eyes. He wasn't ready to go there yet. Maybe not ever. But time waits for no man.

He closed his eyes and pictured his parents, Harold and Margaret. His mind went adrift, and a draft of sleep caught him cold.

Thirty minutes later he awoke, tumbler empty but still in his left hand and a mild chill crawling under his clothes. The fire now just embers.

He grabbed his folding shovel from the molle panel in the truck and worked the fire pit until it was done. He then slipped off his boots, tucked them into the wheel well, and climbed into the back of the LR4, smiling to himself at the cozy confines of his sleeping pad and bag. He slid in, pulling the hood of the bag up over his head, and was out in less than a minute.

2

Joshua Tree, California

Blue hour arrived with soft light bleeding through the tinted windows of the truck. James had slept well with a little help from his friend Tito. He rolled onto his back and rubbed his eyes, yawning and tasting the cotton-mouthed fruit of a night that drank well.

He kicked off the sleeping bag and reached for the keys tucked into the side door bin. Unlocking the Land Rover, he climbed out the rear passenger door and grabbed his boots.

As light rays streaked across the dry mountain peaks, James fired up the propane stove, grabbed the collapsible kettle and filled it with water. He set it on the flame and moved to the other side of the table. Inside the food bin, he grabbed a bag of Seattle's Best No. 5, the coffee press and slipped two filters from the packet.

As he walked over to his chair, he grabbed his phone from his right pocket and pressed the power button. James sat and watched the sun rise as his phone grabbed a network signal and retrieved his emails and texts from the ether. Desert sunrises are pretty magical.

His phone began to buzz incessantly. James stood and walked over to inspect the low rumble in the kettle. The water was beginning to boil, but not quite ready. He made busy work cleaning up the campsite and placing items back in the Front Runner Cubbies.

There was no way he was looking at his messages before he had a tumbler of coffee at the ready.

The metal stove began to rattle under the force of the boiling water. James walked back to the table, grabbed the coffee and the press and scooped grounds into the bottom, shaking the container to spread them evenly over the filter. He placed the container on top of the tumbler—there's one for every occasion and this particular one is red—and grabbed the kettle by the tiny black foldable handles and poured carefully.

The steaming water made a trickling sound on the stainless-steel interior. The grounds began to rise and float. He grabbed a spoon and stirred, mixing the grinds slowly until they sank in the water. He grabbed the press and inserted it, pushing downward with deliberate caution. He could feel the air escaping the sides. This little gadget was ingenious.

With a final push he could feel the press meet the coffee grounds at the bottom. His tumbler was full, and he removed the device, set it on the table and snapped the spill-proof lid onto the Yeti. Setting the tumbler down, a small chimney of steam rose through the sipper.

Back in his chair, he opened his phone and found sixteen messages from Frank Murphy at the top of the queue. Flicking his thumb upward he scrolled through more texts. The usual suspects —friends, his tennis buddies, Taylor. He smiled, thinking of her dimple and innocent doe eyes. He went past a few more, stopped quickly and scrolled back up. *Alyssa. Haven't heard from you in a while,* he thought.

He clicked open her message.

Grandma is sick.

It didn't need to say more. James knew what she meant.

Hitting the back button, he scrolled to the top and opened the messages from Frank, starting at the bottom of a thread that had begun while James was sleeping and finished an hour ago. *Does that guy ever sleep?*

Murphy was often at his desk by 07:00. He worked in a small bureau for the *International Herald Tribune*—whose main offices were in Paris—managing the North American stable of writers and correspondents. A 33-

year veteran of the newspaper industry, he was known as a lifer. The news business consumed his hours.

His wife had left him more than a decade ago, complaining that she thought she was marrying a man, not a rotten lifestyle. In his way, Murphy had shrugged his shoulders, kissed her on the cheek, and said in his finest Boston accent, "Go find that man. I gotta go to work."

In Murphy's messages, James found a few notes about story deadlines, an awards banquet, a link to a *New York Times* piece that was now covering a story James broke five months prior. *Blah blah blah.* Then, at the top of his most recent missive, a simple message that put a knot in James's stomach.

"Our Swiss friend is in town. He wants to meet."

James wrote back instantly.

"Where is he?"

He put his phone down, awaiting Frank Murphy's reply. The Swiss friend he referenced was Francois Thies, a private banker who had worked for Switzerland Bank & Trust for at least twenty years. It was one of several Swiss banks that long held the cash secrets of the world's wealthiest and most notorious. When banking regulators forced the Swiss to stop using numbered accounts and rat on their customers (countries like the US wanted to collect taxes), SBT refused and dared governments of the world to challenge them in court.

Few would.

James's phone buzzed again. He picked it up and rolled his eyes.

"Scottsdale," the message read.

Of course, Thies was in Scottsdale. There were two things the man was known to love: golf and leggy blondes in yoga pants.

For that, Scottsdale was a hedonist's delight.

3

Highway 62
Mojave Desert, California

James decided to drive to Scottsdale to see Thies. He wanted to go home to his loft in Downtown Los Angeles, but he was just four hours from the desert fashion and golfing mecca. Had he driven back to L.A., changed and headed to LAX for a flight to Phoenix, rented a car...well, it would have taken longer.

He took the back roads, past 29 Palms and the mystery world that ensued, as he found beauty in the desolation, where a drought-stricken landscape intersects with cobalt blue skies on the horizon.

What is Thies doing in the States? And what does he portend to know?

Because of his position, Thies was able to peek behind the curtain of not just the wealthy, but the criminal underworld that used Swiss banks to launder money. He had enough information to be dangerous, and James had used him in the past to connect the dots on some major stories, including the international gun runners ring he reported on previously.

Thies got very little from being an informant except to feel important. He was never named in stories. He thought of himself as a player in games of international intrigue. He got to travel to exotic and far-off locales, sampling the local wares, while his wife and two children stayed in Zurich.

———————

Before long, James pointed the truck south on 247, which links up with Interstate 10 at Desert Center. This World War II relic town is barely standing, but it once served as home to US troops trained by General Patton for tank deployments in places like Africa and Southern Italy.

Now, amid the random home-on-wheels and a blossoming solar farm, there was nothing but asphalt and empty skies. James put his foot down, making the 395 horsepower engine roar and the supercharger whine as he hit 100 miles per hour. He smiled to himself before backing off to a modest 92.

Soon, he was on the 10 going east. In a little more than three hours he'd reach the outskirts of Phoenix.

4

Scottsdale, Arizona

Mathieu James wheeled the Land Rover into the Westin Kierland, a high-end hotel in North Scottsdale known for its golf course, lazy river pool, and proximity to world-class shopping and dining. He pulled up to the valet, exited the truck and tossed the 20-something the keys.

He pivoted quickly and grabbed his Filson Ranger backpack from the back seat. It held clean clothes, his laptop, and some toiletries.

Still smelling of woodsmoke and with Mojave dirt under his fingernails, he strode inside and was pleased to find the front desk void of people, save a pretty brunette. Her dark skin, bouncy curls, fake lashes and heavy eye shadow told James she grew up in Arizona but likely had a family tree that very recently crossed the border. Maybe her parents. Or grandparents, perhaps.

This was always a little bit judgy on James's part, but he liked to play this game with himself. As a writer, everyone he met was a character in their own story. He enjoyed rounding out the sketches.

"Good afternoon, checking in?" she asked.

"Yes, thank you," James replied.

"Credit card and ID please. Welcome to the Westin Kierland," she said. "Have you been with us before?"

James was staring at her left breast, where her nameplate read Yvette.

"Hi Yvette. No, not my first time here. Although this is my first time meeting you. Have you worked here long?"

Nothing wrong with some mild flirting, James thought.

"About eight months," Yvette replied.

"Nice," James said.

"Thank you for being a Gold member with us, Mr. James. I have you on an upper floor, away from the elevator. Is that still your preference?"

"Yes indeed."

"Great! How many keys would you like?"

"One please."

"Very well, one key, wifi password is inside here, and elevators are just down the hall to your right. The bar opens at eleven, our fine dining establishment opens at five and you may call the concierge to book any spa services. Please enjoy your stay."

"Thank you," James said. "I will." He smiled at Yvette and looked her in the eyes as he accepted his room key and sauntered toward the elevators, wondering if the young woman noticed how dirty he was.

Room 613 had a king bed and a golf course view. He slung his pack off his shoulder and onto the bed. He unbuckled the strap, opened the flap, and reached for his toiletries bag. He marched into the shower and cranked it hard to the right.

As the water turned from warm to hot, steam poured over the glass and began to fog the mirror. James stepped out of the bathroom, closed the door to keep the steam inside and began to undress. Boots were kicked off, climbing pants unzipped and kicked onto the bed, performance tee pulled over his head with one hand and tossed aside and finally crew length wool socks flipped into a corner.

He walked naked back to the bathroom, pausing to look at his profile in the full-length mirror. He shrugged, neither pleased nor displeased with what he saw. Inside the bathroom, the steam from the scalding hot water created a sauna effect. He reached inside the shower, turned the hot water down a bit and waited for the adjustment, checking periodically with the back of his hand.

Satisfied, he stepped inside and let the water therapy wash over his 6-foot-1 frame, matting his curly brown hair. He stood with his back to the shower head, hands clasped behind him, and closed his eyes.

What does Thies know? Is this really about The Scotland Project?

Twenty minutes later James stepped out of the bathroom with a towel wrapped around his waist. He was still wet, a combination of the moisture from all the steam and maybe a little sweat that had aided his recovery and cleansed him of the Mojave dirt. He inspected his fingernails—clean—and wiped his forehead with the back of his hand.

He grabbed a pair of Lucky Brand jeans and a Poncho short-sleeve button-down shirt. He realized he had no clean underwear, so commando it was. James ran a comb through his hair, wedged his feet into some Combat Flip Flops, grabbed his phone and his room key and headed for the lobby bar.

His goal? Set a meeting with Thies for the morning, so he could get back to L.A. tomorrow night.

James preferred a bar seat—always at the end on a corner and with a mirror to the front and a clear exit strategy. Old habits die hard. He hadn't found himself in trouble in some time, but when it happens once, you can damn well bet it will happen again.

He learned this lesson the hard way during his time in Ranger Regiment. He wasn't some SEAL-team reject or special operator. He worked in communications, helping downrange units stay in contact with command. His time in the Army taught him a lot of things, but the biggest lesson was always to be prepared. For anything. All the time.

James never saw combat himself, but he was the link between those who did and the brass charged with keeping the mission safe. He heard many things over radios, satellite phones, and in-person at unit debriefs fueled by cans of beer and a single bottle of whiskey passed around.

He'd joined the military because his father served in the Air Force and his grandfather served in the Army. With his parents gone, he surmised the GI Bill would be a smart way to pay for college and see the world. Like many his age, he didn't expect America's global war on terror to be entering its second decade when he enlisted.

But there he was, serving in war time just like his daddy and granddaddy.

The preferred seat at the bar became habit when he and some buddies were on a NATO training op in Amsterdam. They hit the red-light district one night looking to blow off some steam. They had found this dive bar with live music, and the four of them were standing at the bar, backs to the door, watching the band, laughing and giving zero fucks about the outside world.

A group of neo-Nazi dickheads had walked in, buzzed on Holland's finest and probably some cocaine. Heads fully shaved, denim jackets with sleeves rolled up revealing swastika tattoos —they definitely wanted to look the part.

The bouncers were trying to get them to leave without making a scene, but they were intent on being the jackasses they were. Two of the skinheads took on two of the bouncers and the other three went straight for Mathieu and his friends.

They never saw it coming. James took a barstool to the back, his buddy Nick took a beer bottle to his head, and Tommy and Fitz had wheeled around just in time to avoid sucker punches before unleashing some version of hell on the bogies.

When it was all said and done, the bar was shattered and empty, the police had arrived and were questioning witnesses, two skinheads were knocked out, lying face down on the floor. Another had a 225-pound bartender with a rugby nose sitting on him. The rest had run away.

A lesson had been learned. Don't turn your back to the door.

"What can I get ya?" asked the bartender.

"Stella, please."

"Sounds great, coming right up. Would you like to see a menu?"

"Not now," James replied. "Thank you though. Just the beer."

"You got it."

The bartender, with slicked black hair, thick black eyebrows, and a palette of brown skin, pulled a chalice off the shelf, inspected its cleanliness, placed it under the tap at an angle and gently pulled on the draught. The glass filled with a golden hue of goodness and a creamy foam top, which the bartender leveled with one of those fancy European butter-knife-looking tools meant to tame an unruly head of beer.

He grabbed a napkin, placed it on the bar and put the chalice on top.

"Cheers!" said the barkeep.

"Cheers," James replied.

He took a sip, lifted his phone from the bar top, and opened his text messages.

"Welcome to the desert, my friend," he typed to Thies. "It's your pal Mathieu. I'm in town. Let's meet at Buzz, 09:30 tomorrow."

He set the phone down, took another sip of beer and glanced sideways when his phone pinged.

Thies liked the message with a thumbs up.

James turned in early and woke just the same. He managed to get thirty minutes in the hotel fitness center before grabbing a protein drink and heading to his room. He called down for the valet to bring the truck around and showered quickly.

He worked his wet skin into those Lucky Brand jeans and pulled on a black v-neck t-shirt. In the truck, he had a nice hat—a flat-brim rustic fedora—and a pair of aviators.

He grabbed his backpack, which also had his MacBook Air tucked inside, and headed for the lobby. He was tempted to grab a coffee but decided to wait. He didn't need the shakes when he sat down with Thies.

James stood outside in the morning glow, the sun warming his skin and squinting his eyes. The desert always smelled good in a way most wouldn't know unless they'd been there.

The valet pulled the dusty Rover up to the door and jumped out.

"Keys are inside, sir."

James handed him a $5 and climbed in. On the passenger seat was the fedora, which he put on while checking himself in the sun-visor mirror. He then grabbed his aviators, slid them onto his face, and wheeled out of the Westin.

Buzz was just down the street at the main Kierland shopping area. No more than a half mile or so. It was tucked away on the north side, around the corner from Anthropologie. With plenty of parking behind the glitzy storefronts, he parked away from others and walked maybe fifty yards to the shop. It was a simple cafe, serving coffees, breakfast, and various pastries. He glanced around at the patrons, looking for Thies.

Three men in golf shirts, barking into AirPods at separate tables. A woman and a toddler, who was enjoying a danish. A young couple, mesmerized not by each other but their phones.

No sign of Thies.

He walked to the counter and ordered an Americano. The girl—no woman working the register was razor thin, probably 20 something, and caked in makeup. Paper-straight hair and fake lashes—*are these a thing now?* She was cute, but in a weird way. Her vibe said woman, but her appearance screamed 12-year-old playing dress up.

"I'll have that right away for you," she said with a big smile and perfect teeth.

James grabbed the coffee from the counter, offered a "thank you" and turned to scan the room. Still no sign of Thies.

Patio tables were set up outside on the sidewalk. It was November and the weather was near perfect in Scottsdale this time of year. He picked a table off to the side, where he could see both left and right down the street.

He sat, grabbed his phone from his right pocket, and checked for messages. Nothing new yet. As he set down his coffee and reached inside his backpack to pull out his laptop, a familiar voice called his name.

"Good morning, Mr. James," Thies said with a mild French accent.

"Good morning, Mr. Thies," James replied, standing and accepting a hand in friendship.

Game on.

5

Scottsdale, Arizona

Francois Thies was a relatively small man—maybe 5-foot-8—and a bit doughy. He had thick, dark hair combed to the side, a beard that wasn't well trimmed, and he favored sweater vests over golf shirts. Paired with khaki pants and some Italian loafers he looked straight out of Central Casting for a white Swiss-French banker.

A gentle breeze encouraged the palm trees to sway, and the sun warmed the pavement. The two men shook hands, and James made a modest gesture.

"Can I get you something?" he asked. "Coffee? A breakfast sandwich?"

"I'll take an espresso," Thies replied.

"Very well," James said. "Have a seat and I'll be back shortly."

As he stepped in line, James glanced at his Stirling Timepieces Durrant dive watch, an emerging British brand started by an active-duty soldier. It was 09:37 and he was hoping to get back to the hotel, check out, and be on his way back to L.A. later that afternoon.

He placed the order and turned to watch Thies while he was waiting. At 55, Thies must have felt like he was in his prime. He was sitting on the patio, making conversation with every hot soccer mom and trophy wife that strolled past. Oblivious, it seemed, to his wife and two kids back in Zurich.

James returned with the tiny espresso cup and set it in front of Thies.

"Merci," Thies said.

James nodded.

"So what's new, Francois? What brings you to America this time?"

"Do I need an excuse, Mathieu? It's never a bad time to come to the enemy of the world."

"I suppose not."

"In fact, I'm looking at bringing new clients into the fund."

"Yeah, which fund is that? The International Assholes Investment Club?" James sniped, knowing Thies would be offended but not show it.

In fact, Thies laughed softly, stirring his espresso with his tiny spoon.

"I see you haven't lost your American humor, Mathieu."

"Humor is universal, my friend. Americans don't have a lock on it. In fact, our British and Canadian friends are funnier than fuck."

"True, Mathieu. True."

James looked to his right, at nothing in particular. Then his left. The shopping center was awakening. Mostly women walking briskly. A few retired couples power walking. Inside, the three men in golf shirts were still expressing themselves verbally via Bluetooth. Everyone could hear. No one cared.

"Francois, I understand you have some information for me."

"Yes, I do, Mathieu. Always quick to the point with you."

"Sorry, Francois. As much as I'd love to talk world politics with you, I need to get back to L.A."

"Yes, of course. Someone waiting for you there, yes?" Francois smiled, pulling his tiny cup to his mouth and slurping the rich espresso blend.

James smiled back and made a circling gesture with his right hand. *Let's get on with it.*

Francois was a decent enough person. The kind you could grab a drink with in Zurich and not regret it. But he also fancied himself a player, someone who catered to people with money. They weren't all *bad* people, but some were, and this was where the line got blurred with people like Francois. Was he in that business because he liked to live on the edge, or was someone holding something over him and he had no choice?

Hard to say, James thought.

"So, Mathieu, you once asked me to let you know if we ever had new money come into the fund that seemed dubious."

"And...?"

"We have someone new."

"How deep?"

"Two million Euros at the moment."

"They've invested in your fund?"

"Yes, but they have an intermediary. Royal Bank of Scotland. RBS is a stand-up bank. They don't play with the baddies, which is the first thing that grabbed my attention."

James leaned back in his chair and ran his fingers through his hair. He exhaled, looked skyward, and then quickly leaned into the table toward Thies.

"What's the origin of the funds? Can you trace it?"

"Oui, Mathieu. Oui. But this is not easy. It comes from RBS."

"But don't you need to know *who* is sending you that money?"

"No, not really, that's not what we're about. Remember, we are about discretion."

"Okay, you're about discretion but you wanted me to know this. Why?" James smirked.

"Something feels off. We are vetting. You know me, Mathieu. Never kiss and tell."

"Of course, Francois. Always."

James paused.

"Our mutual friend, Frank Murphy, led me to believe this may have something to do with London in 2005?"

"It might," Thies answered. "There's something that feels familiar. Call it a tone in the language."

"That's super vague," James said, pausing. "Okay then, let me know when the money is actually sent?"

"Of course, Mathieu."

"Great. WhatsApp or Proton only. Understand?"

"Oui."

James stood. "Nice to see you, Francois. Enjoy the weather."

"I'll be enjoying something," Thies laughed, eyes locked on another leggy blonde.

"Don't change, Francois. Ciao."

"Ciao, Mathieu."

James climbed into the Land Rover, placed his foot on the brake, and hit start. The engine roared to life. He sat for a minute, staring blankly at the palm trees.

Who could this investor be?

And where were they from?

The point of anyone using Thies was anonymity.

They don't want to get caught.

Fuck. James ran his hand through his hair and then clutched the steering wheel.

So much to do...

Grandma is sick. I need to call Alyssa.

And Taylor. I haven't seen her in a week. That dimple and those eyes.

He smiled to himself.

Time to go home.

6

Langley, Virginia

Alyssa Stevens briskly walked down the corridor, one long stride after another. Head up, eyes straight ahead, encrypted phone in one hand, and her notebook in another. Her black pants suit was meticulously tailored, showing her strength, length, and femininity. Her black hair, long with big curls and healthy shine, cascaded over her shoulders. She possessed a beauty and an athletic posture that made men envious.

Stevens held a dual role at the Agency. She was both a handler for a few Non Official Cover operatives and an analyst, tracking money tied to terror cells in the United Kingdom. With its open-doors immigration policy, the UK had long been a hotspot for sleeper cells—cicadas—for those wishing to hide in a multi-cultural land. However, with MI5 handling domestic and MI6 working the world with its CIA and Five Eyes counterparts, the US intelligence community left home soil to its most important ally.

Of course, the caveat there was always "until it becomes our business."

A number of events over the years in the UK had caught Langley's attention, but none more so than 7/7.

The July 7, 2005, terrorist bombings on the London transportation system brought hate and death to Western Europe. Four years after the US experienced 9/11, London found itself in the crosshairs. One fact rattled everyone: The bombers were homegrown. Three were from Leeds, where they had a bomb-making factory. The morning of the attack they left Leeds, joined the fourth bomber in Luton, boarded a train to London's King's Cross station, and split up.

Twenty minutes later, the coordinated attacks began. Three trains and a bus were victimized by these terrorists, who used backpacks filled with 10 pounds of explosives. The 4 bombers died, along with 52 innocent civilians. More than 700 were injured.

Prime Minister Tony Blair told a worried nation that "there is no hope in terrorism."

Yet a country had been terrorized.

In the end, the UK needed to reconcile that four of its own citizens had been radicalized.

Further, there were rumors that a fifth bomber—possibly a foreign operative or mastermind with Al Qaeda connections—may have been involved. This was never proven, but some at MI6 and the CIA didn't discount the theory entirely.

Stevens, now 36, had been a track and field standout at the University of Florida, where she was a medium-distance star, earning All SEC honors in the 400m and 4x100m relay. CIA recruiters often scour college campuses, looking for a specific fit both academically and physically. The recruiters saw Stevens as a potential field agent, but she wasn't interested.

She was too close with her parents, both of whom were still alive and living in Detroit. Although an only child, she had an extended family of cousins that were just like siblings. She settled for an opportunity at Langley. This way, she didn't have to travel or live overseas and was relatively close enough to visit her parents when she had time.

Trouble was, she had little time. The Agency is known for working people raw. The world doesn't stop spinning, and the threats never decrease. In fact, in a post-9/11 world, with so many resources poured into foreign and domestic intelligence, the threat vector grew exponentially. It wasn't that a rash of new threats were popping up globally. With more resources, the Agency knew about them.

As she reached the end of the corridor, her phone rang. She looked at the screen, which read *MJ IHT*. It was James.

"Stevens," Alyssa answered.

"Good morning, or I guess good afternoon on the East Coast," James replied. "How's Grandma doing?"

"The doctors are worried. I have a report I can send you."

"Of course," James said. "I'd like to see it. I hope she's going to be okay."

"I'm not sure. This sounds like it could be serious."

"Interesting."

"Yes."

"Okay, please send me the report and I'll get back to you."

"Will do."

"Bye."

"Goodbye."

James hit the red "end" button on the Land Rover's touchscreen. He was just west of Phoenix, near the growing suburb of Buckeye. Los Angeles was over four hours in front of him. Way too much time to wonder what was in Grandma's report.

He also couldn't dismiss the timing of Stevens' message and Thies being in the States. Little doubt these two were related.

But how?

Four years prior, James and Stevens had crossed paths in an unexpected way. He was working on a story for the *International Herald Tribune* about

Colombian cartels using the coffee trade as a way to launder money. They were allegedly buying interests in roasting companies across South America. James, through an anonymous tip, was told this was just a front. Rather than being responsible business owners, the cartels were paying the roasters to transport cocaine with their coffee shipments.

Naturally, this was part of an effort to gain more coke business in the United States, the world's No. 1 user of illicit drugs.

As James was working the story, he relied on an anonymous tipster to steer him in the right direction. Sometimes that worked, sometimes not. And while he didn't know who this person was, it turned out the tips were more often true.

As the story developed, he learned that it wasn't just the Drug Enforcement Agency that wanted to stop more cocaine shipments from coming into the country. The CIA was looking at the origins of the money. They had reason to believe it was flowing into the cartels from Africa. But the source of the money wasn't clear. Who had an interest in funding cartel operations and what were they getting out of it?

Alyssa Stevens was an up-and-coming analyst on the Africa desk at the time. She also didn't always follow protocol. As James's stories appeared weekly in the *IHT* with new information, she quickly realized he might have better sources than the Agency. He always seemed one step ahead of what they knew.

How, though?

When the fourth story was published and James wrote that he had seen a wire receipt from a shell corporation in Liberia to a bank account in Bogota, Stevens was furious. *How could a fucking reporter know this before us?*

Stevens, being Stevens, called the *IHT* tip line and left a message for James. Her message simply said, "Your source is burning you. If you want to know how, text this number."

Reporters are suckers for this, and James was no different. Like anyone, reporters don't want to be wrong, and they want the story the right way. Well, most reporters do, anyway.

James did a Google hit on the number and nothing came up. He texted it anyway.

"This is Mathieu James."

Two minutes later, a reply.

"I have information for you. Can we meet in person?"

"I need more information about you. I don't just meet random people who claim they have information on cartels and African financiers."

"I'll tell you everything when we meet. To make you feel comfortable, I'll come to you. Earthbar on Wilshire. Thursday. 10:45."

James hit the Google search engine again and discovered that Earthbar was adjacent to the Czech consulate and the FBI field office in Los Angeles. It's a juice bar frequented by flexing feds fueling their morning workouts. And with a consulate adjacent, there's always intelligence operatives lurking in the shadows. The US counters that with its own counter-intelligence operations. It's literally spy vs. spy.

No way a bad actor puts themselves in that orbit.

Unless they're nuts.

Stevens boarded a government jet at 05:00 the next day and took an Uber from Santa Monica Airport to Earthbar. She ordered a smoothie and sat at a small table, her back to a stairwell. She knew two ways in and two ways out. Once it was a part of her training. Now it was just habit. Scan the room, find the exits, position yourself to see both and use both if needed.

James walked in at 10:44 and looked around the space. It was quiet. Maybe Thursdays weren't for juicing. He didn't know who he was looking for, but he made eye contact with everyone in the room who offered it back.

No signal. Maybe the source wasn't here yet.

At the counter, he ordered a pineapple-banana smoothie with a protein boost. He paid cash and turned his back to the bar. The whir of smoothie blenders filled the room. He scanned it again. *Nothing.* He turned back toward the bar, accepted his smoothie, and as he was about to turn again and find a table, someone bumped his right shoulder with their left, and he heard the words. "Let's take a walk."

Startled, he caught wind of a subtle fragrance he couldn't identify. A woman in skinny jeans, suede ankle boots, a close-fitting long-sleeve tee and long, black hair with bouncy curls was holding a smoothie in one hand, a phone in the other, and had a purse securely draped over her head and shoulders.

She was fit, confident, and pretty.

Sure.

James followed Stevens outside. She headed east on Wilshire, away from the FBI complex and the likelihood that cameras and microphones and other surveillance equipment were monitoring any combination of the feds/Czechs or other nefarious actors.

"Soooo..." James said, unsure where this was heading.

"I'm interested in where you're getting your information on the cartels, particularly the African wire," Stevens said.

"I'm sure you're not the only one interested in that."

"Of course not. I bet your name is on a few lists. Maybe even your picture."

"Part of the job," James said.

"Is it now?"

"Can be. Doesn't worry me. I can handle myself."

Stevens laughed. "Spoken like a man."

"Well...okay."

"I know your background. Ex military. Ranger Regiment."

"Sounds more glamorous than it was. I worked comms, never saw combat," he said of his Signal Corps duty.

"Still, you got the training."

"Sure."

"So what can you tell me about this wire transfer?"

"You seem to know a lot about me, but I don't know anything about you. So let me start with this: who's asking?"

"Friends at Langley," Stevens replied.

"I don't have any friends at Langley," James quipped.

Langley? What the fuck is this? James racked his brain...did he know anyone at Langley? He had likely met some Ground Branch operators and maybe some analysts when he was serving.

"How about I be your friend at Langley?" Stevens said.

"I'm not about to give you my sources. Even if I wanted to help you, there's no telling if you're legit or not."

"Fine, here's something you can check to verify me." She handed him a piece of paper with a combination of letters and numbers. It looked like a code, or a registration of some kind. Maybe a tail number for a plane?

"Go ahead," Stevens said. "Check it out on your phone."

James grabbed his phone from his right pocket and typed in the series of numbers and letters. It looked like a military or government jet. He then jumped to FlightRadar.com and entered the same. It showed a jet leaving Joint Base Andrews at 05:00 and landing in Santa Monica five and a half hours later.

This could be a trick. But it seemed like it matched up.

"What's your name?" James asked.

"Stevens. Alyssa Stevens. I work on the Africa desk, and I think you're about to uncover something big. I'm hoping we can work together."

James held eye contact with her for an uncomfortable length of time. She didn't blink. He flinched first, shaking his head and asking aloud, "Why would I want to do that? Seems like I know more than you."

"In this instance, maybe you do. But I promise you the Agency knows more than you do. We can help each other, Mathieu."

This was the first time she called him by his name. It was an obvious emotional-level appeal.

"I'll think about it. Sorry you came all this way to go back empty handed. Have a nice flight back."

As James began to walk away, west down Wilshire to where he parked, Stevens had one more card to play.

"Mathieu?" she shouted over the traffic whipping by. "What if I told you there may be a connection to London? I know about your parents."

James stopped in his tracks and looked down at the sidewalk.

Harold and Margaret James, the one-time US Air Force officer and British school teacher, were among those killed on July 7, 2005, in the terrorist bombings in London. Although they lived in the States after Harold retired, they returned to England every year to visit friends and Maggie's family.

Fate chose them that day and orphaned a young adult named Mathieu James. Being parentless, he found family and purpose later in the military, which paid for his education at Northwestern University in Chicago, where he earned a journalism degree and pursued a career as an investigative journalist. In the back of his mind, he always wondered if the whole story had been resolved regarding the 7/7 bombings and a "fifth bomber or mastermind." No one, it seemed, had uncovered one. Not MI5, nor MI6. Not the CIA or Mossad or Five Eyes.

So he had let it go.

Or tried to.

Stevens stood staring at James's back, her hair blowing into her face from a slight ocean breeze that waved the palm fronds. He turned and looked at her.

"You have my attention."

"Good. I have a plane idling at Santa Monica Airport. Come with me to D.C. and we can talk. Wheels up in one hour. I'll text you details."

"You don't have my cell number," James smirked.

"Of course I do," Stevens said confidently. "I work for the CIA."

Within months, James was on the CIA's Non Official Cover list. His cover was legit. He really was a journalist.

_____

7

London, England, UK

His cigarette had burned down to his fingers, which were pinching the filter. Standing outside in the drizzle of London's Harringay Warehouse District near South Tottenham, Igor Kozlov put the cigarette in his mouth and pulled hard. The final mash of tobacco and paper burned to the filter, crackling just faintly. Eyes squinting, he inhaled a plume of smoke and released it through his nose.

Kozlov inspected the tobacco stick, making sure he got all of it, before flicking it to the ground and smashing it with his right boot. As he stood on the corner, waiting for Andrey to pull up, he scanned the streets, looking for unfamiliar faces or cars.

Five years ago he had moved to this neighborhood, its industrial textile roots almost peeked through its beatnik magnetism. Artists and musicians and writers—creatives of all kinds—gravitated here, where the warehouses were turned into work-living spaces and an eclectic group of citizens bonded over their alternative lifestyles.

Also here, individuals saw themselves as community leaders and activists—whether political, social, justice reform, or immigration.

Kozlov presented himself as an advocate for immigration. The United Kingdom was a melting pot now, for better or worse, and Kozlov was part of a small community of people who had escaped former Soviet Bloc countries.

Born in the Mogilev region southeast of Minsk, he was one of five siblings. His father worked long hours as a fix-it man, repairing plumbing in run-down apartments or sealing windows in dilapidated buildings. His mother kept things sane at home, where a three-bedroom apartment meant Igor and his two brothers shared a room, while sisters Ana and Katerina shared another. It seemed tight, but it was better than his friends, who often shared a room in a one-bedroom with their parents. Mogilev was poverty stricken as long as he could remember.

Like all boys, he fancied himself a professional footballer or maybe playing ice hockey. But the easier way to make a living, he quickly learned, was getting involved with an unsavory crowd.

As a teenager, Igor found himself with the wrong friends at the wrong time. One of them was Andrey Morozov, whose father Sergey was a well-known organized crime boss. These small-time mafia types recruited teens to do "minor" thefts, grooming them for larger roles in the organization as they got older.

On a Saturday night when he was fifteen, Igor and Andrey joined two of their friends, who happened to be brothers. They visited Andrey's father, whose "office" was the back room of a liquor store. He had a proposition for the teens: He would pay each of them 10,000 rubles if they successfully stole a shipment of cigarettes from the back of a semi-trailer.

This is how it starts. Entice them with something they don't have and before long they are hooked. It could have been rubles, hookers, or drugs. It doesn't matter. When you have nothing, and someone presents you with something, that's your new reality.

When Igor Kozlov left Belarus 10 years ago at 29, he had outgrown the enterprise he was running for Andrey's father. The two life-long friends wanted something more. London had a bit of everything: wealth, crime, access to Western Civilization, women. The two were motivated by money and lifestyle now. Yet they were careful not to stand out. Blending into a neighborhood like the Harringay district allowed them to lower their profile and build their network.

Igor and Andrey were seeking to influence Western policy over the former Soviet Bloc. The increasing isolation of Russia under Putin was dragging the Federation's allies under the tide as well. Belarus had declared itself aligned with Russian ideology for some time. The West was pressing its thumb down through sanctions of oligarchs and reneging on promises of aid.

In their short lifetimes, Igor and Andrey saw just one organization be bold enough to stand-up to the Americans and British: Al Qaeda. First, it was the 9/11 attacks that dragged America into their forever wars. Then it was 7/7, showing the pompous fucks in Britain they weren't safe either. Later, ISIS fanatics wanted their turn and Paris was in the crosshairs in 2015.

Igor Kozlov was hoping he could influence western thought without violence. In London, he sought to rally like-minded immigrants to take charge of their world through peaceful solutions, like protests or running for public office.

This was all a cover for the enterprise he and Andrey were running behind the scenes. Scores of burglaries had rocked London's fashion district over the past year, with millions of dollars in clothing and accessories hitting the black market. Igor and Andrey were still criminals, sending the goods to Russia, to Belarus, to Hungary. Wherever the market demanded.

It was enough to get the attention of the detective blokes at 4 Whitehall Place, but Scotland Yard really didn't seem that interested. It also meant these crimes weren't on the radar of domestic intelligence MI5.

All this criminal activity allowed the men to live well above their means. Igor was able to send money home to his parents, who were aging faster than he cared to admit. Andrey preferred to blow through his illicit earnings on weekends in London's trendiest clubs, where he often paid for affection rather than earn it. Of the two, Igor was the thinker, the motivator, the leader. Andrey liked all the stuff that came with life in London.

As a dutiful mama's boy, Igor called home every Wednesday morning. He looked forward to these chats. It was mostly his mother who begged him to come home. His father complained about the deteriorating conditions in Belarus. Igor always cut him off, telling his father it was likely the State Security Committee was listening to everyone's calls.

With each passing week, one thing became more obvious: The more the West cut off Putin and his allies for his attempts to annex Ukraine, the more the people would suffer. It was bad enough that Russian mothers were losing sons in a war nobody understood. But Lukashenko's continued embrace of these policies —even welcoming Russian weapons into the country and allowing Putin to launch attacks on Ukraine from Belorussian soil—had a trickle-down effect on the general population the oligarchs didn't care about: food insecurity, shortage of medicine, banks that were on the brink of failure.

Naturally, Igor didn't see this as a failing of Putin and Lukashenko and their cronies. He saw this as Western influence in a region they didn't understand and where they didn't belong. With each passing week, his parents appeared more hopeless. News from home was never good.

Igor Kozlov wanted to make a statement. He just wasn't sure how.

Andrey Morozov pulled his BMW M5 to the curb and waved at his friend. He slipped the car into neutral and pushed on the accelerator a few times, playfully revving the engine. He got a smile out of Igor, who in Andrey's mind was smiling less and becoming more serious every day.

Igor slinked into the passenger seat and pulled the door shut. The sound system was thumping with the heavy bass beats of EDM.

"Igor!" Andrey exclaimed. "What's happening, my brother?"

Igor reached for the volume dial and turned the music down.

"Let's eat," Igor said. "I want to talk to you about something."

"Why so serious, Igor?" Andrey said in a happy, upbeat voice. "The world is our oyster, let us enjoy its fruits."

Igor looked over at this friend, who was bouncing with excitement. Maybe he was high. Maybe not.

"Just drive, Andrey, okay?"

Andrey checked his side mirror before punching the accelerator and screeching into traffic, pinning his unamused friend back in his seat.

·

8

Los Angeles, California

Mathieu James completed the drive from Phoenix to Los Angeles in just under five-and-a-half hours. He avoided rush hour traffic for the most part, picking up an hour with Pacific Standard Time. He pulled into the underground garage of his downtown L.A. loft and parked. Unlocking his storage cage behind his assigned parking, he emptied much of the camping gear from the Joshua Tree excursion.

The portable stove, water can and cooler were set inside. The rest left intact. He wasn't gone long enough to haul things upstairs for a proper cleaning. As he locked the cage, he received a notification on his iPhone. It was a Proton Mail alert, and the sender was Alyssa Stevens.

It must be the report on Grandma, he thought, smirking at the idea that *Grandma* was a code word.

He briskly walked toward the elevator and hit the number five. Up he rode, the elevator shimmying slightly. These old warehouses were being converted into lofts, condos, and apartments all over the city. Attempts to capitalize on the housing crisis created somewhat affordable living spaces. He managed to buy this place last year for just under $500,000. It was and remained a ridiculous sum for basically a giant room with a kitchen, bathroom, and concrete walls.

But that's the price you paid for L.A.

James pulled his dirty clothes from his backpack and threw them in the washing machine. He grabbed his laptop, set it on the coffee table, and sat on the couch.

As the computer spun to life, James finally took a minute to ponder what exactly Alyssa had, and whether the timing of Francois Thies's visit to America was a coincidence. He'd know in less than a minute.

He logged into Proton Mail and opened the message. It was void of words, but an encrypted attachment signaled something more. He downloaded the document and double-clicked. It launched a CIA-proprietary software that would unlock, unscramble, and make the message readable.

Prompted for a 10-digit code, he entered it from memory—it changed every month or quarter depending on the frequency of use. The document was an intelligence summary outlining a theory. Nothing actionable at the moment, but it involved two things that caught James's attention.

The first was the mention of a financier in Africa.

The second was a further reach to understand. There was a theory that a sleeper cell may be waking in the UK. This wasn't new as the UK is known for being a wasp's nest for terrorists and the intel was rather vague.

Cell phone conversations had been intercepted by General Communications Headquarters between a number in Liberia and one in London. On the surface that may not seem like much. But the Liberia connection caught his eye immediately.

After the 7/7 bombings, there was the "fifth bomber" theory. Rumors suggested this person was a financier based in Africa. Could this be the same person, 18 years later? If so, how could they connect the dots?

There was no mention of 7/7 in the document, only that the intercepted communications were analyzed and further monitoring would be done by MI6. It was shared with Five Eyes—the intelligence alliance between Australia, New Zealand, Canada, the United States, and the United Kingdom—as a matter of routine.

With Stevens working the terror finance connections to potential UK cells, it was internally routed to her inbox. She knew that James had been connecting dots for a long time. He was never sure if they would lead anywhere, but if there was a way he could better understand the senseless deaths of his parents and countless others, or perhaps even prevent another attack by unravelling the shady financial dealings of terror cells, he would do it.

Of course he would.

Two years prior, while reporting another story for which Francois Thies was a source, Thies mentioned to him that his circles were talking about financial ties between someone in Africa and the jackasses that blew themselves up on 7/7. James spoke with his editor, Frank Murphy, who at the time told him to stay focused on his current work.

Then, James looked into a couple of leads based on what Thies gave him, but it went nowhere. He made a file of what he'd learned and labeled it *The Scotland Project*. As an investigative journalist, James often labeled his projects with a slight misdirection, in the event his competition—or worse, the subjects of his work—gained access to his files. It wasn't some CIA level trickery, but the filing system made sense to him, which likely meant it made sense to no one else. Paranoia is a known trait in the journalism community.

James leaned back on the couch, put both hands behind his head, and looked at the ceiling.

Is this anything?

Is it nothing?

Money flows every day from one account to another. Person to person. Business to business. Sometimes it was all too much to comprehend, let alone tie together.

He needed time to think. He needed a shower. And he needed to see Taylor.

James rose from the couch and began undressing as he walked toward the bathroom. Shirt first, then jeans, underwear, and socks last—always socks last. He reached into the shower and cranked the handle hard right, creating his pseudo-steam room. Three minutes later, he stepped into the shower and scrubbed himself clean.

Next up was Andiamo's, the upscale eatery where Taylor worked as sommelier.

He couldn't wait.

9

It was past 20:00 and Alyssa Stevens was still at her desk, still at work, still putting international puzzle pieces together with a stack of data and no clear direction. This was the job. You take what you get and try to put the pieces together. Sometimes it's obvious. Sometimes you fail. Sometimes the data leads nowhere. The hope is always that you don't miss another 9/11.

The ceiling light was turned off; she always considered it "too surgical." She had a reading lamp on her desk, and it was focused squarely on a mound of intel scattered across three piles—three different scenarios she was looking into. All unrelated. But it was the stack in the middle she kept coming back to—one that referenced an intercepted phone call between Africa and London.

The adage "follow the money" had never been truer. She leaned onto her desk, placing her left elbow on the edge and combing her fingers into her hair, finding just the right spot to hold her tired head up. With her right hand, she tapped a pen mindlessly as she read the transcript of the encrypted call.

Caller 1:
"Hallo. Our mutual friend said we should talk."

Receiver 1:
"Yes, he said the same."

Caller 1:
"What type of investment are you seeking?"

Receiver 1:
"What can you offer?"

Caller 1:
"This depends on the situation, and the intended result."

Line is quiet.

Caller 1:
"Are you still there?"

Receiver 1:
"Yes."

Caller 1:
"I ask again, what type of investment are you seeking?"

Receiver 1:
"I...I don't know."

Caller 1:
"What kind of return are you seeking?"

Receiver 1:
"I'm, uh, I'm not sure. I want to be heard."

Caller 1:
"Careful what you wish for, my friend. When you decide how much investment you need, contact our mutual friend and he will arrange another call."

~ click ~

CALLER 1 HAS TERMINATED THE CALL.

Stevens read the transcript again and again. The original analyst notes
surmised that the caller was using a burner phone. The receiver was on a
public phone box. The call was randomly intercepted through a secret
national program that allowed the British to monitor incoming
international calls. They could do this so long as the transmissions were
random intercepts. If they wanted to listen to a potential target, that was
another matter and another process.

This program was modeled after the United States's Patriot Act, which
allowed the National Security Agency to listen to any phone calls it wanted
—controversial for sure, but the Bush administration that forced this law
into existence didn't care. It was all about "protecting the homeland." But
the Patriot Act actually turned everyday Americans into suspects.

There wasn't much to go on here, but maybe it was a thread that would
pull at something else. MI5 decided to tap the particular phone box in case
the same one was used again. MI6 decided to increase its surveillance of
calls from Africa into the UK.

Sometimes you're just playing a hunch.

As the hour reached 21:00, Stevens's stomach grumbled. She hadn't eaten
since lunch. Time to head home. Maybe she'd pick up some sushi along the
way. As she stood from her desk, she arranged the three piles and put them
neatly back into their folders. She stacked them on top of each other and

walked to her wall safe, entered a code by providing her index finger for a scan, and tucked them inside.

Walking back to her desk, she grabbed her purse, her phone, and her overcoat. Clicking off the desk lamp, she exited and closed the door behind her. Perhaps tomorrow, with a fresh mind, something would make sense.

10

London, England, UK

Andrey parked his prized BMW on a side street and exited the driver's side, tucking his hand inside his sleeve and wiping some dirt from the side of the car. Igor slinked out and shook his head disapprovingly at his friend.

"You and this car, Andrey."

"What?" Andrey smiled. "She's a beast. Gotta keep her pretty, too."

"You jack off to this thing at home, don't you?" Igor sniped.

Andrey bellowed.

The two walked shoulder to shoulder to the corner and turned right. There was an ethnic deli just a few meters up the road. As they reached the door, Andrey pulled it open and let Igor enter first. Igor didn't acknowledge this gesture from his friend, who gave him a friendly kick in the ass as he passed.

Igor looked back, giving Andrey a silent scolding.

"Whaaaatttt???" Andrey laughed.

Igor picked a corner table for two, grabbed the chair, and pulled it out, taking a seat with his back to the wall and in full view of the front door. Andrey sat across from him, his back to the door, and removed his cap.

"What's with you today?" Andrey asked.

Igor shook his head, staring outside with pursed lips.

"It's something, what is it?"

Igor paused, then locked eyes on his friend.

"Have you spoken with your father recently, Andrey?"

"A couple of days ago, why?"

"How's he doing?"

"He's the same. Cranky. Misses my mother." Andrey paused here, thinking of his beloved mother, who'd passed away a couple years back. "But he's the same. Why do you ask me this?"

Igor was staring outside the window again, and his face simmered with anger.

"I spoke to my parents last night. Actually, I FaceTimed them," Igor said, still looking outside. "They don't look well. They look thin. Fragile."

"Our parents are getting old, my friend. Time waits for no one."

"I know this, of course," Igor replied, waving his hand in a dismissive gesture.

"My mother said the store shelves are empty. They are mostly eating bread and bone broth."

"My father has said nothing of this," Andrey said.

"Your father is a career criminal, Andrey. Let's not pretend it's different. He's the reason we do what we do today. His circle of friends is not the same as my mother and father."

Andrey looked down, seemingly embarrassed by this statement. He looked up and made eye contact with his friend.

"I'm sorry, Igor. You know I love your mother and father. They always treated me like a son."

Igor nodded.

"Maybe my father can help them?"

Igor shook his head.

"No. They won't accept this act of pity. They are too proud. My father worked far too long and too hard to live the end of his life like this."

"Yes, I know."

"My father said he went to the bank last week to take out some money. They told him he couldn't take as much as he wanted. When he asked why, they told him they didn't have the funds to cover it."

The two friends looked at each other in silence. Then, Igor continued.

"The West is squeezing us. These sanctions they put on Putin are having an impact at home, too. Lukashenko should have stayed out of it," he said, referring to the invasion of Ukraine.

"What was he supposed to do?" Andrey inquired. "You know he will always have Putin's ass. It's a security issue for Lukashenko. We need Russia and Lukashenko wants to stay in power, so he needs to kiss Putin's ass."

"I don't know, Andrey. I understand what you're saying, but why should my parents suffer? All the working people, the good people of Belarus. They are being punished by the West for Putin's insanity? It's not fair."

"Of course it's not fair. But what's the alternative? Join NATO?" Andrey laughed. "Putin wouldn't let that happen. He'd invade Belarus before NATO could get an erection. Plus, that is not the solution for our people."

"I know this."

"So what's the solution in your mind, Igor?"

"I'm not sure. But I know without the sanctions, my parents could eat better. Without the sanctions, we might have more money in our banking system. Without the sanctions, our people would be free from Western thought and actions."

"True," Andrey said, adding a pause and letting it linger. "So, is the answer to go to war with the West?"

"Of course not. Look at what's happening in Ukraine. The Russians are getting slaughtered by a lesser army. There's no way Russia wins a war with the West without China."

Igor laughed.

Andrey joined him.

"Listen to us. We sound like old men."

"We sound like our fathers, Igor. This is what they talked about when we were kids. All the changes. Western influences. All of it."

Both men looked out the window, eyes following a pretty blonde in a pencil skirt. They smiled at each other.

Then Igor spoke.

"There has to be a way to make the West pay. Make them understand they shouldn't be in our business."

"But how?" Andrey asked.

"I didn't want to tell you this, but I spoke with your father last week. I asked him for a contact. Someone who may help us."

"You did what?"

"Yes, I'm sorry. I called your father. He gave me the number for a man he knows. I think the man works for the GRU, but I'm not sure," Igor said, referencing the Russian foreign intelligence unit.

"Did you call this man?"

"Yes."

"What did you say?"

"I told him I needed help with a project. I needed an investor."

"Help with what project? What kind of investor?"

"Andrey, I'm not sure. I don't know yet. Someone who can help our people make a statement."

"What kind of statement?"

"I don't know."

Andrey pushed himself back from the table. He put his cap on his head and crossed his arms, staring at his friend, who was gazing blankly outside again. *What is Igor up to?*

"Andrey, all I know is look at you and me. We got out, but we're doing the same thing. We are still criminals, just smarter and better at it. We have nice flats, you drive a nice car. We eat when we want. We don't even think about these things."

Andrey nodded.

"And back home, my father is wondering if his money—his savings—is gone. It's not right."

"Of course not."

Igor Kozlov slowly put his hands on the table, gathering his swelling emotions.

"I don't want to talk about this anymore. Not right now. Let's eat."

"Yes, let's eat, my brother."

11

Mathieu James wheeled out of his DTLA underground parking garage and pushed his way northwest, toward Brentwood. Given the time of day—just around 17:00—this wouldn't be worth it save the woman he was intent on seeing.

Taylor Hendrix and James had been dating nearly a year. Call it nine months. They'd met at a club in West Hollywood, when James was out with a buddy to take in some live music. Turned out Taylor was in the band that opened for the other band. They were all-female rockers playing mostly alt-punk. Some original stuff mixed in with plenty of cover jams.

Taylor played bass and, frankly, looked like she didn't belong. The band, known as Diaper Pins, definitely had the punk look—heavy makeup, spiked hair, tattoos galore. And while Taylor dressed the part—she put some spray-on color in her hair, wore fishnet stockings that slid into her knee-high heeled leather boots under her cut-off jeans—she wasn't covered in tattoos, and she had no facial piercings.

James had made eye contact with her throughout the night but not in a one-night-stand kind of way. Rather, he was shy about it. He'd watched her almost exclusively, and when their eyes locked, he'd looked away quickly, thinking he wasn't giving his obsession away too obviously.

When the band had finished its set, James went to the bar to order another round. It was crowded, and the line was at least four deep and three wide. As he waited patiently, he heard a voice behind him ask a question.

"What are you having?"

James was listening for the answer, ever the sleuthing journalist who was creating his own stories about people. But he heard none.

"What are you having?"

Still nothing.

He turned slightly to take a peek and saw the bass player over his left shoulder. She was standing alone, looking squarely at him.

"I'm sorry, were you talking to me?"

"Yes, what are you having?" Taylor had laughed.

"Oh...uh...a Stella for me and a gin and tonic for my friend," he'd said shyly.

"Great," Taylor had said. "I'll take a Stella too, if you don't mind." She'd handed him $10, smiled, and walked back toward the stage. He had watched her go until she looked back, waved, and pointed toward the stage, directing him on where to bring her beer. She'd stepped onstage and started packing her gear. The other Diaper Pins were doing the same.

James had turned back toward the bar, smiled and shook his head slightly. *Interesting,* he'd thought. *She's not shy.*

Not at all.

When his turn at the bar came, he'd ordered two Stellas, completely spacing the gin and tonic for his pal Andy. The barkeep poured them quickly. He'd put a $20 down, grabbed the beers and walked back toward the stage. He'd passed Andy, who looked at him and mouthed *"What the fuck, dude?"* as he extended his arms in mock wonderment. James had shrugged and soldiered on, winking at his pal as he marched past.

"Hey," he'd said to catch her attention when he was at the edge of the stage.

Taylor had turned and smiled, showcasing her dimple. "Thank youuuu!"

She'd grabbed the beer from his hand and chugged about a quarter of it, wiping the foam from her mouth with the back of her hand.

"My pleasure," James had said and reached out his hand, offering her $10 back. "My treat."

"Oh, I don't think so," Taylor had said. "I can buy my own drinks."

"I'm sure you can. But I enjoyed the show. It's the least I could do. And really, who doesn't like free beer?"

She'd smiled and cocked her head to the left. His arm was still extended, and his hand still held the bill. She'd reached for it, nodded, and slipped it into her back pocket.

"I'm Mathieu, by the way," he'd shouted above the bar din.

"Taylor," she had said, putting her free hand to her chest. "I gotta get this cleaned up before the next band throws our shit off stage. Thanks for helping me cut the line."

"You bet."

James had walked back to a smiling Andy. He'd shrugged his shoulders and playfully acted bashful.

"You get a number?"

"Nah. Not yet, anyway."

"Dude, I'm gonna be disappointed in you if we leave here tonight without a number."

"All good, I got this."

They'd fist-bumped, and James walked back to the bar, shouting, "I'll get your drink now."

As the next band took the stage and began setting up, James lost track of Taylor. He'd walked the barroom floor and hit the balcony above. Nothing. Now he was disappointed. And pissed at himself.

"Fuuccckkkkk," he'd said quietly, pitching his head back and rolling his eyes.

Two hours later, as he got home still obsessing about the bass player for the Diaper Pins named Taylor, he emptied his pockets, unbuttoned his jeans and kicked off his boots. As he reached in his right rear pocket, jeans slouching over his rear, he found something he hadn't expected.

It was a $10 bill with a phone number written in black Sharpie.

How in the hell did she do that?

An hour and fifteen minutes after leaving his DTLA garage, James pulled up outside Andiamo's in Brentwood. He checked himself in the mirror, gave his pits a sniff, touched up his hair, and climbed out of the LR4. He walked inside, smiled and nodded at the hostess, and grabbed a two-person high-top in the bar area.

As he sat down, he scanned the room for Taylor. She bounced around, from the cellar to the bar to the tables, offering suggestions for wines to pair with meals, and generally just creating conversation about the restaurant's cellar and what she thought about the industry in general. She was warm, genial, and not too pushy. Some sommeliers come across as know-it-alls. Most nights, every table invited Taylor to sit and have dinner with them.

The two locked eyes across the bar and smiled at each other. Taylor held up her index finger and mouthed, *"Be right there."* She disappeared and quickly returned, holding a glass of red wine. She walked over to the high table, set the glass down, and leaned into him, giving him a kiss on the lips.

"It's been too long," she smiled, wiping lipstick from his mouth with her thumb. "Are you having dinner?"

"Can you join me?"

"Depends on how busy we get. Maybe. Stick around for a bit. Tell me what you think about this one. It's a Super Tuscan. Just came in this week."

"Sounds great," he said, reaching his hand toward hers as she started to walk away.

"I'll check in on ya in a bit."

Taylor walked away, and James never stopped looking until she was out of sight.

She's still got that sweet ass.

12

Following dinner at Andiamo's, James stayed over at Taylor's Brentwood condo. It had been a minute since they were together, but the bedroom chemistry hadn't disappeared. He was up early and hit the fitness center in her complex for a 45-minute workout and returned to shower.

Taylor was still sleeping, her hair cascading over the pillow and her right arm hanging over the side of the bed. James went into the kitchen and dialed in the espresso machine, choosing a latte. Fancy shit.

He took a seat at the breakfast bar and was checking out the morning stories on the *IHT* app when Frank's call interrupted his routine. It was 08:45 in Brentwood, which likely meant Frank had been in his office chair for more than four hours.

"Frank," James answered.

"Matty, what's going on in LA LA land? You get your fancy coffee and avocado toast yet?"

"Can confirm on the fancy coffee. I'll get back to you on the toast. What's happening in the news mecca of the universe?"

"You know how it is, Matty, same shit different day. Paris is always on my ass about budget this and numbers that. I'm always chasing your younger colleagues, trying to figure out if they're working on stories or making dog videos for social media. For fuck's sake, Matty, social media is the one thing this planet didn't need, but don't get me started."

James laughed and heard a slurping noise.

"What's that I hear? You on your fifth cup of that dishwater-tasting Dunkin'?"

"Fuck you, Matty. Dunkin' is life."

They laughed.

"Listen," Frank said. "We need to talk about The Scotland Project. I know you've been waiting like your whole damn life to look into this, and I get it. Paris tells me one of the reporters over there has a source who might be willing to talk about what they know."

"What do you mean 'What they know?' What they know about what?"

"This person—I don't know if it's a man or a broad or what—says they know who was behind those assholes that blew up London."

"Yeah? Why now? It's been a lot of years, Frank. Nobody but me has been interested in this for at least a decade. And let's be real, my interest is because they killed my mom and dad."

"I know, Matty."

"So what do you know? What's in it for this person?"

"Paris tells me our writer there has been working on an investigative piece about the Paris attacks in 2015. Rumors are there's still an active cell in France tied to the same group that did that shit. So this source is talking off the record to our reporter and says to her, 'If you follow the money, it flows the same direction to Paris as it did to London.' So she starts asking more questions and this source is convinced the money required to set up both of those attacks can be traced to Africa."

James paused for a moment, letting that sink in. He took a sip of his latte, which was starting to cool.

"Ya still there, Matty?"

"Yeah."

"What do you think?"

"I don't know what to think, Frank. I need to sit with this for a bit. Who's the reporter in France working that story?"

"Ana-Marie Poulin. She's young but aggressive. I hear she'd rip a bull's balls off and juggle 'em if it produced a good lead."

"That's weird, Frank. A little too early for that kind of visual."

"Just sayin'."

"Yeah, okay. Can you text me her contact info? I'll reach out and see what else she might know, then I'll call you back."

"Sure thing, texting now. Later, Matty."

"Bye."

James's phone pinged with the text from Frank. He remained seated, staring straight ahead, reliving the conversation he just had. *A source is talking about someone in Africa funding terror cells. And this source mentioned London.*

He always wondered if the "fifth bomber" theory was just sensationalized. For most, it always seemed like a far fetch that these homegrown men were radicalized on their own and decided to blow up a bunch of people, including themselves. It's rarely that simple. But nobody had proven otherwise, and as the world always does after a massive tragedy, people moved on.

Except for Mathieu James and the families who lost loved ones. Because he could never let go of the thought that his parents' last moments were sitting on a bus in London, probably teasing each other about something insignificant, and holding hands. Then, in an instant, they were gone.

13

Los Angeles, California
Paris, France

A groggy Taylor Hendrix pulled herself out of bed. Still naked from the night before, she grabbed an oversized Foo Fighters t-shirt and slipped it on. As she walked down the hallway of her condo, she was pulling her hair into a messy bun. Her entrance into the kitchen was all legs and sex appeal. She didn't feel sexy in that moment, but James found her so.

"Hey, beautiful," James said as her bare feet padded across the wood laminate.

"Good morning," she said a little froggy, squinting while reaching across the counter with her hand to touch his. She marched to the refrigerator and pulled out a boxed water.

"I'm gonna shower. I'll see you in a few minutes," she smiled, already heading back down the hall to the bathroom. James watched her as she went, and she felt his eyes on him. She playfully grabbed the bottom of the t-shirt, pulling it up ever so slightly, revealing her naked bottom.

"That's what I'm talkin' 'bout!" James yelled.

Taylor turned her head and smiled before disappearing around the corner and into the bathroom. She shut the door behind her, and James could hear the creak of the faucet handle and the rush of water as it slapped the tile.

He looked at his phone, staring at the contact info for Ana-Marie Poulin, then checked his watch. In his head, he did the math. Paris was nine hours ahead. It was past 18:00 there. She might still be working, or she might be heading home or to a bar or wherever. He took a glance down the hall and could see steam seeping from beneath the bathroom door. He smiled, then wrote a text.

AMP - this is Mathieu James.
I work for IHT and live in Los Angeles.
Murph gave me your number.
Can we chat about the story you're working on? Sounds interesting.
I'm on WhatsApp. LMK.
- MJ

James set down the phone, rose from his chair, and walked down the hall. He kicked off his jeans, underwear, t-shirt, and socks. Always last with the socks. He knocked twice on the door and entered the steaming bathroom.

"Mind if I join you?" he queried and was met with devious laughter.

As James toweled off from his second shower of the morning, Taylor ran a brush through her hair, working out the knots. She kept wiping the foggy mirror with a hand towel, trying to get a glimpse of herself.

"What do you have today?" she asked.

"I might have a new story I'm working on. I spoke with Murph while you were still asleep, and he put me in contact with someone in our Paris office who potentially has something interesting. I need to talk with her to see what's what."

"Sounds promising."

"Could be. What about you? Isn't today your day off?"

"It was, but I gotta go in anyway. We had a good week at the restaurant and the cellar is looking a little bare, so I need to place a new order."

"Ahhh, your favorite part of the job. Buying expensive wine with someone else's money."

They laughed together.

"I won't be there long. Probably a few hours. Then the girls are getting together to work on a couple of new songs over lunch."

"Nice."

"Yeah, it's always a..." Taylor searched for a word "... trip."

James leaned over her left shoulder and placed a kiss on her cheek, holding it extra long. Her hand cupped his face, then slid under his chin and squeezed his cheeks. She turned to his now-puckered face and planted a kiss.

"You want a latte?" James offered.

"Yes, please."

"Coming right up."

After delivering a piping hot latte to Taylor, James plopped down on the couch and checked his phone. Ana-Marie Poulin had returned his text.

Bonjour, Mathieu.

Murph is quite a fellow.

I'm on WhatsApp as well. Ring me there?

Au revoir

- AMP

James swiped twice on his phone, slinging apps to the left, and pulled up WhatsApp. He punched in her number, and her contact photo popped up. *She's cute,* he thought. *Young, but cute.* He pressed his thumb on the number to dial Ana-Marie.

After two rings she answered.

"Hallo, Mathieu, nice to meet you by phone."

"Hi, Ana-Marie. Thanks for taking time for me."

"No problem," she said, her accent thick.

"Murph tells me you're working on a story about more cells being tied to the Paris attacks from a few years back."

"Oui, this is true."

"More specifically, he said you have a source who has mentioned a pipeline of money and ties to the London bombings in 2005?"

"Oui, oui. My source tells me this person with the money is also funding more cells in France. They have been sleeping since the attacks here in 2015. He says something might be up."

"What exactly did this source say about London?"

"Uh, nothing more than ties to the money. Why?" she asked.

"This isn't the first time I've heard this. I don't know if you're familiar with this theory, but in the aftermath of the London bombings, there was an idea that a fifth bomber or mastermind existed. After some time, the intelligence communities walked away from it. They couldn't find anything worth chasing."

"This I didn't know. I was very young when the London attacks happened," Ana-Marie said. "But you think there's something to this?"

"Full disclosure: My parents died in those attacks, so I'm motivated to find anyone who's still alive that played a role in their deaths."

"Oh my, Mathieu. I am so sorry. I did not know this."

"Thank you. Of course not. I was told recently there was a random intelligence intercept—a call from Africa to London—that has caught the attention of a few people in British intelligence as well as the CIA."

"You have good sources, Mathieu, if they are telling you this."

"So I'm curious to find out how much you know."

"Not much as of now. Just that my source mentioned the same person allegedly funded the London attacks."

"Do you feel comfortable pressing your source for more information?

"Oui, of course, no problem, Mathieu. Let me talk with him and I'll return to you with what I learn."

"Merci, Ana-Marie. Ciao for now."

"Ciao, Mathieu."

James tapped the X circled in red with his thumb, terminating the call. He needed to get to work. With his laptop at his DTLA loft, he went to say goodbye to Taylor, who was applying eye liner, sitting on a cushioned stool in a bra and panties.

"I gotta get going. Might have a lead," he said.

"Okay. Will I see you later?"

"Count on it," James said. He kissed her on the lips—lingering an extra beat—and headed for the door. "I'll call or text you. Bye."

"Bye," Taylor said from the bedroom, just as the front door closed with a thud.

James double tapped his key fob to unlock the Land Rover, slid inside, put his foot on the brake, and hit the Start button. The engine roared to life, and he quickly spun the shifter to Drive, pulled a U-turn on the street, and pointed himself toward downtown.

14

London, England

Andrey Morozov dropped his friend at his flat after lunch. He was mildly worried about Igor. He had seemed very serious lately. The two were able to enjoy some food before the mood soured again when the television in the deli reported news from the front. It wasn't good for Russia.

The war was not popular in Putin's country. Although he survived a coup attempt and later killed the leader of his paramilitary forces, there was no denying the power of mothers. Russian moms were welcoming home their sons in coffins. Military-aged men were still fleeing over borders, wishing not to serve in an aggression they both didn't understand and didn't agree with.

Russia had already taken Crimea in 2014, and the international community tucked their dicks between their legs and pretended like it didn't happen. But it did, and it empowered Putin, who thought he could make the Ukrainian government capitulate in a matter of hours.

Of course, he was wrong. The West had come to Ukraine's aid, supplying guns, ammunition, tanks, airplanes, training, and more. Ukraine had proven a formidable foe.

This is what worried Igor Kozlov. The longer this war took, the longer the West would impose sanctions on anyone supporting Putin's efforts. This included his beloved Belarus. In turn, that created more problems for his mother and father.

What if the next round of sanctions included medicine? His parents couldn't survive a shortage of medicines. Not at their age.

He had become a worrier. And this was something he didn't have time for.

Igor and Andrey were still running their enterprise and being paid handsomely for their thievery. It provided them a life they couldn't get at home. And yet with all the newfound wealth, there was no obvious way to help their parents.

In Belarus, as in Russia, the social classes are very distinct. If Igor's parents suddenly had food or clothing or cash they didn't have weeks ago, people would start talking. And when people start talking, stories unfold. Often, those stories make their way to the security services, who pay a visit to those in question.

He wanted to avoid all this. He was also selfish. *Don't get caught.*

Once Igor was inside his flat, he pulled his phone from his jacket pocket and dialed Sergey, Andrey's father.

The phone rang once.

Twice.

Then three times.

Sergey answered.

"Yes?"

"Hello, this is Igor, Mr. Morozov. How are you?"

"Ah! Igor!" he answered.

"I had lunch today with Andrey. He is doing well and said to *tell you he loves you* and will call you soon."

Sergey paused for a moment, taking in the message he had just heard. When they last spoke, Igor and Sergey agreed on this very phrasing for whether Igor requested a second conversation with Sergey's GRU contact.

Sergey nodded his head slowly.

"Very well, Igor," he said into the phone. "Please tell *Andrey I love him* and look forward to his call *tomorrow*."

This was confirmation that Igor would be at the same box phone location exactly 24 hours from now, awaiting a call from Sergey Morozov's GRU friend.

"Very well. Good night, Igor."

"Good night."

Both phones went silent. Both men lifted their heads and stared straight ahead.

Things were in motion.

The very next day, at 13:23 hours, Igor Kozlov was standing in a red phone box in his up-and-coming London neighborhood, staring at the handset, wondering if it would ring. He trusted Andrey's father, of course. But the more people you spin the web with, the more you have to untangle.

He checked the time, then pulled his phone from his pocket, as if staring at his cell would make the box phone ring. Holding the phone to his face, he unlocked it, and selected his photo library, casually scrolling through images of his friends, his family...memories both distant and near.

Lost in this space, he physically jumped when the box phone rang. He lifted the handset and placed it on his right ear. He said nothing.

On the other end, he heard silence.

This quiet dance lasted maybe 20 seconds, and the caller spoke first.

"If you are interested in an investment in your project, please say so."

"I am," Igor replied.

"And you have a plan now?"

Igor paused. He did not. Did he lie and tell him 'yes I have a plan?' Or did he tell the truth?

He paused longer.

"I'm waiting," the caller said dryly.

Igor opened his mouth, but no words came out.

He licked his lips.

He stretched and cracked his jaw.

He ran his free hand over his face. His chest was tight. He inhaled, seeking to relax.

Then he spoke.

"I don't have a plan," he said, expecting the line to go dead at any moment.

He held on, listening. He could hear faint breathing and maybe the whir of a fan.

He leaned into nothing, as if getting close to *something* would help him hear better or make the connection more secure.

And then the other end of the line came alive for a brief instance. The GRU agent spoke.

"My parents would like to meet you before you date my sister."

Igor froze. He felt sick. His palms started sweating, and he felt the blood rush from his face. Sweat trickled down his back and into his ass crack. He shivered. *That was the answer. The financier wants to meet in person.*

Igor was not expecting this. All along, he'd second-guessed himself, wondering if his words could meet his actions. In this moment, he didn't have the answer. He pulled the handset away from his ear and moved it toward the device, prepared to hang up and end the call. To move on. To pretend like this never happened.

Should I walk away?

I don't know these people.

What. Am. I. Doing?

Every instinct, every fiber of his being, wanted to hang up that handset. As he moved to complete this action, to walk away from a mess his emotions had clearly started, he thought of his parents. Their gaunt faces flashed in his mind. The subtle desperation he felt in their recent video call. He had to do something. Anything to help them.

Igor Kozlov was an inch away from ending the call. Instead, he quickly pulled the handset back to his right ear and said the words that would put everything in motion.

"It would be my honor to have permission to date your sister."

The other end of the line went dead.

Igor hung up the receiver, opened the phone box door, and vomited on his Air Jordans.

15

Los Angeles and Paris

Mathieu James exited the elevator and turned left, walking down the cold hallway. His boots echoed on the concrete, and the faint hum of the city slipped through the open window at the end of the hall that led to the fire escape.

He reached his front door, entered both a key and a code, and walked inside, tossing his keys on the ceramic surfboard that doubled as a coin holder. With a flip of a switch, the lights turned on over the breakfast bar. He grabbed his laptop, set it atop the bar and opened it.

James clicked on his browser and stared for a moment. *What am I looking for?* He wasn't sure. But he wanted to know everything he could about the Paris attacks. So down the rabbit hole he went. He read stories. He studied images. He watched old news reports.

Grabbing his phone, he opened WhatsApp and sent Alyssa Stevens a text.

Curious to know what impressions your bosses had of the Paris attacks in 2015.

Hearing there might be a tie to London.

He then queued up Ana-Marie Poulin and sent her a text as well.

AMP...MJ here.
Will your source talk to me?

Hours went by without word from Alyssa or AMP. For Alyssa, this was normal. Busy woman doing spy shit. AMP was probably working on a deadline. Either way, he kept checking his phone every ten minutes for a response.

The rabbit hole on the Paris attacks was a good refresher. He'd been finishing j-school then, a little older than most students because of his military service. He'd paid close attention because it was all too familiar. But he'd likely built an emotional wall as well. They were different attacks than the one that killed his parents, but they were carried out by people who hated the West and wanted anyone who felt comfortable to now feel fear.

That is the point of terrorism, after all.

Live in fear.

Lost in a sea of thoughts, a ping from his phone brought him center. It was Alyssa.

Always looking at these things.
As I recall there was nothing obvious.
What are you hearing? Call me.

James thumbed his way to her number in WhatsApp and waited for it to ring. Alyssa answered right away.

"Hi."

"Hello, Alyssa."

"So what are you hearing? Who have you been talking to?"

"There's not much to it right now. You have an intercept. I have a colleague who has a source that is talking about funding for French sleeper cells."

"Yeah, not much yet," Alyssa agreed.

"But then there's another piece," James said. "You know our Swiss banker friend?"

"Yeah."

"I saw him. He's in the States. Says he has new clients. Says it feels, what was the word he used...familiar," James said.

"Familiar," Stevens repeated.

"Right."

"Okay, well I guess that's another piece."

"Yeah, but a piece of what? I have asked my colleague to dig a little deeper with her source. You never know who has an axe to grind. I'll let you know what she says."

"Sounds good. I gotta run. Talk later?"

"Yep. Okay. Later."

Stevens ended the call a nano-second before James hit the red X. He stared at the phone, unsure where to go next.

There wasn't much James could do until he heard from...and there she was. WhatsApp buzzed. It was Ana-Marie Poulin.

"It's late there," James said as he answered.

"Oui, James. It is. How are you?"

"I'm fine. What do you know? Anything new?"

"I just met my source for a drink."

"Was this the first time you met in person?"

"No, this is someone I actually have known. I don't want to say more than that. This person is not a friend, Mathieu. But, how should I phrase it...an acquaintance."

"Okay. So what are you thinking?"

"Well, as you know, I have been looking into these rumors of a sleeper cell here that might be ready to wake. One that is tied to the attacks from 2015. It's possible these people were supposed to participate in the original attacks and something happened. Or maybe they are new. It doesn't matter, either way, because if even a little bit is true that's enough to worry everyone."

"And what is this person telling you, specifically?"

"This person is in a position to know about funding. For every one of these operations, someone has to pay. And those same people, if the terrorists are Islamic extremists, have to pay the killers' families for their sacrifice. There's always a level of money involved. Sometimes it's not much, sometimes it's a lot."

"So this person knows about the money?"

"Oui."

"Did this person mention London again, when you just met?"

"No, but I brought it up."

"And?"

"And, well, he seems to think there's either a person or a group—based probably in Africa—that has been funneling money to sleeper cells in Western Europe."

"How do you think he knows this, Ana-Marie? What do you think his ties to this could be?"

"I'm not sure, Mathieu. He may be a courier. He may be someone who got himself into something he didn't expect."

"What makes you think he's a courier?"

"Because that's how I knew him from before."

Mathieu was taking notes and wrote MALE and COURIER and underlined each three times.

"Can you explain more about your past acquaintance with him?"

"We went to university together. We had some of the same friends. He fell in with a different group and started dealing, small time stuff. Then he dropped out of school because he was making more money than he had ever seen," Poulin said.

She continued, "After a couple of years he earned the trust of some guys, some organization, whatever they are or were, and he was handling more stuff. He was handling money."

"You mean, like laundering money?" James asked.

"Probably. I don't really know. But since then, we have stayed in touch. He has given me some tips. Sometimes they lead somewhere. Sometimes they don't."

"Why you? Why would he tell anyone anything?"

Ana-Marie Poulin sighed. She took a moment to answer.

"He likes me, I think."

"You think?"

"Oui."

"And that's it?"

"I guess."

James thought she was hiding something, or at least not telling him everything.

"Do you think he's a courier for the Africa people?"

"I don't know. Maybe? But I don't know."

"Okay, good. Well, this is something. And it sounds like he trusts you."

"He does. And I mostly trust him. I think he has a decent soul."

Both were silent for a beat, processing the conversation.

"Oh, and Mathieu? One more thing. I asked if he's willing to talk to you. He said yes. But only on his terms."

"What does that mean?"

"The where and the when."

"Okay, what did he propose?"

"He's going to Amsterdam in two days. He's taking a flight. He will meet you inside Schiphol," Ana-Marie said, referring to the airport there. "I think he has a layover. What do you think, Mathieu?"

"I think I'm going to Amsterdam."

16

Los Angeles, California

Taylor Hendrix and the rest of the Diaper Pins had just finished an informal rehearsal. The lead singer had a small bungalow in West Holly-wood with a one-car garage, which they had converted into a makeshift sound stage. The Diaper Pins were a three-person act, with a drummer, the lead singer on guitar, and Taylor on bass.

As she was wiping down her Fender Precision with a soft cloth, her phone rang. Reaching into her right rear pocket, she pulled out her phone and smiled. It was Mathieu. She answered and asked him to hold on a second.

Setting down her phone, she placed the bass in its hard case, locked it and in one fluid motion, stood with the case in her left hand and the phone in her right.

"Hey babe!"

"Hey beautiful. Where are you?"

"Just finished rehearsal."

"Did you eat?"

"Yeah, we ordered in. You know, punk ladies who lunch. Next big story in *Vanity Fair*!"

James laughed.

"Okay, where are you off to next?"

"Well, I'm free for the rest of the day, so I don't know. What are you up to?"

"Turns out I might be leaving. Like tonight, or tomorrow at the latest."

"Oh? Where to?"

"Amsterdam, and then I'm not sure. Maybe London. Could see my cousin Lily. Or maybe I'll come straight back. Sort of depends on what happens in Amsterdam."

"What's taking you there?"

"There's a source that wants to meet. Could be big. I don't know. One of the reporters in our Paris office is setting it up."

"Um, okay. Wow. Sounds interesting." Taylor was trying to be support- ive. Mathieu had been gone a lot, and it felt like their time was limited already. "So can I see you before you go?"

"Of course. I need to pack a bag and book a flight. I'll call you back in thirty minutes."

"Sounds good."

"Okay, talk soon."

"Bye."

James hung up. He needed to get Frank's permission for a short-notice flight like this. It was going to be expensive. Then he had to pack a bag and get back in touch with Ana-Marie Poulin. He needed to know who he was meeting and where.

"Murphy."

Frank answered the phone on the first half-ring with his usual throaty tone.

"Murph, it's me."

"Talk to me, Matty. What's happening?"

"The source from the Paris office wants to meet in Amsterdam in two days."

"Two days from now? What did you say?"

"I said yes."

"You said yes without getting budget approval? C'mon, Matty, you know Paris is crawling up my ass looking for golden croissants."

"You want to charter a flight on the company jet for me instead? Seriously, Frank, what's the option here? It seems legit."

"Fine but keep it under five grand and get your ass back here quickly. I don't want to be paying for your precious lattes while you're wearing a French terry cloth robe in some post-modern boutique hotel."

"Jeez, Frank, you been reading *Travel & Leisure* lately or what?"

"Fuck off."

"Haha sure, I'll do that."

"Can you keep it under $5k?"

"I'll do my best."

"Your best better be better than your usual best, Matty."

Murphy hung up. James opened a travel app on his phone and entered LAX-AMS for today. There was a flight leaving tonight, connecting thru JFK, for $6,500.

He changed the dates and checked the following day. Another airline had a non-stop leaving at 13:50. This one was $4,000.

And with room to spare, James thought to himself. He booked the flight using his personal credit card and picked a return ticket for the following day. Twenty-four hours should be enough to cover a meeting in an airport.

He screen-grabbed the details and sent the image to Ana-Marie Poulin via WhatsApp.

Hope this works. Best I could do. - MJ

James paused for a moment to collect his thoughts.

What's next? Pack a bag, then call Taylor.

He went into his closet and grabbed his duffle and started tossing in clothes. An extra pair of jeans, a couple of flannels, clean underwear and socks. He set out a pair of boots, which were both fashionable and ultra comfy.

After grabbing his toiletries kit from the bathroom, he snatched his laptop and tossed it in his backpack, along with noise-cancelling head-phones, and a notebook. Figuring he wasn't leaving the airport, he grabbed his lightweight puffer jacket and was out the door, turning the lights off as he left.

As he waited for the elevator, he sent a text to Taylor.

Tell me where to meet you...leaving now.

He checked his watch. It was almost 16:00.

He sighed, looking up at the elevator numbers as they fell to his floor.

I don't deserve her, he thought, as the elevator dinged and the doors opened.

As he peeled out of the underground garage, James heard a ping from his phone. It was a text message from Taylor.

How about we stay in tonight? Maybe order some sushi?

At the first stoplight, James sent a reply with a heart, then wrote *Perfect. See you soon.*

Forty minutes later, he pulled in front of Taylor's condo and stepped out of the truck, grabbing his overnight and backpack. He was always excited to see her, but this time felt different to James. He felt like he owed the relationship more. He owed *her* more. And he wasn't delivering.

Should he apologize? Should they discuss it? He didn't want to ruin a nice evening, let alone the last one in town for at least a couple days.

Read the room.

A quick knock on the door and Taylor greeted him with a kiss on the lips. She was wearing a Sex Pistols vintage tee with the sleeves cut off, faux-ripped jeans and ankle-high zippered boots, complete with four-inch heels. Her hair was down, falling softly over her shoulders. Her makeup was subtle, and she smelled glorious.

He followed her to the kitchen and set his bags down just inside the hallway. She had two glasses of Chardonnay waiting.

She handed him one and took the other. They made eye contact, and she offered a toast.

"To tonight, and to us."

"Cheers," James said, and they softly clinked glasses. He leaned in and kissed her, blindly setting his glass down on the counter. She did the same. The kiss grew longer and more intense, and his hands moved down her back. He slid them into her rear jeans pockets and squeezed her cheeks. Chuckling through the kiss, she did the same.

"Wanna work up an appetite?" Taylor whispered.

"You never need to ask me that," James smiled.

She led him toward the bedroom, walking in front with her left hand dangling behind, holding his. With his right hand he patted her butt, and she giggled and skipped. The excitement was palpable.

When they rounded the corner into the bedroom, Taylor turned to find James was already half undressed. His jeans at his ankles, his boxers at waist level and his t-shirt up around his head. As always, socks still on because they are last.

"Best I could do with one arm," he said as he continued kissing her. He kicked off the jeans and Taylor slid his underwear down his legs, moving her hands over him. James had removed the shirt, and he was all but naked, save the socks.

He reached for her t-shirt at the waist, and she raised her arms as he slid it over her head, pleased to learn she wasn't wearing a bra. She pulled him closer, kissing him as he undid her jeans and pushed them down her legs, kissing her chest, stomach and panties as he went. Before long, those were off too, and they fell naked onto the bed, hands busy, tongues exploring as she guided him inside, offering a sensual moan and a playful bite on his lower lip.

17

Los Angeles International Airport

Mathieu James arrived at LAX via Uber around 11:00 for his 13:50 flight. He had left his keys and the Land Rover at Taylor's. That way she could move it around her neighborhood, and it wouldn't get ticketed or towed.

Last night, after a couple of rounds in the bedroom, they'd ordered in sushi and watched a new show. They had a wonderful night together. This morning, Taylor had to work, and they said their goodbyes at her door. A nice kiss, a long hug, and a lingering shot of that dimple and those doe eyes.

LAX can be finicky. Sometimes, you just want to put a bullet in your brain. Other times, it's actually not bad. Poorly designed decades ago, the horse-shoe traffic pattern begs for airport rage, especially around Terminal B, the international terminal located at the bottom of the horseshoe where traffic clogs in the turns.

His Uber driver was unable to get him curbside, which wasn't a big deal. Three lanes out, James stepped out, thanking the driver as he walked into the next two lanes of chaos.

Entering the terminal is a throwback to yesteryear. In fact, it feels a little like a Western European check-in, with vertical lines of airline kiosks, poor signage, deep groves of humans, a layer of stress, and not enough air pumping from the HVAC vents.

Okay, mild exaggeration. But some truth, too.

At the airline kiosk, a bossy woman in a pale blue skirt-jacket combo was pleading with people to do self-check-in. James wasn't checking a bag, but he wanted to be sure he had a paper ticket. You just never know once you get inside those dreaded security ropes.

Reaching inside his backpack, he grabbed his passport, opened it to the picture page and placed it flat on the machine. A few maneuvers later and his paper ticket was printing. He shoved the passport inside his right front pocket where he kept his phone and headed toward the escalator.

The TSA security lines were at the top, and accessible from both sides of the terminal. His gate was in the "C" concourse, so James went up the closest elevator, only to learn the TSA Pre-check/CLEAR entry point was on the other side.

Again, signage would be helpful.

He ducked a couple of ropes and walked the entire width of the security area only to see three CLEAR reps standing together, joking and laughing. He stood and stared, until one paid him mind.

"Can I help you?"

"Yes, I'm Clear and Pre-Check."

The twenty something pointed at the non-existent line.

"Sir, go ahead. You won't need CLEAR today."

Uncertain by this divergence from protocol, James offered a puzzled look and stepped toward the TSA agent, who was staring at him. She asked him to place his passport on the scanner and pose for a photo.

"Please move to your right, sir. The first photo didn't take."

James took two steps to his right and locked on the lens with the most deadpan look he could conjure.

"Thank you, have a nice flight."

The smoothness belied his previous experiences here, but who's going to complain? Security in less than five minutes is a win. He gathered his two bags on the other side of the x-ray machine and made his way into the terminal, which resembled a shopping mall. Ample restaurants, a duty-free shop, and plenty of Euro-inspired boutiques.

LAX has a second international terminal, connected to the first via an underground tunnel. Before James walked across, he stopped at a bar for his pre-flight requisite: a glass of wine and a cheese plate.

Simple pleasures.

While he sipped his drink and waited for his cheese plate, James opened WhatsApp on his iPhone and sent a message to Ana-Marie Poulin.

I'm at LAX.

Flight to AMS leaves in less than two hours.

What's the plan with the courier?

He set his phone down, awaiting a response.

His cheese plate arrived, and he nibbled, taking in the people wandering the terminal. Again, he loved getting lost in the story.

AMP responded quickly.

There's a Heineken bar near concourses T and D.

He will be there, wearing a Tottenham cap, blue scarf and quilted gray jacket. He will have one empty pint and one full pint in front of him.

I have your itinerary. Everything syncs.

Good luck MJ.

-AMP

James re-read the message.

Seems easy enough, he thought.

Tottenham? A popular English Premiere League team, but middle of the pack normally. Interesting choice.

Another sip and a bite of brie paired with a cracker, chased by some grapes and candied walnuts. He texted Taylor with an update, and Frank Murphy as well.

Glancing at his watch, he figured now was a good time to dial in Euro time. Amsterdam was nine hours ahead. He fiddled with the automatic watch and placed it back on his wrist.

Making eye contact with the barkeep, he nodded for the check.

Forty-five minutes later, James boarded his plane and slipped into seat 11A, with a window on his left and the bulkhead in front of him. He immediately identified the nervous flyer sitting next to him.

Mid 20s. Male. Athletic build. He was popping gummies, hitting every button and lever, constantly shuffling items in and out of his backpack. At one point, he asked the flight attendant for two vodkas, and she turned him down.

"Drink service begins after we take off and reach a safe altitude."

He remained fidgety, and James tried to block him from his vision. No reason to raise the anxiety level because someone is a nervous flyer.

James reached into his backpack and pulled out his noise canceling headphones, his MacBook Air, and a book he had grabbed from Taylor's coffee table. It was called *1983*, and it was a real-time account of the Soviet-US freeze that nearly led to nuclear Armageddon.

Those were heady times, he thought, before leaning back in his seat, pulling his headphones over his ears and embracing the sweet, sultry voice of Kacey Musgraves as he made notes and considered an outline for his story.

He'd be in Amsterdam in a little more than ten hours.

18

London, England, United Kingdom

Igor Kozlov was reluctant to share with his friend Andrey the conversations he was having with Andrey's father. Andrey was already a worrier, and he didn't want him calling home and telling Sergey to stop. Not that Sergey would listen to his son. Sergey had never said this to his wife because she was Andrey's mother, but his son never grew into his outsized expectations. It was probably the reason Andrey left with Igor for London all those years ago.

Sergey Morozov had a trio of underbosses running his enterprise now. As he approached 70, he was looking to wind down. Drink less. Maybe exercise more. Find someone other than a Russian escort to dine with. He was starting to weigh the time he had left. Often, he thought of his wife. He did miss her, although he most certainly never told her that when she was alive. Not one for affection or remaining loyal, Sergey was starting to learn the meaning of regret.

As he contemplated the call with the GRU agent, the one who would set the meeting with the money man from Africa, Igor wondered whether he should turn to Sergey for advice. This was his own insecurity, and he definitely didn't want the man he walked away from to think he was weak.

Am I scared? Igor wondered. That cannot be. *I have to be strong for my mother and father. They need me.*

In the meantime, he was watching for a sign. He wasn't sure what came next, and he wasn't even sure where to look. *Would someone call him?* This all made him nervous.

He grabbed a jacket and hat, scooped his keys and a pack of smokes and left his flat, choosing to take a walk, hoping to take his mind off everything. Just outside his front door, he zipped his coat, put a cigarette in his mouth and sucked hard as the flame from his lighter danced in the wind.

Igor looked up and down the walk, choosing to go left while nervously sucking on his tobacco stick. At the first corner, he kept walking, right into traffic that was turning. The driver punched his horn and yelled something indiscernible. Nervous, Igor jumped and swore.

"Fuck!" he yelled. "Fucking watch it!"

He slammed his hand on the hood of the car, the driver cursing something wild through the glass. Igor was at fault, and he was embarrassed. His nerves were burning to the ends. This was a feeling he didn't know well. Ever confident, always the one with brass balls, he was lost in a sea of frustration and hopelessness.

Continuing up the walk, a man in a black pea coat and khaki pants was walking toward him. But Igor didn't notice. He was still looking back at the empty crossing, where the car had almost hit him, cursing an event that time had already forgotten.

Just as he turned back, he collided shoulder to shoulder with the man in the black pea coat. Igor bounced off, surprised by the contact. The man in the coat immediately apologized.

"Sorry, mate! That one's on me."

"Fucking hell," Igor said.

"So sorry. My fault. Cheers!"

Igor grumbled something and offered a half-hearted "cheers" in return. Regaining his composure, he instinctively checked his pockets. Pickpockets have been a thing in London since Shakespeare's time, and Igor had been burned once when he first moved here.

His wallet was still in his left back pocket, his phone and keys in the front right. He felt for his cigarettes as well, as they were in his coat pocket. Not that he was worried about some petty thief stealing his sticks. His right hand found them securely in his right jacket pocket. His left hand, however, found something else.

Stopping in his tracks, Igor ran his fingers around what felt like an envelope in his left jacket pocket. He slowly removed the item. It was beige in color, folded in half and held together by a paper clip. The inside was sealed shut with adhesive. He turned it over, inspecting both sides. No writing or markings. No postage.

This envelope wasn't familiar. It wasn't his.

He turned and looked behind him for the man he'd bumped into, but the walk was empty.

Did that man put this in my pocket?

He began to feel anxious.

Did I even see him? Could I describe him? He was wearing a black coat.

Fuck.

He scanned the neighborhood, looking for anyone he didn't recognize and unfamiliar cars parked along the street. Since he told people he was a community organizer, he knew most of the locals. Knew what they drove. Knew their habits, generally.

Again, nothing stood out.

His mind was racing, trying to piece together what happened.

A man.

A black coat.

Khaki pants? I don't remember.

The car that almost hit me.

Who was that?

Were they connected?

Was he there to distract me?

Am I imagining shit?

Fucking hell.

Igor Kozlov turned around and briskly walked home. Head down, lifting only for the occasional scan of the neighborhood. He reached his front door, fumbled his keys from his pocket and rattled his way inside, slamming the door behind him and locking the dead bolt.

Breathless, he leaned his back against the front door and lifted the envelope toward his face, looking it over once again. With his right hand, he used a key and inserted it into the sealed flap and tore it open.

Squeezing the sides, he looked inside and saw two more pieces of paper. He turned the envelope on its end and let the papers slide into his right hand.

One was a train ticket from London to Edinburgh, Scotland. The second was a plane ticket from Edinburgh to Amsterdam.

Both were leaving tomorrow.

This was the message he wasn't sure he'd get.

He set the tickets on the bureau and noticed a sticky note on the back of the train ticket.

He'll find you. Starbucks. Upper level. Main concourse.

19

Schiphol International Airport
Amsterdam, Netherlands

Post World War II Amsterdam was in the enviable position of being a major transportation hub in Western Europe. Its proximity to the sea, flat terrain and regional tentacles that could touch London, Paris, Copenhagen, and Brussels made it so.

Schiphol International Airport had grown into the world's third largest and busiest airport as the connecting hub for airlines with destinations around the globe.

Ever under construction and now sleekly modern in the traditional European minimalist way, Schiphol has enough amenities for the longest of layovers.

It was here that Mathieu James was meeting the courier.

It was here that Igor Kozlov was meeting the money man.

A coincidence of the highest order?

With about three hours left in his journey from Los Angeles to Amsterdam, Mathieu James decided a nap would be the best course. He had spent the first two of the ten-hour journey going over notes and making outlines for a potential story.

After dining on tuna takaki, he read from the book he borrowed from Taylor, then watched a movie on the in-flight entertainment system. The flight had been smooth so far. His seat neighbor had calmed down some, having put on a neck pillow, hat, sunglasses, and ear buds. James still wasn't sure what was going on there.

Not wanting to be seen or followed, Igor asked Andrey to drop him off at London's King's Cross Station. He didn't tell him why, but the twenty-five minute drive from their Harringay neighborhood was enough to test his patience.

As he was about to exit the BMW, Andrey asked his friend when he would return.

"Probably tomorrow," Igor said. "Maybe the next day."

"Where are you going?"

"I shouldn't say, Andrey. Not yet, anyway."

"Are you in some kind of trouble, my brother?"

"No. Don't worry about me. I'm fine. I'm fine. I'm going to meet someone."

"But you're not even taking a bag," Andrey observed.

"I won't need one. I'll be fine. I'll let you know when I'm coming back."

With that, Igor Kozlov stepped out of the BMW and onto the street. He gently closed the door, good-naturedly mocking his friend's passionate love for the car, and waved goodbye. He then did a slight jog before slowing to a walk as he neared the station's entrance.

Here we go.

Igor would take the next train for Edinburgh's Waverley station. He could then use the tram to take him to the airport, where he would board his flight. He had never been to Edinburgh but heard many of his neighbors talk about taking holidays there, especially during winter for the Christmas Market.

That would be fun to see, he thought.

James's flight that left Los Angeles 10 hours and 20 minutes ago touched down in Amsterdam with a smooth glide and a plume of smoke as the tires hit the pavement.

In seat 11A, Mathieu James flexed his abs and pushed his feet into the floor to combat the force of the plane from chucking his face into the bulkhead as the plane rapidly decelerated. Schiphol has multiple runways, and taxi times can vary depending on where you land. It was 09:10 in the Netherlands, which gave him a long window to wait for the courier at the Heineken bar. Hopefully he was already there.

Gathering his personal belongings, his seat mate—who had the aisle— kindly handed him his bags from the overhead bin and James packed things up, double-checking he left nothing behind. One of the beauties of the plane he was on was a separate exit for First Class, which meant row 11 was first out the main door.

The LAX flight had arrived at gate F5. The arrival/departure halls are lettered at Schiphol, and from prior experience James remembered seeing the Heineken bar. It sits alone near the T and D gates, and to the left of European Union passport control. This was good. No need to enter the mouse maze for transfers to other terminals.

Igor made it to his departure gate in Edinburgh with forty minutes to spare. He boarded the regional flight and sat in seat 5A. Seventy-four minutes later he touched down in Amsterdam, where his flight parked on the tarmac.

Igor walked down steps and got on the first bus, which took him to terminal D. He made his way through the crowded gates and up to the main concourse. At the top of the escalator, he made a U-turn and headed toward the main shopping and dining hall, passing some empty T gates, the Heineken bar, and a cluster of shops and restaurants. As he was walking, he noticed the second level, and saw the Starbucks sign.

At the base of the stairs, the escalator was closed for maintenance. The Christmas tree ever festive to his right.

Igor walked to the top of the stairs and took a right into Starbucks, where he ordered an espresso and biscotti. He picked up his coffee and snack at the end of the counter and moved behind the barista area to a set of tables in the back, along the windows. He positioned himself with his back to the glass facing the tarmac, allowing his eyes to scan the comers and goers on the second floor.

Mathieu James was coming from the F gates, which put him in motion in the opposite direction of Igor Kozlov. After hitting the men's room, he walked beneath the second level where Starbucks was located, past the restaurants and shops and toward the T and D gates. As he approached passport control, he steered left.

The Heineken bar, at 09:35, was oddly busy. He stopped just short, adjusting his backpack and overnight bag, and scanned the bar. At a two-person high-top on the outermost edge of the seating area was a man in a Tottenham cap, blue scarf, and quilted gray jacket. Rather than one empty pint he had two, along with a fresh one, foamy to the top.

The Euros sure love their drink.

James took an educated guess that the second empty pint was just circumstance and walked toward the man. They made eye contact without saying a word. He grabbed the stool underneath the seat, pulled it back, and sat down across from the courier.

20

Schiphol International Airport
Amsterdam, Netherlands

The courier sat still, one hand on his freshly poured pint of Heineken, the other resting on the table, fingers fidgety. Under the Tottenham cap was a mess of blond hair. His skin was pale and his eyes cold, with dark circles underneath. He wasn't intimidating. In fact, he wasn't what Mathieu James expected at all.

Although he wasn't sure what, exactly, he had been expecting, but it wasn't this guy. Nails painted black and tattoos on his fingers, the courier was young. This shouldn't have surprised James since Ana-Marie Poulin said she went to university with him.

James adjusted his bags, placing the overnight duffle at his feet, and slinging the backpack over the chair. He kept everything close to him out of habit. The courier watched him, barely moving, looking frozen.

Was he strung out?

One way to tell. Start talking.

"Waiting long?" James tried.

He shook his head. Although the empty beers said otherwise.

"Good. I appreciate you meeting me. How do you want to do this?"

The courier scanned the bar and the concourse. On the lookout for something. For someone. He didn't answer. This gave James pause.

"Did you come alone?"

"Did you?" the courier replied.

"Of course. I'm a journalist, not a cop."

The courier pursed his lips and shifted in his chair. Clearly, he was uncomfortable.

"So, I'll ask again, how do you want to do this?"

"Off the record."

"I expected as much," James said.

"Don't ask me my name."

"Okay, what should I call you?"

"Call me nothing."

"Okay."

"You ask the questions, I'll provide the answers if I want."

"If you want?"

"Depends on what you want to know. And what I think you need to know. Because I know lots." The courier sniffed twice and wiped his nose on the back of his hand, then looked at James and raised his eyebrows, as if saying *'See?'*

"Alright," James said. "Can I start?"

He nodded.

"Who do you work for?"

"Next question."

"How long have you worked for the person you told Ana-Marie about?"

"A long time."

"How long?"

The courier was annoyed and leaned across the table.

"A long fucking time."

"Ten years? Five years?"

He shook his head.

"Something in the middle?"

"Why is this important to you?" the courier wondered aloud. "How long I've worked with this guy."

"I'm trying to establish a timeline."

"Of what?"

"Of you."

"Why?"

"I need you to be credible. Ana-Marie has told me things. I want to make sure you tell me the same things. I don't want you getting mixed up and not remembering things."

"You know I volunteered to be here. I said I would meet you. Isn't that enough?"

"Depends."

"On what?"

"Your motive," James said.

"My motive?"

"Yes, your motive. What *is* your motive?"

The courier looked away, staring at the barkeep with the long black hair, straight as paper, and the nose ring. She was laughing with a group of patrons. James waited patiently.

The courier avoided eye contact.

This dance lasted maybe three minutes.

James went back at him.

"I need to know why you want to talk. I need to know your motive. What's in this for you?"

The courier turned and locked onto James. His face seemed paler, colder. His eyes burned with anger.

"What's in it for me? How about my life?" he seethed. "How about the lives of my sister and mother?"

"Meaning?"

"Meaning I can't get out of what I'm into. I've been moving money for this guy for years now. He has the goods on me. He knows where I live. Who I fuck. Where I eat. He knows when my mother attends church, and when my sister has classes at the university. He knows all of it. He has the power."

"Power over you?"

"Yes."

"So you don't rat him out?"

He nodded.

"Who would you rat him out to?" James wondered.

"Does it matter? He doesn't want to be known. He wouldn't be happy I'm talking to you, that's for damn fucking sure."

"I understand."

"Do you?"

"Yes. Listen, I work on hard stories all the time, the kind of stories people don't want other people to know about. People talk to me, and they trust me. You can trust me. I'm sure Ana-Marie wouldn't have made this happen if she thought you couldn't trust me."

"What are you going to do with any of this information?"

"I'm hoping to write a story, expose the money pipeline. Ana-Marie and I are working together. She's working on the connections in Paris. I'm looking into London. And that's why I wanted to see you, to talk to you. She said you mentioned London."

The courier was still fidgety. He sipped his beer, wiping his mouth with his sleeve. *He acts like a junkie,* James thought. A waitress appeared, asking if James would like anything. He ordered a pint. Although it was barely 10:00 local time, it was after midnight in L.A.

She walked away, leaving a scent of strawberries and coconut. *Shampoo,* James thought, wondering why in that moment he connected with that scent.

Now James leaned across the table.

"Look, I'm interested in London. 2005. I know you were just a kid. But what happened there, we don't know the whole story."

"Who's we?"

"Everyone. The public, the authorities. Intelligence agencies. I'm right, aren't I?" James insisted.

The courier shrugged. "I guess it depends on what you know."

Frustrated, James leaned back and held back. He was tired. He was anxious. He'd been looking for clues for years—more than a decade. He wondered how much of what he thought was true might actually be.

The waitress with the hair smelling like strawberries and coconuts returned with a pint, laying down a coaster and offering a "Cheers!" before shoving a credit card machine in front of James. He paid and thanked her.

"Here's what I think," James said. "I think there's always been a 'fifth bomber' for London. I think that person was the mastermind, the brains, the money. Whatever. I think those guys, the four of them, were fucking stupid. I think they were radicalized to the point of no return because they weren't grounded. They didn't have lives. They had no future. I think someone convinced them to build those bombs, wear those backpacks, walk into those places and blow themselves and everyone and everything around them up. Someone convinced them that would give them purpose. There is no way—no way!—those four managed this on their own. London has cameras everywhere. MI5 and MI6 are dialed in. These guys weren't trained by ISIS in some camp in Syria. They didn't learn how to make bombs at school. They weren't the two fucking knuckleheads in Boston who threw a bunch of shit into a rice cooker and ran like pussies," James ranted, referring to the Boston Marathon bombers. "These guys lit themselves up. Liquid. Vapor. Poof!"

He paused, leaned back, catching himself getting hotter, his face redder, his demeanor angrier.

"Not just homegrown boys. They had help," he reiterated.

The courier was bouncing his right knee in a rhythmic pattern. Consistent, quick, twitchy. His arms were crossed now. His face was pointed straight at James, but his eyes continued to dart. Left, center, right. *He's not going to calm down,* James thought. *I need to lead him.*

James took a sip of Heineken—much better on draught than in a can or bottle—and sat straighter.

"Okay, look, let me get back to the questions. Let's start with what you told Ana-Marie, okay?"

He nodded approval.

"You told her that you helped a guy in Africa with money, you helped him with his flow of money."

He nodded again.

"Ana-Marie said you believe this guy funded the Paris attacks, true?"

The courier locked eyes on James. "Yeah. True."

"You know this how?"

"My friend."

"What friend?"

"My friend, he told me."

"What did this friend tell you?"

"My friend? He was *me* before me. He was *the guy* for the Africa guy. He ran the money through clubs. Through drugs. Through different things. He washed it and moved it."

"So your friend told you about this guy's connection to Paris, to the attacks?"

"That's what I said."

"How did he know?" James asked.

"How did my friend know about the attacks? The guy in Africa told him. He straight up told him he paid for it. He was the guy who made it happen."

"Why would the Africa guy tell your friend this?"

"Because he asked the wrong question."

"What question was that?"

"He asked the guy in Africa if he was involved in the Paris attacks, and if that meant that he—my friend—was indirectly involved in a terrorist attack."

"When was this?"

"Two, three years ago. My friend put some things together, some things that didn't make sense. Like the cafe that got shot up? That was a drop site. The weapons used? How many semi-automatic machine guns have you seen on the streets of Paris? He had seen those weapons on men he delivered to. This isn't America. Those things aren't everywhere."

James nodded, not wanting to interrupt.

The courier continued. "There were so many questions that my friend had. Often, I went with him and he paid me. He looked after me. In some ways I guess he trained me, or how do you say it, he groomed me."

"Groomed you for what?"

"To take his job eventually. I don't know for sure."

"Where is your friend now?"

The courier took in a deep breath and slowly exhaled. He put his arms up and his hands behind his head. He exhaled through his lips and his eyes watered.

"He's dead," he whispered.

James stayed locked on his eyes.

"They killed him."

"They?"

"Africa. Whoever Africa is."

"So you don't know who the guy is? You don't know his name?"

He shook his head, and continued, "but I've seen him. Once."

"What?" James demanded.

He nodded.

"When?"

"When he shot my friend in the face, right in front of me."

"Why did he do that?"

"Because my friend was asking too many questions. He probably was asking the *right* questions."

Asking the right questions of the wrong people is a great way to get yourself killed, James thought.

"And you were there?"

"Yes, I was there. I left with my friend's brains and skull and blood on my face and in my hair and on my jacket and shoes."

"Why didn't they kill you as well?"

"Because now they had me. Who could I tell? Where could I go? I couldn't run. I wanted to run. I wanted to scream. But I froze."

"Did they say anything to you?"

"Yeah, of course. They said, 'You're next. And this is what happens when you get outside your lane. If you want to avoid what happened to your friend—if you want your mother to return from church and your sister to return from class—you'll do the job, keep your head down and your mouth shut and one thing you'll never have to worry about is money because we will take care of you.'"

His eyes were welling with tears, his nose running. He was slobbering a bit at the memory. *No way he's acting.*

"So now *you* clean the money for them."

The courier nodded, grabbing a napkin and wiping his face.

"For how long?"

"Too long."

"And you heard enough to know this guy was connected to Paris?"

"Heard enough. Saw enough."

"And you said you saw him. Could you remember what he looked like?"

"I don't know."

James paused for a second, reviewing what he'd heard. "You said 'They killed him.' Who's they? Was there more than one person there when they shot your friend?"

He nodded.

"How many?"

"Two others."

"Who pulled the trigger?"

"The main guy."

"And you don't know his name?"

He shook his head.

James leaned forward, ready to ask another question, then leaned back. *What is the next question here? This guy is scared. He can't get out. His family is being watched. Why be the squeaky wheel? That's the next question.*

"Why talk? Why put yourself and your family in danger like this?"

The courier lifted his Heineken and took two big chugs, setting the pint glass down, now half empty.

"Because something else is going to happen. They are planning something."

"How do you know?"

"I just know. More money is coming through, and a few different guys have shown up to take the money. Foreigners."

"Foreigners?"

"Yeah."

"Like, what kind? From where?"

"Russian maybe? I don't know. They are white. They sound Russian, but they don't talk to me. I think they are middlemen. They find new places to clean the money."

"So you think this guy is planning something based on that?"

"Not just that."

"What else?"

"He asked me to meet him."

"When?"

"Today."

"Where?"

"Here."

"Here?" James looked around. "Here at the airport?"

He nodded.

"What time?"

"Three."

James looked at his watch. 15:00. That was almost five hours from now.

"When's the last time you saw him in person?"

"When he killed my friend. At least I know meeting him here, he won't kill me. No way he kills me in this place in front of all these people. He wouldn't be able to escape."

This was likely true, James thought. But still, it's risky.

"Why here? Why today? What are you expecting?"

"Honestly, I don't know. I'm guessing, just like you," the courier said.

"Well, okay. What's your best guess?"

"My best guess is he's already here meeting someone, and maybe he wants me to meet that same person."

James lifted his beer and took a long sip. Then another.

"Let's get back to London for a minute. You told Ana-Marie you think he's connected to 2005. Why?"

"Those foreigners I told you about?"

"Yeah."

"One of them made a comment. He said the boss told him what's next will make people forget about London."

"Was there something else? That seems thin."

"He said the boss wasn't happy with London last time. He said the job wasn't done right. He said, and I quote, 'It's time for the cicadas to sing.'"

21

Langley, Virginia

The CIA's Non Official Cover (NOC) program dates back to the 1940s. The purpose was to put agents in positions where they could infiltrate, gather, and report information that a CIA operative working under diplomatic immunity wouldn't or couldn't.

NOC agents work alone. They rarely have contact with their handlers. If they are caught, they don't have diplomatic immunity, unlike most of the "official" brethren. This means that a NOC officer could be arrested, tried, sent to prison, or even executed.

In the 1980s, CIA director William Casey sought to revitalize a NOC program that had ebbed and flowed over the preceding decades. At the time, there were approximately one hundred NOC operatives in the CIA. By 1986 that number almost tripled. Casey was interested in economic espionage, and he convinced American corporations to let him place NOC operatives overseas.

Today's version of the NOC program varies. It's all need-based. During Casey's tenure—and that of Ronald Reagan as president—the CIA came under fire for a series of gaffes, from failed coups to awkward arms deals. Investigative journalists did much of the yeoman's work, shining a spotlight on the agency's misdeeds. Additionally, as NOCs went largely unsupervised, they were often tasked with handling enormous sums of cash without oversight.

This created another set of problems. But the value of being able to insert someone with no official ties to the agency was too good. It was better to ignore the warts and enjoy the makeup instead.

When Alyssa Stevens had presented Mathieu James with the chance to become a NOC operative, she'd expected him to say no. He was a journalist, after all, and they are the purest of evil doers. To his credit, James's instinct was to say no. It would be counter to his role to shine light on topics, people, and policies that preferred to stay in the shadows.

But then there was that patriotic duty—that sense of honor—that came from serving in the military. The same military that helped pay for his education. And, he wondered astutely, how many stories would he get as a NOC that he wouldn't get otherwise? The pen truly can be deadlier than the sword. And if it helped him tell better stories, with access no one else likely had, what was the harm?

As Mathieu James sat and digested what he had just heard from the courier, his immediate thought was to contact Alyssa Stevens back in Langley. She should know something's afoot. It was only 03:00 there, and he didn't want to step away from the courier to call his handler. That would be weird.

Instead, under the guise of notetaking, he told the courier he was going to open his laptop.

The courier nodded.

"I just need to make some notes," James said. Which was true.

The courier took another sip from his beer as James pulled his MacBook Air from his backpack. As it powered on, James watched the courier. He was still nervous. Fidgety. His eyes still cold, scanning the terminal. *He's nervous. The financier is coming.* Or could already be here.

James typed his password to unlock the laptop and opened a Word document. He made a few bullet points:

- Friend was original courier

- Friend was killed for asking too many questions

- This courier was present and was threatened

- They threatened his family

- This guy has seen the Africa money man/can't remember anything (trauma?)

- Foreigners, maybe Russians, have been around his Paris operation

- Cicadas singing. He underlined this and used bold.

As he was typing, the courier said he needed to use the pisser and got up. There was a chance he wouldn't come back...but what was James going to do? He couldn't force him to stay. Show some trust.

"Sounds good. I'll be here."

The courier slinked away, hands in pockets, shoulders shrugged high, head tucked low. The loo was behind James about thirty yards or so, near passport control. James watched him walk away, then took his phone out and opened WhatsApp. He needed to get a message to Alyssa.

I have an update on Grandma, he typed and quickly slid his phone back into his pocket. As he waited—hoped—for the courier to return, the waitress stopped by, picked up the empty glasses and asked if they'd like to order something else. James declined.

He turned his eyes to his laptop and re-read the notes, recounting the conversation, and added a couple more.

- He feels hopeless

- Doesn't want to be an accomplice

- Is supposed to meet the money guy here

Behind James, the courier was just passing passport control. With his head still tucked low, he didn't see them. The boss and two others had just moved through and were on their way to meet Igor Kozlov at Starbucks.

James had closed his laptop by the time the courier came back to the table. He looked like shit.

"I think we should get some coffee in you before you meet this guy," James offered. "It's better if you're not shitfaced."

"I'm not shitfaced," the courier quipped.

"Not yet, maybe, but you will be if you keep pounding pints. There's a place right over there that has coffee and some food." James pointed. "Let's go get something and we can keep talking over there."

James stood and gathered his bags. He slung the backpack over one shoulder, grabbed the overnight bag with his left hand, and reached for his laptop with his right. He started to move, and the courier just sat there.

"C'mon. At the very least I can keep you company until your meeting. And maybe you'll remember some things you can tell me." The courier stood and joined James as they walked in silence toward the vendor positioned near the D6 sign.

With nobody in line, James stepped to the counter and ordered.

"Two lattes please...you want a latte?" he asked the courier. He nodded.

"Two lattes and two croissants. That's all, please."

James reached into his pocket for his phone and paid the vendor with Apple Pay. As he did so, he saw a notification from WhatsApp. A message from Alyssa was waiting.

Call me.

22

Schiphol International Airport
Amsterdam, Netherlands

The financier and his two goons nearly ran into the courier as he walked to the loo. Having exited passport control they now made a beeline for Starbucks.

The trio walked confidently but stood out. The financier was a short man, about 5-feet-7 inches. He had dark skin, curly cropped hair and walked with swagger. He was wearing a navy blue Adidas velour track suit, a scally cap and carried a hand-carved wooden cane. His belly bulged slightly, and his wrists were adorned with beaded bracelets and a Rolex Submariner. The two goons were security. White, both over 6 feet and fit. They were dressed in jeans, polo shirts, and blazers. All three of them wore sunglasses in the airport.

They definitely didn't care if they were noticed as they made their way to Starbucks on the floor above.

Inside the coffee bar, Igor Kozlov was sitting in the same seat, against the bank of windows. His back toward the tarmac.

The financier and his men reached the stairway and were miffed at the escalator being under repair. They started swimming up the stairs, against the flow of people coming down. Out front were the two goons. They made a path for their boss. At the top of the stairs, they turned to check on their man, and the three walked inside together. The financier stopped and removed his sunglasses. He scanned the room, looking for a face he had been shown in a photograph.

He spotted Igor in the back, snapped his fingers, and pointed first at a goon, then at the barista. One goon got in line for coffee. The other walked to the back with his boss.

Igor was buried in his phone, head down, oblivious to the two men approaching. The goon walking with the boss pulled out a chair and sat at the table next to Igor, which got his attention. As he lifted his head from his phone, he made eye contact with the goon first. Then with the boss. He recognized the situation immediately. Igor Kozlov stood and held out his hand, smiling. The financier did not accept this gesture. He pulled a chair out and sat across from Igor.

Igor was still standing, with his hand out, expecting a handshake that wasn't coming. Embarrassed, he withdrew and lowered his hand, smiled shyly, and sat down.

Igor and the financier locked eyes. It seemed like minutes but was less than ten seconds. The financier was measuring Igor, evaluating the unknown man in front of him. Igor was trying not to shit himself. He was nervous and felt the sweat beads forming on his forehead. His palms were clammy. He put his hands under his legs briefly, then back on the table, not wanting to make any suspicious moves or gestures. He waited for the financier to speak.

And then he did.

"Mr. Kozlov, is it?"

Igor nodded.

"You know who I am, correct?"

"Of course."

"I am the man who can help you."

"That's pleasing to hear," Igor said. "Thank you. Thank you for coming to meet me."

"I'm here on other business. But maybe we can do business together, you and I."

"Yes, of course. That would be wonderful."

"What's the nature of your business, Mr. Kozlov? What, exactly, do you want my assistance with?"

Igor leaned in and lowered his voice.

"I want to get the West's attention."

The financier maintained eye contact and nodded, encouraging Igor to continue.

"I want to disrupt their fat, comfortable lives. I want them to feel pain. To be afraid. To suffer. I want them to learn what it means to have something important taken away from them."

The financier moved his head approvingly.

"Tell me what you have in mind."

"I don't know. I'm not an expert at this. I've actually never done something like this. But I saw the power of terror in Paris, in London. The West thinks they are above it all. I want to bring them pain."

"What's in it for you?"

"It's personal."

"How so?"

Igor adjusted his chair and squirmed a bit. The second goon arrived with three espressos, handing one to his boss, one to his counterpart, and offering a shit-eating smile to Igor. He sat to his boss' right. Across from Igor now, the three men were seated. Goon, boss, goon.

Igor folded his hands and placed them on the table. He looked the boss in the eyes.

"I am from Belarus, originally. I grew up poor, but my parents worked very hard to provide a life for us. Since the collapse of the Soviet Union, things have not always been great for friends of Russia. At times, we in Belarus prospered. At other times, we suffered. We are suffering now. Putin's war in Ukraine has rallied the West against not just Putin, but his allies. Lukashenko has been targeted, meaning the people of Belarus aren't getting the food, the shelter, the medicine.

"My parents are still there, still in the same tiny place where they raised me. They don't have enough food to eat. They are losing weight and aren't well. My father tried to get money from the bank last week. They told him they didn't have enough cash on hand. The sanctions from the West are hurting innocent people. They need to pay! They need to suffer like my mother and father. I am so tired of the imbalance."

The financier studied Igor's face, which had reddened with anger. Veins bulged on his forehead. Sweat beads glistened.

"So your solution, Mr. Kozlov, is what?"

Igor took a deep breath and searched carefully for the right words.

"I was told you could help. That you were someone who had the means and the expertise to help me make a statement. My business, with my partner, we do fine. We eat well. We have nice things. But that's not enough. I need—I want—someone who can help me make a statement."

He stopped and locked on the financier's eyes.

"Are you that person?"

The boss chuckled.

"I'm always that person. I'm whatever the fuck I want to be."

Igor nodded.

"I have means and I have expertise. But you still haven't told me what you want. Or what you're willing to do personally. I agree with you, Igor. The West is out of control. They like to stick their noses in places they shouldn't. They shouldn't care what Putin does or doesn't do. They shouldn't punish people in Belarus.

"I consider what I do as an equalizer. I try to restore balance. I want the West on their toes, scared. Because then they are looking at everything. Then they are a mile wide and an inch deep.

"Tell you what, Mr. Kozlov. Bring me a plan. If I like it, if it makes a statement, if it makes their white skin turn yellow with fear, maybe we can do business together."

With that, the financier stood and turned to the goon on his left. He patted his stomach and said, "I'm hungry. Let's find something nice to eat."

Igor took the cue and stood as well. With a half smile, he asked a final question. "How should I get in touch with you?"

The boss turned his back to Igor and, as he walked away, said, "same as always. Use the channels. Goodbye now."

As the three men exited the Starbucks, they managed the impossible given their flamboyance. They disappeared in a sea of people.

Igor sat down and stared at nothing. *Holy shit,* he thought. *HO-LEE-SHIT.*

23

Falls Church, Virginia

Alyssa Stevens was wide awake, lying alone in her bed. Her face illuminated by her phone screen. She was mindlessly scrolling through Instagram, checking in on the lives of her college friends and teammates.

Marriage. Kids. Beach vacations.

Someday, she thought.

She flipped back and forth between social media and WhatsApp, waiting for the next missive from Mathieu James. He had been a low-key yet reliable contributor for her, feeding information that was often helpful. He would be a good agent, she believed, because he was detail oriented. That was why he was a successful investigative journalist. He knew how to ask the questions and get the most from his sources.

Stevens was normally up and out for a run around 05:00. The clock was ticking slowly. She could use another few hours of sleep, but it was now past 04:00 and she was awake. Hoping for another thirty minutes of sleep, she set the phone on the charger on her nightstand, rolled over, and closed her eyes.

As she lay there, tucked warmly under her comforter, she thought of James's message, and wondered how it was going. As her mind wandered, her body flirted with a light sleep. She rolled onto the opposite shoulder for a few minutes, before settling on her back. Once more on her right shoulder, then her back again. Giving in and giving up on sleep, she opened her eyes and stared at the ceiling.

Reaching for her phone with her left hand, she pulled it close to her face. It unlocked, and she checked WhatsApp again.

Nothing.

I did ask him to call. Maybe he can't.

Maybe he's still working on this guy.

With that thought in mind, she grabbed the corner of her comforter and top sheet and swung them open. Stevens sat up and pivoted her feet to the floor.

Time for a run.

Upright and walking toward her closet, she untied the drawstring to her silk bottoms and let them drop to the floor. She pulled on a performance thong and running tights, then removed her tank top, replacing it with a sports bra and long-sleeve thermal quarter zip. She grabbed some socks, her running shoes and a performance beanie, and walked into the living room.

Realizing she had forgotten her phone, Stevens went back into the bedroom and grabbed the phone and her AirPods from the nightstand.

In just a few minutes, she would be in the damp morning cold of Virginia, with eight miles of pavement awaiting her long stride.

24

Schiphol International Airport
Amsterdam, Netherlands

Mathieu James took his latte and croissant and sat at a high-top table, where he could charge his devices and open his laptop. With eight seats available, just two were taken. James chose the empty end on a corner.

The courier was pacing the concourse, sipping his latte and picking at his croissant. He was lost in his own head. Every once in a while, he'd give James a side eye, probably to see if he was watching him.

James typed some additional notes—and questions—into his laptop. He wasn't convinced, at this point anyway, that he had enough for a story. He thought it would be a good idea to check in with Ana-Marie Poulin to update her and see if she'd learned anything new.

Pulling out his phone, he opened its camera by swiping left on the home screen and took a quick image of the courier, still pacing in the concourse. Then, he opened WhatsApp and typed a message to AMP, attaching the image.

Here's your friend.
He's a hot mess.
Have learned a lot. Will fill you in.

-MJ

Checking his watch again, James decided to give Alyssa Stevens a call. It was way early on the East Coast, but she did say to call. Reaching into his backpack, he grabbed his AirPods and wedged them into his ears. With the familiar musical cue of connection, he hit Stevens's number in WhatsApp and waited for her to answer.

Across the Atlantic, Stevens was two miles deep into a cold morning run. With Beyonce serenading her inner ear, she was brought back to reality by Siri's voice. *Call from Mathieu James. Answer it?*

"Yes."

James heard the call connect and some heavy breathing on the other end.

He laughed and said, "catch you at the wrong time?"

"Ha ha, Mathieu," Stevens answered breathlessly. "I'm on a run. Talk to me."

"So this guy I met with, the courier. He knows some things."

"Such as?"

"He's been working for a guy in Africa. Sounds like he launders money in Paris before it's moved into legitimate accounts, which I'm guessing are in Switzerland and probably tied to my buddy Francois Thies."

"Okay, so there's the Africa connection. Did he give you a name?"

"Negative."

"Anything? Description? Phone number?"

"Well, he did say he's meeting the guy today. Here in the airport in Amsterdam."

"What? He said that?"

"Can confirm."

"When?"

"15:00 local."

"Do you have eyes on the courier now?"

"I do."

"And?"

"He's a hot mess. Been drinking since before I got here. Nervous as fuck. Looks a little strung out, but it's probably the stress of it all."

"Mathieu, I'm going to need eyes on that meeting. Can you do that?"

"Shouldn't be an issue."

"And pictures. If you can get some images, please do and send them to me."

"Of course."

"You gotta be discreet, Mathieu. You can't be seen."

"Not my first rodeo, Alyssa."

"Right. But we don't know who we're dealing with. And the last thing you need is to get yourself tangled up in something we don't know anything about."

"Agreed. But I'm already tangled. You know that. I'm doing my job for the *IHT* and I'm helping you and yeah, let's say the quiet part out loud, I've got some skin in this."

"Yeah, I know," Stevens said. She was approaching mile three and wanted to pick up the pace. The conversation had energized her, and she wanted to get to the office as soon as possible, especially knowing James would potentially have eyes on the Africa connection.

"Listen, Mathieu, I'm gonna jump off. Be safe and keep me posted."

"Sounds good. Talk soon."

"Bye."

"Bye."

James set his phone down, sipped his latte and pulled off a small piece of croissant and placed it on his tongue. He was watching the courier, who suddenly had his phone in his hand. He looked at James and nodded. James waved him over.

"What's up?"

"Got this just now," the courier said, holding his phone up to James. It was a green SMS text message. It read *E9*.

"You think that's from the money guy?"

"What else would it be?"

"I don't know. Were you expecting a text?"

"I was expecting anything. There was no communication on where to meet. Just the time."

"Okay, so they probably have scouted some place that will be pretty quiet."

"Or pretty busy," the courier said.

"Yeah, but I doubt that. He's not going to want anyone overhearing anything."

"True."

"My flight this morning arrived at F5, but honestly I didn't look around. We still have more than three hours. Let's take a walk and check it out."

"Okay, yeah."

"But not together, okay?" James said to the courier. "I can't be seen with you by them."

"I know. I get it."

"Why don't you get a head start? I'll pack it up here and be a few minutes behind you. Look around at everything near E9. Look for cameras, vendors, bathrooms, exits. Make a mental note of all of it."

"Okay, yeah. Makes sense."

The courier walked off, dumping his latte cup into a bin and taking the last bite of his croissant. He held his phone in his hand and adjusted his Tottenham hat, pulling it off his head and placing it back on.

Yeah, he's nervous as fuck.

The financier and his goons were in a first-class lounge on the second level, enjoying the free buffet, free drinks, and free entertainment. The goons stayed alert, avoiding alcohol and keeping eyes on the lounge's patrons. It was their job, after all, to keep this guy safe.

The financier had a mimosa, drained it, and ordered a second. He snacked on chickpea finger sandwiches and a Mediterranean pasta salad. He had sent the text to the courier using a burner phone—he always carried extra burners and SIM cards.

With his mind on Igor Kozlov, he wondered if this guy could deliver. He was definitely an amateur in the world of terror. But he had some money, he had enough clout and contacts to get in touch via the GRU. So he knew some people. That could be useful. He'd had his people run Kozlov's credentials. You can never tell if someone is CIA or MI6 these days. His story held up. He seemed to be who he said. And the parent story checked out. His GRU friend made sure to verify that.

With a final swig of his mimosa, he snapped his fingers at the goons, put his thumb and forefinger together and his pinky out, making a sipping motion to his lips.

The goons headed to the espresso bar and brought one back for the boss.

25

Paris, France

Ana-Marie Poulin was at her desk in the *International Herald Tribune's* Paris office. She had just returned from lunch with a colleague and was working through her notes on the possible sleeper cell lurking somewhere in the city. The horror of the 2015 attacks was still raw in Paris. Poulin found it unfathomable that something like that could happen again.

Yet here she was, almost a decade later, with decent information. This could be real. She was poring over news accounts from that time when her phone rang, startling her. It was Mathieu James calling on WhatsApp.

"Bonjour, Mathieu," she answered.

"Ana-Marie, hello. Things good in Paris?"

"Oui, oui. Things are fine here. Trying to connect some dots, you know? Put this puzzle together."

"How's it coming?"

"Hmmm, slow, Mathieu. Very slow. What's happening there? Are you still with him?"

"He's off doing a little recon. I'm not too far behind him. He has a meeting soon, and I'm going to do my best to observe."

"How are you going to do that?"

"I'll just look like another passenger and try to keep a line of sight. I mean, I am another passenger, so it shouldn't be strange."

"Okay, sounds good. What else? Has he given you anything you can use?"

"He's getting us closer to London, that's for sure. He seems to be confident there's a link that goes straight to this African financier."

"I see. Okay, well stay in touch and let me know how it goes."

"Will do."

"Ciao, Mathieu."

"Ciao."

Poulin terminated the call and stared at her laptop. She was visualizing her college friend in the airport in Amsterdam. *What has he gotten himself into? Hopefully, he's not in over his head.*

Time would tell.

Then she thought of her colleague. She hadn't met Mathieu James in person, but he seemed like a stand-up guy. Her curiosity always got the best of her, though. Probably why she was a good journalist. But she wondered, *Is all this too personal for James? Can he be objective?*

At Schiphol, James had gathered his things and was on his way to explore the area around E9. As he strolled past the Heineken Bar and into the plaza, he took a moment to take in his surroundings. Luxury brands, upscale eateries, personal care. You really could live in a well-run airport.

The number of travelers had increased since James landed. The plaza was busier than earlier in the day with occasional passengers sprinting through the maze of people with looks of fret and dread as they tried to make a connection.

James also noticed that airport security randomly stopped travelers, asking to see their travel documents and swabbing their bags for explosives. A necessary normal in the wake of 9/11. But it also seemed sketchy. Most of the travelers stopped were young men, many with beards and long hair. No question there was some profiling happening here. *Maybe a good story down the road?*

The courier had made his way to the E concourse and walked the full length before turning around. There were security cameras everywhere. Some gates were empty, but it was fairly busy. If the boss wanted to be alone, this wasn't the place.

Intent on following instructions, he noted everything he could around E9 and headed back toward the plaza. He was holding his phone in his right hand when he felt it vibrate. As he lifted the screen to his face to unlock it, butterflies filled his stomach.

There was a message that would turn those butterflies into nausea.

Change of plans.

Airport library. 5 minutes. We will find you.

26

Schiphol International Airport
Amsterdam, Netherlands

As the courier was coming out of E concourse, James was heading in. They crossed paths almost immediately and made eye contact. The courier's eyes got big, he held up his phone, and nodded quickly, as if to say, *this way*.

James picked up on both and checked his phone, to see if the courier had texted him. He hadn't. He continued to walk further down the E concourse to put some distance between himself and the courier, then did a U-turn and headed back toward the plaza.

Up ahead, he could see the Tottenham cap weaving through pedestrian traffic. He kept his eyes locked on the hat, careful to keep his distance while mindful of looking casual. Inside the plaza, James stopped at a kiosk, then a sunglasses shop, pretending to browse while keeping tabs on his mark.

Just across the plaza was the airport library, a sitting space with comfy chairs, power outlets, and a generally relaxed vibe. James saw the courier looking for a place to sit. At the far end, a couple of empty chairs caught his attention, and he moved that direction.

With that decided, James needed to figure out where he could get eyes on all of it. Some tables were nearby, as well as a couple of restaurants.

There was the second level, which could offer a view from above, but he wouldn't be able to get a look at his face or take a photo with his phone.

He settled on an empty table with four chairs. There would be considerable foot traffic between him and the courier, but that should also provide him cover. Nothing too obvious, and he should be able to get a couple of images and a line of sight.

James sat down and placed his bags on one of the chairs. He pulled out the book he'd grabbed from Taylor's place and set his phone on the table. He made eye contact with the courier and nodded, wishing him good luck. Just as the courier gave a single nod back, a man sat down next to him.

He was wearing a navy colored Adidas track suit, a cap and sunglasses. He carried a hand-carved walking stick of some kind. His skin was dark, and he was sporting a beard and was twirling a toothpick in his mouth.

Must be him.

James quickly scanned the immediate area around the courier and his boss, looking for anyone that seemed out of place. Nothing registered. He settled in with his phone at the ready, making mental notes, and looking for a chance to get some pictures with his phone.

"Good to see you again," the boss said to the courier.

The courier didn't respond. He glanced at the boss, who was seated to his right, and then looked straight ahead again.

"We have a project we are working on," the boss continued. "It's going to require some special attention."

"What does that mean?" the courier asked, still looking straight ahead.

"It means you will be working with some different people. My Russian friends who have been helping you in Paris will still be around, but for this project they cannot be involved. Things are—how should I say it?—complicated with this one."

"But you're still moving money, that's what you need me to do, right?"

"Yes, money will always be part of the transaction. But in this case, there will be another shipment."

"Of what?"

"This is not your concern."

"It would help me to know exactly what's happening so I can prepare for contingencies," the courier said.

"I understand, but in this case, you just need to do the job."

"Why are we having this conversation here?"

"It is important for you to see the faces of the people who will be involved in this transaction. They are here with me now."

The courier leaned forward and looked on the other side of the boss. There was an empty chair, then a woman who had headphones on, watching a cooking show on her iPad.

"Where?" the courier asked, leaning back in his seat.

"One is to your left. Jeans, sport coat, built like a boxer, hair shaved close."

The courier looked to his left, scanning the sea of humans scurrying about. He spotted him, standing alone, holding a phone in his hand. He looked like a security agent, also scanning the area, hunting threats.

"And the other one?" the courier asked.

Across the plaza, James was watching the conversation unfold. He wasn't a lip reader, but he was trying with no success. The gestures the courier was making—leaning forward and looking, then turning to his left—were clear signs that he was searching for someone else.

James scanned the plaza. There were so many travelers moving through the airport, and those stopping for food, or shopping for gifts, it was hard to get a bead on anything.

He placed his phone vertically, pretending to be reading something on it, and opened the camera. Clicking the tiny 2x on the screen, he activated the short telephoto lens, trying to get as much length as possible so his images would be clear. He took two quick photos and inspected them.

Decent, but not good enough.

James did the same thing once more, lining up the camera, trying to get a clear image of the boss. He was too intent to think about who he was truly looking at, the person who may be involved in planning the London attacks that killed his parents. One thing James was good at was compartmental-izing things. Just ask Taylor.

He was feeling good about his angle when he noticed a large group of tourists moving from his right to his left. They were led by a person with a sign, and everyone was wearing the same shirt and badges.

Missionaries, James thought.

He'd have to wait for the school of fish to swim past.

"The other one," the boss said, "is right over there, standing behind your friend."

What?

The courier glanced immediately at James, who was still in his position at the table. James was looking around the plaza as the tour group moved in front of the courier's field of vision.

"My friend? What are you talking about?"

"Your friend, seated over there. Tall, handsome with wavy hair."

"I don't know anyone here."

"Do you always drink with strangers, then?"

What is he talking about? Oh shit, the courier thought. *Did he see us together at the Heineken Bar?*

"I don't know what you're talking about," the courier said.

"I think you do. That man, you were sitting with him at the bar earlier today. And then you got up to hit the loo, and walked right in front of us as we came through passport control."

What is he talking about? I don't remember seeing him. But I did go to the loo. Fuck.

The courier was beginning to sweat. His hands felt clammy and cold. He squirmed in his seat.

"Who is that person?"

"I don't know"

"Yes, you do know."

"I'm telling you, I don't know."

"C'mon now, I'm supposed to believe you were having beers with someone you don't know."

"Okay, look, this guy saw my Tottenham cap and was friendly and wanted to talk football."

The courier made brief eye contact with James. In doing so, he tried to make a gesture, opening his eyes wide and quickly tilting his head, trying to make James aware of his surroundings.

"Not a believable story, my friend. What are you not telling me?"

Across the plaza, James took the non-verbal cue as a sign of distress. As the tour group finally moved past, he again trained his iPhone camera on the boss and had a clear line of sight. He snapped a couple of photos.

Suddenly, he felt a hand on his left shoulder. He turned around to see a hulking man standing over him.

"Give me your phone," the man said.

James immediately made the connection. This guy was with the boss, and the courier was trying to point him out. His mind raced. *That's one. Where's the other? Think. Say something.*

In his worst attempt at being a foreigner, James said, "Parlez-vous français?"

"Your phone. Hand it to me."

James quickly processed the accent. *Russian. Keep going. Think, Matty. Think.*

"Je suis désolé, parlez-vous français?"

The hulking man standing above James had the strategic and tactical advantage. Being seated made James vulnerable. He was trying to buy time while he planned his exit.

The big Russian didn't ask again. He reached down and tried to grab James's phone. James pulled it away quickly, muttering, "I don't think so" in English. Here, his instincts kicked in.

James pushed with his legs, scooting his chair back to give him space. With his phone in his right hand, he balled his fist and quickly punched the Russian in the groin. The Russian groaned and buckled.

James grabbed his bags and took off, glancing back to see the Russian on his knees, bent over, with onlookers curiously assessing the situation. He eyed the courier, who together with the boss had seen this unfold. The boss looked to his left and made eye contact with his other bodyguard, putting his index finger in the air and making a circling motion.

Get moving.

The second Russian began walking swiftly through the terminal, eyes locked on James.

In this moment, and for this moment, Mathieu James didn't have a plan. He was trying to get space between him and the problem, but another problem presented itself. He was in a secure airport, with a ticket back to Los Angeles the following day, and no obvious way out.

He couldn't board another flight or purchase a new ticket without exiting the departure hall. If he wanted to exit the airport, where would he go?

Think.

Zig-zagging through the plaza area was easy. The plethora of shops and dining areas allowed him to weave seamlessly about. Whenever possible, James checked his six, trying to determine if he could remain evasive.

And then it occurred to him. *The hotel.* James was planning to stay a night but hadn't made a reservation. He was trying to remember where the hotel was. Schiphol offered easy access outside the terminal to an assortment of hotels. There was also one inside, the Mercure. He rattled his brain to recall where it was located.

On his next glance behind him, James saw the second Russian. While he hadn't picked him up earlier, this guy was dressed for the part. He wasn't sure if the Russian had eyes on him, so he kept the pattern, slipping in and out of shopping areas, slowing down to be less noticeable. *Don't run,* James thought. *You'll stand out.*

At once, two things popped into James's head. He had a tuque in his backpack, and he'd seen the hotel sign when he came out of the F gates. He set his bags down, opened the pack, digging inside with his hand, feeling around for the tuque.

Found it.

While kneeling, he placed the tuque on his head and tucked his hair inside. He then slipped off his jacket and shoved it inside the backpack.

He stood and surveyed the scene. He spotted the second Russian. He had gone past James's location and was standing near a sunglasses shop, scanning the plaza. He then looked to the opposite direction—where he was sitting originally—and noticed some airport workers in yellow vests around a man on the ground. *Probably EMTs. Must have gotten him good.*

James began to move toward the F gates. As he did, he walked directly in front of the airport library. Still in his chair, watching the action unfold, was the boss. James wasn't sure, but he felt confident he got at least one photo of the guy.

To the left of the boss, an empty chair. The courier had left. Probably panicked. He was already nervous.

James grabbed his phone from his pocket and slid his thumb left across the home screen, opening the camera. He selected video and hit record as he walked past the seated boss. The two locked eyes immediately. James picked up the pace. The boss sat alone, watching him go, calmly tracking his newfound prey.

This wasn't lost on James.

See you soon, motherfucker.

27

Mercure Hotel
Schiphol International Airport
Amsterdam, Netherlands

Mathieu James continued his brisk march toward the F gates, Lounge 3, and ultimately the Mercure Hotel. If he could get in there unseen, he would have the upper hand. At the bottom of the stairs, he took a detour in case he was being watched or followed. He performed a circular route and spotted no one.

He made a beeline for the stairs and moved swiftly, taking every other step. At the top, he turned right and entered the hotel, removing his tuque and tousling his hair. James approached the check-in counter and asked for a single room.

Wish granted.

Following registration and payment, he grabbed a complimentary water and a bag of nuts and found his room.

What's next? How do I get out?

Back in the plaza, the courier was in full panic mode. If they saw him talking with James—even if they didn't know who James was—they were going to ask more questions. The courier didn't want to end up like his friend, with a bullet in his head.

Exhausted by living in fear, the courier thought maybe it was time to run. Escape. Get out from under the thumb of this man. *But where? Where would I go?* There was no answer. And then he thought of his mother and sister. They knew his mother went to church. They knew his sister was at university.

Shit.

With his mind racing, he was entering fight or flight mode. Panicky and motivated, he needed to find a place to think. *I can't put my family in danger.*

The courier scanned the plaza. There was still a commotion near the tables, where James tried to make that Russian a permanent soprano. His mind went straight to the loo. Get inside a toilet stall and wait it out.

Another check to his right and the path to the loo near passport control and the D gates appeared clear. He started to move, taking off the Tottenham cap and shoving it inside his jacket.

Twenty-five yards away, the second Russian caught a glimpse of him removing his cap. *Target acquired.* He locked onto the courier and began moving. He played an angle that would put him ten yards behind when the courier reached the loo.

The courier, feeling like he was in the clear, increased his pace, seeking cover as soon as possible. The Russian matched him step for step. The two turned right, heading down the hall to the loo.

Sensing someone behind him, the courier looked back.

Fuck.

He increased his pace, getting inside the bathroom.

Fuck, fuck, fuck.

Looking left, he went right. He needed a stall. *There!* He started running.

The Russian was right behind him, getting closer, within reach.

The courier was looking at the door handles, hoping for an empty stall.

Red.

Red.

Red.

All occupied.

There, green!

He reached for the door, pulled it open and stepped inside, quickly turning to close the door.

And there it was. A big meaty paw on the door. The Russian cursed in his native tongue as the door slammed on his hand. It bounced open just enough and he was able to get inside by reaching with his forearm to block the door from closing again.

The courier was trapped. Nowhere to go.

He couldn't fight the big Russian. There was no way he could handle him. He backed up, stumbling over the toilet.

"Okay, okay, okay," the courier said, pleading with his pursuer, hands in the air.

The Russian balled his fist and delivered a jab to the courier's nose. His face felt like it had exploded. Blood splattered onto the walls. Instinctively, he put his hands to his face, covering his nose, concealing his pain.

Hunched over, the courier was at the mercy of the big Russian, who reached inside his pocket and pulled out a thick gage, pre-cut spool of fishing line. Wrapping the line around his hands, he kicked the courier in the stomach, sending him backward, stumbling over the toilet again.

The Russian grabbed the courier and spun him. With the courier's back now facing his assailant, he feared for his life. *Is this it?*

The Russian had a taut grip on the fishing line and reached over the courier's head. The line met his neck. The courier's hands reached for it, but the Russian was twisting and pulling with all his strength. The courier was digging with his fingers, his nails, anything to get something between that wire and his throat. He flung his elbows wildly, kicked his feet backward, anything to disrupt his attacker.

But the man was too big, too strong, and had the tactical advantage. The courier kept fighting, trying to kick, punch, scream. His face turned red, his eyes bulging and snot firing from his noise. Spit and foam covered his lips. His neck, his face, his forehead turned blue. His brain said scream, but his body couldn't. Life was literally being choked out of him.

His attacker could sense the end was near. He rolled his wrists, tightening the fishing line one last time. Elbows out and back, he flexed his traps and deltoids in a quick, snapping motion, and felt life leave the smaller man.

The Russian loosened his grip and unwound the wire. His hands and wrists were a reddish-blue and bleeding. The line had cut into him as they fought. The courier's body went limp, and the Russian positioned him hunched over the toilet, as if he were vomiting. He stepped out of the stall and closed the door.

Another traveler walked in, and they made eye contact. The Russian was sweating. He turned to the sink, splashing cold water over his face, then washed his hands. He looked at himself in the mirror, glanced at the stall door behind him, grabbed a paper towel from the dispenser, and wiped his face. With another he wiped his hands and exited the bathroom with a calmness only a killer could possess.

28

Mercure Hotel
Schiphol International Airport
Amsterdam, Netherlands

Mathieu James held the keycard over the lock on Room 202 and entered the single. European hotel rooms always made him laugh a little. The "single" room was literally that: a single bed, meant for one person, with half the space of an American-style hotel room. At that moment, he was beyond grateful for the small refuge.

James put his bags on the bed and sat down. Time to think.

So now we have images of the African connection. I need to get those to Alyssa immediately.

He grabbed his phone and held it to his face to open it, noticing the battery was running extremely low. Inside his backpack he grabbed a power adapter and charger and plugged the phone into the wall socket above the tiny desk.

Opening WhatsApp, James quickly typed a message to Alyssa.

Sending you images and a video of our friend from Africa.

I was spotted and confronted.

Shit got real.

Safe for now. Need an exfil plan.

As he attached the images, he finally took a minute to look at them closely. While he didn't recognize this person, he was relieved to know they had something to work with. He assumed Alyssa and her colleagues at the CIA would be able to run some kind of facial recognition algorithm on the images and the video. With any luck, this man was in the database somewhere.

James hit send.

What's next? Probably update AMP.

Still on WhatsApp, he punched a message to Ana-Marie Poulin in Paris.

Afternoon meeting went sideways.

Have video confirmation of African connection.

Lost contact with your friend.

Safe for now.

-MJ

Across the Atlantic, Alyssa Stevens was at her desk when her phone vibrated with James's message. She quickly opened it, curiosity getting the best of her.

Holy shit, she thought to herself. *There he is.*

She pinched the screen and zoomed in, studying the face of the man possibly behind two of the most heinous terror acts in Western Europe. *Do I know this man?* She took a long, deep look at two images and the video. As much as she wanted to know who this was—wanted to recognize him and pull a name from memory—she was stumped.

Stevens typed a quick reply to James.

Thanks James. Good work there.

Are you sure you were spotted?

I'll get these images to our team and I'll get back to you with a new travel itinerary.

Stevens rose from her desk and strode out of her office and down the hall. A left and a right later, she scanned her access card and entered a room buzzing with activity. This is where the agency tracked criminals and terrorists in real time.

She stopped and searched the floor, looking for a familiar face. She found one. Ben Wilson was someone with whom she'd entered the program. She nodded and acknowledged him by raising her hand. The two walked toward each other, meeting in the center of the bustling space.

"Hey, Ben! Haven't seen you in a while."

"Stevens, always great to see you. Do they lock you in your office and slide a food tray under the door?"

"Ha, sometimes I wish."

"Yeah, I hear you. What's up? You need help with something?"

"I do, actually. I have some images of a person of interest —potentially a high-value terror target—and I wanted to see if your team could help ID him."

"Yeah, of course. Let's see what you have."

Stevens handed him her phone with the images already pulled up.

"There's two pictures and one video taken by one of our NOCs in Amsterdam."

Ben studied the images.

"These are pretty good quality. That will help. Can you upload those to our internal server? That will get things started. Then I can assign a team member to it and hopefully get you some answers. We'll start with the Interpol database and go from there."

With its global reach, Interpol had an extensive pool of images and the best facial recognition software available. It was their best bet to ID the man.

"Thanks Ben, that's super helpful. Our NOC is on the run and I need to see if I can assist in getting him out of there."

"Copy that. Let's stay in touch. I'll let you know when I have something."

"You're the best." Stevens turned and headed for the door.

"Hey Stevens, let's get that beer you owe me sometime soon."

"You got it!"

In his hotel room, James took a minute to organize his bags. *Ah shit. I left Taylor's book on the table in the plaza. Gonna need to replace that.* He chugged the water he'd received at check-in while snacking on the nuts. Thinking it would be a good idea to change clothes, he grabbed a clean pair of jeans and a shirt from the overnight bag, along with his toiletries kit.

He took a quick shower, brushed his teeth and ran a comb through his hair. Looking at himself in the mirror, he acknowledged he was tired. The adrenaline was wearing off from the altercation in the airport plaza, and that come down always made him sleepy.

James pulled on some underwear and tossed the towel onto the bathroom floor. He moved his bags from the bed to the desk, checked his phone, and laid down.

I could use ten minutes, he thought. Closing his eyes, James zonked right away.

He awoke to the sound of his phone buzzing. *Messages.* He quickly sat up and looked at his home screen. There were a dozen messages from Alyssa Stevens and Ana-Marie Poulin. Plus one from Frank Murphy. All on WhatsApp. And an iMessage from Taylor.

James checked the time. His ten-minute nap had turned into an hour and fifteen minutes.

29

Schiphol International Airport
Amsterdam, Netherlands

Still in his navy blue Adidas leisure suit, scally cap and shades, the boss from Africa gathered his two bodyguards in Schiphol's plaza. His hair still curly, and his wrists still adorned with beaded bracelets and a Rolex Submariner; the custom walking stick he carried stood out.

The hulking Russian brought to his knees by the fist and iPhone of Mathieu James declined further medical attention. His testicles were likely to be black and blue for reasons he didn't care to remember. His partner helped him up, keeping an eye on the boss, who was more interested in the shitshow he just witnessed.

The boss wanted answers.

"What happened here?"

"Boss, we should probably move quickly and get out of here," the Russian killer said, his accent thick, his mind racing and his body language intense.

"What's the hurry?" the boss demanded, his belly bulging slightly, and that curly hair tangled under his cap showing just enough.

"The courier is in the toilet. And we don't want to be here when someone finds him."

The boss glanced around at the ceilings and walls. Security cameras everywhere, which meant the actions of his men would be seen. It also meant the courier and whoever the other guy was would also be seen. But how much?

Not worth finding out.

"Okay, here's the plan. We are going to leave the airport and take a train to Paris and my apartment there. Let's go, now!"

The three men moved toward baggage claim, leaving behind a whirl-wind of problems inside Schiphol. The courier was dead. Was any part of that caught on security camera? The confrontation with the unknown man, also likely caught on camera, brought eyes onto his bodyguard, who was injured and unable to walk for a short while. Had anyone asked him for ID? Or asked him any questions?

It was best to not talk about it here, or at all really, until they were in a secure location in Paris. As the trio exited the airport and headed for Amsterdam Central, life around them went on. PA announcements and the mechanical whir of baggage belts. People talking on phones; kids chasing each other. Outside the terminal, horns honked, filling the air with tension, as cars positioned themselves for pickups under a canopy of carbon monoxide clouds. Couples embraced in the foggy, damp air. Reunions of love. Businessmen and women went off to the city. Police officers patrolled the area, numb to potential threats that existed.

The boss absorbed the scene around him. His situation was urgent, but he couldn't help get past how normal life seemed in that moment, just outside the doors of Schiphol.

Normalcy wasn't acceptable. Time to put the West back on their heels.

30

Edinburgh, Scotland

Igor Kozlov boarded his flight in Amsterdam bound for Edinburgh unaware of the mild chaos and eventual murder that had transpired, involving people he had just met. He had a window seat on the flight out, and dozed off, dreaming of his family.

The holidays were approaching, and he had fond memories of his siblings and parents, grandparents and cousins all gathered for food and merriment. Always a festive time.

As the plane's wheels touched down in Edinburgh, he was alert and thinking back on his conversation with the man from Africa. He wanted a plan. *Why did he want me to come up with this plan?* Igor knew this wasn't his forté.

Being a small-time criminal wasn't the same as being a terrorist and planning a catastrophic event to get the West's attention. This guy was supposedly able to provide the means—money and whatever else—to carry out an attack.

So that's how I have to think. What kind of attack would make the statement worth it? What would rattle the West? Could it possibly lessen sanctions against the people of Russia and Belarus?

Igor deplaned, walking down the steps, and onto the tarmac, following the roped lines into the terminal, up three flights of stairs, down several hallways and into customs. He followed the queue, weaving back and forth, until he was at a kiosk where he scanned his passport and got his photo taken.

From there, he exited the baggage area, took a left out of the arrivals hall and headed toward the tram. After purchasing his ticket at the automated vending machine, he boarded the tram, bound for Waverley Station and a train home to London.

He had so much to consider. With the outskirts of Edinburgh rolling past him, he thought of this city he had never spent time in. He remembered people in his neighborhood talking about the Christmas Market, and how they made a holiday out of visiting.

The tram's ticket agent appeared, asking Igor and those around him to show their tickets so he could validate them.

"Excuse me, mate," Igor said to the ticket agent. "If I wanted to visit the Christmas Market, which stop is that?"

"You'd be keen to get off at Princes Street or St. Andrew's Square," the agent replied.

"Thanks mate. Cheers."

"Cheers."

Why not? Igor thought. May never get the chance again.

St. Andrew's square was also the stop for Waverley Station, so Igor chose to exit the tram there.

A very short walk later, he entered the Christmas Market. It was full of holiday cheer. Amusement rides, festive lights, food vendors. Families milled about. Flocks of teens squealed and laughed. Toddlers ran in circles, high on sugar. Adults sipped mulled wine, pounded pints or held coffee with both hands, keeping warm.

The temperatures were unseasonably cold, and a blustering wind from the south produced gusts that made your eyes water.

Igor was surprised at the sheer size of the festival, with dozens of vendors offering everything from pizza to Christmas ornaments. There was an ice rink for skating and a stage for concerts. This was something to behold.

He strolled the East Princes Market and continued on to the second market on George Street and Castle Street, snacking on donuts and playing with snow globes.

Before long, he checked his watch and saw that he had already been there for two hours. He pulled out his phone, checking train times for London. There was one left, and it departed in forty-five minutes.

Igor made his way toward an exit. The air around him filled with laughter, with joy, with a traditional holiday spirit. People were enjoying themselves and the season. Distant screeching from the carnival rides, the occasional crying child, adults offering toasts, and consuming holiday cheer.

He should be enjoying this. But the more time he spent inside the Edinburgh Christmas Market, the more it grated on him. All of the money and the happiness and the...freedom. Was it actually the freedom he despised? He, too, was living that life in London. He was living much better than his parents and siblings and extended family.

Now, with every step toward the exit, the scenes unfolding before him caused his muscles to tighten. He clenched his jaw, he balled his fists. He pursed his lips and shook his head. *Here, they are happy and carefree. Yet my parents are worried about food, about losing their money to the bank.* His frustration and anger at the disparity put him on a low boil.

Fuck the West, he thought. *Fuck them.*

Igor Kozlov finally exited the Christmas Market and walked up Constitution Street toward Waverley Station. His mood had soured considerably, and he was already frustrated, scared, and angry after his meeting in Amsterdam.

He entered the station and checked the board, finding his platform. The train was still on time. As he waited on a bench, his thoughts jumped back to his meeting with the African boss. 'Bring me a plan,' he'd said.

Igor had an idea. Perhaps he had just found his target. *What better way to get the West's attention than to take away the very traditions they loved?*

With this thought swimming freely in the open waters of his mind, Igor lowered his head and smiled.

The target had been acquired.

31

When Mathieu James's phone buzzed again, it was Alyssa Stevens on the other end. She sent a text, assuring him she was working on two things.

MJ:
Running images now. Will let you know.
Working on exfil. Standby for further instructions.

James had no qualms about Stevens and her colleagues doing everything they could. She had been nothing but fair to him since that original meeting adjacent to the FBI's Los Angeles Field Office. His decision to get on that government jet in Santa Monica that day was easier than he'd expected, looking back. Since he left Ranger Regiment for school at Northwestern, he'd missed being of service to his country.

This relationship—his Non Official Cover—allowed him to put duty before self without sacrificing any responsibility he had to his employers at the *International Herald Tribune* or his sources.

In so many ways, what the CIA does and what investigative journalists do is the same. They gather and process information. They analyze it and write about it. They develop sources and methods. It's really the end game that creates the divergence. For the Agency, it's about national security and protecting the public. The public doesn't necessarily need to know what's going on behind the curtain.

For journalists, it's about sharing information with the public. Creating transparency that governments—and others, like criminals, terrorists and dictators—aren't willing to provide.

James was working both sides of that fence, and it didn't faze him.

While awaiting word on an exfil plan, James decided to clean up his notes and create an up-to-date summary of key points. He planned to share this with Ana-Marie Poulin in the Paris office.

- *Met with Thies in Scottsdale. He suggested new money coming into the fund.*
- *Source has intel on intercepted call with cryptic language. Could be Thies's guy?*
- *AMP has a source who claims to work for someone taking credit for Paris and London attacks. He is a courier; agrees to meet me in Amsterdam.*
- *At meeting, source confesses to witnessing the murder of his friend*
- *Source says he is also at AMS to meet the African boss*
- *Source meets with African boss, and disappears after I get blown*
- *African boss has two rugged bodyguards, likely Russians, likely ex-military or Wagner Group*
- *Was able to get images of African boss*

Those were the highlights. But they created so many more questions. There wasn't anything like a smoking gun at this point, although AMP's courier, who she considered a friend of sorts after attending university with him, had given her reliable information.

James then wrote down some questions and a to-do list.

- *Contact Frank with an update*
- *Reach out to Francois Thies and see if that transaction from RBS went through*
- *Will the courier keep talking?*
- *Would he reach out to AMP and tell her what was said by his boss?*

- Who is the African boss? Can we get a positive ID?

And, perhaps the most important question of all:

- If the African is laundering more money, and it's eventually going through Thies's fund, what is the intent? What are they planning?

James emphatically underlined that last sentence three times.

He glanced up from his notes and looked out the tiny window in his single. Outside, a highway bustled with trucks. It was still foggy. Naked trees stood together in single file, at the most distant end disappearing into the hanging haze. The pavement was wet, and the deep bass rumble of jet engines rattled the window frame.

Always an adventure, James smirked to himself. *Always.*

Almost thirty minutes later, his phone buzzed with a message from Alyssa Stevens. She was always on it. Reliable as fuck.

Move to EDI.

Indirect travel.

Cash only.

Next update in 5 hours.

James re-read the message. *What is EDI?* He opened a private browser window on his phone and typed it in. EDI is the airport code for Edinburgh, Scotland. James couldn't remember if he'd ever been to Edinburgh. With his mom's family in the UK and his dad being stationed at RAF Lakenheath, home of the US 48th Fighter Wing, it was possible he and his parents traveled around England, Scotland, and Wales during their time there. He was just so young, and he remembered so little.

Okay, so indirect travel. That should be easy, James thought.

Cash only. Well, this could be tricky. James made decent money. He could access a couple thousand dollars in a savings account, move it to checking, and hit a couple of ATMs.

Would an ATM be a good idea? Probably not. Maybe one withdrawal here at Schiphol because anyone looking would already know he was here. *Yeah, that makes more sense.* Get what he can from here and figure it out later.

James opened the US Bank app on his phone to move some money into his checking account. After the facial recognition software confirmed his identity, the app opened to his account summary. He took a quick glance, and then a longer one. The balances of his checking and savings were higher than expected. *What the...?*

He opened his checking account and looked through the line items. It didn't take long for him to see where the extra money had come from. It was a $2,000 wire transfer from 'Atlantic-British Holdings' which wasn't a company he recognized. It had dropped into his account fifteen minutes earlier.

That's gotta be Stevens, James thought. *A little play money until we figure shit out.*

James decided not to move any more money and logged out of the app.

Wary of using his phone too much, James gathered his bags and packed them. First, he wanted to get to Amsterdam Central, the city's train depot. From there, he could investigate routes to eventually take him to Edinburgh.

James pulled on his backpack and grabbed the overnight bag by the hand straps. He exited room 202 and placed a 'Do Not Disturb' sign on the door. He walked out of the hotel and found an ATM in the baggage claim area. His daily limit was $1,000 for a withdrawal, so he took all of it and boarded the airport train for the city. He would be in Amsterdam Central in 10 minutes.

32

Langley, Virginia

Alyssa Stevens was in her office, looking through a top secret list of Agency safe houses in the UK. Although Britain was the United States's closest ally, one can never be too careful or discreet. The Agency and its partners at DOD, NSA, and even foreign intelligence agencies often needed to move internal and external assets through different countries. Having plenty of options was key.

Stevens picked Edinburgh and chose to route Mathieu James there because it was a lower-profile city and had direct flights to New York. If she needed to get James out on a commercial airliner, it would be simple. Edinburgh's airport was smaller than many of its European counterparts and he could move by rail from his current location all the way to departure if necessary.

Yet Stevens wasn't willing to bring him back just yet. James could be useful in Europe. Until they figured out who and/or what they were dealing with, it was best to keep him safe. The agency had a safe house in Leith Ward, near the port. This offered another exfiltration opportunity. Ships were routed all over the North Sea from there, including Norway, which was roughly thirty hours away by train and ferry.

Impatient, she picked up the phone and dialed Ben Wilson's desk.

"Wilson."

"Ben, it's Alyssa."

"Yep."

"Anything?"

"Not yet, my friend. Still working it. We have a lot on our plates, but I've made it a priority."

"Okay, appreciate anything you can do. I have an asset on the move. Would be nice to know what he's dealing with."

"Copy that," Wilson said. "Do you have anything else on this UNSUB?"

"Just some notes from the field. We think he's a money launderer at best. At worst, he could be a terrorist."

"Whoa, okay. Yeah, that could be big."

"Agreed."

"Do you have any idea if he's actually African? I mean, could he just be there? Looking for any nuggets to help my team unearth an identity."

"I don't really know anything. This was a huge get for us, Ben. A bit of a happy coincidence. It's possible it leads somewhere we aren't expecting, like this guy is just moving money around to sell drugs or he's involved in human trafficking or something else. It sounds like he had a couple of Russians with him. Probably bodyguards."

"What was happening? And where again?"

"We had an asset meeting with someone else at Schiphol. Actually looking for information on the guy in the photos and video. Turns out the guy our asset was meeting with was also in Amsterdam to meet with the African guy."

"Yeah, wow, that is a happy coincidence. Okay, will get back to you as soon as I know something."

"Appreciate you."

Alyssa hung up the phone and began prepping a message for Mathieu James that she would send, most likely, in a few hours as promised. It would contain the details for the safe house and other instructions as needed.

Glancing at her watch, she decided she could use a coffee and a snack and headed toward the cafeteria.

33

Amsterdam Central Station
The Netherlands

The train from Schiphol to Amsterdam Central Station knifed through the fog and haze, arriving in just over ten minutes as advertised. James exited on Platform 4 and walked into the main terminal, pausing a minute to orient himself.

Central Station was stone and featured both a Renaissance and Gothic architectural flare, with high arches, wide concourses and a sharp, angled roof. James took an appreciative glance around before re-focusing on his situation.

He needed to get some messages out quickly, then figure out his next move. First, he had to respond to Taylor. He slid his phone from his right pocket and opened iMessages. Here he saw a few messages from friends—his tennis buddies looking for a fourth for doubles and another buddy looking to get some tacos. He pressed his thumb on Taylor's conversation and began typing.

Hey babe.

Sorry I'm late getting back to you.

Things here have been busy.

I'm good, and I hope you're great.

See you soon I hope.

- MJ

He hesitated with his initials. They'd been together awhile and never really had the "love" conversation. He was sure he loved her in many ways, but neither of them signed messages with "love" nor, to his recollection anyway, said it to each other. It was probably one of those instances where she was waiting for him to say it first, and he her. Lessens the inevitable heartbreak if one says it and the other doesn't reciprocate. *Thoughts for another time, Matty.*

Next up was Frank, via WhatsApp.

New leads.

Gonna chase.

Will be here longer.

- MJ

And finally, Thies. *Should I text him or call? I'd probably get more out of calling.*

James opened the phone portion of WhatsApp and found Thies's number. He pressed with his thumb and put the phone to his ear.

It rang once, twice, three times...

"Bonsoir, Mathieu! What a pleasant surprise!"

"Hello, Francois. It's been a minute."

"Oui, Mathieu. What's new? How can I help my American friend?"

"I wanted to check on that transfer you referred to. Has that happened yet?"

"I don't believe so, Mathieu. I would have had a notification of funds transferred from Switzerland Bank & Trust. I haven't seen it yet. How is everything? Have you learned anything new I should know?"

"Nothing," James lied, knowing he couldn't trust Thies with anything important. "But do me a favor and keep your eyes open. It would help me a ton if you could alert me when that money comes in."

"Okay, Mathieu, I will see what I can do. I'll be in touch."

"Ciao, Francois."

"Ciao."

James stood up and grabbed his overnight bag and headed toward the departures board, scanning for London, and also for divergent routes, like Dusseldorf and Paris. Those didn't make much sense if he wanted to get to Edinburgh quickly. There was a train leaving for London in an hour.

That's the one.

James headed toward the nearest ticket kiosk and paid cash for the ticket to London. He was booked on a non-stop Eurostar that left Central Station at 16:45 and arrived at London's St. Pancras International Station at 19:47.

With a little less than an hour before departure, James needed to eat, and sought a sandwich and a cold pint. It had been quite a day, and it wasn't over yet.

34

Eurostar bound for London, England

Mathieu James was seated comfortably in his Standard Premier class seat en route to London. Traveling by Eurostar was normally a top-notch experience and this time it didn't disappoint. Catering at his seat for drinks and food along with high-speed rail service would put him in London in a matter of hours.

As the train exited Amsterdam Central, he got comfortable and thought it best to contact Lily Jameson, his cousin on his mother's side. Lily worked in banking in London and was a couple years younger than Mathieu. Like Mathieu, she was an only child.

Lily's father Mac had passed away two years prior from cancer, likely a result of burn pits associated with his service in the SAS. He was a larger-than-life character, and Mathieu respected him not just for his service, but how he treated others.

Her mum, Mary, was still alive and living in Glasgow. The family had a cottage near Aberdeen, where Uncle Mac lived until he passed.

James had come over for his uncle's wake but hadn't seen his cousin since then. He didn't want to drag her into anything, but also thought if he needed help with something, better to let her know he's in the region.

He texted her first, with a simple message.

Lily it's your cousin.

How's London?

I'm in Europe. Wanted to say hi.

Hope you're well!

Rather than give his location or destination, he at least put her on alert. Nothing like a relative showing up unannounced and screwing with your plans.

James pulled out his laptop and decided to start working on the primary elements of his story. Sometimes journalists know what goes up top straight away. Other times, it takes some work to get there. James wanted to go through this exercise to see if he had enough to contribute to Ana-Marie Poulin's story.

The International Herald Tribune has learned that the 2005 London terror attacks on the transportation network, and the 2015 Paris terror attacks that locked down the city, were financed by at least one individual with ties to Africa, an anonymous source confirmed.

A second source told IHT that this person was still active in funding terror cells and networks, and that money was being laundered through a criminal enterprise in Paris, and later invested in a fund managed by a Swiss firm.

He paused here, contemplating what he wrote. In theory, both statements were true. His anonymous source was the courier, whose name he didn't know but who was a friend of AMP. His second source was Francois Thies, who he met in person.

The hangup was that Thies didn't finger the African. He only suggested that money was coming from an enterprise or individual that looked familiar.

James didn't think Frank Murphy, his editor, would let him run with this, but it was worth a discussion.

It was late morning when Frank Murphy's phone vibrated on his desk, nearly working its way onto the floor. He had his land line to his ear and a cup of Dunkin'—probably spiked with a splash of whiskey—in his left hand.

The WhatsApp notification read *Mathieu James*, and Murphy told the caller on his other line he'd get back to them.

"Matty, report!" Murphy said, answering and putting James on speaker. "Where the fuck are ya?"

"I'm on a train, let's leave it at that," James said.

"A train to nowhere. I like it. Wanna trade seats?" Murphy joked. "Paris is up my ass again and I'd rather be dunked naked in a tank of marinated skunks."

"Again, Murph, with the visuals. I can do without."

"Haha yeah yeah. So what's happening?"

"I'd like to read you something. I've got a couple of grafs and I want your take," James said.

"Let it rip, Matty."

James read his first two grafs to Murphy without additional comment. He let the seasoned editor absorb it.

"Matty, read that to me again."

James did so and waited for his boss to comment.

"How many sources are involved in this so far?"

"Two."

"You know the identity of both?"

"Sort of."

"Sort of? What the fuck is sort of?"

"I met the guy, in person. But I don't know his name."

"How did you meet him?"

"Ana-Marie in Paris. She is using him as a source and put us together."

"She knows his name, right?"

"For sure. They went to university together, apparently. She's known him for a bit. I just haven't asked her for a name yet. I was worried he'd get buggered and disappear."

"Where is he now?"

"Last time I saw him was in an airport. We had ourselves a situation. We got split up, then I needed to leave, and I didn't see him again."

"Got it. And the other source?"

"Yeah, you know him, our Swiss-French friend."

"I'd sure like more, you know. Is there a way to get some backup on this?"

"Working on it, Frank. I will contact Ana-Marie and see what else she has, and we can coordinate from there."

"Sounds like a plan. When are you coming back?"

"Well, here's the thing..."

"Ah, fucking hell, here we go," Murphy said.

"That situation I referenced was enough to alter my plans. That's all I should say for now, Frank. I'm going to keep working on the story and I'll check in when I can, okay?"

"Alrighty, Matty. Be smart. Cheers."

"Cheers, Frank."

James put the phone down and stared at his laptop. *Frank is right, there's not enough there yet. Keep working the story, keep in touch with AMP, and stay low, watch your six.*

Mathieu! So great to hear from you!

Where are you???? Are you coming to London??

Please tell me you're coming to London!!

It's been too long. Ring me when you're able!

Let's catch up!

Cousin Lily was as solid as they came. Fun, polite, bright, attractive. She wasn't married, had no kids, and seemed to be enjoying the single life. James was sure she was never short on suitors.

He pressed his thumb on the message and selected the heart emoji. As much as he'd love to see her, best to stick with the plan. James glanced at his watch. London was just under three hours away.

Schiphol International Airport
Amsterdam, Netherlands

One of the perks of traveling through Schiphol is the cleanliness of the airport. From the lounge areas to the plaza to the toilets, workers in yellow vests are buzzing about with mops and brooms.

In the men's toilet off the plaza, across from the Heineken Bar and adjacent to passport control, a female airport worker entered the men's toilet area and announced herself. She was neither shy nor bashful. Just doing her job.

The men taking care of business paid no mind. They went about their duty, washing up, and checking themselves in the mirror before moving on. A new wave of travelers would enter, and the scene would repeat itself. Consider it like waves in the ocean—repeatable and mostly predictable.

The female was the first wave, checking supplies like toilet paper and hand towels and soap. The next wave was the mop bucket and the sanitation crew. They scrubbed the urinals, the toilets and sinks and floors.

Most public bathrooms in Europe have private stalls for sitting down and doing your thing. Unlike in North America, the walls of each stall go floor to ceiling, usually, creating a sealed closet for privacy.

This particular crew had just come on for the evening shift. As the mop man worked the floors, a second worker opened each unoccupied stall, holding a spray bottle of bleach in one gloved hand and a toilet brush in the other. He worked his way down the row of stalls until he reached the second to last.

The green indicator on the lock announced the stall was unoccupied, so he pushed open the door. It hit something, stopping the door's momentum. He pushed harder, encountering the same problem, and the door slowly swung back toward him.

"Hallo?" he said, giving a verbal warning to someone inside who may have forgotten to latch the door. "Hallo?"

The man peeked inside and saw a person hunched over, sort of kneeling on the floor. The upper body was sprawled over the toilet. On the floor next to him was a Tottenham cap. The man was wearing a quilted jacket and scarf and appeared to be sick or vomiting.

"Is everything okay? Do you need assistance?" the worker asked.

There was no response.

The worker backed out and motioned to his colleague mopping the floor. He walked over and peeked inside. They both shrugged their shoulders and said nothing. The female worker noticed the two together and came over to investigate the fuss.

"There's someone in there, looks ill. He's not responding."

The female worker peeked inside and tried to rouse the man.

No luck.

She then tapped his right foot with hers.

"Sir, are you okay? Can we get you some assistance?"

No response.

"I think we should call security," she said.

The worker with the mop stepped into the stall, grabbed the man's jacket near his shoulder and tried to roll him over. The body crumpled off the toilet and onto the floor. The worker jumped, startled at the appearance of the man.

With the body stuck between the wall and the toilet seat, they could now see his face. It was ashen. His lips were purple, and his eyes were open, severely bloodshot, with a look of shock and horror. His neck had obvious bruising.

He was dead.

The female employee pulled her talkie off her belt and radioed for help.

36

St. Pancras International Station
London, England

The trains in Europe really make travel easy and efficient. Mathieu James's Eurostar arrived at London's St. Pancras International Station at 19:47, just as advertised. He grabbed his bags and, mindful of the gap on his way off, stepped onto the platform in full stride.

His connection to Edinburgh was set to depart in thirteen minutes on LNER from King's Cross Station right across the street and would place him at Waverley Station at 22:20. James checked the departures board and found his platform, turning his brisk walk into a light jog, his curls bouncing a bit as his bags flopped at his side.

The four-plus hour journey would give Alyssa Stevens enough time to get additional exfil details to James. Hopefully she would have an update on those images he sent, perhaps even an ID on the boss from Africa.

He darted in and out of pedestrian traffic. This station is London's busiest, and it was still buzzing at this hour. Pigeons poked around on the concrete floor, and the smells of coffee, stale beer, and exhaust filled the air.

Passengers with roller bags dawdled, and skinny men with single-gear bikes walked their two-wheeled transportation to destinations known only to them.

As he made his way through the heart of the station, he accidentally bumped into a handful of people, offering a "Sorry, mate" along the way—whether the receiving end took it well or not. James tried to be polite, tried not to stand out, was certain to avoid knocking anyone over and making a scene. Most important was making his connection, so he kept moving.

Given his current state of mind, it never occurred to him in the moment that King's Cross was where the 7/7 attackers split up. It all unfolded in the confines around him.

James had no idea if anyone was following him. The likely answer was no. But he wasn't willing to take the chance.

He reached Platform 5 with six minutes to spare. As he glanced in the windows of each car on the train, he took note of the number of passengers. Most cars looked half full, and he climbed aboard the C car.

He selected a pair of seats facing backward and put his bags down near the window. He unzipped his jacket and rolled it over his hands like a towel, folding it neatly and stuffing it inside his backpack. Just as he sat, his phone buzzed, and he pulled it from his front right pocket.

It was Ana-Marie Poulin calling.

"Good evening. What's new on your end?" James asked, his eyes scanning the train car and making notes on faces and seat locations.

"Mathieu, I have been trying to reach our mutual friend with no luck. Do you have any updates?"

"Not really. We left at different times and went in different directions. I haven't heard anything."

"Okay, I will keep trying him."

"Ana-Marie, I have some notes I want to send you. I'd like your feedback. I also took a crack at the first few paragraphs. I'll send that as well and would welcome your input."

"Oui, of course, Mathieu. This is no problem. When can you send?"

"Shortly. I'll email you with Proton and please return the favor."

"Okay. Where are you now?"

"I'm on the move. I probably shouldn't tell you where, but I'll keep in touch with you. Let's keep working the story. I shared with Frank the same thing I'm sharing with you. He wants better sourcing, which I understand. Maybe we'll find that."

"I'll watch for your email. Be safe, Mathieu."

"Ciao."

"Ciao."

James hung up and slid the phone back into his pocket. Outside, the whistle blew from the platform conductor, indicating the train was ready for departure. He heard the clacking of the car doors closing and felt the tug of the locomotive as it pulled from the station.

Sliding his laptop from the zippered sleeve of his backpack, he decided to take another crack at the story. More detail, perhaps, would give credibility to the anonymous sourcing. Readers, in general, didn't trust anonymous sources, nor did they understand how journalists used them.

The truth is any news organization worth its salt has a strict policy on anonymous sourcing. It's intellectually tight, responsible, and has consequences for the journalist if shit hits the fan. Editors then hold journalists accountable, and journalists hold their sources accountable, sometimes through the simple threat of outing them if they are burned.

It's a weird dynamic that has consistently failed to capture the public's trust. The only way to change that perception, James knew, was to be right one hundred percent of the time when using anonymous sourcing. A tall ask, but one that must be returned with a sobering truth.

Just as Mathieu James's LNER was departing London, Igor Kozlov's train was pulling into the same station. Igor was eager to get home. As the train slowed to a roll and eased into its platform, he stood and stretched.

Igor decided to take a taxi home. The queue was situated just outside the station on Pancras Road. The line was about six deep by the time he worked his way out of the cavernous depot. Igor lit a cigarette, sucking hard on the first taste, creating a longer burn. He held the smoke in his lungs until his body forced an exhale. He tilted his head skyward, blowing a long white cloud into the dark London night.

The train from Edinburgh had given Igor time to consider his next moves. The Christmas Market seemed almost too perfect. It went after every ideal coveted by the West: capitalism, commercialism, status, making an economic boondoggle out of a religious holiday. All the festivities and smiling faces and credit card debt. All of the commercials and advertisements and crowded shops. All of the joy and time with family.

Why should those people embrace a state so unfamiliar to his friends and family back home? Why should some suffer and others not? Again, he acknowledged it was likely foolish for Lukashenko to be in lock-step with Putin. But if Belarus wasn't an ally, what was it?

Igor shook his head and looked down at the pavement. He took another hard draw on the cigarette, pinching it with his thumb and index finger against his lips. This time, he blew the smoke from his nose. He was next in line, and moved toward the taxi, flicking his lit cigarette into the gutter.

As he sat in the back seat and announced "Harringay" to the driver, Igor laid his head on the back of the seat and closed his eyes. He put himself back in the Christmas Market, this time with a backpack full of explosives, and imagined where he would drop it. Maybe the ferris wheel? Or slide it under one of the shop tables? Security was so weak. *They would never know.*

Would one be enough? The London bombers had four separate tasks. Three took the subway and one took a bus. In Paris, teams fanned out across the city. Together, they combined for larger attacks that stoked panic and fear.

This much he knew: he would need help. The bigger the message, the better.

That's how you send a message, he thought. *Make them suffer.*

Igor lifted his head and looked out onto the nighttime streets of London as his taxi glided toward home. He was starting to feel at ease with this concept. Less panic, more certainty. Certainty that his cause was just. If not him, then who? This was egoism at its finest, but he regarded himself as some kind of vigilante.

So much to do, so little time.

Now that he had a target, he needed to get back in touch with the man from Africa.

If Igor Kozlov thought things got real in Amsterdam, he was about to take this shit to another level.

37

Langley, Virginia

Ben Wilson walked into his small office that sat just off the floor of a bustling AI and facial recognition task force. Lifting the receiver to his ear, he punched an internal extension and waited for Alyssa Stevens to answer.

"Stevens."

"It's Ben. We got something. Come down and take a look?"

"On my way."

Stevens rose from her desk, reached for her cell and a Yeti water bottle before heading for the door. In less than three minutes she was inside the task force center and found Wilson.

"What'd you get?" Stevens asked, with hands on hips and an aggressive posture.

"We found a partial hit. Someone that is more likely than not your person of interest. A variety of hits through on-the-ground assets in Africa produced these images."

Wilson turned his desk monitor so Stevens could see.

"These two images here," he pointed with a pencil, "are more than ten years old. They were taken in Somalia by someone we had embedded in a UN vaccination program.

"These here are from about four years ago in Liberia. Look who he's surrounded by," Wilson said, pretending to circle two burly white men that looked like security. "Looks like the same guy."

"Agree, I can see it. What else?"

"We found these from airport security cameras in Amsterdam, and this one from Amsterdam Central, the train station. They are very recent."

Stevens leaned toward the screen, examining the images closely. She was looking at a man who appeared older, wearing a Boston-style scally cap, sunglasses, and a track suit.

"What makes you think this is the same man?"

"AI makes me believe that," Wilson said. "The algorithm is pretty good. The recognition software has matched features on his face, like jaw angles and the width of his eyes."

"Okay, I get that. So you're comfortable if we hunt for this man?"

"I wouldn't have called you down here if I wasn't sure," Ben smiled, feeling confident and looking cocky.

"So you have a name?" Stevens asked, pulling her hair into a bun.

"I actually have two names for you."

"What? How's that work?"

"I have what we believe is his real name—Aadan Mukhtaar of Somalia. And I have a very different name that he is using on what is probably a forged Venezuelan passport—Eduardo Dominguez.

"That's a stretch," Stevens said, stifling a laugh. "So, you said Aadan Mukhtaar? What kind of hit did you get on that?"

"Well, Alyssa, that's not our purview. We just ID the baddies, it's up to others to piece it together. I'd start with the Africa desk and see what they know."

"Right, right. Of course," Stevens said, her mind racing with images and names and fake names and Russian ties and big burly white men and utter confusion. "Thanks, Ben. I'm going straight to Africa desk now."

Stevens exited Wilson's fiefdom fueled with excitement but felt her stress level and anxiety growing by the second. *Now we know. Now we have a real person. Connecting the dots should get a little bit easier.*

The next person that needed to know this was Mathieu James. He should be close to Edinburgh now, and Stevens needed to not only pass this on, but also get him to the safe house there.

She pulled up WhatsApp and tapped a message to James.

Aadan Mukhtaar

And then another.

Eduardo Dominguez

She then gave him the instructions for finding the safe house.

Best drink I ever had was sitting on the far corner stool at the Port O' Leith. It was two fingers of Writer's Tears and a side of club soda with ice and a lime.

She hit send and continued on her path to Africa desk.

38

Near Edinburgh, Scotland

As the LNER locomotive chugged its way through English villages and rolling countryside dotted with farms and grazing sheep, Mathieu James woke from an unintended nap. His phone was buzzing.

He took a swig of water and scooped the phone off the folding table in front of him. It was Alyssa Stevens on WhatsApp.

Aadan Mukhtaar was the first message.

Eduardo Dominguez the second.

And this was the third.

Best drink I ever had was sitting on the far corner stool at the Port O' Leith. It was two fingers of Writer's Tears and a side of club soda with ice and a lime.

Clues on how to find the safe house. James opened a private browsing window on his phone and typed in Port O' Leith. A match confirmed it was a bar on Constitution Street in the Leith Ward of Edinburgh.

He zoomed in and around the area, getting a lay of the land. The port was within walking distance, and a tram offered service through the heart of Edinburgh, including a stop just outside of the bar.

Perfect.

Swiping to the right, he moved the map to find Waverley Station. It was among three train depots in Edinburgh, but by far the main one and the busiest. Trains ran through a steep ravine below the old portion of the city. At the top sat Edinburgh Castle, with its stone walls, moat and cannons aimed at the Firth of Forth, and beyond the North Sea. Invaders would have a rough go approaching.

From the castle, a road led through the ancient portion of the city. This was known as the Royal Mile and ended at the Queen's residence opposite the castle. Gothic-inspired churches and monuments paid homage to saints and offered sinners reprieve and a place of shelter. Edinburgh is known as one of the world's great cities because it has painstakingly left its heritage intact, choosing to live within its history rather than escape from it.

As he surveyed the map, James noticed there were two tram stops near Waverley. It looked like St. Andrew's Square was closest, although Princes Street wasn't too far either. Which one he chose would likely depend on how he exited the station.

James moved the map toward Leith again, preparing to study every bit he could. Safe houses tended to be nondescript, but offered multiple escape routes in case that was necessary. Not all were equipped with cars, so James would need to memorize streets and routes in case he had to leave sooner than anticipated.

The quickest path out of the city was the port. Multiple vessels of various sizes and shapes were supported there, along with the Royal Britannia, official yacht of the British Royal Family. The Water of Leith was a largely unused and unnavigable river now. The tram had another three stops before circling back on the same route with a final destination of Edinburgh International Airport.

Access to motorways was decent, and routes on foot would suffice in a worst-case scenario. James did his best to sweep everything into active memory for recall later.

Next, he wanted to check out the two names Stevens had sent.

Aadan Mukhtaar

Eduardo Dominguez

Neither triggered a thought for him. He typed the first into Google. The search engine returned a sea of hits.

He tried the second.

Same thing. Plenty of hits. Eduardo Dominguez would be a fairly common Latino name. Aadan Mukhtaar less so for a Somali name, but he might be able to tighten his search parameters.

James scrolled through pages of the search engine, clicking on stories and images. Nothing registered with him. Grabbing his phone, he typed those names to Ana-Marie Poulin via WhatsApp.

He added the word *leads* to the names, and then *lmk*.

Who knows, something might hit with her.

Within seconds, AMP responded with a question mark. James wrote back.

Possibly our African friend. The man in my images that met with your friend the courier.

AMP responded.

Got it. Still no word from him.

James was a bit surprised.

Is this normal? he asked

Nothing is normal anymore, she wrote.

Now was the time to ask Ana-Marie what her friend's name was. She might be willing to say, yet she might wish to protect him further. What's the harm? Maybe best to avoid text, even if WhatsApp is end-to-end encrypted.

He found her number and pressed it with his thumb. She answered in half a ring.

"Bonjour."

"Good evening, Ana-Marie. I want to get right to it. I have a question to ask and you don't need to answer it. But maybe answering it will help us move things faster. It's also possible it goes the other way and makes things worse. So your call. No pressure from me."

"Okay, yes, I understand. Go ahead and ask, Mathieu."

"Your friend, the courier...what is his name? I don't want to put you or him in any danger. But the reality is he's probably in deep trouble right now after what went down in Amsterdam. And if he is in trouble, me knowing his name might be able to help everyone's situation."

The line was silent, save the background noise from the Paris bureau of the *International Herald Tribune*, bustling as always to get the next edition into the hands of readers around the world.

Ana-Marie remained quiet.

"Again, this is your call. I'm not going to pressure you into something that doesn't sit right."

"Oui, of course."

She let out an audible sigh. James remained patient.

"Okay, Mathieu, I will tell you. But only use his name if you think we need to."

"Understood. Right now we don't know anything, so there's little we can do anyway. But I think it would be of use to me in case I need to find him."

"His name is Henrique Perron. We call him Henry."

"Henrique Perron," James repeated, careful to avoid writing it down in case anything gets stolen. "Henrique Perron," he whispered once more for his own benefit.

The name meant nothing to him. But he now associated it with the man at the Heineken Bar in the Tottenham cap, scarf, and quilted jacket. The same man who nervously sat with the boss in the airport library at Schiphol. And the man James lost sight of when his instincts kicked in and he punched a nosy Russian in the dick.

"Thank you," James said. "I will protect his identity. I'm nearing my destination. I will be in touch soon. Please reach out if you learn anything."

"Okay Mathieu. Be safe. Ciao."

"Ciao, Ana-Marie."

James tucked the name into a safe place in his brain and began to pack his things securely. He stowed his laptop in his backpack, grabbed a tuque, and put on his jacket. When the train stopped on the platform, he wanted to be ready to move quickly. Finding the nearest exit and route for the tram was his only goal. *Read the signs and react. Don't stop, don't ask questions, keep moving with purpose.*

39

Paris, France

Aadan Mukhtaar began keeping an apartment near Paris-Nord three years before the 2015 attacks. Easy access to the city's primary rail hub was desirable and necessary. He was involved in the planning and found it helpful to see potential targets firsthand. Yet he never was interested in doing the deed. He left the details and the parade of death to those beneath him—those he felt were disposable.

The apartment was simple and barely furnished. It had a table with three chairs, a couch and a toilet and shower. In the United States it would be called a studio. The kitchen area was small, with a gas stove, small refrigerator, and a few cupboards.

Over the years he would occasionally bring items to the apartment, like dishes, a tea kettle, and cups. These usually came from second-hand stores in the neighborhood. The bathroom had one towel that hung from a hook and smelled like mildew and body odor. The shower had a bottle of body wash and a rusty razor. The tile grout was moldy and stained.

A single key worked both the handle and the deadbolt, and Aadan led the way in, even though the two Russians insisted on sweeping the apartment first.

"No one even knows about me, let alone this place. Everything is fine," he reassured them.

The two charged with his safety still took a quick look around. Given the size of the apartment, this took about four seconds.

"It's fine, boys. Sit down. I'll get us a drink and an ice pack for your nutsack," he laughed.

Aadan walked toward the refrigerator and opened the freezer door. Inside were two bottles of Russian Standard vodka and a blue ice cube tray. He grabbed a bottle and the ice and set them on the counter, then took three small glasses from a cupboard.

With a different finger inserted into each glass he carried them and the vodka to the table, where he poured the chilled liquor. The first Russian was seated facing the door. The second with his back against the wall. He was still looking pale from the punch to his groin.

Aadan returned to the kitchen, grabbing a towel from the edge of the sink and spreading it out on the counter. He twisted the ice tray back and forth until all the cubes fell onto the towel. Folding the towel neatly, he handed it to the second Russian and smiled.

"Good luck with your blue balls," he smirked.

The Russian groaned with disapproval.

Aadan pulled out his chair and sat. Three hands reached for a glass and raised them. There wasn't anything to toast, so the men threw them back and set the empty glasses back on the table. Aadan poured another round for each.

"Let's get to it. What happened in Amsterdam?"

The two Russians looked at each other, and the second nodded at the first. The first Russian spoke.

"I had eyes on you, boss, talking with the courier. Next thing I know, there's a commotion at some tables and I look over and see him buckled on the ground. I started moving in that direction, but so did other people, maybe looking to help."

The second Russian was shaking his head slightly, reliving the moment he nearly blacked out from pain.

"As I started moving his way, I tried to get into a strategic position, where I could keep tabs on his situation and still see what was happening with you."

Aadan held up his hand, indicating he wanted the Russian to stop speaking. He looked at the second Russian, who was staring at the ice pack soothing his groin.

"What happened with you? What were you doing?"

The second Russian lifted his head and explained in the thickest of accents.

"There was a man seated at a table. He was decent size, fit, possibly military age or older. He was pretending to read a book, but I saw him trying to take pictures of you, boss."

Aadan nodded.

"So I tapped him on his shoulder and asked for his phone. I was trying to avoid a scene. I had strategic advantage above him, and he didn't seem like much of a threat, so I thought I could intimidate him into deleting the photos, or maybe just walking away with his phone."

"Did he say anything to you?" Aadan asked, keeping eye contact and sweeping his left hand across the table.

"He spoke French, I think."

"You think?"

"It didn't seem right. He had an English language book on the table."

"What was the book?"

"It said *1983*."

"So what did he say to you?"

"He pretended like he didn't speak English, so he asked if I spoke French, I think."

"And then what?"

"I don't remember exactly the sequence, but it wasn't long before he punched me in the dick."

Aadan smiled and took a sip of vodka.

"I bet that stung a bit."

The big Russian stared back at him.

Aadan held his gaze, smiling still.

"And then?" Aadan asked.

The first Russian spoke.

"By then I had moved to the opposite side of them. I had them in between you and me, so I could see everything. I saw the courier get up and move, so I stayed on him. I was confident you were in no danger, boss."

Aadan nodded. The second Russian downed his second vodka, and pushed his cup toward the boss, seeking another. He obliged, pouring two ounces of the icy spirits.

"Is there more?" Aadan inquired.

"Yes."

"And?"

"I locked onto the courier. He was heading toward the toilets. I found my angle and cut the distance in half and..."

Aadan interrupted.

"What was your intention here? Remember, we want to avoid a scene."

"My intention was to avoid a scene and bring him quietly back to you."

"I see."

"It didn't work out that way, boss."

"Of course not."

"He started moving quicker toward the toilets. I followed him in, and he found a stall near the back. He went in, and I followed him."

"You followed him into the stall." Aadan wasn't asking. He was repeating, again sweeping his left hand across the table.

"That's right. And then we had a struggle."

"A struggle."

"Yes."

"And?"

"And it escalated."

"To what?"

"I wouldn't call it a fight. I had the advantage. He wasn't a big man, and I knew I could eliminate any threat. I knew you didn't want a scene, and we were making one, so I neutralized him."

"How?"

"With fishing wire."

"I see."

Aadan went silent. He finished what was left in his cup and poured another, pushing the bottle toward the first Russian, who took it and topped his cup.

Aadan sighed, then he spoke.

"So he's dead," he said flatly.

"Yes."

"Did anyone see you?"

"Yes."

"Who?"

"I don't know. Another passenger. Maybe two. I don't know if they heard anything. They saw me washing my hands. I was calm when I left."

All three men were quiet. The Russians threw back another round and refilled their cups. Aadan looked at both, staying calm and in control.

Or so it seemed.

"Damnit!" He slammed his left hand down on the table, palm down, making a loud smacking noise, startling his men. "Henrique was one of us! He was an asset! He fucking worked for me!"

The Russians made eye contact, then looked at the table, trying to disappear. The empty room was silent. A single light in the kitchen, glowing warmly, drew harsh shadows on the men's faces. Anger was brewing. So was distrust.

40

Waverley Station
Edinburgh, Scotland

The locomotive eased to a rest, and the PA announced the train's arrival to Edinburgh's Waverley Station. Mathieu James had risen from his seat and moved toward the door, awaiting his turn to exit. In the moments before the doors opened and the passengers washed over the platform, he made eye contact with a man.

He was maybe 6 feet, about 185 pounds. He was wearing a black wool peacoat, gray scarf, and crimson tuque. James did not recognize him from his earlier scans of the train's interior. *Perhaps he came forward from another car?* Or maybe James had missed him altogether.

James glanced down at his boots, and then raised his head and looked out the doors. He was anticipating his moves and directions to rid himself of Waverley and get to the tram as quickly as possible.

Right on the platform, left toward the ticket gates, rescan your ticket, straight toward Princes Street exit.

After that he wasn't sure but would need to be alert.

He stretched his neck and moved it side to side looking for relief in a pop or crack. He was stiff from the hours spent on trains that day. As he did so, he glanced again toward the man in the peacoat and crimson tuque. He was still standing there, and the two made eye contact again.

Coincidence? James wondered. Maybe. Maybe not. He tried to get a glance at his hands. *Was he carrying a bag? Suitcase? Roller?* Just then the doors spread like aluminum wings and a hundred-plus passengers spilled onto the platform like waves on a beach. They flowed as a malformed amoeba toward the ticket gates, scanning bar codes as they exited the secure platform and mixed with the masses.

James walked briskly, with ever-increasing tempo—enough to pass many passengers. But he wasn't running; therefore, he wasn't drawing attention to himself. As he approached the exit gate, he placed his phone face down on the scanner and waited for the doors to swing open. He stepped through and took a glance back, capturing a glimpse of the man in the black wool peacoat.

He was maybe fifteen yards behind James, who could now see his hands were free of luggage. Only a mobile phone, which the man was preparing to scan. James continued his brisk walk, taking note of signs and exits. He followed the arrows toward Princes Street, which led him to the first in a series of steps and escalators. He could take one or the other.

For the first choice, he picked the escalator. Best to dial it down a beat and see what transpires. He stepped onto the crowded escalator and rode silently to the top, taking notice that the man remained behind him and also took the escalator.

At the top, James stepped off and turned right. A crush of humans was coming toward him; passengers entering the station. He returned to a brisk walk and weaved in and out. As he approached the stairs, he turned and saw the man again. They locked eyes.

Trouble, James thought.

This time he chose the stairs, taking two at a time as he worked his way from the underground station to the exit at Princes Street. Looking ahead, anticipating, he saw even more steps.

Time for a workout.

It was probably three stories of stairs to the exit, and James put the pedal down, willing himself to crush the stairs two at a time and put some distance between him and the man in the black wool peacoat. With the final flight in sight, he looked back to see the man had closed the distance. He was maybe ten yards behind now, and James's mind began to calculate the possibilities.

Was he part of the boss's crew?

Someone tied to the courier?

Guns were uncommon in the UK. Did he have a knife?

Was it still a coincidence?

Probably not, given the number of times they had made eye contact now.

At the moment, James had nothing to defend himself save his wit and his fists.

James put himself in a dead sprint up the last flight of stairs. His overnight bag bouncing off his leg and his curly hair pushed by the winds of momentum. He was working up a sweat, and his breathing was getting heavier. While he was in good shape, stairs can get the best of anyone, and he had been sitting on his ass for the past eight hours.

The top of the stairs put him on the sidewalk on Princes Street. As he looked ahead, it was a wall of humanity. Multiple streams. This was a tricky area, dense enough so it would slow James, meaning the man in the black wool peacoat would likely close the gap.

He had memorized the map and knew how to get to the tram stop at St. Andrews Square. He slithered into the crowd and began swimming upstream, going against the grain, dodging left and right to make time and space for himself.

To his right, cars whizzed past, headlights shining brightly on wet pavement. Buses idled at the curbs, spewing diesel, their metal frames vibrating with the gurgling shimmy of the engine. He listened for a moment, picking up at least four languages from people around him. Not uncommon in Europe.

Twenty-five yards later James reached the crosswalk and looked to his right. He scanned the area quickly.

No sign of the man.

Did I shake him?

Was I mistaken?

Keep moving.

On the pavement was a painted warning that read 'Look Right.' A reminder that traffic patterns are opposite from his home in the States. He did so and moved quickly to the center median, where he looked left and moved to the opposite sidewalk.

The corner was busy. A coffee shop was still open, with friends and couples seated at window tables sharing smiles over lattes or tea. James decided to get closer to the building, protecting at least one side of himself. Any surprise element would come from his left or from behind.

He steered himself around the corner, looking left at the crosswalk.

Still good.

Shifting his eyes ahead, he identified the tram stop. Maybe 100 yards away. The outbound tram heading toward the airport was just leaving, its signal bell audible above the wind and bustle of the city. The tram he needed to board would be coming up Princes Street and making a hard left toward the stop, where it would pick up passengers and then make a hard right, gliding toward Picardy Place and stops beyond.

Just then, James saw his tram rounding the corner, making that left turn. He had just crossed an alley and was now in front of the Cheval Edinburgh Grand Hotel. He checked his six and considered it clear. He moved toward the curb, looking to cross the street diagonally and make it to the center island that was the tram stop. He looked right at oncoming traffic.

Clear.

Then left, where he saw his tram gliding up the street. And there, on the opposite sidewalk, was the man in the black wool peacoat. They locked eyes once again.

Fuck.

The tram moved in front of the man in the black wool peacoat, obscuring James's view. James went into a full sprint, crossing the street and stepping onto the platform and running toward the far end, which would put him in the first car. As the tram's bell signaled its arrival, James realized he needed a ticket.

Shit. Nothing is ever easy.

He spotted a kiosk, which had one person purchasing a ticket, and waited. With a completed transaction, that person stepped aside. James slid his wallet from his pocket, pushed a Visa from the stack of cards and inserted it into the machine. This was less than ideal. People with means can trace credit cards, but his only other choice was to enter the tram without a ticket and risk a scene.

Not smart, Mathieu.

The transaction went quickly. James pulled his paper ticket and arrived at the front car just as the doors were opening. He peered inside and to his left. He looked out through the windows, toward the other side of the street. It was hard to see with the lighting inside the tram casting a glare on the windows.

Edinburgh's streets and buildings were in full Christmas cheer. The rides at the Christmas Market, adjacent to Waverley Station, lit the night sky with neon colors. Screams of joy and terror filled the air as kids and adults braved the giant spinning swings.

James couldn't locate the man in the black wool peacoat. It didn't matter. He needed to get on the tram and get to his next stop, which was The Shore and the Port O' Leith bar.

Stepping inside, the front row seats were empty. Two on each side. He took the furthest seat, next to the window and convenient to the opposite door. If he had to bolt quickly that's the plan.

He sat and turned to his right and then over his shoulder, scanning the inside of the tram car. Nothing. There was a plexiglass divider in front of him, which housed the tram's driver on the other side. It offered a soft reflection of what was behind him. He would keep an eye there, looking for anyone moving toward the front that resembled his pursuer.

The tram driver rang a single bell with the push of a button. The doors closed, and the electric motors whirred, propelling the streetcar ahead. James relaxed briefly and looked outside the window to his left.

There, on the sidewalk next to the square, stood a man. His eyes locked on James. And James's on his. Hands in his pockets, he was standing next to an iron and brick fence, his crimson tuque and gray scarf offering a muted contrast to his black wool peacoat. He stood and watched as James's tram rounded the corner.

Who the fuck is following me?

41

London, England

Andrey Morozov drove his BMW to Igor Kozlov's flat late that evening. It was past 22:00, and his friend invited him over for a drink. Andrey was interested in learning where Igor had been and what he was up to. He also had some updates on their mutual business he needed to share.

The evening was cold and damp, and a light snow was beginning to fall. *'Tis the season,* Andrey thought. He found a street parking spot about two blocks from Igor's flat and nestled his beloved BMW in between a Mini and a Suzuki.

Inside the flat, Igor was doing his best to avoid any digital footprints. He was at his dining table, drawing a sketch from memory. He heard Andrey's approach outside, his heavy combat-style boots plopping on the walk. Andrey paused at the door and stomped his feet to rid the soles of dirt and slush. He knocked three times hard, paused, then knocked twice softly. He heard his friend approaching from inside, and then the heavy metal sound of the dead bolt sliding and the door handle twisting.

Igor opened the door; his skin met by a rush of cold air.

"Come in. Come in."

Andrey stomped his feet twice more and shuffled inside. They clasped hands and completed the ritual with a classic bro hug, complete with the requisite single back-slap of the free hand.

"What's new, brother?" Andrey asked.

"A lot, actually. Come into the kitchen. Can I get you anything?"

"A beer would be nice."

"Perfect."

Igor led him back toward the dining area, where Andrey took off his tuque, scarf, and jacket and placed them on an empty chair. Igor continued toward the kitchen; Andrey followed. He grabbed a bag of pretzels and tossed them at his friend, and moved to the refrigerator, pulling out two bottles of lager. He opened them and set them on the table.

"Sit, Andrey. Please sit."

His friend obliged.

"How are you, Igor? Is everything okay?"

"Yes, I'm fine. I'm sorry I didn't tell you where I was going. I wanted to make sure I had some things lined up."

"What kind of things?"

Igor paused, grabbed a couple of pretzels from the bag and munched them before taking a swig of beer.

"I met with someone who can help me send a message to the West."

"You're still on this?"

"Yes, I'm still on this, Andrey. This is about my parents, your parents, our people, our way of life."

Andrey looked into his friend's eyes. He said nothing. Igor continued.

"There is someone who can provide the means and the resources to help me execute an attack on the West."

"What?"

Igor nodded.

"This person, he has real experience. He has funded other attacks, including London in 2005 and Paris a few years ago."

Andrey leaned forward, putting his elbows on the table, closing the distance between him and his friend. His face had a look of shock—his eyes wide, his mouth slightly open.

"Igor, what are you talking about here? You want to carry out a terrorist attack? Are you a terrorist?"

.   .   .

Andrey stood.

"Are we terrorists?" he asked, gesturing his hands wildly back and forth, pointing at himself and Igor. He began to pace the floor. "You cannot be serious, Igor."

"I am deadly serious, Andrey. I need your help. And even the two of us cannot do it alone."

"What are you talking about? And what is that?" Andrey asked, pointing at the sketch on the table.

"This is the Christmas Market in Edinburgh, Scotland."

Andrey put his hands on top of his head and clasped them together. He was still pacing, but quicker now, as if to keep up with his racing mind.

"Andrey, your energy is nervous. Please sit and let me tell you about this."

Igor gestured to the chair where Andrey was seated previously. His friend had now re-entered the kitchen, hands still on his head.

"Andrey, please."

"No, Igor. We cannot talk about this. We cannot. This is not something we do. We steal shit, brother, and we sell it back home. That is how we help people. We send home cigarettes and booze and clothes. We help our people by getting them things they can't buy at home for the prices we can offer. We are not terrorists, Igor! We are thieves!"

"We are also sons of Belarus, Andrey."

"We are the sons of our parents!"

"Yes, exactly. Remember my parents, Andrey? Remember what I told you?"

"Yes, Igor. But that's not a reason to attack a Christmas Market. I am sorry for what is happening to your parents. How about I send them some money? Why won't you let me talk to my father about this?"

"You know why. We have talked about this already," Igor snapped. "And you should know, Andrey, that your father is involved in this as well."

"What? How?"

"I called him, Andrey. I asked him for help. He made a connection with someone who has helped me meet the person I met on this trip."

Andrey returned to his chair and sat down. He grabbed his beer and took three consecutive pulls. He stared at the sketch on the table.

"Listen, my friend. We have a chance to send a message to the West. They fear nothing more than the unknown. Terror attacks are known to alter how they think. This could give people like Putin and Lukashenko a chance to negotiate. Maybe get some sanctions removed. Maybe get some food and some medicine into Russia and Belarus.

"The West will not tighten the screws if they are worried about terror attacks going off in major cities. They will not continue the hostile rhetoric if scores of their own are dead and it's being shown on television every night."

"Every night? How many of these are you planning?"

"Just the one, Andrey. But I would also do whatever it took to help my parents, to help our people. One attack would play out on news networks around the world for weeks. This is their Christmas season. This would hurt them. There's no way they could return to normal after this."

Andrey Morozov was staring at Igor Kozlov in wonderment. His mouth open, his head shaking left to right. He could not believe what he was hearing from the friend he grew up with. They had made a nice life for themselves. They escaped the poverty and the iron thumb of rule in Belarus—has Igor forgotten what life was like back then? They were helping people back home. He was convinced of this. They were doing *something*, and it didn't involve murder, mayhem, or terror.

And it sure as hell didn't involve some guy who masterminded other attacks.

Andrey stood and grabbed his jacket, his scarf, and his hat. He stared at his seated friend, who was watching him.

"This isn't you, Igor. And this sure as fuck isn't me. Don't talk to me about this again."

Igor watched his childhood friend walk toward the door, put on his jacket, then his hat and his scarf, and slip into the snowy English night.

42

Edinburgh, Scotland

Seated at the front of the tram, Mathieu James's mind was racing. The man in the black wool peacoat was clearly following him and wasn't shy about making it known. He had run through the possibilities earlier and still had no concrete understanding of who that man was.

He carried nothing but a phone and was dressed ordinarily enough. Perhaps the thing to note was that after he closed the distance on the stairs coming out of Waverley Station, he separated himself from James by going to another crosswalk and coming up the opposite side of the street.

He was intent on watching. On making his presence known, James thought.

The trolley tracks offered a smooth ride as the tram accelerated. It was largely full, with revelers and shoppers enjoying the holiday season. James glanced above the door at the tram's map. Multiple tram cars ran a loop between the airport and Newhaven, with more than a dozen stops in between. When he got on at St. Andrew's Square, it was five stops to The Shore. They had just stopped at Picardy Place, meaning four more— McDonald Road, Balfour Street, Foot of the Walk and The Shore.

He had checked the map on his phone earlier in the day from the train, and noticed the bar was adjacent to the tram stop. Wanting to make sure he got the exchange right, he consulted his message from Stevens once more.

Best drink I ever had was sitting on the far corner stool at the Port O' Leith. It was two fingers of Writer's Tears and a side of club soda with ice and a lime.

Got it.

After that, James lost himself in the smooth glide of the tram. Looking outside, he saw rows of restaurants, bars, and shops. Graffiti littered store-fronts with youthful expression. Buses pulled past, two stories high, reminding him of the bus his parents were on when that bomb went off long ago.

Headlights cast a yellow hue on the glistening pavement, and city lights twinkled with an array of background color, adding texture to a waning day. At each stop, the cars emptied and refilled as locals scurried about. After the stop at the Foot of the Walk, James gathered his things and stood at the door, glancing once more down the middle aisle that connected all the cars, taking in the faces. A variety of skin tones and ages. Men and women, young and old. Headphones and deep conversations, laughter, and silence.

Others stood as well and migrated toward the doors as the tram pulled into The Shore. This stop is considered the easiest to access the heart of Leith, an Edinburgh hamlet known for its bar and restaurant scene, new housing developments, and relatively young population. Leith was recently named one of the world's coolest cities by some magazine who does such things. James wondered if he'd have the chance to find out why.

James stepped off the tram and took a sweeping view of his surround-ings from the platform. This panorama presented stone buildings that were likely apartment homes. The platform divided the road, and traffic in front of him moved from left to right. He turned to get a look at the opposite side of the street and waited for the tram to move on before assessing.

Here he saw a cluster of shops, bars, and restaurants. Directly in front of him was Printworks Coffee, which was closed. Nobles was a bustling restaurant; next to it was Rock Salt, also a coffee house, also closed. It was approaching midnight.

Further to the left he saw two bars—Malones and the Port O'Leith. Outside each, tables sat empty. Patrons stood near the doors, sucking on tobacco sticks and shivering without coats.

He moved down the platform, looking for a place to cross and stepped across the tracks into the street. A car was approaching, its headlamps putting James in a momentary spotlight. He stepped up on the curb and approached the Port O' Leith entrance, making note of every face and person he could process along the way. Perhaps eight or ten total.

The bar sat on the corner in an old brick building. It had two windows facing the street, a wooden door with a glass window, and side door that led to an alley. It was decorated in Christmas cheer and was fairly busy this night.

He opened the door with his right hand and slid inside, carrying his overnight in his left and his backpack strapped over his shoulders. The bar was on his right and stretched toward the back. Two barkeeps were working a merry scene. On his left, small tables were filled with couples and friends, spilling stories and laughter.

The space was small but cozy. Definitely a locals' bar. James worked his way toward the back end of the bar and noted the side exit door into the alley. As he moved toward the bar, an empty stool awaited with a small, hand-written sign that said 'Reserved'. Every other seat was taken, and those without one were standing two deep.

James made the correct assumption the seat was reserved for him. He set down his overnight bag near the front of the stool and took a seat. Looking down the bar, he saw the young faces of Leith and the old faces of Edinburgh. The crowd was a mix. It seemed to make sense.

He did another quick scan around the room before he put eyes on both barkeeps—a tall, skinny man with a beard and thinning hair; an older woman, probably in her 50s, with a curly out-of-style cut and a pear-shaped figure.

The male bartender shuffled toward the end and made eye contact with James.

"What can I get you?"

James looked at him and replied.

"Two fingers of Writer's Tears, please, with a side of club soda and a lime."

He had intentionally left out the "ice" portion, testing the barkeep. Precision was always key in these exchanges.

"Say again?" the tall, skinny man said.

"Two fingers of Writer's Tears, a side of club soda with ice and a lime."

The barkeep nodded, and pulled a bottle of the copper-pot, triple-distilled Irish whiskey from the shelf. When he returned with James's order, he slid two glasses in front of him, one with the whiskey, one with the soda water, ice, and lime.

He also reached into the back pocket of his jeans and pulled out a small, folded white envelope and set it in front of James, who discreetly retrieved it by placing his left hand over it. He glanced at the writing on the envelope.

13/8 Mitchell St.

James put the envelope in his coat pocket, feeling a key inside.

He now had access to the safe house.

43

London, England

With or without his friend Andrey, Igor Kozlov decided to put his plan in motion. His anger and frustration grew by the hour, compounding by the days. The more he read about sanctions, the more he read about the West continuing to support Ukraine while punishing Russia, Belarus, and others, the more determined he was.

So far, the *action* for Igor Kozlov has been the outreach via Sergey Morozov and the conversations with the financier. If he wasn't already a homegrown radical, he was steps away from completing the process. And it was not lost on him that the London bombers in 2005 were also homegrown.

Igor had already called Sergey to arrange another meeting with his contact. When they met in person in Amsterdam, the financier said to reach out the same way if Igor developed a viable plan. He believed he had one.

Sergey relayed to Igor the instructions: Public phone box, 14:00 today. Igor left his flat at 13:45, lit a cigarette, and took a walk. It was cold and blustery, and he zipped his leather jacket higher and scrunched his shoulders inward, trying to keep the chill from his bones.

The phone box wasn't far, and he arrived early. He stood outside the box, smoking dart after dart, extinguishing them on the sidewalk with his shoe. He checked his watch. It read 13:59. Out of habit, he scanned the neighborhood, searching for nothing, and stepped inside the phone box. His face was about twelve inches from the receiver. He stared at the analog relic, this time determined not to be startled when it rang.

He was not. The tinny sound barked from the phone, and he quickly picked up before the first ring was complete. He listened.

"Go ahead," the GRU agent said on the other end of the line.

"I enjoyed my date with your sister. I would like permission for another one."

Igor listened intently. He could hear a television or radio faintly in the background. That same whir of a fan was there, too.

The GRU agent answered.

"This was expected. You will receive an answer soon. Goodbye."

The line went dead. Igor continued holding the receiver to his ear. He repeated the words to himself in a whisper.

This was expected.

You will receive an answer soon.

He quietly set the receiver back and calmly walked out of the phone box. *Very well*, he thought. *I guess he read my intentions.*

44

Edinburgh, Scotland

Mathieu James slept heavily. The night prior, he left Port O' Leith in search of the safe house and easily found it just two blocks away. It was a residential apartment, top floor, no lift, two doors accessing the shared stairwell, eight units total. He wasn't sure what to expect, but it wasn't an apartment with baby strollers and kids' bikes in the hallways and a community bookshelf at the base of the stairs.

He found his way inside and checked the place over, discovering a simply furnished two-bedroom, two bathroom apartment. His guess was the CIA used one of its many foreign shell corporations to lease or purchase it furnished, so it looked like a rental.

After checking the place, James had set his bags down, laid on the bed, and was out in less than two minutes. He woke up twelve hours later, local time 14:00.

Damn, he thought. The crash from adrenaline can't be overstated. Not to mention he was working on minimal sleep, in a high-stress environment, and battling jet lag to boot. A lot had happened in the last few days. He was spent.

He rolled off the queen mattress and opened his overnight bag to retrieve some fresh clothes and toiletries. One bathroom had a strangely narrow walk-in shower; the other a soaking tub. He chose the shower and made quick work of it, stepping out and snatching a folded towel from the shelf.

Dressed, he made his way to the kitchen to find an electric kettle, which he filled with water and plugged in. A can of instant coffee sat beside it. *Not ideal.*

Nonetheless he searched the cupboards to find a mug and flipped the switch on the kettle. It took maybe sixty seconds for the water to boil. With a spoon found in an adjacent drawer, he put three scoops of grounds in the mug and poured the hot water over them. The aroma quickly found his nose, and he stirred the coffee into a foamy whirlpool.

Hot mug in hand, he took a daylight tour of the safe house. A white paper in a plastic sheath sat on the breakfast bar. It held instructions for working the washing machine, the dishwasher, the internet, where to find the trash bins. *Clever.* The kind of thing you'd find in a short-term rental.

He went room to room, opening doors and closets, before ending in the bedroom where he'd slept. There were two nightstands and a chest of drawers. This is where things got interesting. One nightstand held a Glock 17 pistol with two loaded 17+1 magazines. He picked up the pistol and inserted a magazine, pulling the slide back to load the chamber.

The grip felt good but didn't conform to his palm the way his Springfield Armory XD-9 did. After James left the military, he owned guns for both personal safety and the thrill he got out of going to the range and hitting targets. In addition to the XD-9 he owned a Beretta 1301 tactical shotgun that might be the most fun shooting he'd ever had. When home, he would hit the Los Angeles Gun Club whenever time allowed.

James hit the magazine release button and caught the mag as it slipped from the pistol. He set it down and pulled the slide once more, ejecting the loaded bullet, which launched in a half-arc and landed on the bed. He returned the bullet to the mag and slipped it—along with the pistol—in the drawer. *Good to know*, he thought.

The opposite nightstand had a zippered vinyl pouch, which contained stacks of British Pounds, Euros, and American Dollars. Flipping through them, it appeared each stack was the equivalent of 2,000 in cash.

Finally, he inspected a bureau in the entry way, where an extra set of door keys lay next to keys he recognized as Land Rover. He picked these up and gave them a close look, guessing they were likely 1990s vintage. He walked back into the bedroom and looked down from the third floor window to a parking area, where he saw a tricked out 1995 Land Rover Defender, with lift kit and oversized wheels, a partial soft top in the back, finished in black.

Sick.

James had some calls to make. He had made it to the safe house, and Alyssa Stevens said this was the first step in getting him safely home. He expected within twenty-four hours they'd have him on a flight to JFK, and then either to Langley or back home to Los Angeles, where they'd send someone to debrief him.

Meanwhile, he needed to make some notes. He grabbed his backpack and took out his MacBook Air and returned to the kitchen breakfast bar, taking a seat with his coffee still steaming. Opening the laptop, he clicked on the Notes app and started a checklist.

Calls:
Stevens
AMP
Taylor
Murphy

Things to do:
Food
Escape routes

And then he wrote, *Keep connecting the dots.*

With the whole scene at Schiphol, he had a lot to figure out. The whereabouts of the courier. More information on the African boss. Who were the Russians?

And then there was the guy in the black wool peacoat. Who was he? Why was he following James?

Finally, in all caps, he wrote *WHAT DON'T WE KNOW???*

James took a minute to think about that last part. What he did know to this point was leading somewhere, but he wasn't sure where yet. Thies talked about new money coming into the fund from a familiar source; AMP was working on a possible sleeper cell in Paris, tipped off by the courier; the courier mentioned something about London and agreed to meet James in Amsterdam, but was really there to meet the financier/boss from Africa; the courier was convinced something new was happening based on what he was seeing in Paris as he laundered money.

These were tangible, linkable things. But what did they point to? If Henrique the courier speculated another attack was being planned, how would they find out?

There are two options here, Mathieu, James told himself. Find Henrique or find the man Alyssa Stevens said was Aadan Mukhtaar.

45

It was just after 06:30 and Alyssa Stevens was on her morning run. The Eastern Seaboard was expecting a huge snowstorm to begin later that day, and temperatures were plummeting. Her long strides ate pavement as she glided through her neighborhood. This morning it was Taylor Swift in her AirPods, helping her keep a pace that would make her college coaches proud.

Stevens ran with both her phone and an Apple Watch. Although the watch would be enough for most, the rising analyst wanted to make sure she was accessible for calls on a number of platforms.

And that was fortunate for Mathieu James, who rang her on WhatsApp.

Stevens unzipped her chest pocket and pulled out her phone, maintaining full stride. She answered, and slid the phone back into her pocket, taking the call on her AirPods.

Her heavy breathing welcomed him once again.

"Are you always running?" James joked.

"Always someplace to be," Stevens breathlessly replied.

"Of course, of course. Listen, I won't keep you. Wanted to confirm I'm in a safe place," he said, referring to his successful acquisition of the safe house.

"Good. Any issues?"

"None with the place. But I did have a visitor on my way here."

"What kind of visitor?"

"The kind that boards a train somewhere between London and here and follows me, watching me."

"Male or female?"

"Male."

"What did he look like?"

"Six feet, maybe 185. Similar to me."

"What happened?"

"I noticed him on the train as we were disembarking. We made eye contact a couple of times. He then followed me out of the station, and as I tried to put distance between us, he kept coming, closing that distance. There was a lot of direct eye contact. It wasn't coincidental. I made for the tram as fast as I could and picked him up on the other side of the street, where he was just watching me. He watched me get on the tram and leave."

"What was he wearing?"

"Black wool peacoat, gray scarf, crimson tuque."

"Notice anyone else?" Stevens asked as she continued to glide through the chilly morning, her breathing labored-but-even as her lungs repeatedly exhaled small clouds of vapor.

"I was too focused on him."

"Okay."

"Okay what?"

"Okay, so he's nobody to be worried about. He's MI5, and he was assigned to make sure you got to the tram and ultimately to the safe house. He boarded in London. Just keeping you safe, Mathieu."

James paused for a moment, taking in the context of the man in the black wool peacoat. *Why was he so obvious? It seemed like he wanted me to know he was there?*

"Interesting. Not at all what I expected. Will I see this guy again?"

"Doubtful, unless you need help with something. He's in your area, so if you do need something let me know and I'll reach out to my contacts. We also have our own assets, but they've been busy with other things. I called in a favor."

"Understood."

"What else, Mathieu? Anything more on Mukhtaar? Have you heard from the courier?"

"Nothing more from me, although I plan to call my colleague in Paris right after we're done. She's hopefully had a head start on the day. I slept like a baby."

"I bet."

"So if I learn anything there I'll let you know."

"Okay, sounds good."

"When am I leaving here?"

"Well, have you seen the news here, Mathieu?" Stevens asked, her breathing getting noticeably heavier.

"No, I've been a little distracted," he laughed.

"A bomb cyclone is going to sweep the Eastern Seaboard. They are already starting to cancel flights for the next couple of days. You'll be staying put, I think. There's cash available to you in the house to get things you need. Don't use your credit cards..."

"Yeah, about that. The tram ticket was card only."

"Shit, okay. Didn't know that. I'll see if we can get someone in there and scrape it," she said, referring to the transaction on his statement. "You probably noticed there's a vehicle. Use it only if you need it."

"Copy that."

"And then sit tight."

"I'll find some entertainment."

"Be careful and stay in touch. Gotta run, the final mile is coming and it's uphill. Bye for now."

"Have fun."

James terminated the call and promptly dialed Ana-Marie Poulin. She answered on the first ring.

"Mathieu, I'm so glad you called."

"Ana-Marie, what's going on? Is everything okay?"

"I don't think so, Mathieu."

James furrowed his brow.

"How so? What's happening?"

"I got a phone call earlier from Henrique Perron's sister. She was hysterical. She said the police paid her mom a visit."

"And?"

"They told her Henrique was found dead at the airport in Amsterdam."

"What?"

"Oui, I know."

"How? Where?"

"They didn't offer a lot of details, but they said the death was suspicious and under investigation."

"Holy shit, Ana-Marie. I wonder what happened."

"I don't know for sure. I have some colleagues in Amsterdam who might be able to talk with the police to get some more information."

"Right, well, yeah, that would be a good idea."

James's mind was racing again. If the other Russian continued pursuit of the courier after he punched his buddy in the balls, this might be a really simple case of Henrique getting killed by the people he was there to meet.

But he also looked strung out, so maybe drugs had something to do with it? At this point the cause of death mattered, but not as much as the fact he was dead. He was the primary source for their story, and someone who had access to leads and information that could be important not just for investigative journalists like James and Poulin, but law enforcement and intelligence services as well.

"Ana-Marie, did you know the family? I mean beyond Henrique?"

"No, I didn't."

"So how did the sister know to contact you?"

"Always curious, aren't you? That's a great question, one I asked her myself."

"What did she say?"

"She said more than a year ago, Henrique gave her an envelope, and told her that if anything ever happened to him, open it, and follow the instructions."

"So Henrique wanted you to be notified in the event of his death."

"Oui, seems right."

"Why?"

"I don't know. I've been thinking about that. He probably knew he was involved in some shit, Mathieu. He was probably trying to spare his mother and sister the details. Keep them out of it."

"Was there anything else in that envelope?"

She thought for a moment, then answered.

"Honestly, I didn't think to ask. I was too stunned with the news."

James turned silent. He was processing. *Zero chance he just died in Schiphol. They killed him. But why? There's no way they arranged the meeting to kill him. You don't do that in an airport. So something went wrong. Or someone went rogue. Either way, he's dead.*

"Ana-Marie, I'm going to think on this for a bit. I'll get back in touch with you and we can go over our story notes. Things are changing rapidly. Sound good?"

"Oui, sounds perfect."

"I'm sorry about your friend."

"Mathieu, you were among the last people he saw or spoke with."

"Seems like it. I am sorry. Let me know if your colleagues in Amsterdam learn anything."

"Will do. Ciao, Mathieu."

"Ciao."

James set the phone down and took a sip of lukewarm coffee, crinkling his nose at the experience. He lifted his phone again and opened the photos app, reviewing images of the man he now knew as Aadan Mukhtaar. He also looked at the video he took as he was exiting the plaza when he had locked eyes with the terrorist.

He watched it over and over. And his sentiment was the same now as then.

See you soon.

James just needed to figure out how.

46

London, England

With his day spent running errands and talking to hired help about the business he shared with Andrey Morozov, Igor Kozlov had just one last stop to make. It had been a while since he had shopped at the market, and his refrigerator was bare. He swung by Dostlar to get some fruit, vegetables, and dairy before heading home to his flat.

His front walk had a dusting of snow. The crunch of his boots was followed by perfect imprints of his soles, creating a path of lonely, ghostly steps leading to his door. He set down the grocery bags and fumbled with his keys, looking to unlock the door and get out of the damp and cold. As he did so, he noticed a thick envelope shoved into his mail slot. Using his fingers, Igor pushed the package inside before unlocking the door and gathering his groceries.

Kicking off his boots, he marched to the kitchen and set three bags on the counter, quickly putting the perishable goods in their proper places, before walking back to grab his mail.

Save the package, there was one other envelope, probably a bill. Intrigued, he rotated the package, finding it blank. This was curious. It hadn't come from the Royal Mail. Instead, someone hand-delivered this. He shook it, held it to his ear, rotated the package again and, for no obvious reason, sniffed it.

Nothing weird. *No idea*, he thought.

He walked back to the kitchen, carrying the package, and still inspecting its blank exterior. He grabbed scissors and cut his way through one end. Looking inside, he saw a small box. Tilting the envelope, he let the box inside slide onto the counter. It was a prepaid phone—a burner—with a sticky note affixed to the box.

First, there was a telephone number. Then...

21:30 today

Use once + destroy.

Igor correctly assumed this was a direct way to reach the African financier. He checked his watch. It was still early evening.

Be prepared, he thought to himself. He sat at the dining table and continued working on the sketch of the Edinburgh Christmas Market. The festive market ran adjacent to Princes Street, stretching from Waverley Station to the Scottish Royal Academy and National Galleries of Scotland. It was a horizontal strip with limited security. The small stalls for merchants and vendors made for a naturally enclosed space. He marked the three primary exits, one at each end, followed by a set of stairs that led to a park below—Princes Street Gardens.

The entire area, including the retail corridor across Princes Street, was heavily trafficked, especially this time of year. On most nights there would easily be thousands of people working their way between Waverley and the museums, and those beginning to ascend The Mound toward the touristy Royal Mile district and Edinburgh Castle.

Igor was excited about this possibility. He was certain an attack on something as sacred as a Christmas Market would force the West—the Brits, the Americans, the Canadians and more—to refocus on security at home. The public outcry would be enormous.

He kept himself busy working on the sketches, identifying possible escape routes and snacking on fruit. Before long, the call time had arrived, and

Igor pulled the phone from the box and powered it on. The battery was fully charged—someone had done this prior to placing the phone in his mail slot.

Igor dialed the number from the sticky note and listened as the tone buzzed three times on the other end. A voice spoke.

"Yes."

Igor froze at first, uncertain what to say next. Then he found his courage and continued.

"Following up on our meeting. You asked for a plan. I have one. I think it would be great to take the kids to the Christmas Market," Igor said, proud of himself for speaking vaguely and in a code language he made up.

This was met with silence before a question came back at Igor.

"Where?"

"Edinburgh."

"When?"

"I was hoping you'd tell me. But soon."

"Have you been there?"

"I have."

"Security?"

"Limited."

"Collateral damage?"

"Substantial."

"Carnage?"

"Enormous."

"How large?"

Igor paused, tapping his index and middle fingers on the table.

"Thousands."

"Not people. How large is the space?"

"Large, two blocks maybe. Borders a busy street. Next to the train station."

"I like this. This has potential."

"I thought you would like it," Igor said, kissing ass a little.

"I have a crew I can bring. Who else have you talked with about this?"

"Just my partner, no one else."

"Partner? Like your girlfriend or boyfriend?"

"No. My business partner."

"Is he trustworthy?"

"Yes, I think so."

"Why do you say 'think so'?"

"Because when I talked with him about this idea of weakening the West, he was against it. But I don't think he will say anything. He won't be a problem."

"So you don't think we can trust him?"

"I trust him," Igor replied.

"That's fine, but I don't. So he's not a player?"

"Not with this, I don't think so."

"And what will you do about that?"

"About what?"

"You told your friend your thoughts, your plans. What's keeping him from telling someone else, like the police?"

"He wouldn't do that."

"We can't take that chance. He's either in or he's not. And if he's not, you have to solve that problem."

"Solve what problem?"

"Let me make myself clear: If you have spoken with *anyone* about this, and they are not helping, they are a liability. I don't like liabilities. Liabilities talk, and they must be eliminated."

"Eliminated? You mean..." Igor swallowed hard here.

"It must be done. No questions. I have a team where I am. It will take me twenty-four hours to organize, but we will be in Edinburgh in thirty-six hours. Make your way there tomorrow. Destroy the phone you are using now. We will get you another. I will call you next. Be ready. Sounds like a good find."

The line went dead, and Igor smiled. He'd found a willing partner.

"This shit is happening," he said to no one.

Just then, he heard a strange noise near the front door. He stood from the dining table and walked quietly. There was another package dangling from the mail slot. It looked identical to the one he'd received earlier.

He pulled it from the slot and confirmed the exterior was blank, and the inside felt like the box containing the burner phone. He ripped open the envelope, and sure enough, it was another prepaid phone, with a note scrawled in Sharpie on the box: *Keep.*

Igor shuddered and looked behind him.

They're watching me.

He peeked outside the front window, pulling the blinds back ever so slightly. It was dark, and the street was poorly lit. A dog barked in the distance; a car drove past as the sounds of slushy pavement leaked through the glass. He moved to the other side to change his angle, and here he could see his walk.

A fresh set of footprints in the icy mush, leading up to his door and back, then down the sidewalk and out of sight.

Igor let go of the blinds, and the blood drained from his face. His world would never be the same.

47

Zurich, Switzerland

Francois Thies sat on his fourth-story veranda bundled up and sipping an espresso, reading the *Financial Times*. He had recently returned from his visit to the American Southwest, where he was unsuccessful in bringing new investors into his fund.

Such was life. The recruitment of new money was like a good baseball batting average. If you were able to get a hit one-third of the time, you were likely making yourself a millionaire.

Thies had a lot of irons in the fire, as usual. He operated a number of funds, each with a distinct goal. But the fund that got everyone's interest was the one where you had to be in a select class of criminals. He knew it came with risks, but the reward was too bountiful to turn a cheek.

On this day, he was expecting a new infusion of capital into the fund, likely via Royal Bank of Scotland. The transfer would probably originate with an offshore shell company. He would only know the owners if they wished to reveal themselves.

Over the years, he began noticing patterns in how money entered and left his fund. This was unsettling because it was possible now to put together the pieces of a puzzle. There were too many coincidences where money would enter the account, and one or two weeks later a news-making event would happen.

Recently, the most obvious newsmaker was the assassination of the former Japanese Prime Minister. In the past, violence in drug cartels or a series of pirated merchant vessels would be part of the pattern. Money in, money out.

For some enterprises, Thies's fund was the end of a laundering process. For others, it was the beginning. He preferred not to know what the motives were of his clientele, but sometimes it was too obvious.

The most recent incident that ate his soul was the 2015 terror attacks in Paris. He was able to assemble that puzzle rather easily. He also knew that if he ever spoke, ever hinted at or ever made a call to the authorities, his wife and two children would be killed. And chances were, the perpetrators of such hate would make him watch before torturing him and leaving his body to bleed out.

These are the stories he told himself. This is how he justified who he had become. He hadn't set out to be the investment chief of the criminal underworld. His younger self had dreams of managing money for the world's non-criminal elite. He saw himself living in the tiny Swiss village of Davos or the glitzy resort of St. Moritz.

Faced with a cross-roads when he married, he chose to stay with Switzerland Bank & Trust due to his father-in-law's influence. By his late 30s, he was managing global funds for international clientele. And then, one day, he had a meeting request from a handler for a notorious international arms dealer. This person was in the news frequently, supplying black market military equipment to spawn civil wars in Africa, to arm rebels in Chechnya, and to equip some of the world's largest drug cartels.

That's how it starts. You take one meeting, you manage it right, and word of mouth spreads. It opened new doors to a lifestyle Thies envied. But once those doors are opened, and you walk across the threshold, there's no going back. Even if he wanted to. Lately, he often did.

Thies set down his espresso cup and saucer after savoring the last sip and picked up his iPad. He had a secure network at home, complete with VPN to mask his online whereabouts. He went through his email and messages quickly, deleting most and moving two into client folders. He then logged into his private portal at SB&T, where he could see his fund's performance and track incoming funds.

There, it was—just three rows down on the incoming transfers list. A wire from Royal Bank of Scotland, with an account number ending in 3981, for two million Euros. He was expecting this, as he had shared with Mathieu James in Scottsdale.

This account, through his own analysis, was likely tied to the Paris attacks in 2015. He also had reason to believe the same person was tied to other terror attacks. This person was probably a financier, if not a mastermind. He surmised this fund was used as a temporary holding station, and then days later withdrawals would be made to pay those responsible for ill deeds. The investors kept the short-term gains—or writing off losses—in exchange for another trip to the money laundromat.

Thies felt a pit in his stomach. *What could be happening?* He opened the Proton Mail app on his iPad. He had an account with a generic handle—swiss_skier4399—and sent a simple message to James.

The transfer we discussed is complete.

48

Paris, France

Aadan Mukhtaar now had a direct line to Igor Kozlov. The latest burner phone had been slipped into his mail slot within seconds of their last call ending. Igor had presented a plan that was music to Aadan's ears—large masses of people, few exits, Western-style celebrations.

Boom.

Mukhtaar had waited patiently for an opportunity to renew his personal war on terror with the West. He was 'encouraged' to finance and lead these operations by heads of state, criminal enterprises, and men with axes to grind.

He didn't accept every opportunity. If he did, he'd probably be dead. Being patient meant lulling his enemies to sleep. Hit them hard, then lay low. Build your teams, pay them well, let them blend into society. Wake them when it was time.

Mukhtaar had built a network of sleeper cells. He had them in France, Wales, Turkey, and throughout Africa. They were experts in mass destruction: bomb makers, snipers, former intelligence experts, and the worst kind of all, suicide bombers. He funded the operations; he approved the hits; the sleeper cells carried out the missions.

Along with his two Russian goons, Mukhtaar was still in the Paris apartment he kept. Aside from going out for take away food and replenishing the vodka supply, the three kept a low profile.

With a target package identified, it was time to start the operational planning. Aadan called the two Russians to the dining table to fill them in.

"Boys," he said, looking each in the eyes, "we have a new opportunity. We are going to awaken our friends in Wales. They will need things, probably extra cash. Maybe something more. They have weapons stashes, but they will likely need to build some explosives. Our cells have been stockpiling necessary items for years. We consider it an ongoing cost of doing business."

"What does that mean for us, boss?" the first Russian asked, as the second Russian listened closely, still feeling the dull ache from his balls getting crushed.

"From now on, communication happens in person. We stay off anything that's not a burner. No computers, no iPhones, no internet. You understand?"

The Russians nodded their heads in the affirmative.

"I have a team in the UK that we will activate. The three of us will head to Scotland. We are planning something big there, and I need to see it for myself."

"How will we get there?" the second Russian asked.

"By train, hopefully. If not, then by bus. Maybe both," Aadan answered.

The Russians looked at each other. They had been working as Aadan's heavies for a while. They were provided by the Russian GRU, who paid them a salary. And then Aadan paid them a 'duty hazard' fee. They made great money, but their entire world now was protecting an international bomb maker, financier, and terror mastermind.

The GRU had locked onto Aadan more than a decade ago for his work in Africa. Both Russia and China had been sending teams there to pilfer the mining and mineral rights on the continent. Aadan was the guy who got things done, getting crews together, laundering money, falsifying documents—whatever they needed.

As his place in that underworld gained a foothold, he was able to branch into other things. Among his favorite pet projects?

Terror plots.

"Boys, let's be clear on something. Whatever you see and hear stays in this group," he said, motioning his finger in a circle at the Russians and himself. "Plan to leave tomorrow for Scotland. We will get tickets at Paris-Nord and pay cash. I want the two of you to visit our warehouse here and bring back 30,000 Euros, three pistols, and extra magazines and ammo. We need to travel light, so don't get carried away. While you're doing that, I'll set things in motion."

Aadan pulled his burner phone from his back pocket and dialed a number. It rang twice.

"Yes?" The caller on the other end said.

"Edinburgh, tomorrow night. Picardy Inn and Suites."

"Got it," Igor said nervously.

Aadan hung up, stood and went to the kitchen. The first drawer on the left contained silverware. He pulled everything from the drawer, then removed the drawer from the cabinet, flipping it over and setting it on the counter.

Written on the underside of the drawer was a series of numbers. They all corresponded to the sleeper cells he had around the world. Aadan located the number for Wales and dialed it.

No one answered.

He dialed the number a second time.

His call was answered on the first ring.

Aadan spoke.

"Hello, my son. This is your father. It's time to wake up. We have a new project developing in Edinburgh. I will see you soon."

Aadan hung up the phone, returned the drawer to its slot in the cabinet, and replaced the silverware. He would make his moves one at a time, like a master chess player. Always playing steps ahead.

49

London, England

Igor Kozlov had a lot to do before heading to Edinburgh. He had no idea how this trip would end. He tried to imagine his plan unfolding—he and a like-minded group pulling off an attack that would shake the West to its core.

Given he had never done something like this, his mind wouldn't play the movie for him. Instead, he was left with a lot of questions whose answers hopefully would come after he checked into the hotel at Picardy Place.

His rage, fueled by Western arrogance, had reached a new pitch. His news feed was filled with press reports about a speech given by the Belarus leader Lukashenko. He admitted what most intelligence agencies already knew—Belarus was now hosting Russian nuclear weapons. Two months prior, in October, Putin had sent a shipment of short-range and tactical nuclear warheads to the neighboring country. The goal was to deter NATO member Poland from eyeing any aggression toward Belarus.

This, of course, was nothing more than showmanship by Putin and Lukashenko. While the Poles were supporting Ukraine in its struggle for survival from Russian invaders, NATO and its member countries had been extremely thoughtful in their attempts to support Ukraine while avoiding anything that ignited Armageddon from a paranoid Russian leader.

Nevertheless, Igor saw this through the lens he preferred: NATO was intent on flexing its power, what with Finland and Sweden's applications to join; Poland training troops and pilots while allowing shipments from the US military to be staged on their turf before sending them into Ukraine.

This reinforced Igor's notion that Putin was wise to react in the way he did, forcefully trying to take Ukraine while the West was rallying to save an undermanned, burgeoning democracy. No, it was certain the West was propping up its allies, making strategic plays in the region for forward bases and tactical advantages should things deteriorate.

Meanwhile, Igor planned to make one last attempt at recruiting his life-long friend, Andrey Morozov. Although the weather had turned sour in London, he invited his friend for a walk along the path at Woodberry Wetlands. It was a calm, serene setting amidst the bustle of city life. The two could talk freely. Igor hoped his final plea would appeal to his friend.

The one thing he did not want to do was what the African boss suggested: eliminate any threats. While he had no qualms planning the mass murders of thousands of innocent men, women, and children, Igor couldn't stomach the thought of killing Andrey.

However, what must be done should be done quickly. There was no sense in holding back a plan that was already in motion. Igor asked Andrey to meet him near the Coal House Cafe off Lordship Road. From there they could take a stroll and talk.

Andrey pulled up in his BMW right on time, waiting in the car with the heater running until he saw his friend. Igor was normally on time but wasn't within sight when Andrey arrived. He gave it fifteen minutes or so, listening to EDM, and scrolling through social media.

With no signs of Igor still, he dropped him a text message.

I'm here. Still coming?

Igor responded right away.

Here already. Been waiting for you. I'm outside the cafe.

Andrey shrugged his shoulders, turned off the engine of his BMW, and grabbed his gloves from the passenger seat. Stepping out of his car, he blew on his hands to warm them, then slipped on his gloves, his breath faintly visible in the chill.

The sun sets early in the UK during winter. Days are short, and darkness falls in midafternoon. Blue hour clung to the city, offering a faded photograph of life in London.

Andrey's boots crunched on top of the crusty slush that was freezing over. It was slippery, but he paid no mind. Growing up, he had seen winters that people in London couldn't fathom.

As he made his way toward the cafe, he saw the silhouette of his friend Igor. He was smoking a dart, his face aglow with each hard suck on the filter. He was wearing jeans and a zip-up fleece hooded jacket that Andrey had never seen before. Igor had the hood up and was also wearing a tuque on his head. His hands were sleeved in thin leather driving gloves.

Odd, Andrey thought of his friend's fashion choices.

"Hey, brother!" Andrey exclaimed.

"My brother," Igor answered as the two men embraced.

"It's cold out here. Why couldn't we meet at your place?"

"Let's take a walk," Igor answered, ignoring his friend's question.

From the Coal House Cafe, they took the southern path. The route was tree-lined, though winter had left the branches naked, void of their leafy canopies. On the opposite side of the trees was a neighborhood of clustered homes. The soft evening light was accented by windows in those homes glowing in warm tones of yellow and orange.

"Where'd you park?"

"Just up the road," Igor answered.

"Oh, I didn't see your car."

"Yeah, honestly I couldn't remember where the parking was, so I just grabbed the first spot I saw. Had to walk a bit. It's been a long time since I've been here."

"Nature never seemed like your cup of tea," Andrey laughed. "So what's on your mind?"

"I think you know."

"Actually, I don't. Fill me in."

The two walked side by side. Andrey to the left, closest to the water, and Igor to his right, nearest the tree line. Igor finished his cigarette and flicked it to the ground, stepping on it as he reached in his pocket for another. He stopped for a moment, covering his lighter from the wind, then flipped it closed, putting both hands in his pockets and holding the cigarette between his lips.

The silence was awkward, so Andrey tried to make a joke.

"You got girl problems, my brother? Need some advice on getting your dick hard?"

Igor chuckled.

"No, I'm good thanks. Listen, Andrey," he said, pulling his right hand from his pocket and grabbing the cigarette from his mouth. "What we talked about at my flat? You remember that?"

"You're still on this 'sending a message' thing?"

"It's happening, Andrey. And soon. I could use your help. I could use someone I trust. I'm working with people I don't know, and I could use someone who has my back."

Andrey stopped in his tracks. Igor kept walking another few steps before turning toward his friend.

"Igor, have you gone mad? There has to be a better way. Why do you need to kill innocent people? I was thinking about all of this. Do you remember a long time ago, we were very young but we learned about this...do you remember when Al Qaeda bombed the American warship in Yemen? Do you remember this? They drove a boat with explosives right next to the ship and detonated it. They killed a bunch of American sailors and injured more. Why not target their military? Why does it have to be women and children?"

Igor pulled hard on his cigarette, the burning tobacco creating a large orange circle that illuminated his eyes. His nose and the hood from his jacket drew sharp angles across his face. He looked deadly serious.

"Because killing their military doesn't put fear in their people. They expect their military to die, to sacrifice themselves for their freedoms. But when people look at death and see themselves, it cuts a little deeper. It puts fear in their stomachs. It makes them feel vulnerable in the places they feel most comfortable."

Andrey held his gaze on his friend, shaking his head slowly.

"C'mon, it's cold, let's keep walking," Igor insisted.

They resumed, no longer side by side. Igor was slightly ahead; Andrey unsure what to say.

"Andrey, what if you had a job that was, I don't know, not part of the action? What if you were a driver, or a courier? What if I kept you at a distance? Would you help me then?"

Andrey kept walking, hands in his jacket pockets, head down. He was feeling emotional about his friend, wondering what darkness had found its way into his soul. This part of Igor he didn't know. He wanted to forget this part of him. He wanted to go back to being friends who were stealing truckloads of cigarettes and booze. Ripping off fashion warehouses and sending the goods back home. They had a good life. A tight network. They didn't feel vulnerable.

But now Andrey felt vulnerable. And a little bit scared. He stopped once again to address his childhood friend.

"Igor, I can't. I won't. And I hope you won't either. I hope you will reconsider and get as far away from these people as you can."

Igor also stopped but didn't turn to face his friend. "It's too late for that," he said quietly.

Andrey shook his head. "It's not too late. I love you, brother. But you need to stop with this. I'm going home. I'm cold and I'm tired and I don't want to think about this. I don't want to talk about this ever again."

Andrey turned and began walking back the way they had come, toward the cafe and his car.

"Andrey, wait..." Igor said, still facing away from his friend. He tossed his cigarette to the side, where it landed on the damp brown grass. With his right hand he pulled his jacket off his hip, and grabbed the 12.8-inch, full-tang Bowie knife sheathed inside his jeans. With the black blade exposed and his gloved hand gripping the contoured wooden handle, he turned and lunged at Andrey, who didn't see it coming because he never imagined his friend would be the person who sent him to the afterlife.

Andrey reacted late, and the tip of the knife pierced his jacket, ripped through his shirt and sliced into his abdomen. Instinctively he grabbed Igor's arm, trying to fight him off, looking first at the knife that was inside him, then at his friend's face. Igor had glazed over, showing no fear or panic. His eyes were hollow; his face expressionless.

They wrestled there on the path of the wetlands park, Igor grunting as he tried to turn the blade inside his friend, carving through his abdominal wall and organs. Andrey screamed and fought, throwing punches at his friend. Fearing the noise, Igor leveled a left hook on his friend's jaw, knocking him to the ground, his head bouncing off the path. With his right hand, he continued to grind, twist, and skewer as his friend no longer fought back. Andrey was slumped over on his left side. Through the thin driving glove, Igor could feel the warmth of Andrey's blood as it drained from his friend.

He pulled the knife from Andrey's stomach and stood, looking around and listening. The distant hum of traffic. Dogs barking. Darkness brought silence, and the end of Andrey Morozov's life. He lay motionless, his eyes open with fear. Igor knelt down and whispered "I'm sorry" to his friend. He reached inside Andrey's jacket and found the keys to the BMW and put them in his pocket. He took Andrey's wallet from his pants and wiped the blood-soaked blade on the dying man's sleeve.

If there was ever a question if Igor Kozlov was fully radicalized, it had been answered. He stood and checked his shoulders, making sure no one was coming or watching, before beginning a purposeful walk toward the BMW. Igor had not driven to meet Andrey. He planned this to look like a robbery if he couldn't talk his friend into helping him. With Andrey out of the picture, he would take the BMW to Edinburgh and ditch it.

As he distanced himself from the man he'd stabbed, a pang of guilt shuddered through his body. He turned and looked at Andrey, a pool of blood now visible on the path, inky black, a faint source of light mirrored on the surface. Igor whispered, "God help me. Goodnight, Andrey."

50

Edinburgh, Scotland

The sleeper cell Aadan Mukhtaar controlled was based in Wrexham, an industrial town in Wales best known for its emerging football team now owned by two Hollywood actors. The four cicadas were recruited after the Paris attacks. They were Muslim immigrants and were radicalized long before turning up in Wales. This was the moment they lived for.

The four men didn't socialize and didn't work together. Each knew of the other, and they all knew the combination to the storage unit that contained a panel van, various explosives including military-grade C4 and industrial grade dynamite. Also in storage was a wooden case of Soviet-era automatic rifles with extra magazines; three crates of ammunition; a dozen Beretta PX4 Storm handguns; two rocket propelled grenade launchers; and a host of chemicals for making home-made improvised explosive devices.

Aadan had arranged rooms at the Picardy Inn and Suites for the four men from Wales, plus Igor Kozlov. Each would check in under a company name and false ID except for Kozlov. There was no time to get him a false ID. He would be checking in under his own name. The rooms were pre-paid with a debit card tied to a bank in Copenhagen. Aadan had opened this account after the 2015 Paris attacks in the event any of his funding had been tracked. Very little money went in and out, making it less suspicious and more like a frugal retiree was in charge.

The two Russians and Aadan would be staying across town in more luxurious accommodations that sported a posh, regal interior in sharp contrast to the budget single rooms near Picardy Place. Aadan wanted some distance from the group. And he was the boss. He was the financier. He was the mastermind. If luxury suited him—and he believed it did—so be it.

The sleeper cell and Igor would meet in person with Aadan and his goons just once, at the coffee shop on the street level of Waverley Station. Easy in, easy out with multiple access and exit points if needed. From there, they would walk the Christmas Market, essentially plotting their attack in real-time. The final assignments and go or no-go would be Aadan's call.

Aadan and the Russians arrived by train and walked to their hotel. The sleeper cell would arrive later by van, which was loaded with explosives and weapons. They planned to park in one of the many public garages near Picardy Place and walk the short distance to the hotel.

Igor was to travel by train from London as well. The fact he would be arriving in his dead friend's BMW would not be welcome news.

51

Edinburgh, Scotland

Mathieu James felt a burning need to explore his neighborhood. Getting out of the safe house wasn't part of the plan, but he felt like he'd blend in easily. The Leith area of Edinburgh was trendy and young enough that no one would be wiser.

The bomb cyclone hitting the Eastern Seaboard of the United States meant he'd be here longer than planned. He'd assumed Stevens would get him out on the first available direct flight, but now a couple more nights were likely on tap.

Searching the map on his iPhone, he found a coffee shop that was around the corner. In fact, there were multiple coffee shops and cafes nearby, but BAM Coffee seemed a little off the beaten path, and that put his sensibilities at ease.

He packed up his backpack with his computer, headphones, a second hat and some charging cables. Bounding down the three flights of stairs to the exit, he felt like a new man. He wasn't sure why. Maybe the crush of the past few days drifted away in his sleep. Or maybe it was the simple thought of getting out in a new city and exploring a bit, even if he was going less than a quarter mile away.

The directions to BAM were simple. Left out the door, left again at the top of the street. Stay straight to Salamander and turn right. The cafe was tucked into the first floor of a multi-use building with other shops and apartments above.

The cobblestone streets were slick from an overnight rain and cooler temperatures. James stayed on the narrow sidewalks, avoiding the surprisingly large amounts of dog poop left behind by inattentive owners. Nevertheless, Edinburgh is considered one of the world's great cities.

Approaching Salamander Street, he saw the port straight ahead, with a couple of large commercial vessels visible. The waterfront was under development, with an assortment of apartment homes and the occasional commercial project. He took note of the access points to the port and planned to check more later in the day.

Stepping inside BAM, he was greeted with a smile from a large man with a shaved head and bulging belly. He was wearing a t-shirt and shorts in December, and his feet were tucked into tube socks and ankle-level leather hiking boots.

"Welcome, take a seat anywhere," he said in a thick Scottish accent, making a sweeping gesture with his hand. The cafe had maybe seven tables, a booth tucked in a corner, and a small breakfast-type bar at the window.

James chose a table in the far back corner, adjacent to the kitchen sink and dishwashing area. This gave him a full view of the entrance, but also placed him at the farthest point from the door. *Not ideal*, he thought. But it should suffice.

The wait staff were two young women, dressed casually but both sporting facial piercings that seemed to be a thing with young Scots. A tiny redhead wearing a wool watch cap and a shy smile handed him a menu, and James requested a cappuccino.

Pulling his laptop from his backpack, he opened it and connected to the hotspot on his phone. The less use of internet connections, the better. Logging into Proton Mail first, he scanned the couple dozen unread messages before noticing one in particular from *swiss_skier4399*. He knew that handle to be Francois Thies.

James smoothly dangled his index and middle finger over the MacBook

Air's track pad, clicking on the message. It had no subject line, and simply read: *The transfer we discussed is complete.*

The waitress with the shy smile returned with a frothy cup of goodness and set it on the table.

"Do you need any sugar?" she asked.

"No, I'm good, thank you."

"Would you like to order?"

"I'm fine for now, maybe later."

"No problem, I'll check back with you."

James watched her disappear around the corner and lifted the cup to his lips, taking a sip. He decided his next task was to inform Frank Murphy and Ana-Marie Poulin of the development.

He created a new message in Proton Mail and addressed it to both.

Good morning. Will keep this brief, but my source in Switzerland has confirmed the latest wire transfer has arrived. This is believed to be from an account or entity that has supported terror in the past. He has previously told me his gut feeling is that with each new transfer from this entity, the likelihood of a new plot is high. Suggest we work any sources to learn more. Stay in touch on usual channels. - MJ

After hitting send, James took another sip of his cappuccino and held the cup near his face with two hands, taking in the aroma. He closed his eyes for a moment and thought of Taylor. He missed her, those big doe eyes, cascading hair, and cute dimple. What he was doing now, though, was the reason she often provided regarding her uncertainty about their relationship. He was on the other side of the globe, hiding in a safe house from a possible terrorist. He was largely unavailable, which would be a problem in any relationship.

His mind continued to wander. He suddenly thought of his parents. The UK was his mother's homeland. His cousin Lily was in London. Their family cottage was north near Aberdeen, not far from the salty breeze of the North Sea. Next, a memory from his time with Ranger Regiment at Fort Gordon, Georgia. A scene from J-school at Northwestern. He smiled faintly and snapped out of it.

Opening the document for the story he was working on, he decided to try adding a new piece of information to the structure. After a few minutes of tapping the keyboard, teleporting his thoughts to the screen, he read this back to himself:

The International Herald Tribune has learned that the 2005 London terror attacks on the transportation network, and the 2015 Paris terror attacks that locked down the city, were financed by at least one individual with ties to Africa, an anonymous source confirmed.

This same source has confirmed to IHT that a new wire transfer has been received by a Swiss bank. The sender has been previously flagged as having possible terror ties. IHT is working to confirm the sender's identity and is in possession of information that could reveal who's behind the money.

A second source told IHT that this person was still active in funding terror cells and networks, and that money was being laundered through a criminal enterprise in Paris, and later invested in a fund managed by a Swiss firm. IHT has recently learned this second source is deceased, and the death is considered suspicious by international authorities.

He felt the same now as he did with the last draft. It was true on the surface, but it was probably not enough to print. Maybe AMP would have some thoughts. He selected the text, pasted it into a new email and sent it to his Paris colleague, placing just a question mark in the subject line.

His stomach was grumbling after the latest sip of cappuccino, and he picked up the yellow, single-page menu from the table and looked it over. It was inspired for a small cafe, and the Bamacado Toast would be just the thing to order to send Frank Murphy over the edge.

52

London, England

Two young Indian women met at the Coal House Cafe for their morning walk. It was 06:00 and the sun wouldn't rise for another two-and-a-half hours. One was a nurse with the National Health Service. The other a stay-at-home mum, who cherished her one-hour alone to exercise and socialize.

Barely five minutes into their gossip-fueled giggles and brisk pace, they spotted a dark, shadowy pile on the path ahead. Thinking it might be a dead animal, they made a joke about dinner before realizing their mistake.

As the women drew nearer, it was obvious the shadowy pile was a person.

"Drunk and passed out," the nurse laughed.

"Kicked out by the wife, no doubt," the mum quipped.

The oncoming morning light barely offered enough lumens to see a watch, let alone identify a person in distress. The women walked with trail runner-style head lamps to keep themselves safe. About five feet from the body, the nurse saw a thick pool of liquid on the ground, and she gasped.

Quickly moving toward the man, the nurse rolled him over and saw his face was ashen, his eyes barely open and his lips a light shade of blue. She called to him and slapped his cheek a few times. The nurse checked his pulse on his wrist, finding nothing. Next, she checked his neck, repositioning her fingers several times.

"He has a weak pulse! Call an ambulance now!"

Her friend pulled her cell from her fleece pocket and ripped off her gloves, letting them drop to the ground. She dialed 999 and planned to stay on the line, reporting real-time information to the dispatcher until emergency crews and police arrived.

The nurse found his stab wound and removed her coat and her performance zip, leaving her in just a sports bra. She used the performance zip to keep pressure on the wound and spoke to the man in a soft, reassuring tone, telling him help was on the way. He was unresponsive, with the faintest pulse, when the medics arrived on scene.

Two police cruisers weren't far behind. As the medics rushed the man to the waiting ambulance, yellow tape was wrapped around trees to cordon the area. Officers interviewed the two women who found the body and inspected the scene for signs of a weapon—or something else.

Inside the rushing ambulance, medics worked to stabilize the patient and searched his pockets for identification. They found a cell phone.

A medic held the phone to Andrey's face, ready to search for an ICE contact—In Case of Emergency. When the phone unlocked, it revealed the man's open calendar, which had one entry in it from the previous day: Meet Igor, Coal House Cafe.

Back at the crime scene, investigators were tagging and bagging items found near the body. Of special note were two discarded cigarettes, which were retrieved by a latex-gloved hand and a pair of tweezers and placed into an evidence bag. A stupid person, it turns out, is often among the most dangerous.

Andrey was stabilized at the hospital and sent to surgery soon after. It took doctors four hours to stitch together his insides, with no guarantees he would live. The cold night temperatures had lowered his body temperature enough to give him a chance to survive. He had lost so much blood, and the risk of infection was real. If he could make it through the next 36 hours, his chances for recovery were good. This was the best-case scenario for a man who should be dead.

As police waited for a chance to speak with him, they continued following the leads they had, including searching his phone and checking those cigarette butts for DNA. The obvious clue was Igor's name in his calendar. Police were able to locate his phone number in Andrey's contacts, which they linked to an address in Harringay. Two detective constables were sent to Igor's flat, only to find no one home.

They also visited Andrey's apartment, which they were able to ascertain through his cell phone billing plan. There they searched outside for a BMW that appeared prominently in his camera roll. It was nowhere to be found.

A bulletin was soon released by police with details of the car. Furthermore, a man named Igor Kozlov, of Harringay, was missing and wanted for questioning regarding a stabbing incident at a local park.

As this drama unfolded, Igor was on his way to Edinburgh in Andrey's BMW. The nearly eight-hour drive on the A1 and M1 happened overnight, with Igor staying alert on over-caffeinated energy drinks, as he tried to erase the previous night from memory. He arrived in Edinburgh just after 06:00 certain he had killed his childhood friend. He had no idea that back in London, a random nurse and her friend may have saved a man who was clearly left for dead.

53

London, England

The detective constables working the case of Andrey Morozov's stabbing were running into some serious questions. Among them, the fact that his beloved BMW was missing, as was the contact in his phone he was supposed to meet the night he was stabbed.

By the time Igor Kozlov arrived in Edinburgh and checked into the hotel at Picardy Place, the bulletin issued earlier with the BMW's plate numbers and a possible suspect ID had made its way into UK law enforcement circles. Igor didn't know this, of course, and rather than ditch Andrey's BMW at the earliest moment, he'd found parking near the hotel.

Another curious aspect of the case for the DCs was Andrey Morozov had a British Citizen Card, essentially a national ID card that was approved by the Home Office and law enforcement. But it was not the same as a driver's license.

While they waited for a search warrant to be approved for both Andrey's apartment and Igor's flat, cursory background checks showed very little. Neither had extensive files in the UK. The DCs suspected Andrey's Citizen Card—discovered in a national database—could be a fake because so little was known about him. They couldn't locate a valid UK passport, and no medical records turned up in the NHS search.

This raised enough suspicions to warrant a phone call to MI5. Perhaps the broader reach of the UK's domestic intelligence service could unearth clues about the two men with Russian-sounding names.

MI5's threat assessment desk received the query and immediately began a database search. As part of ordinary routine, they shared details with GCHQ, the third branch of British intelligence that focused on cyber security, counter terrorism and other online/IT threats and safeguards. GCHQ worked a nexus with MI6, MI5, and Defence to be the tip of the spear in all things cyber.

Within an hour, MI5 and GCHQ were looking at bank records, lease applications, loans, large purchases, travel habits—all routine, but all necessary to build a pattern of life. If unusual activities were part of a person's lifestyle, this was where the clues were stitched together.

For Igor Kozlov, the efforts to unearth information about his life was the worst thing he could imagine. While the same was true for Andrey Morozov—both men had been running a criminal enterprise for years right under the noses of London law enforcement. Andrey was seen as a victim for now.

And while the lack of depth in his personal profile made the DCs uncomfortable, the more urgent threat was a man on the loose who they suspected of attempted murder.

It didn't take long for MI5 and GCHQ to start asking questions of their own. The first thing they identified was recent travel patterns by Igor Kozlov. Thanks to the extensive surveillance network in the UK, they noted he had traveled by train from London to Edinburgh, where he flew to Amsterdam and returned the same day.

This by itself was a head scratcher. Getting to Amsterdam via London is rather easy. Train, plane, or automobile would be more efficient than traveling four-and-a-half hours by rail to Edinburgh, taking a tram to the airport and flying for one-hour-twenty minutes to Amsterdam.

The question was why did he do this?

The next question was, what was he doing there?

Bank records showed no activity in Amsterdam or any other European city around that time. In fact, they couldn't trace his purchase of rail or plane tickets for the trip.

Phone records were also part of the search. They were able to acquire his cell phone records, which showed routine calls in and around London, and occasional calls to Belarus. A simple trace of the numbers bore fruit.

The most common number he called in Belarus in the past month belonged to a Sergey Morozov. Same last name as the victim. There was also another frequently dialed number. Every Wednesday it came up. That search yielded the name Kozlov. Probably family. Both numbers were land lines and were soon entered into the database of numbers to watch. Any future calls from the UK to those numbers would trigger an internal alert.

With this pattern of life starting to unfold, many more questions arose. The simplest thing they could do at MI5 was ask for a trace on Igor's cell phone. If he was dumb enough to still be in possession of it, he was dumb enough to be found, arrested, and questioned in the attempted murder of Andrey Morozov.

A stupid person, it turns out, is often among the most dangerous.

As a low-level criminal specializing in burglaries of fashion warehouses, shipping trucks, and other coveted black-market commodities, Igor was always careful. He did things as simply as he could. Paid cash for everything whenever possible. Had a bank account but rarely used it. He tried to keep a low profile, just in case. Because the life he was living was better than prison, but the life he was living would also put him in prison if he was caught.

The work he did when he and Andrey were younger—the work for Andrey's father—gave him the basic tools to be a successful 'importer/exporter.' His passion for defending the ways of the old Soviet Bloc gave him a platform as the community organizer he used as cover.

But what Igor Kozlov had gotten himself into now—selling a terror plan to an international mastermind and financier who then encouraged him to kill his best friend—was a different level of seedy shit. He had no experience at this level, and he had already made key mistakes.

With a simple trace of his phone, which was pinging off towers on the A1 and M1, along with location services pinging his GPS coordinates, it was far too easy to locate the lead suspect in the stabbing of a man in a London park.

MI5 and GCHQ had a lock on his phone, which was transmitting now from the city center in Edinburgh. As they continued to build a profile on one Igor Kozlov, the officers shared this information with the London DCs, who promptly dialed their counterparts in Edinburgh.

A most wanted man was in their city. Be on the lookout.

54

Edinburgh, Scotland

Eight men gathered inside the street-level Costa Coffee shop at Waverley Station, right off Princes Street. They sat at two tables toward the back, enabling them to see the entire cafe, plus the shopping atrium below, accessed by stairs inside the shop.

Outside, grey skies bled mild flurries over the Scottish capital, lending a seasonal bent to the adjacent festivities. The Christmas Market was close by, with rides, shops, and food vendors running full steam nearly all day.

As the group's leader, Aadan Mukhtaar led a brief meeting.

"My brothers, we are here to honor Allah by continuing our crusade against infidels of the West. Time and again they push their ideals on our friends, our people, our communities. We must push back, always. The West desires to be the maker of policies, the choosers of right versus wrong, and the bully to the weak. This is why we are gathered here today."

The men listened intently, nodding their heads while sipping flat whites, Americanos, and tea.

"We all understand the mission. The goal today is to walk the site then choose our methods. When it's done, not everyone at this table is going home. For your sacrifice, we thank you and Allah is grateful.

"Let's get on with it."

The men rose and naturally split into small teams, choosing different exits from Waverley and different entrances to the Christmas Market.

Aadan left with Russian number one. Russian two went with Igor. The four from Wales split into two groups of two. When their sweep of the Christmas Market was done, they would return to their respective hotels, awaiting final instructions from Aadan, who would seek input before planning the attack.

Outside, Aadan and his goon strolled into the nearest entrance, adjacent to Waverley Station. The wind was gusting hard, watering his eyes. The crowd was growing slowly, and the smells of mulled wine mixed with aromatic foods like kebabs, spiced chicken, and pizza.

Young adults and kids lined up for rides on the ferris wheel and giant swing, which soared well above the market, offering 360-degree views of the medieval city as it spun wildly. Occasionally, a small blanket of vomit would fall from above, a grotesque offering from someone who couldn't stomach the ride.

Aadan adjusted his jacket to brace for the stiff wind and tucked his scally cap lower on his forehead. With his walking stick at his side, he carved a path through the sea of people, inspecting everything from security (limited, no bag checks) to bin access (possible, mustn't be obvious). It didn't take long for him to understand this was a target primed for destruction. So many places to drop bags, not to mention a busy street just steps away, with a tram, public buses, shopping, busy sidewalks, and then, of course, the train station.

It was perfect.

He could see the execution in his mind, but it would also take input from the Wrexham crew. What Igor thought wouldn't matter. While it was his idea, the idealistic Belarusian didn't know that Aadan planned to pin the entire thing on him, while making sure he wasn't alive afterward to say anything different.

55

Langley, Virginia

Like most of her colleagues, Alyssa Stevens packed an overnight bag before heading to work. There was a good chance anyone working at CIA Headquarters would be spending the night—maybe two—with the region getting clobbered by the latest bomb cyclone.

Hunkered in her office, dressed down given the weather in leggings, a sweater, and her hair pulled back in a pony, she thumbed through the daily classified reports. As the person responsible for the UK, there was seldom much of interest. Internally, MI5 usually had things dialed in. The culture of security was much stronger in the UK than elsewhere.

With that said, MI6 was a tempest of activity. As the strongest ally to the United States and a fervent defender of freedom and democratic processes, the UK was in the crosshairs of bad actors one hundred percent of the time.

Knowing she had a NOC asset stuffed away in a safe house, Stevens was looking for anything that might tickle her brain and help unravel the sequence of events Mathieu James entered in Amsterdam, those that put him on the run and what it would take for Mathieu to exit Europe.

Stevens squirmed in her seat, the athlete in her wanting to stay in motion. She stood and leaned over her desk, spreading the analyst reports from the UK in front of her. She rubbed her forehead and squeezed her eyes shut. Then opening them, she tried to gain focus. She hadn't worked out yet and hadn't injected enough coffee into her veins.

The reports were often dull and dry. She read them to herself in a British accent to bring some personality to the pages before her. As she turned one page over and moved onto the next, something jumped from the flat white paper and grabbed her attention.

A Belarusian national living in London was wanted in connection with an attempted murder. He had recently traveled to Amsterdam by way of Edinburgh. Security cameras at Schiphol International Airport captured several images of a man named Igor Kozlov. He was seen deplaning his aircraft and walking through the departure halls and into the plaza, where he went into Starbucks.

The airport's cameras couldn't reach inside every store, vendor, or shop. But cameras did pick him up at the back of the coffee house, near the windows. He was visible by his shirt. At one point, he was seen talking with at least two, possibly three people sitting across from him.

Analysts scoured the footage, looking for men in pairs of two or three who entered Starbucks and may have left together as well. Multiple potential suspects were identified, and screen grabs from the video feeds were copied into the reports. The facsimile of images was poor, but they had Stevens's attention. She had the images and video that James had sent her of the person they later identified as Aadan Mukhtaar.

She knew exactly who she was looking for.

On the third image, in a small crowd of people, a dark figure wearing a scally cap, a track-style suit, sunglasses, and carrying a walking stick or cane, was flanked by two large white men in blazers.

"Motherfucker!" she said quietly, tapping her finger on the image. *That's him.*

Stevens tagged the page with a pink sticky and thumbed through the rest of the images, finding the same trio departing Starbucks before disappearing in a sea of people.

British intelligence had already ID'd Igor Kozlov entering and exiting

Starbucks. For the first time, Stevens had eyes on the person law enforcement in the UK was hunting.

She thought of James and reached for her iPhone, opening WhatsApp and sending an encrypted message.

I have an update. Call when secure.

56

Edinburgh, Scotland

Believing he may have just eaten the best avocado toast ever, a satisfied Mathieu James exited BAM coffee in Leith, turning left up Salamander Street. This took him on a route along the port, past the Leith Assembly Rooms and into a retail corridor straight from the early 1800s. Along the way, the street changed names twice—from Salamander to Baltic to Commercial. He chuckled, having never thought of the Scots as being indecisive.

Stone and masonry buildings towered above the narrow street with gothic spires and false cannons among the creativity shown by early architects. The buildings literally lean into the street.

At the narrowest point, he reached a bridge, and the simply named Water of Leith, a small river that feeds into the strangely named Firth of Forth, which leads to the North Sea.

Here he crossed the street, passing the warm, sugary smells of the Clock Tower Cafe and the bougie nouveau Granary restaurant.

Soon he found the posh Malmaison Edinburgh hotel standing watch over a Scottish maritime memorial. It was a beautiful slice of waterfront, with all of Scotland's charm laid bare under gunmetal skies and glistening cobblestones.

James grabbed a seat on a park bench at the water's edge. As he did so, his phone vibrated in his right pocket, and he slid his hand inside to retrieve the device. He had a WhatsApp message from Alyssa Stevens.

I have an update. Call when secure.

With seagulls swarming overhead and geese pedaling in the Water of Leith, James felt as secure as he had in days. He dialed Stevens on the encrypted app.

"Mathieu, how's everything? Do you feel safe?"

"Hello, Alyssa," he beamed, as the low-riding sun sliced through the clouds and cast a combination of cinematic shadows and warm glow on the set below. "I feel good, thank you."

"We have some interesting news from our friends at MI5 and MI6. Some local police in London were looking into a stabbing in a park and as they started pulling threads, they passed it up the food chain. British intelligence cast a net on a person of interest and found something interesting."

"Okay, this is getting good," James said.

"Are those seagulls I hear in the background? Are you outside?"

He laughed. "I've gone for a stroll. I needed some fresh air. Don't worry. I blend in nicely here as long as I don't talk to anyone and give away my American accent."

"Be careful. It's called a safe house for a reason."

"Copy that. So, continue please. What did they find?"

"A Belarusian national named Igor Kozlov has been living in London for about a decade. He's wanted for questioning in the stabbing of another Belarusian national named Andrey Morozov."

"Those names don't mean anything to me," James interrupted. "Should they?"

"Probably not. But get this: As they dove deeper into Kozlov, they started tracking his whereabouts. Turns out he took a circuitous route to Amsterdam—to Schiphol—the same day you were meeting the courier."

"Interesting. What do you mean by 'circuitous'?"

"Rather than take the easy way out, like leaving from Heathrow or taking a train, he traveled to Edinburgh, and flew from there to Amsterdam. Same on the return."

"He did this in one day?"

"Yes."

"Did he leave the airport?"

"No."

"What do we know, then? Why was he there?

"Evidence strongly suggests he was meeting with our man and your new best friend, Aadan Mukhtaar."

"No fucking way," James said.

"Yes fucking way," Stevens smirked.

"How do they know this? Wait," James interjected. "Let me guess, security cameras."

"Correct."

"Of course."

"So," Stevens continued, "I have seen screen grabs of Kozlov entering a Starbucks at the airport, and then later Mukhtaar and his boys entering. There's some footage that's hard to see on the inside, but it looks like the four of them were seated together in the back of the place."

"Did they leave together?"

"No. Mukhtaar and his boys left and disappeared into a crowd. I'm sure if we asked, we could find them again on surveillance footage."

"No," James said, now standing and pacing along the water's edge. "I'm willing to bet they went straight from that meeting to the meeting with the courier, Henrique Perron."

"Certainly possible."

"I'm sure nobody knows why they met."

"Not really, but could it be anything good? We have a guy who's believed to be a small-time criminal in London wanted for questioning in the stabbing of someone who might be his friend, and this same guy is seen earlier on video talking with a terror-minded financier from Africa. They weren't exchanging Christmas cookie recipes," Stevens quipped.

"Where is this Kozlov guy now?"

"According to MI5, his last known location was on the A1 motorway driving the stabbed guy's BMW. They think he's heading to Edinburgh, Mathieu."

"For what, do you think? Maybe fleeing? Flying out of the airport here?"

"No idea. But since you're out and about, are you up for meeting our MI5 contact?"

"Is this the guy in the black wool peacoat, gray scarf, and crimson tuque?"

"One and the same."

"Set it up."

"I'll be in touch. Watch your six, Mathieu."

"Good copy."

James terminated the call and slid the phone back into his right pocket. His mind was a traffic jam of information.

Slow down. Think.

So we know the African boss met on the same day with this Kozlov guy as well as the courier, Perron. No way that's a coincidence. Two meetings in the same airport on the same day is something you plan.

But what's the plan? What were they discussing? The courier felt something was brewing.

James began walking down the cobblestone street, the Water of Leith on his right. He wasn't sure where he was headed next, but his mind was like a Formula 1 race, thoughts darting to the fore, only to be overtaken by another, more immediate thought or idea. His mind was in competition with itself to sort the problem and deliver a thesis on how all these people are connected.

Need to call Ana-Marie, and see if any of this makes sense to her.

57

Paris, France
Edinburgh, Scotland

Ana-Marie Poulin had been figuratively chained to her desk for days. Journalists get married to their work, and her pale skin, sagging eyes, and frazzled hair were telltales of an overworked, overstressed reporter.

Her desk in the *International Herald Tribune's* Paris office was in a prairie of tall grass, each one looking the same, obscuring the next, feeling worn and wind-whipped. Colleagues could walk through the newsroom and not realize she was hunkered down. But she was dogged, and if her desk and the desks of her colleagues were aligned like tombstones, well, there was irony in that.

Ana-Marie had been pleading with sources within French law enforcement to guide her on this story about an emerging sleeper cell. *Was she right? Was she close? Is the path worth following?* In their way, the sources understood what she was trying to report, but were reluctant to help her.

Ana-Marie, they would say, *if you report this, then the sleeper cell knows they have been blown. Those people will disband, flee the country, and set-up shop someplace else. We need more time to build a case, so when we perform the raid, any charges will stick.*

Bullshit, she would whisper to herself, incessantly pulling her hair back into a pony, then undoing it, and doing it again. Her nervous tic, she thought.

In one of those harried, stressful moments, she was relieved to see Matthieu James's name arrive on her home screen.

"Bonjouuuurrrr!" she exclaimed with a smile.

"How's my favorite French reporter?"

"I'm—how would you say it—frantic as usual."

"Ah, of course. This is our life."

"Oui. What's happening?"

"A lot actually, but before I get into it, is there anything on your end? Have you spoken with Henrique's family again or have they heard from the police in Amsterdam?"

"Nothing new there. I haven't heard from the family lately. The police said they will likely release his body to the family in a couple of days. Otherwise, the police are still digging through video and interviewing people at Schiphol."

"Got it."

"So what do you know?" Ana-Marie asked, twirling her hair with her fingers.

"A lot and nothing. The African guy that was meeting Henrique in Amsterdam was also meeting someone else at the airport. It looks like it happened earlier in the day. Someone named Igor Kozlov. He's a Belarusian national, wanted for questioning in an attempted murder in London."

"What? That's crazy. Do you think they're connected, Mathieu?"

"The meeting and the attempted murder?"

"Oui."

"I don't know. It doesn't feel right, but right now I'd never say never."

"Do they know where this Kozlov guy is?"

"Apparently he's on his way toward Edinburgh, Scotland, driving the BMW of the guy he stabbed."

"Oh wow. That's some intrigue!"

"Sure is."

"Have you spoken to Frank lately?"

"I haven't. I did work on revising my piece earlier today, and I've been on the phone for a bit since. How about you?"

"Oui, he was asking how it's coming. I told him we weren't really close, but still reporting."

"How'd he take that?"

Ana-Marie started laughing, working her way into her best Frank Murphy impression. "'Fucking get on with it' I think is how he phrased it."

They laughed hard together before wrapping things up.

"Okay, Ana-Marie. I'm supposed to meet with someone here that might be useful. Will see where it goes."

"Sounds interesting. Please keep me posted. Ciao."

"Ciao."

James decided to head back to the safe house. He checked his Apple Map and plotted a course through some side streets and alleys.

He picked up the pace, turning left at Innis & Gunn, another left when the street came to a T, then a right. If he stayed straight, he should make it back in a few minutes.

The sun continued to knife through the gunmetal sky as clouds broke open briefly. The shadows in the alleys and side streets were long and black, like three dimensional shapes projected from the buildings' time-worn facades.

In short order, he came along the side of the Port O' Leith and peered into the emergency exit. A few patrons with pints sitting at tables. The bar seats empty for now. Here he triple checked before crossing Constitution Street and the tram tracks and made his way without incident up Mitchell Street and to the safe house.

When he was just inside the apartment door, his phone buzzed again in his pocket. He put the keys on a shelf in the hallway and hung his coat, walking into the living room, where he put his backpack on the couch. He slid the phone from his pocket. It was Stevens via text, and another number he didn't recognize.

Mathieu James, say cheers to Conan MacGregor. 16:30. Lady Libertine, inside the Edinburgh Grand.

58

Edinburgh, Scotland

Aadan Mukhtaar and the two Russians took the tram from Princes Street to Picardy Place. They could have walked, but winds were gusting heavily and temperatures were plummeting. The African blood in Mukhtaar was averse to the Scottish climes.

The four from Wales, plus Igor Kozlov, walked across the street from their Picardy Place budget-minded hotel. The eight terrorists were to meet in front of St. Mary's Cathedral, a stunning house of worship built in 1814.

With cloudy skies everlasting, the men stood on the steps of the city's cherished Catholic Church and laid bare their plans for the mass murder of innocents. The wind gusts rippled their jackets and tousled hair, and more than once Aadan had to grab his signature scally cap to keep it from blowing off.

"My brothers, the plan is quite simple," Aadan began. "We will use explosives to rain destruction on this tiny slice of Western obedience. They will not soon forget the carnage we will sow. Our brothers from Wales, you each will carry backpacks into the Market.

"Our brother from London," he said, looking at Igor, "you will drive the van onto Princes Street. There is no parking. You will set yourself free directly in front of the Market."

The sleepers from Wales all nodded and whispered praise to Allah. The death sentence just now bestowed to Igor Kozlov did not resonate. Instead, he asked a question.

"And what about you and these two?" Igor said, pointing to Aadan and the Russians.

"We will be on overwatch, above the chaos, prepared to give the final go or no-go."

Igor absorbed the response and felt a deep pit developing in his stomach. It was finally registering that he was assigned to drive a van laden with explosives and detonate it with himself inside.

This wasn't what he expected. It then dawned on him that his plan, his proposal to Aadan that set all of this in motion, would also kill the four men from Wales standing next to him. This wasn't his world. He didn't understand the ramifications, the consequences or the finality. Igor thought they could plant explosives and escape, and he now wanted to know why five of them had to die.

"Wait a second, I want to make sure I get this right," Igor said, looking directly at Aadan.

"Go ahead," Aadan answered.

"Five of the eight men standing here are going to die. We are doing that on purpose, is that correct?"

"Yes."

"Why? Why not set the bombs inside the Market and detonate them remotely? That seems like it would make the same statement."

"I see your point, Igor. But there is no parking on Princes Street, so we would lose the biggest weapon we have, which is a van filled with explosives. Second, if we placed backpacks inside the Market and left to detonate them, the chances of someone spotting them, or us, and alerting authorities is rather high. Then they evacuate the Market, and potentially isolate and disarm our devices."

Igor was shaking his head, maintaining eye contact with Aadan, who continued, speaking in low tones as the men huddled together to hear amid the wind and street noise.

"The point of doing it like this is the element of surprise. They never see it coming. They didn't see us coming in London all those years ago. We were just passengers on the tube, a passenger on a bus. They didn't see it in Paris either. Our men on Vespas, racing around the city creating confusion and chaos, and a bomb going off during a football match. You have to own the moment, seize on the element of surprise.

"This, Igor, is why they call it a terror attack. Terror freezes you, immobilizes you. We make our sacrifices for the greater good."

The foursome from Wales nodded and whispered, "Allahu Akbar."

They stood in silence, making weak eye contact with each other, weighing the moment of truth. Igor thought of his parents. His death would crush them. This is not what he intended. He wanted to make a statement to the West, pushing them off their sanctions, scaring them into backing down, which in time would help the people of Belarus and Russia. People like his mother and father.

Simply put, he was not planning to die. *What have I done here?*

Igor stepped toward Aadan and asked for a word. The two men moved away from the group. Instinctively the Russians followed, their only job was to protect the mastermind. Igor looked at Aadan, asking a silent question: Can the two goons step away? Aadan raised his hand, instructing them to stand down.

With the wind at his back, Igor closed the distance to an uncomfortable measure, putting himself face to face with the Somali-born Mukhtaar. His eyes glistened from fear and anger, his muscles were tight from anxiety and the cold.

"This is not what I had in mind. I did not expect to come here to die, and have those four do the same thing," Igor said, flustered and angry and searching for words of strength that eluded him.

"That is exactly what you asked for," Aadan replied smoothly. "Why did you think you would come here and kill hundreds and injure thousands and pay no personal price? Did you think you would sacrifice nothing? If so, you are a coward. In this war we have been waging with the West, there is always sacrifice. That is how the message is sent. We choose to do the unthinkable. That is how we get their attention. That is how we chip away at their arrogance and security."

"I can't do it," Igor said flatly, shrugging his shoulders. "Not what I wanted. I can't do that to my parents. I wanted to help them, and people like them. If I die here, a part of them dies here."

"Igor, my brother, you are going to die here either way."

A confused look washed over Igor's face, now contorted by further anxiety and fleeting hope. Aadan continued.

"You have no choice. You perform the mission—your idea, I remind you —or my two Russian friends help you commit suicide in your hotel room. This is your choice, of course. I cannot let you leave here without completing the mission because you might say something to people who would love to find me. That's not going to happen. So you choose, Igor. An uncomfortable death in your room, or strap on your ball sack and execute the mission with the rest of the team."

Igor was numb. He had no words. He looked down at the pavement, then up and to his right at the majestic cathedral. He turned and stared at the six others, standing loosely together, not talking.

"And to make sure you don't try something stupid, Igor, I'm going to send one of my Russian friends back to your hotel to keep an eye on you. Whether you leave that hotel again or not is your choice."

Aadan walked back to the group, and whispered in the ear of Russian number two, captain blue balls.

"My brothers, begin your preparations. Our mission is set for tomorrow night at 18:00. May God be with you and accept you in his arms and celebrate your courage."

With that, Aadan and Russian number one walked away. The four men from Wales headed to a nearby crosswalk, where they would walk to the public garage and begin assembling backpacks full of explosives and wiring the van.

Igor looked at his Russian handler. Tears welled in his eyes.

What have I done?

59

Edinburgh, Scotland

The tram bell rang faintly in the waning light of day, a blue-gray hue clinging to the cobblestones and mirrored in lifeless windows. The sound was dull enough that Mathieu James knew it wasn't at The Shore stop just yet, but it was close.

Exiting the safe house and making a right on Mitchell, he jogged lightly to the end of the street at Constitution, where he looked right and saw the tram easing into the stop. Picking up the pace slightly, he bounded across the street and hopped up the curb, just in time to board.

He worked his way back until he found two empty seats on the left side. He sat closest to the window, and put his backpack on the aisle seat, his arm still through the loop as a quasi-security measure.

James stared out the window as shops whizzed past. The stops at Foot of the Walk, Balfour Street and MacDonald Road were just pauses in momentum; he paid little mind to those boarding and exiting. Rather, he was lost in thoughts draining from his mind.

At Picardy Place, he took note of the Playhouse and a handsome cathedral that was known as St. Mary's. The Conan Doyle pub looked promising, and he shook himself from the momentary lapse in consciousness to remind himself his stop was next.

As he snapped to the present, a pair of men walking the sidewalk caught his attention. A white man, large with cropped hair, jeans, and a leather coat. A black man, short, bulging belly, track suit, puffy jacket, scally cap, sunglasses, and a *motherfucking walking stick*.

James stood in his seat and moved to a nearby door to get a better look as the tram slid forward on its tracks, preparing to slow for the sharp left turn toward St. Andrews Square.

There's no way that's the financier, Aadan Mukhtaar. No. Way. But the outfit stood out, and the silhouette of the big white dude certainly could have been either Russian—the one he eluded or the one whose nuts he turned into oatmeal.

His gut was full of anxiety. His mind was a spinning top. James checked his watch and saw he had some time to spare before meeting Conan MacGregor. He had to get a closer look.

Disembarking at St. Andrews Square, James sprinted across the street from the platform and headed for Harvey Nichols, an upscale department store. If the suspected mastermind and his goon were still on a path to somewhere, it might be Waverley, and they would walk right past James.

He slipped inside the store and scurried about the first floor, looking for a view from the two giant picture windows that housed clothing samples and sales signs. It was difficult to find both a spot and an angle where he could get a continuous look at passersby. Instead, he stood five feet off the entrance, amidst perfumes and makeup and nail polish stands, locking onto every person who walked from his right to his left.

Checking his watch again, he looked up to see the same two figures he spotted from the tram.

Holy shit, James thought. *That's him. What's he doing here?*

A flurry of thoughts sent his mind into overdrive, and then he thought of the man known as Igor Kozlov, who supposedly met with Mukhtaar in Amsterdam and was on his way here in a stolen BMW. Chances were he'd arrived by now.

James let the two men gain about twenty yards before exiting the store.

He knew enough about SDRs from his time in the Army and his limited guidance from the CIA to keep himself out of sight. He wondered, though, if the two men he now followed would activate their own surveillance detection routes. His goal was to maintain visual contact, avoid detection, and assess the situation.

As Mukhtaar and his bodyguard reached the crossing at Princes Street, the throngs of people waiting to cross were slowed by a pedestrian light that said *stop*. Buses and cars criss-crossed, headlamps bounced off glass and reflected off wet metal and roads. James ducked into Black Sheep Coffee and leaned against the near wall, looking out through the giant plate of glass. He could see them, standing silently together.

The pedestrian light turned green, and a school of humans walked as one, crossing and diverging, some going left toward the entrance to Waverley Station; others going right, toward the Christmas Market and points behind.

James trailed behind, actually jogging across the street after the light had turned, earning an enthusiastic punch of the car horn from an unamused Scottish taxi. The two men he was following kept a deliberate pace—neither too fast nor too slow—and continued past the Christmas Market until Lothian Road. James slowed, blending in, living in the shadows, conquering darkness and bending it as his friend. As they crossed Lothian, the boss and the bodyguard veered left, up the steps and into the lobby of an upscale hotel.

Lingering a few minutes in case they were checking their tail, James broke his pursuit and turned back, double-timing it to meet Conan MacGregor at Lady Libertine. Eight minutes later and perspiring a little, he entered the cocktail lounge and scanned the bar and tables, seeking the man he last saw watching him pull away in a tram right across the street from where he stood.

His eyes went left, then right, then left again before catching the stare of a man seated at a two-person table near the window. The man nodded, and James sauntered over, reading the eyes of one Conan MacGregor. James took note of the black wool peacoat draped over the chair, and the gray scarf still elegantly tied around his neck.

Conan MacGregor stood and offered a hand to James, announcing his name in what sounded like a syrupy Irish accent.

"Conan MacGregor," he said, "by way of Belfast. Welcome to Scotland."

"Mathieu James, by way of Los Angeles," he smirked, peeling off his backpack and setting it under the table. "You'll never guess the ghost I've seen."

60

Edinburgh, Scotland

"You say you've seen a ghost? Well, have ya now."

Mathieu James couldn't tell if that was a statement or a question. The man seated across from him was an intelligence officer from MI5, a friendly assigned to keep tabs on James while in country, and now a colleague with whom information must be shared. Conan MacGregor spoke with a sparkle in his eye, a half-smile and the pale-yet-ruddy complexion of an Irishman who knows his pubs. He was also lean, fit, and impressively buried a shock of red hair under his crimson tuque.

"That's what I say, indeed," James replied, both hands on the table, palms-down and his eyes locked on the man from Belfast.

"So you work with Alyssa, do ya now? She's a fine one."

"Sort of...she is a fine one, as you say, but I don't technically work for her. We help each other out."

"What does that mean, exactly?"

"I'm an investigative journalist. I write for the *International Herald Tribune*. Alyssa, how should I say this? Alyssa recruited me at a time we both needed information and we could help each other."

"I see. So you're not an Agency guy then?"

"I'm not."

"So you're a journalist then, that's it? That's your background?"

"Not exactly," James said, feeling exasperated by the flurry of verbal inquiries.

"Not exactly, I see then. Okay. Care to explain?"

"How about we order a couple of pints and slow down. There's a fair amount of information I can share with you."

"Sounds amazing, let's do that." Conan turned and raised his arm, snapping his fingers at the nearest server. He was wearing a festive Christmas sweater—the kind you wear when you lose an ugly sweater contest—and a pair of horn-rimmed glasses, which added to his geek motif. Yet his build, his square jaw that seemed injected by steroids at birth, and that general Irish swagger said he was a man not to be fucked with. "Two Guinness, please and thank you. Cheers, my girl."

He's not shy, James said to no one.

"So where were we?" Conan asked.

"My background," James replied. "Served in the US Army, Ranger Regiment, Signal Corps. Helped me pay for college at Northwestern University, where I was a journalism major."

"Where's that now?"

"Chicago."

"Okay then, carry on."

"Have worked in some different markets in the US. Got into the investigative journalism side a few years back, stories on gun dealers, cartels, terror—the glamorous lives of international criminals. That's what led to a meeting with Stevens. When we have a fit, we help each other out. Right now we are working on a fit."

"Alright, I'm following you so far," Conan said. The server returned with two pints of Guinness, asking if they'd like to open a tab. Conan instinctively said yes. "So what's going on now? I was told to follow you from London, make sure you got where you needed to in Edinburgh. Then I hear about this fellow wanted for questioning by some London DCs and maybe he's problematic, he's been seen with a known terror financier. How I'm doing so far?"

"Pretty good actually."

"I'm told you have a link to all of this, but I don't know what. I guess that's why we're meeting. I'm also told the guy from London might have stabbed someone, and he could be on his way here, to Edinburgh."

"Still pretty good. I'm guessing he's here." James grabbed his pint and offered a cheers to his festively dressed colleague. They clinked pints and drew a sip of smoothness, their retreating lips styled with enough foam that both required a backhand swipe to clear the distinctive finish of Dublin's finest.

"Why do you think that?"

"Because the ghost I just saw? His name is Aadan Mukhtaar. He's a known terror financier and mastermind. There's still a small circle of us that believe the London bombings in 2005 had a fifth bomber—someone they never caught."

"I remember this vaguely. If I recall, in the aftermath of the tube and bus attacks, there was chatter about a mastermind or fifth bomber who got away, without detonating anything."

"That's right."

"And you think that's him? You think this is real?"

"I do, and yes. Let me tell you why."

James delivered the backstory to Conan, replete with details from the story Ana-Mari Poulin was working on, how her source was a college friend named Henrique Perron, who ascended to be a key cog for someone laundering money through small-level criminal stuff in Paris. How he became "the guy" because his friend, who brought him into the criminal life, was the original courier, and got himself killed for asking too many questions.

"And then this courier, this Henrique guy, mentions to Ana-Marie that he thinks his boss was also behind the 2005 attacks, and that's when she brought me in."

"Why you? What's your connection to it?"

"My parents were on the bus that was targeted. They were killed that day. Ever since, I've been looking for that fifth bomber, the possibility that another terrorist eluded capture, someone who maybe can give me answers, give me closure."

"Holy shit, James, I'm sorry to hear this. That's absolutely fucking terrible stuff. Raise a glass to your mathair and the ould fella."

They did, and James thanked him.

"Cheers to you, Conan. Much appreciated."

"So then what? This courier guy, Henrique is it? Did ya talk to him?"

"I did. He agreed to meet me in Amsterdam, at the airport there. So I flew from Los Angeles. I also had some other leads I was working, including following some money headed for a notorious fund managed by a wannabe flyboy in Zurich. I can explain that later."

Conan nodded, draining his pint and again raising his arm and snapping his fingers. When he had the server's attention, he pointed to his empty glass and signaled for another. James was still nursing his first.

"So I meet the guy, and he's probably a little buzzed at that point early in the morning, and he's super jittery."

"Is he on something?"

"Doubtful, but hard to say."

"Go on."

"So he gives me some interesting stuff, right? And then he drops a bit of a bomb on me. He tells me he's meeting his boss, the African guy, that same day, also in the airport. The boss shows up with two bodyguards —Russians—"

"Of course," Conan interrupted.

"And turns out they have two meetings planned as well. Security footage found them meeting with our friend from London, who is likely already here."

"If you didn't before, you've got my attention now," Conan smirked. "And then what? They all have a big criminal orgy in the men's room?"

"You're closer than you think."

"Okay then, please, continue. I won't interrupt!"

James smiled. "So the courier meets with his boss, and I'm trying to get some pictures of the guy. I get spotted by one of his Russian goons, who wants my phone. I refuse, he gets angry, I punch him in the balls and try to get away amid the confusion. I see the courier also getting up, probably to leave, and I'm just thinking every man for himself. I managed to get away, and out of the airport, and here I am. But before I left, I got video of the African boss, and he had eyes on me the whole time. It was like a mutual 'fuck you' showdown. So that video helped Alyssa and her colleagues get us an actual ID."

"Nice play by you, mate. Cheers!" Conan offered, practically inhaling his second pint.

"So I get out, turns out the courier is later found dead in the men's room, and on my way to meet you, I see the boss—the African guy, Mukhtaar—walking down the street right outside here, with one of his Russian friends. So I followed them. They are at the Carlton, not far from us."

"Congrats, you're quite the storyteller," Conan said, shaking his head. "You should be writing books."

"It's all true, my friend. You can check with Stevens."

"Nah, I believe you. There's always shady shit going on here. I work closely with the Joint Terrorism Analysis Centre, which helps coordinate a lot of information between a lot of agencies here. That's why they assigned me to you."

"Okay, makes sense, I suppose," James said, getting a couple more swigs of Guinness inside him.

Conan nodded. His stare was distant, toward something behind James. It seemed blank, as if he were pondering a scenario.

"Two guys who are known trouble meet in an airport. Those same two guys later show up in Edinburgh, at the same time? That's probably not a coincidence."

"Probably not."

"So what's the play? How do we find out what they're up to?"

"We know where the boss is staying. We can get a tail on him," James offered.

"Keeps getting merrier!" Conan laughed, raising an eyebrow in irony.

"The other man might be here with the BMW of the guy he tried to kill. If he was dumb enough to keep driving that, and dumb enough to keep using his phone—that's how I'm told your people at MI5 found him, they tracked his phone—can we get some current data and see where it leads?"

Conan pulled his phone from his pocket, his eyes focused on Mathieu James. He unlocked it, hit a number from his 'Favorites' list and waited.

"Yeah, MacGregor here. *Pause.* Still in Edinburgh. *Pause.* Yeah, I'm with him now. *Pause.* Something could be going down. There's a lot that doesn't make sense. Can you get me the latest tracking on that cellphone, the one from the guy in London I've heard about." He winked at James. "Right, well I need something up to the minute. We need eyes on this guy. *Pause.* Got it. I'll watch for it. Cheers."

Conan hung up. He finished his second beer, and silently waved the server over. "Two shots of your finest Irish whiskey and bring the tab. Please be quick, we need to go."

James smiled and nodded. "Leaving in style, are we?"

"Always."

"So what did you learn?"

"They're going to ping that phone again and see if they can zero in on a location. If he's here, let's take a walk, shall we?"

"I like it," James said.

"I figured you might."

"So what's your backstory, Conan? Other than Belfast and MI5? What else is there to know about you?"

"We need more pints for that, friend!"

"Tease me then."

"Like yourself, I served. I wore the boots. SAS."

"Ah, is that where you learned to dress yourself?" James teased, pointing at Conan's ugly sweater.

"Very funny! Not bad for an American."

"I'm half British, too. My mum was from here. My dad met her when he was stationed at Lakenheath."

"Ah, alright then! A bastard child of the Imperial Empire! This gets even better!"

The server returned with two shots and the tab, asking cash or card. Conan said cash, inspected the amount and laid down thirty pounds. He raised his whiskey glass to his new friend Mathieu James and offered a toast.

"Always remember to forget the things that made you sad. Cheers, Mathieu."

They threw back their whiskey, which was smooth and clean, and gathered their things. James reached for his backpack, and Conan donned his black wool peacoat, gray scarf, and crimson tuque.

They walked in single file to the door, Conan leading, and he held it open for James.

"Let's go find us an ugly son of a bitch and see what he's cooking for dinner."

They stepped into the dampness of the night, streets glistening, revelers bustling, cars streaking through puddles. The familiar sonar ping from an iPhone pierced the air. Conan MacGregor reached into his pocket and read the missive from MI5.

"We got a hit," he said. "This way, let's go."

61

Edinburgh, Scotland

"You okay with a brisk walk, Mathieu?"

"I am, let's do it."

Conan MacGregor and Mathieu James turned right, passing in front of the Edinburgh Grand and headed toward Picardy Place on foot. It would take maybe five minutes, but the men were now fueled by adrenaline from a lead. The pints and whiskey did little to slow MacGregor, who looked much larger than he was. James stayed light on the spirits, and easily kept pace with his new shadow.

"So what did you learn?" James inquired, pulling even with the man from Belfast.

"They found his phone pinging on towers near Picardy Place."

"That's the direction the African and his Russian pal were coming from when I spotted them from the tram."

"I think that's no coincidence, in fact, it smells like trouble to me," Conan said, keeping a strong pace, working his way through pedestrians like a slalom skier with James now tailing from behind.

"What are we looking for? Do you have a picture of this guy from London?"

"The crew is sending me one. But I think the obvious thing we're looking for is that BMW. If we can find that, maybe we can find our guy."

To James, this seemed an impossible task. Edinburgh was a large city, and Picardy Place was maybe its busiest spot, with shops, restaurants, the Playhouse, hotels, a movie theater and a path to popular Calton Hill. With car parks and residential side streets, one white BMW could turn into 20. Or none.

"Do we have a plate number?"

"We do."

"Can you share it?"

"I can. Got yourself an iPhone?"

"Yes."

"Open it up, I'll AirDrop you a screen shot."

The men married their phones briefly, and Conan dropped a plate number for the BMW.

"Ah, here we go, this just came in as well," Conan added, downloading and dropping a copy of Igor Kozlov's national ID card.

James studied the picture, still keeping pace with the man from Belfast. He pinched and zoomed, asking himself over and over if he had seen this man in Amsterdam. Or anywhere.

He couldn't place him.

Conan took a few glances, still leading the two through the pedestrian slalom course, looking to keep his phone in his hand and avoiding knocking anyone to the ground.

James asked if he recognized the photo.

"I don't, no," Conan said. "But let's burn his face into our skulls, so when we do see him, we know it."

James chuckled at the wording 'burn his face into our skulls' as the two men were coming on Picardy Place. They stopped outside The Conan Doyle without comment, but James couldn't resist.

"Friend of yours?"

MacGregor shot him a puzzled look, and James pointed at the sign above them.

"My uncle, yeah? Probably. Who the fuck knows."

"Named after your uncle? Good to know. Conan, I think we should split up. There's a lot of ground to cover here. If we're looking for a white BMW we can eliminate a lot of possibilities."

"Agree, Mathieu. Agree. Tell you what, you take the car park there," he pointed across the triangle-shaped intersection. "I'll hit the side streets across the way, over there. Let's give it fifteen minutes and meet on the tram platform, which looks like the middle. Good, yeah?"

"Copy."

"Mark your watch. Fifteen minutes. Tram stop."

"Good hunting," James offered.

The two men split, with Conan MacGregor running across traffic like a madman, reaching the opposite walk in a dicey game of Frogger. James headed up to the nearest crosswalk, at the foot of St. Mary's Cathedral, and stood with a band of tourists pulling suitcases, waiting for the crosswalk light to go green.

James turned 360 degrees, taking in his surroundings, making notes of landmarks, walkways, and where people congregated. It was a busy night, the streets were heavy with steel—cars, buses, trams. Patrons spilled out the doors of restaurants, waiting to be seated.

This won't be easy, he thought. *But let's get moving.*

Finding a hole in the traffic, James darted across the street, losing patience with the sign to turn green, and flared right, following the car park sign around the corner of a modern building that stood out for its conformity to twentieth century standards.

At the end of the glass and concrete monolith, he went left, and the car path curved hard behind the structure and into a garage. He figured the best way to eliminate all possibilities was to walk the garage, working his way from bottom to top.

Three blocks away, Conan MacGregor was navigating his way up and down residential side streets, making mental notes of the ones he'd covered, trying to canvass as much space as possible. He knew the likelihood was that the target—Igor Kozlov—was either staying in a hotel or an apartment. Maybe he was shopping, but unlikely. There were a few hotels in the area, and hundreds of apartment homes.

He covered the first three streets at a light jog, working a heavy sweat under his ugly Christmas sweater. He unbuttoned his peacoat and pulled his crimson tuque from his head, revealing his shock of red hair matted with sweat, and a hint of steam pillowing skyward.

"Fucking hell," he muttered. He had covered York Lane, Albany Street, Forth, Hart, and Broughton, which was full of parked cars.

Nothing.

He made his way up Union, checking his watch. Twelve minutes expired. He was probably two minutes from the tram platform. He stopped at the corner of Union and Picardy Place, pacing now, scanning the streets for both a white BMW and his American counterpart, Mathieu James. He was wandering a bit, working his way toward the tram platform, when he walked in front of the Picardy Inn and Suites.

The hotel was nondescript, with steps leading from the walk to the lobby. Near the foot of the steps, two men stood smoking cigarettes. Conan looked away, and then it registered. After a glance back, he pulled his phone and checked the national ID photo of the man they were hunting.

Bloody hell, that must be him, Conan thought.

The man next to Kozlov stood close enough to be with him, but the two didn't interact. Conan decided it was best to watch from a distance. He continued to the crosswalk and moved to the tram platform, where he could blend in with the tide of humans ebbing and flowing from the trams and into the night.

Across the way and out of sight, Mathieu James had cleared the first two parking decks, finding every kind of car except a white BMW. As he approached the third, the hair on his neck and arms stood tall. He was thirty yards from a gray panel van, where four men worked furiously unloading crates. Something felt off, and James kept eyes on the men while walking backward and sliding in between two parked cars, looking for a cleaner line of sight.

Maybe it's nothing, he thought.

Scanning the rest of the deck, he saw no white BMWs. There was one deck to go, and he slithered back and walked down the ramp to the stairs, choosing to head to the top floor and out of sight. He climbed two levels of eight steps each and opened the door to the top deck, giving a full visual sweep.

Nada.

He walked about ten yards and found a vantage point for the van, looking down between two cars through a diagonal slot in the concrete floor. Here he could see the back of the van, and the four men—one was inside, with the back right door open. Two were on the side, with the left sliding door open and wooden crates on the ground. The fourth was stuffing backpacks with what looked like cylindrical sticks, round and bound together somehow.

Is that dynamite?

Just then, the man in the back of the van swung open the second door, and James could see two plastic drums inside.

That doesn't look good. He checked his Stirling Durrant watch, and the minute hand was rotating toward the mark on the bezel, indicating his fifteen minutes were almost up. He slid his iPhone from his pocket and turned on silent mode before opening the camera. Snapping some quick images, he tried to zoom in and capture a couple of angles before working his way back to the stairs.

With quick feet and a racing heart, Mathieu James made easy work of the stairs, finding an exit through the middle of the complex that led him onto the front walk, in full view of Picardy Place. Gaining his bearings, he spotted the tram platform and Conan MacGregor. He made a beeline for the MI5 intelligence officer, who greeted him with a shit-eating grin.

"What'd you find, anything?" James asked.

"Take a look over there," Conan nodded toward the Picardy hotel. "I think that's our boy, stomping out his cigarette. The bloke he's with looks Russian to me. What about you, anything?"

"Great find, man. Well done. Negative on the BMW, but I may have found something worse."

He pulled his phone and opened the photos app, showing Conan his images from inside the garage"

"Shit, that looks nasty."

"Whatever those four are doing is pretty bad..." James paused, looking at MacGregor, who shared a knowing look and a nod. "Something's happening here."

62

Edinburgh, Scotland

From the tram platform, Conan MacGregor walked away from the cluster of people, so he couldn't be heard. Mathieu James stayed within earshot as the British intelligence officer rang MI5 headquarters and spoke with his supervisor. MacGregor knew there was a situation brewing in the Scottish capital, and they needed eyes, ears, and units in place quickly.

James caught bits and pieces of the conversation, which was relayed with calm urgency by the red-haired man from Belfast. It was obvious to James that MacGregor's military service was helping him deliver a deliberate and nuanced situation report.

"I'm with an American counterpart...

"We have identified at least two known persons of interest...

"Each are housed in different hotels in the city approximately one kilometer apart, with Waverley Station in between...

"A van has been identified by my American counterpart with four additional persons and a highly questionable cargo load...

"Yessir, we have its last known location. A car park in Picardy Place...

"Yessir...

"Yessir...

"Copy that sir, standing by. We will have eyes on this location...

Conan covered the phone with his hand and turned to James.

"Hey James, what hotel did you say the other two were seen at?"

James stepped closer.

"The Carlton. I watched them both enter."

Conan returned to his call, covering his ear with his free hand to block the street noise.

"The Carlton, sir. That's right, near Princes Street Gardens and the Christmas Market, not far from Waverley."

As the call concluded, James and MacGregor came together. The MI5 officer pulled his cap back onto his head, his hair still matted with sweat, and placed both hands in his pockets. James spoke first.

"What's the plan?"

"Well, you and I are going to keep eyes on this location. I'll take the hotel, you take the car park. HQ is going to mobilize some of our assets, and some local tactical too. They are sending two officers to the Carlton immediately, should be there within minutes. A team will relieve us shortly."

"And then what happens?"

"Well, so far we don't have much other than a man wanted for questioning in London by local DCs and a suspicious van."

"We also have a known terrorist in town," James exclaimed, realizing his voice was too loud.

"Right. Relax, mate. So we watch, see if they are making a move, and if so we take them down."

"And if not?"

"If not, we get the guy across the street and return him to London."

James was hoping for something more immediate. Sometimes he needed to be reminded that he was a journalist, he was no longer in the military, and he was certainly not law enforcement. *Watch and observe, help as needed.*

Conan was on the move and gestured for James to do the same.

"I'm heading back across the street. They went inside. I need to figure out if there are other exits that need covering. Keep your eyes on that car park. There's only one way in and one way out."

"Copy," James said, as he turned, checked traffic and moved across Picardy Place, away from the tram platform and closer to the glass and concrete building that housed the car park.

Inside room 230 of the Picardy Inn and Suites, quarters were cramped for Igor Kozlov and the Russian assigned to look after him. Igor sat on a chair in the corner, and the Russian was no more than three feet away, sitting on the end of the single bed, quietly watching the man in the room with him.

Igor was going through a crisis of conviction. Those radicalized by religion or ideals can experience this, but they often put their faith in whichever god they believe will absolve them. Igor had no god, and now he wondered how his plan to make the West pay for sanctions that led to suffering back home was worth his life.

He fidgeted with his phone, making subtle eye contact with the Russian, trying to figure a way out of this mess. *Maybe I should talk to him*, he thought.

"Hey...brother. Where are you from?"

The Russian looked at him but didn't answer. Igor gave it a minute.

"I'm from Belarus. You're Russian, right? We are neighbors—we are on the same side."

The Russian maintained silence and uncomfortable eye contact.

"My brother, I feel like this thing has gotten out of control. Maybe this isn't a great idea, you know? Can we talk about it?"

Finally, the Russian spoke. "You have a job. I have a job. Do your job."

"Does your job mean giving your life?"

"My job is protecting the boss. And if that means I give my life, the boss will take care of my family back home. That's the deal."

Igor ingested that comment, and it didn't sit well with him.

"Look, there's a difference. You signed up for that, right?"

"And from what I can tell, this was your idea, right?" the Russian replied.

"This is pointless," Igor yelled, standing now. The Russian stood as well, towering over the Belarusian. "Fuck it, I'm not doing it. I'm leaving."

Igor headed for the door, determined to walk out, challenging the Russian to do something about it, which was the wrong call. The Russian stepped in his path and pushed Igor hard in the chest, knocking him back a couple steps.

"Sit down," the Russian said calmly.

Igor charged again, this time more aggressively. The Russian countered with a right fist to the face, stunning Igor, who was now bleeding from the nose. Pride and fear swelled simultaneously in the Belarusian. His heart was racing, his stomach felt empty and sick. *You can take him.*

He exploded at the Russian like an American football player, looking to tackle the bigger man. The Russian caught him and held his ground. It was now hand-to-hand combat in a tiny hotel room, the Russian holding the advantage in size and strength. They exchanged punches, tangled together, wrestling for space. Neither landed anything hard, and the Russian put Igor in a bear hug and tossed him onto the bed, where he bounced off and onto the floor.

Igor scrambled to his feet, looked the Russian in the eyes, and lifted his fists. He couldn't remember the last time he fought. Probably as a kid. But now his life literally was in his own hands. He was scared, bleeding, brimming with anxiety. He didn't even think. He went right at the Russian with a right-left combo, which the Russian easily blocked, returning two right-handed jabs to Igor's face, crushing his orbital bones, then a left to the stomach, punching the air from his lungs.

Stunned by the triple barrage, Igor tumbled and fell to the floor, holding his face with his right hand and placing his left arm across his stomach. He couldn't catch his breath. He struggled to get up, to regain a defensive position, as his body spasmed for air.

Sensing his opponent was stunned, the Russian went in for the knockout, taking two steps forward, bringing his fists together and clasping his hands while raising them over his head, he was looking to bring the hammer down on top of Igor's skull.

Just then, the Russian felt the familiar sting of a blade slicing his skin. Igor had a small river knife in his right hand and was swinging it desperately at his attacker, ripping through his pants and opening a gash on his thigh. Igor jabbed the knife toward the Russian's stomach but missed. The big man moved back, then reached down, grabbing Igor by the arm. In one quick motion, he was in control, snapping Igor's arm and breaking his bone below the elbow, causing a compound fracture that left Igor screaming in agony.

The Russian needed to finish this quickly. The noise from their struggle was surely drawing attention. He moved around the Belarusian, attacking him from behind now, his right arm around his neck while his left fist pummeled the left side of his head. Igor fought with his left arm, but it was futile. With complete control of his combatant, the Russian positioned his left forearm on Igor's neck, and ended his life with a vicious twist and snap, breaking his neck.

He let go, and Igor Kozlov fell to the floor, losing a fight he was never going to win. In his final moments, he didn't think of his parents. He didn't think of the Christmas Market or his anger at the West. He thought only of himself, a fleeting sense of regret washed over him before the room went dark forever.

The Russian went into the bathroom, grabbing a towel and ripping it into strips. He wrapped one around his bleeding leg and tied it off. He took Igor's limp body by the ankles and dragged him into the tub, searching his pockets and pulling out the keys to the BMW and his wallet. He scanned the room before leaving, sure not to leave anything obvious. Reaching into his jeans back pocket, he withdrew his phone and dialed a man who was not going to welcome these new developments.

"Boss, we have a problem."

Outside the Picardy hotel, Conan MacGregor kept his distance from the entrance while staying vigilant. He continued to scan Picardy Place in case the men left through a back exit. He was expecting help to arrive any minute, likely local police first but possibly officers from MI5. He glanced at his phone, checking for messages, before looking up toward the corner at Union Street. There, turning right into traffic was a white BMW. As it sped past, Conan raced toward the curb to look inside.

Just one passenger was visible, and it was the guy standing with Igor Kozlov earlier, near the front steps.

Fuck...

63

Edinburgh, Scotland

Aadan Mukthaar was sipping a 20-year-old Speyside gem in the bar of the Carlton when his phone vibrated in his pocket. Reaching for the device that interrupted his momentary pleasure, he saw a familiar number. It was his Russian bodyguard, assigned earlier to Igor Kozlov.

"Yes?" Aadan answered, pulling on his scally cap, then wiping his hand across his face.

"Boss, we have a problem."

"And that is?"

"The guy got frisky, and I had to deal with it."

"Define frisky."

"Uh..." This one stumped the big Russian. "He tried to use his hands on me..."

Aadan was silent.

"And, well, I..."

"Yes, say it, you...what?"

"I had to solve it."

"I see."

"Sorry, boss. He wouldn't listen."

"And where is he now?"

"He's taking a bath."

"I see. And you?" He took another sip of his smooth whiskey.

"I'm on my way to you. He loaned me his car."

"Hmmm. This is unwelcome news. Park the car nearby and meet us here," he said, thinking of the second Russian who was seated across from him, sipping a Stoli.

"Be there soon, boss."

Aadan terminated the call, lifting his glass from the table and slinging back the remnants. He looked at the Russian seated across from him and shook his head.

"Everything okay, boss?"

"No, but we will solve it. Get me another drink, will you? And one for your brother. He's on his way."

The second Russian nodded and stood, walking awkwardly to the bar. *His balls must still be black and blue*, Aadan smiled to himself, a moment of levity in a cloud of evil. Reaching for his phone, Aadan looked through the call history, finding the number for the Wrexham crew. He tapped it with his thumb and moved the device to his ear.

A man answered.

"Change of plans. The show has been moved to tonight. Take what you can. Put a timer on the big gray oven. It won't be part of the show. Set it for two hours from now. Fireworks start in one hour from the end of this call. Godspeed, my brothers."

And with that, the plan set in motion by a now-dead man was on. In one hour, the West would receive its most vicious message in years.

The black-and-blue-balled Russian returned from the bar carrying three glasses—one whiskey, two vodkas. His brother walked in just then, nodding and grabbing a seat. Each took a glass from the table, and Aadan raised his.

"We go tonight to fulfill the dream of one man and to guarantee the destiny of others."

The three men merged their glasses over the marble table and threw them back. The Russians looked at each other with surprise.

The alarm had sounded.

64

Edinburgh, Scotland

The four men from Wales had packed four backpacks full of explosives. Each was wired with both a trigger—for suicide—and a timer—for delayed detonation. Circumstances would dictate which would be used, although each of them, radicalized long ago and firm in their convictions, knew the hate that filled their hearts would send them to a welcoming afterlife.

The gray panel van, filled with plastic drums holding fertilizer, fuel, and nitrogen designed to take down a city block, was set with two timers. With a go-time in less than one hour for the Christmas Market assault, the van was set for two hours from now, per Aadan's instructions.

Although the plan was maximum chaos at the Christmas Market, this would achieve the same result. The Welsh sleeper cell relocated the van to the opposite side of the car park, positioning it closest to the interior retail mall and movie theater. The chaos there would come after the first wave of horror. Picardy Place was a busy hub in the capital city. Hundreds would be killed. Perhaps thousands injured.

This was the true definition of terror.

With the van set to take down a large piece of real estate, the four men each slid on a backpack. They confirmed the detonation time, making sure their watches were in sync. They shook hands, hugged, and said their good-byes. Allah was with them now.

A pedestrian exit from the car park spilled them onto the plaza and they split in pairs. Two would approach from Calton Hill, heading down Princes Street where they would split from each other, one entering from the entrance nearest Waverley, the second from the steps below in Princes Street Gardens.

The second pair veered right, toward the tram stop at Picardy Place. They would take the tram to the Princes Street stop, nearest the National Museum. From there, they would enter the opposite end. When the four suicide bombers were inside the market, the plan was to detonate at the three primary entrances, with the fourth bomber located in the center of the market.

This guaranteed maximum coverage and maximum carnage.

———

Moments earlier, as the BMW sped past him, making that hard right turn from Union Street onto Picardy Place, Conan MacGregor had some deci-sions to make. Coming across the street from him were four uniformed Police Scotland officers, likely part of the response team. Already gone was the Russian in the BMW.

As the officers approached, Conan ID'd himself and delivered a brief SITREP.

"Gents, we have a suspect in that hotel, wanted by London DCs for questioning in an attempted murder. We have the man he was with just now speeding past me, heading that direction," he pointed to his right, toward St. Andrews Square. "We need to track that car immediately, can either of you help me with that?"

One of the officers confirmed he could assist, his car was parked across the street, adjacent to St. Mary's Cathedral.

"Perfect. Now the rest of you, this is what I'd recommend. One cover the opposite side of the hotel. The other the front entrance, right here. The third one, you," he pointed at the youngest officer, "go inside and check with the front desk. Show them the picture of the man wanted in London—you all received that info, yes?"

They nodded in the affirmative.

"Yeah, perfect, that's good. See if they can remember his face. Tell them you want to do a wellness check. Keep your radio hot, got it? If you find him in his room, radio these two and move for an arrest."

Conan was in full control of the situation, at ease with the stress, the immediacy and the plan given for the locals to handle. Wiping his nose with the back of his hand and adjusting his tuque, he turned to the fourth officer and said, "You and me, we gotta move now. Time's wasting."

The two checked traffic and sprinted across the street toward the patrol car.

Diagonal from the side street where the parked patrol car was now revving its engine and whirling its emergency lights, Mathieu James was pacing, trying to keep warm and keep his mental focus. The area was filled with holiday revelers. Generally, he knew what he was looking for. But if they came out and went in different directions, there was a chance he'd miss them completely.

During a fit of mental gymnastics, where he tried to read and track every face that passed him by, two military-aged males emerged near the Edinburgh Street Food sign, which was tucked away in a small courtyard. James put a mental bead on their path and quickly scanned the rest of the area, looking for the other two.

He didn't see them.

A bird in the hand is better than two in the bush, he thought, smiling at the colloquialism his father used often.

Quickly searching the crowd, he spotted the two men, both wearing backpacks, both heading toward the tram platform.

Shit, that's not a good sign. Will they use the tram? He immediately thought of his parents, who died all those years ago on a bus in London. And he thought of the others who also perished in the tube. All at the hands of men who justified their actions through religious approval.

As the two bombers neared the platform, the tram was rolling into Picardy Place, heading toward St. Andrews Square and Princes Street—both stops for the Christmas Market. There was no way James would make the tram, and deep down he wasn't sure he wanted to be on it.

Yet he couldn't escape the sinking feeling that something imminent was happening.

He rang Conan on WhatsApp. Conan answered quickly.

"Yeah, what you got?"

"Conan, I got eyes on two guys from the van. Both wearing backpacks, both boarding a tram with next stop St. Andrews Square."

"Copy, I'm with a local officer in his patrol car, trying to track down the person driving that white BMW. He came wheeling around the back of the Picardy hotel. I don't know how I missed the car when searching."

"Did the guy look Russian?"

"Maybe, yeah."

"The African boss had two Russian bodyguards. I saw him walking with one, which means the other one is out there. Decent chance you'll find him at the Carlton."

"Good copy, James. Appreciate the footnotes. Why do you sound out of breath?"

"I'm running, Conan! Trying to keep up with the tram. Keep your phone handy, I'm going to need you."

With that, James clicked off and found himself nearly keeping pace with the tram, building a robust sweat and wishing he was wearing workout gear instead of jeans and boots.

―――――

Conan and his police escort were ninety seconds from the Carlton. He dialed into MI5 headquarters to relay an update. He wasn't sure what was happening, but everything he knew, everything he'd learned, fueled the instinct that trouble was brewing, and it might be on a scale larger than they'd seen.

On the other end of the call in London, the supervisor-in-charge listened to Conan's plea.

"Sir, we have a developing situation in Edinburgh. We have the London suspect possibly cordoned. More details on that soon. We have our American friend chasing a tram with two, I repeat, two military-aged males with backpacks likely filled with explosives. And finally, I'm with a Police Scotland officer and we are in pursuit of a white BMW... That's right, probably the same one... We believe two additional suspects remain at the Carlton and the third guy, the one driving the BMW, is heading there to meet them..."

Conan listened as the supervisor repeated his SITREP nearly verbatim, ordering additional officers into the area, requesting a tactical weapons squad from the Ministry of Defence (MOD) Police. He ordered an MI5 command unit to take charge of coordination and wanted someone to find his counterpart at Police Scotland and the MOD so they could start communicating.

"Sir, one more thing," Conan interjected. "You're gonna need a bomb squad at a car park at Picardy Place, behind the movie theater. They are looking for a gray panel van. We've had eyes on it—definitely something suspicious... Copy that sir, good luck, I'll be in touch."

Conan disconnected the call as the patrol car roared up to the Carlton, onto the paved walkway, and within feet of the entrance. As they exited the car, Conan saw three men just across the street, turning to see the commotion. It was a black man and two white men.

He rang James immediately, who answered in full stride, huffing and puffing, his chest heaving as he was now taxed by a full sprint toward St. Andrews Square. The tram made time on him, beating him there as he rounded the corner.

"Yeah?"

"The African...what was he wearing?"

"Track suit. Scally type hat."

"Is he short?"

"Kind of. Maybe 5-8, 5-9 at best."

"We got eyes."

Conan hit the red X with his thumb and motioned for the patrolman to come closer. The three men across the street picked up the pace, no longer turning back, seeking to blend into the crowd of revelers.

"I'm going to follow those three. Radio that in with descriptions, three suspects heading toward the Christmas Market. That has to be the target. Also, tell them we have two military-aged men with backpacks being tracked on a tram, but we are missing two more of the same. There were four at one point. They have likely split up. We need to find the other two."

"Yes sir, I've got this. Straight away."

Conan set off on foot, his phone ringing once more. He checked the screen. It was James.

"Conan here."

"Conan, it's got to be the Christmas Market...the target. It's right in the middle of the two hotels and, Jesus Christ, it would be devastating."

"Just had the same thought. I had the local officer radio in the latest. They know you're tracking a tram. I've now got the African and his boys in sight. We need to find the other two with backpacks. You're sure you didn't see them?"

James was at peak lung capacity, breathing hard and trying to speak.

"I'm sure. I looked," he gasped. "Listen, just rounded the corner. The tram is at St. Andrews. I see two of them, they are getting off."

"Good copy, James. Stay with them if you can. We have help coming."

"Save the African for me, Conan. It's personal."

James slowed to a walk in front of the Harvey Nichols department store, keeping close tabs on the two bombers leaving the tram. It occurred to him, in this moment on a cold night in December on a street in Edinburgh, Scotland, that he found himself in the center of a plot he couldn't have fathomed just days ago. Moreover, within reach was the man believed to be the mastermind, the "fifth bomber", from the London attacks of 2005.

He could hardly wrap his head around it all.

Now, as his heart rate slowed and his breathing calmed, he was soaked in sweat. He could see his breath in the air, and he tried to blend into the crowd as he stalked the would-be mass murderers. James was now wishing he had taken that Glock 17 from the nightstand of the safe house. He suddenly felt naked and alone. His instincts no longer driven by the story, but by survival.

65

Edinburgh, Scotland

The two bombers nobody had eyes on left the car park and went left, up Leith Street, past Calton Hill, and toward Princes Street. This was a road less traveled, but when Leith Street dumped them onto Princes Street, all bets were off. Waverley Station was coming up on their left, then the Christmas Market.

This was a popular bus stop area, too. Where double-deckers belched diesel and the sound of grinding gears mixed with the ear-piercing squeals of rusty brakes brought them to a stop.

The bombers walked side by side, slowly up a small hill that curved to the right. Soon they would be in clear view of the killing fields, where they would deliver their souls to the afterlife. Indeed, their Valhalla was in sight.

———

Further down Princes Street, Aadan Mukhtaar and his Russian protectors had cleverly used the high volume of people to disappear. They crossed from the Carlton on the pedestrian walk and were swallowed by humanity.

This allowed them to get the temporary slip on Conan MacGregor, who was in fast pursuit.

From there, the trio bled right onto a pathway that carried them through the park and under the shadows of Edinburgh Castle. This route would take them parallel to Prince Street. Ahead, they could exit toward The Mound, the famed road that curves up the volcanic outcropping, host to the old city and its fortress.

Near the top, they could look down on the revelry, the celebrations, the family fun, the amusement rides. They could see the lights twinkle in greens and reds, the gothic salute to Sir Walter Scott knife skyward through the blackness, lights painting his Gotham-style shrine in the colors of the season. They could see the tram and the train station, the shops and the vendors, the museums and the bustle.

From here, they would see a morbid show.

***

Mathieu James kept tabs on the tram riders, their backpacks stuffed with death. The bombers chose the opposite side of the street from James, nearest to St. Andrews Square. They walked calmly, blending into the scene, save their blank expressions.

At first, they looked poised to take George Street, one block parallel with Princes Street. But they recognized a growing police presence, as Conan had promised. Marked and unmarked cars began arriving with urgency, double parking and taking over sidewalks as plain-clothed and uniformed officers fanned out, some with assault rifles at the ready.

The heavily armed police stood out. A show of weapons might be found at airports and large train stations, but never on the streets of Edinburgh.

Not unless it was necessary.

James noticed the two bombers had aborted the George Street plan and continued toward Princes Street. He stayed on the opposite walk, confident he could maintain visual contact.

***

At Picardy Place, a bomb squad arrived at the car park, pulling into the drive and blocking it. Two technicians painstakingly pulled on their blast suits, entering the garage as uniformed officers blocked entrances and urged passersby to keep moving. Yellow caution tape was unfurled, wrapped around light poles, bike stands, and trees. The vibe in the city shifted from celebratory to tense in minutes.

Across the way the uniformed officers who had met Conan MacGregor near the Picardy hotel were now standing outside the room of Igor Kozlov, pepper spray and Tasers at the ready. Beads of anxiety percolated on their foreheads, eyes were filled with angst because they knew that the first knock on the door could be the last thing they ever did if the man on the other side was intent on killing everyone.

MI5 didn't have significant assets in the area to lend, but they put out the alarm and it was all hands. The Ministry of Defence Police's primary role is counter-terrorism and deterrence. They arrived as well, specially suited for such cases of national emergency.

In this case, MI5 and the Edinburgh police were eyes and ears, fanning across the Christmas Market and funneling out from Waverley Station like rats fleeing a flood.

Law enforcement and intelligence officers spread out from Waverley, looking to set a perimeter that would visually filter the throngs of people. Inside the Christmas Market, undercover teams that were covertly armed—pistols in waistband holders and shoulder harnesses, at the ready but out of sight—were human predators, stalking an unknown prey in a garden of festive ebullience.

The first test of their resolve was about to meet the pressure point. The two bombers heading up Leith Street and onto Princes Street were fifty yards from Waverley Station.

As the local tactical units fanned out, the duo was spotted by a team of five—three Police Scotland officers, one armed MOD policeman, and one officer from MI5. The targets were known to be military-aged males wearing backpacks and had split in groups of two. The probability this contact was positive? Better than 90 percent. The sole armed officer took charge.

"Halt!" he shouted, as the other four spread out, creating a semi-circle around the duo.

"Halt!"

The bombers were conflicted, sharing a puzzled look with each other. They hadn't expected resistance, let alone being ID'd by law enforcement.

"Hands where we can see them above your head and drop to your knees!" the officer screamed.

Onlookers, passersby, and holiday revelers alike scattered amidst the chaos. Screams filled the night air, mixing with those from the giant swing ride at the Christmas Market. Yet these were screams of horror and fear. Families grabbed their children and ran, leaving behind strollers. Women in heels kicked them off, sprinting down the sidewalk barefoot. Others froze in fear, crouched low, instinctively covering their heads and processing a scene that looked straight from a movie.

One last warning was delivered. "Halt! Stop now!"

The bombers didn't comply. Instead, they spread apart, analyzing, planning, coping. They had three choices: Detonate on scene; run and detonate closer to the train station; comply and give up.

The last one was never on the table.

With his M4 trained on the bomber to his left, the armed officer communicated calmly with the others in his group.

"I got left. I can only get one. Clear for contact."

"Confirm your left."

This was the dreaded choice in times like these. He could take one. The other would no doubt detonate. The result devastating. The carnage unknown.

The MI5 officer tried this time, verbally challenging the bombers to give in.

"This doesn't have to happen. Let's take a deep breath and talk. Why don't you both keep your hands where we can see them and kneel on the ground, so we can talk."

The bombers shook their heads in defiance. They were whispering something, probably a prayer. The MI5 officer knew this wasn't going to end well.

"Green light for target."

"Copy, green light," the armed officer confirmed.

Two seconds later, after checking for clear background and getting a good red dot on the bomber to his left, the MOD police officer fired two quick rounds from his M4.

Crack, crack!

The target on the left was a bullseye, his head snapping back, chasing a misty spray of blood and brain matter as the bullet exited his skull.

He fell backward and crumpled to the ground.

The second bomber saw the writing on the wall, watching this unfold in real time, knowing his moment had come. As the MOD officer trained his weapon quickly to his right, seeking to line up the target and checking again that the background was clear, he was too late.

The bomber moved aggressively, raising his right hand holding the trigger, shouting *Allah Akbar!*

The officer held down the trigger, firing a burst of hollow points at the subject, striking him multiple times as he detonated his backpack. The explosion was loud, it was violent, and it was deadly. The four officers were blown onto their backs. Bystanders were screaming and running. A pile of limbs, flesh, blood, and organs filled the street.

Pandemonium ruled this corner, just outside of Waverley Station. Dozens were injured. Many were dead.

Adjacent to the Christmas Market, across The Mound, Aadan Mukhtaar and his Russian guards stopped in their tracks. The mission was already off the rails. The sound of the explosion, followed by the silence of fear, was chased by blood-curdling screams. It left Mukhtaar capped at the knees. He was no longer in control. It was time for him to escape.

He had three choices: return to his hotel and the BMW; head for the train station, which may be shutting down due to the attack; go on foot, perhaps toward the Port of Leith.

His original exit plan was to lay low, then head north to Aberdeen, where he had arranged for transport on a commercial shipping vessel to Bergen, Norway.

Still the best option, he thought. He turned to Russian no. 2, mister black-and-blue balls, and issued an order. "I need a head count on our brothers from Wales. Nobody leaves here alive. Make sure they committed to the mission...or take care of it."

"Yessir," the Russian replied, less than thrilled with this assignment that could go more than one bad way.

Aadan turned to his favorite bodyguard.

"Let's try for the train station," he told the Russian. "Market Street entrance. If we can't get out, to the port on foot. Now! Let's go!"

The trio split, with the second Russian heading on foot toward Waverley, along Princes Street, into the vortex of death.

Aadan and his sidekick started uphill, with The Mound connecting them to Market Street.

Behind them, closing the gap, was Conan MacGregor.

As Mathieu James approached Black Sheep Coffee, just across the street from the Princes Street entrance at Waverley, the shock wave and heat from the blast rushed past him. His skin felt hot and tight, his ears ringing and his brain frantically processing the fog of war unfolding before him.

The glass windows shattered in the coffee shop, sending shards of razor-like shrapnel into the crowded store. In one instant, people were sipping lattes and flat whites, enjoying an evening out. In the next, they were on the ground, bewildered; they were stepping over others bleeding out, their arteries sliced clean by flying glass. The chaos and confusion and panic consumed the entire area.

James managed to refocus, shifting his eyes from the bloodshed inside the coffee shop. *Find those bombers.* He spotted the two he was following on

Princes Street. They were splitting up, with one pointing toward the Waverley entrance to the Market, the other running, likely for the far end.

Crack! Crack!

The familiar sound of an automatic weapon echoed off the concrete and stone walls of the towering buildings. James saw the bomber nearest to him crumple to the pavement, two tactical officers moving in and pumping one more round in his skull. His brains spilled onto the pavement, severing his motor skills and ability to trigger another backpack.

This isn't over.

The fourth bomber also knew it wasn't over. He could still make his last stand. The bomber stopped dead in his tracks in the middle of Princes Street, raised his arms and closed his eyes. As panic within the Christmas Market spilled over into the street, the sidewalks filled with fear. The purest of evil unites mass murderers, encouraging them to give their lives. All of this was on full display. Empty shoes. Body parts. Blood. Wailing sirens. Wailing humans. Panic, fear, shouting. People running in all directions. People frozen in place. Children wandering aimlessly, searching for a familiar face.

The Christmas Market lights still blinked green and red. The rides still ran. The smells of mulled wine, grilled food, and sugary treats wafted above a scene from hell. All of that...and then this.

Boom.

66

Edinburgh, Scotland

Inside a poorly lit hallway with papered walls and an orange glow, Police Scotland officers were getting no response from anyone inside Igor Kozlov's room. They had secured a copy of the key and inserted the electronic card. The lock released with an audible click, and the green light and two-tone beep signaled success.

They entered in a defensive posture, prepared for the worst-case scenario—gunfire or another suicide bomber. What they found instead was the drone of the air conditioning unit, and the bathroom door cracked ever so slightly. After clearing the bedroom, they took caution and threw it to the wind, opting to surprise whoever might be on the other side with a bull rush and take down.

Two officers made eye contact as the leads and counted to zero with their fingers...three, two, one, closed fist. The third held the taser, prepared to stun the subject to oblivion. Bursting through the door, the officers discovered their cautious plotting was for naught. Inside, they found the ashen body of a man who looked like Igor Kozlov, his face and lips blue, but otherwise matching the photo on his national ID card.

Checking his pulse, the officers announced him deceased over the radio, unsure if anyone could hear through the blaring sirens and general mayhem unfolding outside.

Across the street, two Scottish bomb technicians waddled their way toward the gray panel van in the car park at Calton Square, one using a mirror to inspect the undersides, the other carrying a bucket of oversized tools manufactured to work seamlessly with the oversized blast suits that limited mobility.

From a distance, another member of the bomb squad operated a remote-control robot with a camera, looking for trip wires or clues to what the men might be facing.

Despite the chilly December weather, the blast suits were hot, and the techs were leaking sweat. The remote-control operator gave the all-clear, and the two veterans of the war on terror moved to investigate whether anyone was inside the van.

"Negative," one reported. "No suspects inside. Repeat, no visuals."

"Copy," the reply came amidst static.

The techs split and performed a survey around the van, looking for any signs the doors might be wired, or attempts to access the van would ignite whatever was inside. They merged at the rear double doors, giving each other a thumbs up. Their inspection was clean.

"Preparing to breach the doors," the second tech said into his mic.

"Copy that, breaching," the on-site commander replied.

The second tech put his hand on the handle and pulled. He was met by a flash of light, followed by darkness.

Boom.

The three officers at the Picardy Inn and Suites first felt the building shudder, then the blast wave brushed against their skin, pushing through windows and open spaces. The sound of it all, a terrifying sonic expression of terror, registered last.

Shaken, they exchanged looks and ran toward the lobby. The glass doors had been shattered. A man and a woman stood still, paralyzed with fear, bleeding from the face and arms. Stepping outside, the sound of glass crunching beneath their feet added to the surreal atmosphere that lay before them.

Across the street, a partially collapsed building lay silent in the foreground as a plume of smoke, dust, debris, and flames rose to the heavens, likely carrying the souls of many.

67

Edinburgh, Scotland

Three devastating explosions within minutes. Terror and panic the United Kingdom hadn't seen since the Manchester concert bombing in 2017, and of course the events of 2005. This was the plan. *Shake them to their core.*

On Market Street, Aadan Mukhtaar and his Russian were quickly moving downhill, toward the train station's entrance of the same name. The final two explosions stopped them cold. Amidst the pandemonium, the night was calm. Aadan could feel the dampness in his lungs, the cold air against his face. He could feel anxiety in those running around him. He was composed yet carried a sense of urgency. His feet hurt and his back ached.

He knew a big, red-headed man was on their tail since the hotel pedestrian crossing. Watching the aftermath of destruction he'd orchestrated—the smoke and fire; the screams and pain; the death—brought him warmth and satisfaction. Demented, no doubt.

"Boss, we need to keep moving."

He nodded at the Russian, and they continued a deliberate march downhill, and into Waverley Station. Conan MacGregor was not far behind.

Inside the train station, rail officials and the police decided that every available train would be used to evacuate this part of town. Loudspeaker announcements and rail workers told those seeking a way out to board any available train. All trains were heading to Haymarket, a smaller station a few kilometers down the tracks. From there, destinations could be sorted further.

Officials rushed to open emergency exits and disable the automated ticket turnstiles—the fewer impediments the better. Trains were filled quickly, with standing room only, and the whistles of platform conductors pierced the air as they moved as many cars out as quickly as possible.

Conan MacGregor had reacquired his targets. Fueled by adrenaline, he battled through the lactic acid buildup in his legs and the burning in his lungs. He was struggling but determined. His job was about to get harder, as a massive wave of panicked revelers were looking for a way out.

Ahead, he had eyes on Mukhtaar, who along with his Russian had moved into a slow-moving mob. The crowd was being steered toward platform 10, which appeared to offer one of the last rail cars out.

Conan reached into his pocket and dug out his phone, calling Mathieu James, hoping above all hope he answered and wasn't a victim.

The line rang once. Twice. Three times. Then a fourth.

"Conan..."

"James," a relieved MacGregor said. "You good? Where are you?"

"Uh, I'm a little beaten, not too bad I think. My head is throbbing. I'm near Black Sheep, outside the Princes Street entrance to Waverley. Where are you?"

"Heading into Waverley. I have eyes on the boss and one of his goons. The other one was heading your way. Listen, mate, they are evacuating people by train—everyone heading to Haymarket. It's chaos in here, just madness."

"I don't think I can get into the station," James said. "Two bombs went off pretty close to the entrance here. There's so much carnage."

"I don't need you here. At this point I need you safe. I got this for now and will get further help. Get to your safe house and stay there. Be on the lookout for that other Russian goon. Await further instructions. Talk to no one but me or Stevens. Copy that?"

"I can help you, Conan. Let me find a way in there."

"I don't think so, James. Get to your spot. I'll contact you."

With that, Conan terminated the call.

James was unhappy, and he briefly made his way toward the Princes Street entrance, determined to help Conan. More than anything in this moment, he wanted Mukhtaar. Every passing moment it became clearer this man was directly connected to the deaths of James's parents.

With that singular thought of vengeance, he moved toward Waverley. Within ten yards, he was met by first responders.

"Sir, turn around, you can't go past here. Please, sir, turn around."

"I have to get in there. I need to get on one of those trains."

"Sir, this entrance isn't accessible. There's half a double-decker bus blown to bits and wedged into the stairs. Please, sir, turn around and head back toward the square."

James tried to step past the man but found it futile. Indeed, the bus wreckage was wedged into the stairwell, parts aflame and smoldering. He could see dismembered bodies, and a red hue streaking across the walk. His stomach became unsettled at the sight. This was how his parents died. He looked to his left, up Princes Street where Leith and Regent streets merge. He saw an e-bike lying on its side, and a person on the ground next to it.

He ran through the killing field, seeing police officers down, a smoldering pile of flesh and bone that must have been the first bomber. He could hear someone yelling for him, but he kept going.

At the e-bike, he checked the man on the ground. He was face-down and not moving.

"Hey buddy, can you hear me?" James shook his arm and shoulder. No response. James rolled him over. What he saw made him gag. The man's face had melted to the bone, his eye sockets black and void, his teeth and jawbone visible and charred. *He must have been burned by the blast,* he reasoned.

Again, James heard someone yelling for him. He ignored the pleas, pretending not to hear.

James stood and grabbed the e-bike. *How do I get from here to the safe house?* He looked around, searching for something that would trigger a mental map for his location. In the distance, he heard the familiar clang of the tram bell. *The tram tracks.* He mounted the e-bike and within seconds saw the tracks near Black Sheep Coffee, where inside first responders were just arriving, assessing the scene.

He steered the bike to his right. Standing there, waiting for him, was mister black-and-blue balls. The second Russian had spotted James moments earlier when he was standing on the corner talking to Conan. He made a beeline for the American, yelling at him—his was the voice James had ignored.

Stunned by this development, James almost came to a complete stop on the bike. Trying to maintain his balance, he swerved to the left of the now-lunging Russian, who grabbed James's jacket and yanked him to the ground.

James fell onto the pavement, landing on his back. Within moments, the Russian was on top of him, raining hard rights to the side of his head. James had but one instinct: he jerked his knee toward his chest as hard as he could, crushing the Russian's groin once more. He then grabbed him by the lapels as he recoiled, and James forcefully pulled the Russian toward him as he flexed his core tight and threw himself into the bear. Their heads violently collided, Jame's forehead meeting the Russian's nose, which collapsed and exploded, blood coming from his nostrils like a tap was turned on.

Stunned by the double barrage, the Russian was in a fog. James took advantage, throwing him off and to the side. With a double-barrel roll, he sprung to his feet and grabbed the e-bike, his head throbbing in pain, his eyes watering, and a pressure cut trickling blood from his forehead. James started the slight uphill climb, past Lady Libertine and the Edinburgh Grand, past Harvey Nichols and right toward Picardy Place. He followed the tracks, confident he would find his way. It was starting to feel familiar.

Pedal, Mathieu. Pedal.

Ahead in the distance, swirling blue lights bounced off buildings and windows. Sirens wailed and people were running. *Picardy Place*, he thought. *The gray van.* In all the commotion outside of Waverley Station, James had forgotten about the van packed with drums of explosives. As he pedaled on scene, slipping in between cars and the people who had flooded the streets, panicked, still stunned, still scarred by the urban battlefield in the midst of the Christmas season. To his right, he could see the face of Calton Square, obliterated. A pile of rubble and flames. Fire trucks shooting water cannons at the smoldering ruins.

His mouth agape, his eyes wide, he left his body momentarily. He couldn't feel anything. He couldn't process what he was seeing, what his eyes and his brain were telling him in real time. He was floating through the intersection when the *whoop! whoop!* of a siren snapped him back to the present. An ambulance was on his tail, needing him to slide over.

The whir of the e-bike's motor caught his attention, and he pedaled faster, processing, thinking, evaluating, planning. He had to help Conan. *How?* He couldn't let the African boss escape. An image of his parents projected before him, his pain laid bare on a devastating, cold December night.

It stung, as it always did. He had resolved to fight. For them. This wasn't over. He was less than two kilometers from the safe house, and he started a mental checklist.

- Look up Haymarket.

- Check alerts for train movements from there.

- Call Conan for a status check.

In the mental tornado that was swirling in his mind, two brief images brought him sober.

The Glock 17 in the nightstand.

The keys to the Land Rover.

He felt a smirk forming on his face. Pedaling furiously, the electric motor propelling the e-bike down the middle of the tram tracks, he was focused, even if he was pedaling on the wrong side of the street. Some American habits are hard to break. The cold wind chilled him to the bone, the sweat running down his back caused him to shiver. His face flushed from the rush of adrenaline, the increased heart rate, the determined spirit. It was all starting to feel like his time in Ranger Regiment, where the challenge was real. The challenge then, as now, was life or death. And he welcomed that feeling.

He was still in the fight.

68

Edinburgh, Scotland

Haymarket Station, normally just a few minutes by train from Waverley, wasn't equipped for this. The volume of people and rail cars converging on the smaller of Edinburgh's two primary rail depots was creating havoc.

Because of the number of trains that had stopped there delivering those escaping the mass murders at the Christmas Market, platform space was at a premium. Crews were tasked with getting passengers off of trains without platform space, meaning they had to climb down onto the tracks, in the heart of the rail yard, and scramble to safety.

Conan MacGregor believed he was two cars behind the African boss and his Russian bodyguard. The man from Belfast made attempts to move between cars, but the wall of people made it impossible. He sought to avoid a scene and more panic. *Play it safe.*

MacGregor's train was one that had to unload on the tracks, nothing but steel, wood cross-ties, and loose gravel. As one of the last to leave Waverley, there was little danger of getting crushed by a locomotive. He was surprised with how smoothly the evacuation was going, and how well the mass of people were handling their emotions. Sure, there were tears and screams and anxiety and tension. But generally, order was peaceful and cooperative.

Declining the hands of the rail crew who were helping people off the cars, MacGregor jumped and landed squarely on the gravel below. He straightened his jacket out of habit, tweaked his tuque as a measure of focus, and set off to locate a 5-foot-8 black man in a track suit and a 6-foot-plus white man in dark jeans.

E-bikes largely remove the workout from cycling, and Mathieu James was making time, pedaling hard and zooming down Constitution Street into the heart of Leith. He passed familiar tram stops, mostly vacant as news of the bombings spread and people sequestered indoors.

As he passed the Brass Monkey in Leith, on the corner of Queen Charlotte Street and Constitution, his peripheral vision caught the flashing lights of an emergency vehicle behind him. He couldn't hear a siren, but also knew across from the Brass Monkey there was a police station.

He paid it little mind, still pedaling the wrong side of the street, anticipating his turn at Mitchell coming on quickly. The squad car behind him was closing fast, and James was suddenly feeling under pressure. He turned to grab a glance and saw the police car was also on the wrong side of the street. *I'm on the wrong side of the street—why is he?*

Within seconds, the car was inches from James's rear tire. He felt panicked, with little room to get over without smashing into the curb. *What is going on?* The police car pulled even with James, who was doing his best to pedal fast, maintain balance, and not break his neck. He snuck a glance to his left, wondering if the police officer was after him. Inside he saw a familiar face.

Mister black-and-blue balls.

The Russian must have stolen a police cruiser amidst the chaos outside of Waverley Station and chased James since spotting him near Picardy Place. The Russian grinned, and James knew he was in trouble. Just as the Russian pulled hard to the right on the steering wheel, expecting to crush the American on the e-bike, James hit the brakes. The cruiser swerved violently in front, crashing into the curb and now riding two wheels on the walk and two on the street.

The front tire of the bike tangled with the rear fender of the police car, knocking James off balance momentarily. He skidded to a stop, regained his composure, and instinctively turned the bike around, an unexpected pivot that would give him just enough time to make one move that might save his life.

The U-turn put James in the proper lane, going the direction he'd just traveled. He made a quick left at Queen Charlotte Street, in front of the police department and past the Brass Monkey. He could hear tires squealing behind him, probably the police cruiser changing directions to chase him down.

Fueled by fear and adrenaline, James dug as deep as he could and pedaled hard. He was sweating profusely, his mouth pasty, mealy, wide open, and sucking air. He rode off the street and onto the walk, hoping the shadows would hide him if only momentarily.

He remembered a park ahead. *Thank god, I got out and explored.* He knew a back way to the safe house. The question was, could he get there in time? And if he did manage to get there, would the Russian see him? Would the safe house then be blown?

Keep going.

James saw the pavement on his right illuminate from the headlights of a car. Soon the blue and red lights were bouncing off the stone walls and windows of Queen Charlotte Street.

Here he comes.

The Russian was actually enjoying this, feeling he had the advantage. Car vs bike. Machine vs man. He hadn't picked up the trail just yet and stepped on the accelerator.

James could hear the engine roar behind him.

Now or never, Mathieu.

Now gliding, James prepared to jump from the e-bike, his left foot bearing his body weight on the pedal as he swung his right leg over the seat. He was nearly to the corner of Elbe Street. He remembered a small convenience store there. He was half-a-block from the safe house.

He leapt from the bike and pushed it toward a building on his left, where it crashed into a fence. A dog barked in the yard, startled by the crash, amped at protecting its turf. James was now sprinting, seeing his shadow running before him, the headlamps of the police cruiser making him a claymation silhouette.

After a hard left at the convenience store, he hugged the stone walls and fencing. The walk was narrow, uneven, and the cobblestones bent the soles of his boots. Another left and he was on Mitchell. The safe house was on the right. Two entrances. One on the street, the other in the car park behind, where the Land Rover sat alone, with a single light overhead, glowing in the darkness.

The Russian also turned left at the convenience store, but he had lost sight of James. He slowed, scanning the street and walks in front of him. The Bowlers Rest, a local pub, was ahead on the left. Patrons standing in front, smoking darts and shivering, amused by the flashing lights coming toward them, tossing jokes in accents made thicker by pints of lager.

James had now reached the entrance to the car park and was out of site, behind the building, slowing to a quick walk, breathing hard, spitting mucus, his face a mixture of salty sweat and blood from the cut on his forehead.

Keys...keys, where are the keys? He remembered he'd tucked them in an inside pocket. He reached in, grabbed them, and unlocked the door, stepping into the stairwell. Outside, he could see the blue and red lights twirling, penetrating the empty spaces in the neighborhood, searching, licking the hidden crevasses. He worked his way up the stairs, mindful to stay away from the windows on each level, until he reached the safe house. Once inside, he held the door so it closed quietly, and leaned against it with his back, sliding down into a seated position on the faux wood floor, exhausted, exhilarated, anxious, tired.

Just down the street, the Russian had stopped in front of the pub and asked The Bowlers Rest patrons standing outside—a cloud of tobacco smoke aloft above them—if they had seen a man running. This, they found funny. All of them pointed a different way and laughed, and the Russian spat at them and swore in his native tongue. The cruiser now slowly rolled down the cobblestone street in search of a man he desperately wished to kill.

At Haymarket Station, Conan MacGregor swam through a sea of people in search of Aadan Mukhtaar and his bodyguard. Announcements were drowned by the din of the crowd. The electronic departures boards updated with trains now running to Glasgow to the West, Dundee to the North, and Manchester and Newcastle upon Tyne, both in England, to the South.

This was ScotRail's way of clearing the station. They would send two trains back to Waverley to further assist the evacuation. The rest would move to larger stops, with calls along the way, dispersing the cluster of rail cars that would make a welcome target should others be looking.

Glasgow was a good bet, Conan thought. Big city, easy to get lost, lots of options out. The other choice he thought the African might make was to stay in Edinburgh, maybe even double back to the hotel. The second Russian had peeled off. *Would he leave him behind?*

Conan scanned the crowded platforms, watching as people climbed from the tracks and worked their way into the station, and out onto the streets. Normally a tram stop could be found at street level, but the likelihood of trams running now was doubtful.

He scanned for a scally cap and black skin. Raw as it may seem, Scotland had few Black people, and Aadan Mukhtaar, the Somali-born terrorist, mastermind and financier, would stick out just the same as any other. The Russian was a lesser bet, although his burly physique and ruggedness might be noticeable in a crowd largely consisting of families, couples, and the elderly.

Once up on the platform, Conan found a bench and jumped on top. His elevated position gave him eyes on the tops of heads. He made three sweeps of varying depth, each one looking a bit further than the other, going from his left to his right, slowly, carefully.

On the fourth sweep, he spotted two individuals knifing through the crowd, elbowing their way, knocking people off balance. A sign of panic. Or desperation. Conan locked on the area, which was getting further away, his eyes struggling to maintain focus at such a distance. And then, a face he recognized. Aadan Mukhtaar had turned ever-so-slightly to say something to his trailing bodyguard. Conan caught a glimpse of his face and that damned scally cap.

Zeroed in on the location, he leapt from the bench and moved swiftly through the crowd, pivoting himself sideways left and right to make his profile smaller. He had a line on them, and he needed to re-acquire visual contact.

Mathieu James gave himself roughly two minutes to collect his thoughts and recover his breathing. Finally, he stood. The apartment was dark, and he chose to leave the lights off. With blinds partially open, there was enough ambient light from the street for him to navigate the apartment.

He walked into the kitchen and pulled a water from the refrigerator. Twisting the cap, he chugged almost the entire bottle, carrying it to the bathroom with him. Here, he pointed his cell phone at his face, allowing the home screen to glow just enough so he could inspect the wound on his forehead. It wasn't terrible. A couple of stitches would close it, but the bleeding had stopped, and the wound was crusting and scabbing.

He poured the remaining water from the bottle onto his face, taking a towel from the rack and dabbing himself dry. He popped four Advil from the bottle on the sink and swallowed them dry, contorting his face, neck and tongue to get the chalky tablets to slide into his throat.

Next, he moved into the bedroom, opening the nightstand and withdrawing the Glock 17 and two magazines, each loaded with 17 rounds. *Gotta be smart.* He slid a magazine into the pistol, pushing the bottom hard with his palm until it clicked, then pulled back on the slide, putting a live round in the chamber. *Instinctive.* The second magazine went into his left rear pocket, and he slid the Glock into his waistband, centered on his lower back.

The apartment had four primary windows, two overlooking the car park in back and two overlooking Mitchell Street. James carefully peered out all four, looking for signs of the patrol car, or the Russian, or both. The Land Rover Defender was parked in back, facing forward, ready for a quick exit. *Would it start?* He'd find out soon. *Where am I going?*

Conan had told him to stay put, that he would contact him. "Don't talk to anyone but me or Stevens," he'd said.

Stevens...I should check in. She's probably frantic.

James clicked open WhatsApp on his iPhone and punched her number. She answered straight away.

"Mathieu?"

"It's me."

"Thank god. Are you okay?"

"I am. A little beaten up, but I'm good."

"Where are you?"

"Safehouse. I was followed. One of the Russians protecting Mukhtaar has a special interest in me, it seems."

"Did he see you enter?"

"I don't think so, but he's nearby. Stole a police car and tried to run me over."

"Okay, let me see if we can get an exfil team to get you out ASAP."

"No, Alyssa. Not yet. Conan is going after Mukhtaar. I want to help him."

"Mathieu, this is probably a good time for me to remind you that you're a journalist. MacGregor is MI5. You're in Scotland. Let him do his thing."

"I'm not just a journalist, Alyssa. I'm a son who lost his parents. I'm an Army Ranger, Signal Corps be damned. I can handle myself. If I couldn't, would I be helping you?"

"Always with the valid points. Listen, if you need to run, take the cash. Take the Land Rover. Take the Glock. Be safe first, then make contact and we can get you home. But let me be clear, my preference is that you stay put and we send a team to get you out."

James was silent.

"Mathieu?"

"Copy on all that, Alyssa. You know where my head and my heart is at. We now can feel certain a fifth bomber existed all along, and it's Mukhtaar. We may never get closer. *I* may never get closer."

"Mathieu, hold one second..."

James could hear muffled voices and Alyssa saying "Where? When? How certain are you?" She came back on the line.

"Mathieu, I have something. One of our assets was in touch with a counterpart at MI6. Both working in Scandinavia. They received intel that a boat crew based in Bergen, Norway, was drinking it up about 48 hours ago, and one of them mentioned they were on their way to Scotland to pick up some human cargo. To the source it came across as human trafficking, so our asset poked around a little, buying a round of shots, and one of the crewman said it was a 'VIP' from Africa. When the captain overheard this, he punched the crewman in the mouth and told him to mind his manners."

"Mukhtaar."

"A good bet."

"Did they say where?"

"No, but we're tracking. We have the merchant vessel number and can probably get a charted course that was filed before they left."

"How long for that?"

"Soon, I would think," Stevens said. "I'll let you know, Mathieu. Be careful, stay out of sight."

James smiled into the receiver. "Of course. You know me."

And with that, he ended the call, collected the rest of his belongings, checked the windows one more time for any sign of mister black-and-blue balls, and slipped the key to the Land Rover into his jacket pocket. His plan was to find Conan MacGregor.

And deliver justice to Aadan Mukhtaar.

69

Edinburgh, Scotland

When he stepped out of the rear entrance to the safe house, he was careful to check his surroundings, scanning the small car park for signs of mister black-and-blue balls. There was only one way in for a vehicle, and someone wishing to sneak in undetected could do so easily.

Mathieu James slid the key into the lock and turned it, pulling the handle to open the door and tossed his bags on the passenger seat. Being in the UK meant driving not just on the opposite side of the road but operating from the opposite side of the car. This would be an adventure.

The iconic 1995 Land Rover's boxy yet functional lines sat on oversized tires. James had to climb up and pull himself in. The lift kit was impressive, taking the ruggedness to another level. The cabin being on the wrong side threw him off more than he expected. He took a moment to get situated, finding the controls, the ignition, the gear shift...*fuck, that's going to be weird.*

He adjusted the mirrors, made sure the radio was off, inserted the key, and stepped on the clutch. Pumping the gas once, he turned the key and the engine roared to life.

Hallelujah!

A light drizzle had settled over Leith, and the glow of the single lamp post offered clarity against the mist and haze pushing in from the Firth of Forth. He reached for the wipers and accidentally hit the turn signal—*wrong side*—before correcting his mistake. He felt for the light switch in the dark, fumbling a bit, leaning forward to get a closer look in the black-on-black cabin.

Satisfied he had found the correct switch, he turned the headlights on and adjusted himself in the seat. With the wipers screeching and the lamps burning, he was ready to ride. He put the manual shift in first gear and released the clutch, lifting his head to peer out the windscreen.

A startled James jumped in his seat. Standing in the drizzle, his imposing figure outlined by the headlights of the Defender, was mister black-and-blue balls. James's first thought was *escape-at-all-costs*. He cranked the steering wheel hard right and released the clutch. The Defender jerked forward, choking a bit, and stalled. The Russian had jumped out of the way, his hands now on the hood, bracing himself for a rush at the driver's side door.

Fuck! James had forgotten to give some gas as he released the clutch. It was like driver's ed class all over again. He scrambled to re-start the Defender, pushing the clutch in, and fumbling with the key. He managed to turn the key, cranking the ignition and the engine once again roared to life.

The Russian was coming full bore for James now, and he was unsure how to lock the doors. The Defenders were rather spartan on purpose. His instincts were to go on the offensive, so as the Russian was lurching toward his door, James grabbed the handle and punched it open, swinging the door into his attacker, knocking him back momentarily. The Russian stayed on his feet, though, and primed himself for another run at his nemesis.

James correctly fed the engine some fuel and released the clutch, and the Land Rover lurched forward once again, graceless in its efforts, but it didn't stall. He needed a hard right and an immediate hard left to exit the car park. It would be tough to build speed, but he put more pressure on the accelerator and wrestled the truck.

The Russian now grabbed the door, which was dangling open, with a grip firm enough to be dragged along by the American. He was able to reach in with one hand and grab for James's arm. James fought him off, shrugging and punching with his dominant right fist, but this meant he had no hand on the wheel.

The Defender lurched again, and James struggled to control it while trying to rid himself of the Russian. The Defender crashed into the wall of the adjacent apartment building at a low speed. With his focus now on his Russian aggressor, James released the clutch and the truck stalled.

Time for a scrap.

Using his legs to catapult himself from the cabin, James flew into his attacker, the Defender's lift kit gave him the advantage of his full weight coming from above and on top of his nemesis. The Russian had a solid tactic in return, looking to catch James and flip him onto his back. He managed the first part well, but James's momentum took the Russian to the ground.

The two men struggled for control, James on top and the lighter of the two. He delivered a right to the face, then dropped a forearm on the Russian's throat. The two exchanged more blows, with James staying on top but losing his advantage. The Russian was reaching for his eyes, his nose, anything he could grab, poke, gouge, rip, tear. James fought back—mostly defensive maneuvers with his forearms—he shifted just enough to give the Russian a clear shot at his throat. He didn't hesitate, putting both hands on James's neck and squeezing as hard as he could, pressing his thumbs into his windpipe, seeking to crush it.

A panicked James now grabbed the Russian on both wrists, trying to pry certain death from his neck. He was in survival mode now, his attacker gaining the upper hand as James struggled to breathe. His strength diminishing, James fell off the Russian and onto his left side, his neck still suffering from a vice-like grip. The two wrestled on the ground, each on their sides, the Russian starting to see the American turn from red to blue. He smiled slyly at the thought.

Fight, motherfucker, fight!

James summoned every ounce of strength and grit he had left, flexing every muscle, fighting, pulling, kicking. And in this moment, the Army Ranger returned. With his left arm he weakly started punching back at the Russian, who still had a deadly grip on James's neck. And with his right, he reached around his back and felt for the grip of the Glock 17. He pulled on the pistol, which briefly snagged on his jeans before releasing, and stuck the muzzle into the Russian's stomach. Knowing he already had a round in the chamber, James slid his finger inside the trigger guard and pulled four times, the pistol unleashing a fury of lead at point blank range.

The stunned Russian released his grip, rolled onto his back and reached for his stomach, crying out in agony. James scrambled to his feet, hands on his knees, spitting and choking as his lungs heaved to intake life and exhale death. Standing over the Russian, he pointed the Glock at his forehead and looked him the eyes. The Russian stared back.

James glanced at the blood spilling from his attacker's stomach, soaking into his shirt and spreading like an amoeba. He could finish him with one to the forehead or let him bleed out.

James chose the former. He bent over and picked up the four casings ejected from the Glock and slid them into his pocket, keeping the pistol trained on the dying man. He looked at him one more time and spoke.

"So long, asshole."

Thinking of his parents, James squeezed the trigger once more, releasing a hollow point 9mm bullet into the Russian's head, which exploded the right side, fragments of his skull and brain matter spilling onto the pavement.

He instinctively leaned over and picked up the fifth casing, sliding it into the same pocket as the others.

The investigative journalist and former Army Ranger had never killed a man until now. He felt sick to his stomach. But he also knew it wouldn't be his last. Aadan Mukhtaar was still out there.

Climbing back into the Defender, he turned over the engine which reliably roared to life, threw it in reverse, then first, and wheeled from the car park, taking a right on Mitchell and a left on Constitution.

As he raced back into the devil's den, the drizzle persisted, leaving drops of water on the windscreen that created colorful bokeh balls refracting the city lights. *Things had gone from bad to worse*, he thought.

No turning back now.

70

Edinburgh, Scotland

With the city under siege, the mood at Haymarket Station was orderly. While tension filled the air, there was no panic, no running or mobs threatening to stampede their way out. The station's concourse on the main floor, with its glass exterior and limited seating, could have been a painting. From the outside, it was brimming full of holiday revelers, the windows dripping with condensation, festive lights blinking from above. The UK has seen its share of misery and desperation over the years. This is where that famed stiff upper lip shines.

Conan MacGregor had been threading himself through the crowd knowing he had sight lines on Aadan Mukhtaar and the Russian just moments ago. He found himself wishing he had been gifted great height, like 6-foot-6 or more, so he could peer over the tops of hats, heads, and hair. Instead, he relied on intuition that had served him well, and continued searching for the terrorists.

Not far ahead and easier concealed in the throngs due to his height, Aadan Mukhtaar was relying on his original escape plan—Aberdeen, with a commercial vessel to Bergen, Norway, waiting for him. He trusted his planning, and when things went awry, as they sometimes do, he believed in doubling down and trusting it even more.

Fortunately for him, the team at ScotRail had a train heading to Dundee. From there, he could easily reach Aberdeen and points beyond if necessary. Dundee was a normal call on a popular route from Edinburgh to Aberdeen, so he thought this might present the best option.

The Russian kept his boss in front for visual and physical contact, and continued to survey the station, looking for signs of trouble. The boss had just confirmed moments ago that Dundee was the plan, so they moved in that direction as expeditiously as possible.

The smell of sweat, that stale stink of winter coats that haven't been washed in years, mixed with fear and angst. The hundreds of people still looking for a way out of Haymarket had no idea the person most responsible for the terror just reigned on this beloved city was in their midst. How could they? Knowing this, Aadan walked without fear of retribution from the masses; rather, he needed to escape but one man at the moment, and that man was near.

Flying down Constitution Street in a burly Defender on the "wrong side" of the road was both frightening and exhilarating. As he navigated the challenges of locating street lights, dodging pedestrians, and people on bikes, Mathieu James was fumbling in his backpack for his AirPods. The driving was one thing; the stick shift made it something more.

Ever organized, he found the charging case and managed to flick it open. The AirPods went tumbling—one to the floor of the passenger side, the other onto the seat. He grabbed that one and placed it in his ear as it automatically paired to his phone.

Dialing Conan MacGregor on WhatsApp, James realized the only way he knew how to navigate through town was following the tram tracks. The Defender was built before automobile navigation became a thing. He also knew this route would only take him so far, as the streets and tracks around Waverley were going to be shut down with first responders attending to the mass casualties.

As he came upon Picardy Place and the second scene of devastation, he slowed to absorb the enormity of what had happened. Yet another terror attack in the United Kingdom. For all of its strengths and faults, the UK has emerged as a world leader, distancing itself from its imperial past and codifying the monarchy to maintain tradition. With the strength of its military and intelligence services, though, it's fair to wonder how this has happened again, and whether sleeper cells can truly be stopped.

As he pondered these larger questions, James only knew there was a strong connection to Aadan Mukhtaar, which made it even more infuriating that the theory of a fifth bomber was ignored so many years.

As the ring tones bounced through his inner ear, Conan MacGregor finally answered on the sixth ring.

"Yeah James, what ya got?" It was loud in Haymarket, and Conan was pushing the phone's speaker into his ear while cupping his left ear with his hand.

"I'm heading toward you, I think. Where did you land?"

"I thought I told you to stay put? You should be in the safe house. Let me and the rest of my team solve this."

"Things changed. I had a tail. I managed to lose him until I didn't..."

"A tail?"

"Yes."

"Who was it? The other Russian?"

"Damn right it was the other Russian."

"Where is he now, Mathieu? Still tailing you? And where are you? Are you *driving?*"

"Good news/bad news. Good news is he's lying in a pool of his own blood in a car park behind the safe house. Needless to say that safe house is coming out of rotation."

"Holy fuck, what happened?"

"He eventually found me...not sure how, but he did, as I was leaving the safe house. The Agency had a Land Rover there for emergencies. This felt like one of those."

"Did you run him over?"

"I tried, but it turns out I didn't know how to drive this thing. So instead, I put five hollow points in him after he tried to choke the life out of me."

Conan paused, letting that sink in for a moment. The man from Belfast, who knew violence growing up and the history of strife in his homeland, thought about an execution of a Russian by an American on British soil.

"James, where the fuck did you get a gun?" an exasperated Conan asked.

"Do you really want to know all the details, Conan? Point is, he's eliminated, and yes, I'm driving the Land Rover on the wrong side of the road—well it's right for you crazies—and I'm coming to help you catch that motherfucker... So, Conan, where am I going?"

"I'm at Haymarket. Can you find it?"

"I'll figure it out. Listen for me when I arrive. I'll be the ugly American with a bruised neck blaring the horn from the curb."

Conan managed a smile and hung up, continuing his pursuit of Aadan and the Russian. Thanks to the well-organized ScotRail personnel, they had the new routes up on the departures board, and he headed for Platform 4.

Just ahead and now out of reach, as the whistle from the platform conductor blew signaling last call, he saw the terror mastermind and his Russian goon board the last car, looking and acting like citizens of Scotland, escaping a city under attack, seeking refuge in a distant place.

En route to Dundee, Scotland

Mathieu James had done as promised. His arrival at Haymarket Station was a scene, pulling partially onto the walk and honking like a mad man. Conan MacGregor was waiting, confident his American counterpart wouldn't let him down.

Conan had watched Aadan Mukhtaar and his Russian bodyguard board the last train car headed for Dundee. It was packed and pulled from the station before he could reach the platform. Had he been able to board, no telling what he could have done anyway. He would have been outmanned—which didn't scare him—but the potential collateral damage aboard that train wasn't worth it.

He had phoned HQ and given details on which train the terrorists boarded and its final destination. MI5 coordinated with Ministry of Defence police and General Communications Headquarters to make sure armed tactical teams were at every potential stop, anticipating a possible hijacking of the train and perhaps an unscheduled destination.

With that, Conan had also relayed the description and plate number of the Land Rover Defender he and James were traveling in, knowing the high rates of speed required to chase down a steaming locomotive. There was no time for being pulled over and queried.

The drive from Edinburgh to Dundee was just sixty-three miles. Aberdeen was twice that. As they drove, James began to fill in the gaps for MacGregor.

"I spoke with Stevens earlier. They had sourcing in Scandinavia that a vessel was chartered out of Bergen, Norway, for a round trip to Aberdeen. Some drunken sailor was guffawing about a VIP from Africa. At first everyone was thinking human trafficking, but Stevens is pretty sure we're talking about Mukhtaar. He probably planned his exit all along."

"Right, sneak out of the country amidst the chaos, with little chance of being detected. No passports, no ID, no cameras like in airports or train stations."

"My best guess then is he's hoping to jump a train in Dundee that will take him to Aberdeen."

"Solid guess, Mathieu. Let me find out what's happening in Dundee with the train schedules."

As James drove, getting more comfortable with the 'wrong side' shenanigans, Conan pulled up the ScotRail app on his phone and tried to check for options out of Dundee that would connect to Aberdeen. The app wasn't responding, either shut down by order of the Home Office due to the attacks or ScotRail simply didn't have information to deliver.

"Nothing here. I have to imagine they really don't know which trains are running when and where right now."

"So what would the contingencies be?"

"I feel confident that we have a bulletin out and every stop along the route is going to be covered, even though the train isn't supposed to stop until Dundee. They will have pictures out to the necessary agencies. If those assholes manage to get that train to stop before Dundee, they'll be met by tactical teams."

"Okay, so if you were Mukhtaar, what do you do?"

"If I have an out in Aberdeen, I'm doing everything I can to get there. And I mean everything."

James took a moment to consider the range of possibilities behind that statement. It was almost too many scenarios to grasp. He offered a question to Conan.

"If they are on the train in Dundee, what happens? How do we avoid collateral damage? What if it goes sideways and they take hostages?"

"I think the right play is let the train empty out and watch them. If there's a moment to take them down, we do it. If there's a chance for them to board another train, I think it's a read-and-react situation, right? The important thing is we believe we know their destination. But ultimately, it's up to command, you know? I'm not running this; I can only give them feedback on the ground. Someone upstairs is calling the shots."

"Understood," James said. His eyes remained fixed on the highway as he pushed the limits of the Defender's capabilities. At 125 kph, he was getting a lot of shimmy from the oversized, knobby tires. The lift kit might have improved clearance, but it didn't improve balance. He had to be careful here—any sudden movements of the steering wheel would send them both into an ugly barrel roll and certain death.

They rode in silence for a while, lines on the highway skipping by in the darkness. Dundee was twenty-three kilometers out, and the emotional toll of the day was beginning to grip them both. In the moment, they were surviving on instincts and adrenaline. After forty minutes on the open road, the mind and body start to decompress. Reality settles like a lead blanket, the mind wondering if everything it just processed was real. Suffocation of the soul is an ugly reality.

Fifteen minutes out, Conan's phone buzzed in the console, rattling around inside the cup holder, the annoying dance snapping them both into focus.

"MacGregor."

James glanced over as Conan was listening intently to the caller.

"Right, okay... Right... Copy that. We are less than fifteen minutes out. Yessir, we can both ID Mukhtaar."

James confirmed, nodding his head.

"I believe we can both ID the Russian as well. Shouldn't be too hard."

James nodded again.

"Yessir. We will be on site shortly."

Conan ended the call and glanced over at James, who returned the gaze with a quizzical look.

"Well?" James prompted.

"They have a plan. It's risky and it could implode."

"How so?"

"They have three MOD tactical teams in Dundee. Two came by helo. The plan is to empty each car one at a time, clearing people one by one until everyone is off. If they haven't found them, they will search the cars, two teams from each end, row by row, toilets, galley, all of it. They're looking for a peaceful resolution. They want him alive, if possible. Charge him with this and put him on trial for 2005 as well. And I'm sure the French have something to say about all of it."

James listened quietly. He wanted justice for his parents. As much as he'd prefer to deliver it personally, this plan made sense—mostly.

"I get it," he said quietly. "It's the right call. Let's get there and support those teams, see if we can get an ID and an arrest. I just worry about a potential hostage situation if Mukhtaar is feeling boxed in."

James pushed a little harder on the accelerator, his personal agenda fueling his desire to see this through. The two men rode in silence for the final ten minutes. An unimaginable day perhaps coming to a welcome end.

72

Cheltenham, England

In 2003, GCHQ moved into new digs in Cheltenham, a futuristic, circular building known affectionately as "The Donut."

Here, teams work intelligence angles through cyberspace, focusing on counter terrorism, organized crime, strategic advancement of UK goals and supporting Department of Defence initiatives.

With the terror events unfolding in Edinburgh, GCHQ had dedicated teams in place tracking and analyzing real-time streams of information, from cell phone towers to internet hackers to real and perceived threats to London financial institutions—when you're distracted, other harbingers of ill will take notice and will attempt to take advantage.

Command had requested a review of CCTV and other surveillance footage around Waverley Station, Picardy Place, and the Edinburgh airport. Those were priorities. A second team was monitoring the Port of Leith, Haymarket Station, incoming and outgoing traffic on major highways and any civilian aviation.

It was this second team that would find the most important piece of intelligence of the hour. With tactical teams set-up in Dundee, and smaller units prepared for unplanned stops along the train route, everyone's focus was on that set of train cars rumbling toward Dundee.

Capturing the precious cargo they were expecting—Aadan Mukhtaar and his Russian bodyguard—could possibly put an end to the most horrifying day in the UK since the Manchester concert bombing in 2017, when an Islamic extremist blew himself up, killing 23 and injuring more than 1,000.

Deep inside GCHQ, a young female analyst, combing through hours of CCTV footage at Haymarket Station, raised her hand from her cubicle. Her immediate supervisor was over her shoulder almost immediately and uttered a phrase that chilled the room.

"Son of a bitch."

Nearly 400 miles away, Conan MacGregor's phone buzzed yet again. This time, he and Mathieu James were fully focused as they closed in on Dundee in the darkness of a cloudy night.

"MacGregor."

James rolled up his window, which was cracked an inch for some fresh air, quieting the cabin.

"Bloody hell, are you fucking kidding me? When? Right... And then what happened? Fuck! Fuck fuck fuck!"

The man from Belfast lost his temper, throwing his phone into the dashboard, cracking the screen.

"What is it?" James asked.

"They aren't on the train."

"What?"

"They aren't on the fucking train! They got off."

"Where?"

"Haymarket. They got on that last car, apparently walked through to the gangway connection, into the next car and pulled open the doors on the non-platform side, then jumped down onto the tracks below. Footage has them walking along the tracks until the train departs, then just fucking casually walking back toward the platform and climbing up with the help of a rail yard worker."

James was silent, reflective, taking in the developments.

"I'm sorry, Mathieu. I should have anticipated something like that. I should have stayed at the station longer to make sure we had the all-clear."

"Hey man, listen, this isn't on you. These guys are pros..."

"And so are we! At least I am. Fuck!" Conan screamed, punching the dashboard with his right fist.

James tried to defuse the tension and bring his counterpart back to center.

"Okay, look, we can't do anything about that now. What we can do is focus on finding them. What do we know? What else did they see, anything?"

"They were on CCTV leaving the station. They are checking external camera sources now to see what they can find."

"All right, what do you want to do about this?" James asked, pointing to the roadblock and inspection point ahead, as he slowed the Defender just outside the tiny Dundee depot.

"Let's stop and check in. Maybe they have something useful."

James pulled off to the side of the road, and they were met by two armed MOD police officers, asking for ID. Conan talked through it, showing his MI5 ID and vouching for James. The two walked toward the command post, taking in the action unfolding. The train was about to pull into the station, and news of what they found at Haymarket was just being relayed to the agent-in-charge.

"Looks like they just learned what we learned," Conan surmised, surveying the faces of those in charge.

The two stood at a distance, watching some intense conversations happening at the command post between Police Scotland and MOD tactical leaders. Minutes later, the two units delivered on helicopters a half-hour earlier were loading up and heading out. The threat wasn't in Dundee.

On the M90 near Perth, a black Audi A7 was about to cross the River Tay, merging onto the A90, just 22 kilometers from Dundee, and 86 kilometers from Aberdeen.

Back in Cheltenham at The Donut, another analyst on the second team found something else. He raised his hand, asking for a supervisor review of footage found two blocks from Haymarket. This time, a team of three gathered around the young analyst's screen and reviewed a black man in a track suit, and a white man in a sport coat and possibly jeans, step into traffic and ask a car to stop for them.

The woman in the car slows down as the two men step in her path. She stops and watches them. The black man stays in front of the car. The white man moves to the driver's side and gestures with his hands. He appears to be asking for a ride—maybe for directions—before asserting himself fully and violently.

The white man reaches through the window and grabs the woman by her long, blonde hair. He yanks her head out of the window and reaches inside with his free hand to open the door. The terrified woman falls onto the wet pavement, her hands grasping at his, fighting his grip on her hair. He kicks her in the stomach, hard enough to draw a gasp from the GCHQ team watching the soundless footage, and she turtles in pain.

The attacker grabs her by the feet and pulls her away from the car. She doesn't fight back; instead, she's still, holding her arms across her stomach.

The attacker then enters the driver's side and calmly adjusts the seat as the black man in front of the car saunters confidently to the passenger door, opens it, and seats himself. The doors close on both sides, and the black Audi A7 leaves the scene, as two bystanders come into the frame, offering aid to the woman in distress.

73

On the road to Aberdeen, Scotland

Mathieu James and Conan MacGregor commiserated on the sidelines at the Dundee train depot, trying to figure out a plan that would put an end to this. While Police Scotland, the MOD police command, and MI5 worked through the red tape, the two former military men began to hatch a plan.

Alyssa Stevens had given James the intel about the Norwegian vessel chartered to Aberdeen. That was still the most likely bet for the final two terrorists to escape the UK. Knowing they had stolen a car, there was more than one way to Aberdeen. Traffic cameras would be scoured by GCHQ, and a limited aerial reconnaissance could be launched if the weather held. But the low clouds and incessant drizzle made tracking hundreds of miles of highways coursing like veins through the countryside a challenge.

With vengeance at the fore of his current state, James wanted to take control. He pitched his plan to Conan.

"Listen, we know they have an exit strategy, and we know exactly what that is. Any minute now we should have a vessel registration number, a description, and probably a crew manifest from the CIA. Why don't we—you and me—set up a surprise ambush? Let's drive to Aberdeen, beat them there, locate the vessel, and make these motherfuckers pay."

Conan chuckled a bit, suppressing his laughter to avoid offending his American counterpart.

"You and me? We're gonna do that? With what, stones? Maybe find some sticks in the park?"

"Don't forget, I have the Glock. You must be able to get some tactical gear from the guys here," James said, pointing to the cluster of heavily armed MOD police.

"Not a chance. Not how it works. This isn't some American cowboy movie, and Bruce Willis isn't showing up to save Christmas."

An incredulous James snapped back. "Then what's your plan? You have something better? More bureaucratic bullshit? More red tape? More personnel without weapons? Jesus, Conan, I get I'm in your country, and you do things differently here than we do, but I'm a vet and so are you. We can handle ourselves just fine. Plus," he paused for effect, grinning slightly, "I know where we can gear up."

Conan flashed a non-verbal quizzical facial contortion at James, who smirked and pulled out his phone, punching a number quickly.

Putting it on speaker, he locked eyes with Conan, maintaining a steady smirk.

"Hey, Lily, it's cousin Mathieu."

"Mathieu, it's late, are you okay? You weren't up near those bombings in Edinburgh, were you?"

"Unfortunately, I was in the city at the time, yes. I'm lucky to be standing if I'm being honest."

"Oh my gosh, cousin! Where are you now?"

"I'm with a friend," he said, winking at Conan. "We're okay. I'm wondering though, is the cottage available tonight?"

"Yes, of course, whatever you need," Lily Jameson replied. "I haven't been up there in over a month, so it's probably freezing cold but there's plenty of wood, you can get a fire going, and there's some canned goods in the cupboards, and lots of whiskey. I can text you a photo of where the spare key can be found."

"That's amazing, Lily, thank you so much for the generosity. We'll keep it clean."

"Of course, don't worry about it. You're family, whatever you need.

You're welcome here, too. My flat is small but we can make room."

"No, this is perfect, and much closer. Really grateful..." James was smiling and nodding at Conan, who wasn't really understanding what was unfolding. "Hey, Lily, one more thing...Uncle Mac's gun safe, is it still there?"

"Yeah, of course. My dad would be pissed if I got rid of that thing."

"Ya know my buddy is ex British military, so we're just a couple of gear nerds. He'd love to see what your dad had left over from his SAS days. Any chance you can share the code?"

"Ah, yeah, sure. Sounds like a total dude night—a fire, some whiskey and some guns!" Lily joked. "The safe is both biometric and it has a keypad. Don't touch the biometric pad, just enter the code. It's pound 0779 pound."

"Got it, pound 0779 pound," James said slowly, nodding at Conan to write it down or remember it. Conan tapped it into the Notes app on his phone.

"Lily, thanks again. Hoping we can hang soon. Come to L.A. sometime, I'll show you around."

"And maybe I can meet that girlfriend of yours, the wine sommelier and rock star? You still together?"

"If she'll still have me when I get back!"

"Okay, Mathieu, let me know if you have any trouble getting in. That key photo is coming now."

"Thanks, cuz, love ya."

"Bye, Matty, love to you."

James looked at Conan, nodding his head, feeling the fire burning deep, ready to see this to a close.

"Problem solved, friend. We'll have more weapons than we know what to do with. My uncle passed away some time ago, former SAS, and the family cottage is on the way to Aberdeen. He'll have a nice little gun safe for us to pilfer."

Conan shook his head. He still hadn't bought in.

"Not sure this is the best plan, mate."

"How about you talk me out of it on the way? Time's wasting."

The American and the man from Belfast climbed into the Defender, setting course for a cottage near Newtonhill, where they could secure the means to create the end for Aadan Mukhtaar.

74

Near Newtonhill, Scotland

The Defender ate the gravel like a champ as James and Conan MacGregor left the highway near Newtonhill and traversed several back roads en route to the family home. James's mother had spent considerable time here years ago, and Mathieu was familiar with the land and had distinct memories of the cottage. It had always smelled of cedar and lavender, a hint of woodsmoke from the fireplaces, and fresh bread.

When the paved roads turned to gravel, the duo was getting closer to their destination. A small stone bridge, which arched over a rolling stream, signaled to Mathieu that the long dirt drive was just ahead on the right. He took his foot off the accelerator and let the Land Rover slow to a roll before taking a sharp turn and heading up a small hill that turned slightly right, then left before coming upon the house.

It was dark, and the curtains were pulled tight. There was no light in the driveway, only a soft glow from the moon hidden above a blanket of clouds. The air was thick with moisture. The ground was wet and gathering beads of drizzle—tiny, nurturing gifts from the clouds above.

James and MacGregor climbed out of the truck. James activated the flashlight on his iPhone and pointed to the north side of the house. A bird feeder stood in the garden, about fifteen yards from the kitchen window. He remembered his Aunt Mary washing dishes and commenting on the birds that would feast there. Inside, he could see a tiny black box. He lifted the top from the feeder and put his hand inside, pulling out the plastic rectangle that slid open, revealing a key to unlock the deadbolt and door handle.

Following his counterpart's lead, Conan stopped at the covered wood-shed and grabbed an armful of tinder. They weren't staying the night but could use the warmth as they inspected Uncle Mac's wares.

The key opened a door to Mathieu's past, and he went in with mixed feelings. So much family history here, and a few small memories of his own. His mother's spirit felt close, giving him comfort near the end of a trying day.

Inside, he turned on a single lamp, and they worked quickly to extinguish the chill from the air. Within minutes, the crackling percussion of a fire just beginning to percolate filled the air; the orange glow lent warmth to an otherwise cold room.

"It's been such a long time since I've been here," James said, looking around at a cottage that hadn't changed in twenty years—if not more. "My mom spent a lot of time here growing up. My cousin Lily spent most of her young life here. It was a good spot. Goes back a couple of generations."

"It feels like a home," Conan offered. "Now, did I hear something about whiskey?"

This brought a good laugh to them both, and James's demeanor softened as he retrieved a bottle of Macallan and two tumblers from the cupboard. He set the glassware down on a dusty table, pulled the cork and measured two fingers each, leaving the bottle open as he let it rest on the counter. They raised their glasses and offered a silent toast. Not much to be said now. The mission was clear.

"Let's go take a look," James said, leading the way toward the back bedroom. His Uncle Mac had built the safe into the wall, inside a small closet. James felt around in the dark for a light switch, finding the protruding nub and pushed it on. A weak glow filled the closet, the light yellow with a hint of orange, adding another layer of perceived warmth to the cold air that hung low in the cottage.

James went to the safe, asking Conan to repeat the code, which he typed with his index finger into the pad. A soft beep and a click signaled the lock had released, and he pulled the door open.

"Whoa," an astonished Conan said.

"Yeah," Mathieu smiled.

Inside the safe, a small special forces team would be pleased to find a C8 assault rifle made by Colt Canada, a Heckler and Koch HK33 with two 30-round magazines, two versions of the Remington 870 shotgun—one from 30 years ago and another modern version, along with a Sig Sauer P226 handgun and a vintage piece of gun porn, the WWII era Welrod Silenced Pistol. It was meant for assassinations, and according to some internet fanboy sites, the Welrod was used as recently as the 1991 Gulf War.

Conan reached for the Welrod first.

"I'm taking this bad boy," he grinned mischievously.

The two men took turns checking out the tiny arsenal in between sips of the smooth Macallan and took note of the limited ammunition stored inside the safe.

"We'll need to be smart," James said, pulling his Glock from his belt and popping the magazine loose to count the rounds. Having spent five on mister black-and-blue balls, he had twelve left and a full second mag. He grabbed a Remington 870 and a box of shells while Conan replaced the Welrod and snapped up the more practical P226.

"That all you taking?" James asked.

"All I need," Conan answered wryly.

James closed the door to the gun safe and turned off the closet light as the duo walked into the kitchen and spread their kit on the table.

"Let's get 'em ready. No telling how much time we have."

Conan reached for the bottle of Macallan and filled the void in the tumblers, taking a nip from the bottle before replacing the cork. Just up the road, in a seaside town known for its universities and coastline, an unknown fate awaited not just the hunted, but also the hunters.

75

Port of Aberdeen, Scotland

It was after midnight, and the empty pint glasses held the stories of the day. Seasonal revelers had turned their joyous evening into a somber remembrance, thinking of national unity and the horror in Edinburgh.

Aberdeen is home to multinational companies that operate off-shore petroleum platforms. The port is full of ships supporting those endeavors, along with car ferries, container ships and commercial fishing vessels.

Mathieu James and Conan MacGregor sat quietly in the blacked out Land Rover Defender, tucked away on Church Street, just off Regent Quay, which ran parallel to port operations. They'd arrived twenty minutes prior and did a slow sweep of the roads leading to and around the port, looking for an Audi A7 with a Russian behind the wheel and a Somalian in the passenger seat.

Sitting at her desk in Langley, where she'd been overnight without sleep while keeping tabs on the developing situation, Alyssa Stevens texted James on WhatsApp.

Satellites have found the ship from Norway.
It's sitting one mile off the coast of Aberdeen.
Appears anchored. Hasn't moved in three hours.

James read the message aloud to Conan, who listened silently, carefully reflecting on the words and the situation as it evolved.

"Thoughts?" James inquired.

"Plenty," Conan replied. "Simply put, if it's all true and they are here to transport a terrorist, they are sitting out there waiting for him to give a signal that he's ready."

"Okay, so whatever that looks like, then what? They just pull into the harbor, he steps on like Thurston Howell III, and he's off on a three-hour tour?"

"Nice *Gilligan's Island* reference," Conan said, rolling his eyes. "I don't think it would be that simple. This port is pretty small. It's narrow. There aren't a lot of places to hide. But what do I know?"

"Right. But it's the middle of the night, they could just come in and turn around and leave."

"They could, but there are cameras everywhere. Ships coming and going. The port authority surely knows what's happening. I'd be stunned if they didn't."

"Can they help us? Maybe they've had contact with that ship from Norway."

"If we're looking to ambush these motherfuckers, it's probably best we don't let anyone know we're here," Conan said. "Besides, our chances of seeing them aren't great. There's no way we can cover the entire port. I'm sure MI6 is talking to MI5 about what they know, and they're putting a plan together. Hell, if the CIA had a satellite over the North Sea and found this ship, you and I might be outnumbered here pretty soon."

James's eyes glazed over as he was soon lost in the throes of a silent rage. The man that many said never existed was within reach: The man who likely played the key role in the murder of his parents. James had seen him up close and personal. They'd exchanged looks, locked eyes even. He wondered if Aadan Mukhtaar had any idea who Mathieu James was.

Fidgeting in the seat next to him, Conan brought James back to the fore, rubbing his hands together, and pulling his jacket collar up.

"Should have brought some of that whiskey," he laughed. "It's getting cold."

"You want me to start the engine? Get the heater going?"

"No, I'm fine, mate. We don't need anyone seeing that exhaust. Let's keep our eyes peeled."

The big Russian covered his yawn with his left hand, keeping his right on the wheel as he navigated downtown Aberdeen. The streets were moderately busy, with taxis shuttling drunken patrons home and the last trains pulling into the station some time ago. The universities were on break, but in Scotland, no one needs a reason to enjoy a freshly poured pint.

"Pull over here," Aadan said, pointing to a parking lot near the port. "I need to find out what happens now."

The Russian pulled off the A956 and into a surface-level car park adjacent to some big box stores, including Decathlon Sporting Goods. He turned off the lights but kept the engine running in case the two were surprised and needed to move quickly.

Aadan reached into his track suit pocket and pulled out his phone, opening WhatsApp to find a message waiting for him.

Offshore. Signal when ready.

Aadan typed a reply.

Arrived. Where is the exit?

The reply was quick.

North pier lighthouse. Zodiac will be waiting. Iron ladder to the water.

Aadan contemplated this, resting the phone in his lap and looking out the passenger window. He didn't like it. He pulled up Apple Maps on his phone and searched for the lighthouse. It was close, but at the end of a long seawall they certainly couldn't drive on. He pulled up his phone and typed back.

Is there another option?

Again, the reply was quick. And this time, it was blunt.

Negative. Zodiac arrives in 30 minutes. Will wait 5 minutes before leaving. Will not come back.

Aadan rubbed his jaw and chin. He lifted his cap and ran his hand across his skull, placing the cap on the console. He sent one more message.

Understood.

He then turned to the Russian and relayed the escape strategy.

"They are sending a small Zodiac craft to the North Pier Lighthouse in thirty minutes. If we aren't there, they wait five minutes and then they're gone for good."

"Is it close?"

The Russian looked at his boss, whose lips were frowning as his head nodded.

"It's close. We will need to ditch the car and walk a bit. There's a ladder on the seawall apparently."

"Okay, so this is no problem," the Russian said. "We do this easy."

"I hope so," Aadan muttered, and for the first time since he started working for his boss, the Russian sensed a lack of confidence, an uncertainty—perhaps even a nervousness—from Aadan.

"Let's go check it out," the Russian replied, turning the lights back on and pulling the Audi A7 out of the lot and onto the road.

Wrapped under the shadow of an adjacent building, the black Defender was stealthy. James and Conan sat quietly, scanning, yawning, tapping their fingers. Every hint of light woke their senses. Every sound left them guessing. Three cars had rolled past in the last thirty minutes. None were Audis, and none had visible signs of the terrorists they were hunting.

Growing impatient, James broke the silence.

"Maybe we should move. We can't see everything from here. We should mix it up, right?"

"Not a bad thought, Matty. What are you thinking?"

"Maybe we drive over to the other side of the port, at least make another scan for that Audi. You never know."

"Yeah, okay. Let's make it happen."

James stepped on the clutch, turned the key and pumped the gas. The big engine roared to life, and a steady stream of exhaust slipped away from the rear, like ghosts escaping into the night.

He pulled off Church Street and turned right onto Regent Quay, recognizing his headlamps were off. He flipped them on and slowly crawled up the road, looking to his right and checking side streets as Conan searched left between the ships and cargo containers. Just ahead near Commerce Street, Regent veered to the left, hugging the water.

Coming toward them on Regent was another vehicle. Both had their lights on, temporarily blinding the other driver. As the two passed, Conan turned to check the make and model.

"There they are, Matty! That's a good X on an Audi A7. Nice and easy, mate, keep moving ahead, and when you can't see them anymore in your mirror, let's turn this thing around."

Another twenty-five yards put space and that slight curve between the Land Rover and the Audi. James checked his shoulder and pulled a U-turn on Regent, heading back the way they came.

"Turn your lights off, Matty, and hug the curb. Stay in the shadows."

James did his best, rolling along in the darkness. Ahead, Regent turns into Waterloo, which forks at York Place. After a slight curve the Audi was within sight again, turning left on York. Conan pulled out his phone and opened Apple Maps.

"There's not a lot of choices ahead. Keep some distance. I see a couple of docks ahead. Maybe that's where they make a move."

The Defender crawled the port streets like a stalker. The brake lights of the Audi occasionally threw a red blur as the Russian casually steered them toward the sea. Conan checked the map and found the most direct route to a stretch of beach and the North Pier Lighthouse.

James increased his speed to keep the Audi in sight. Ahead, they could see the Audi turn left, and tuck behind a building. James slowed again, and he and Conan watched closely.

"They might be ditching. The map says there's a restaurant there, right near the water. Let's close the gap and see if we can spot them."

Another fifty yards brought an uncomfortable closeness between the man from Belfast, his American counterpart, and two of the most wanted men on the planet. Conan pulled the Sig Sauer P226 from the door bin, inserted a fully loaded magazine and yanked back the slide, allowing a 9mm hollow point to roll into the chamber. James reached behind his back and slid the Glock 17 from his waistband. It was already loaded, and he placed it under his leg, easily within reach.

With a boot on the clutch, James moved the stick shift into neutral and let the beast roll quietly on its own as he cut the power. Just ahead, two figures emerged from the side of the restaurant and walked toward the pier. A stone and mortar wall reached into the cold December waters of the North Sea, capped by a lighthouse offering guidance into to the harbor. A pedestrian path allowed the public to enjoy the views.

"We go on foot," Conan announced.

James tapped the brakes bringing the Defender to a full stop. The men climbed out, and James reached behind his seat to grab the Remington 870. They strode forward, under the sharp edges of shadows, their boots crunching on pebbles and dirt, sounding louder as it echoed in the silence.

Ahead, the Russian pulled a 360 degree turn while walking, checking his surroundings. James and Conan slid along the facade of a faceless building before continuing their pursuit.

"Close the gap," Conan said, turning to a light jog, surprising James, who scrambled to catch him. Aadan and the Russian were now on the pier, walking with purpose but not panic. James and Conan passed the restaurant, their accelerated pace closing the distance to forty yards. There was nowhere left to hide.

The Russian must have heard their boots because he turned again and saw two armed men approaching. "Go, now! I'll deal with this." He pushed Aadan in the shoulder as the terror boss looked behind him, assessing the situation. There was just one way out now that didn't involve death: the Zodiac. Neither man was armed, which meant almost certain death for the Russian—his goal was to occupy the armed men approaching, giving his boss enough time to slip into the darkness.

Conan raised his Sig Sauer P226 and locked his sights on the Russian.

"Stop!" he yelled into the night, his voice sounding loud in front of him, yet stunted by the incoming sonic wall of waves and wind. "I said stop! We will shoot!"

James pumped the Remington 870, sliding a slug into the chamber and moved into a tactical walk, the butt of the big shotgun on his shoulder, right eye looking down the barrel and through the site at his target, Aadan Mukhtaar.

"I got the boss," James said coolly.

"Copy, you got the boss," Conan replied.

The Russian's job was to create chaos, a diversion, allowing his boss to get to the end of the pier, down the ladder, and onto the rubber boat that would shuttle him to the Norwegian vessel offshore. The Russian knew they'd shoot him, so he slowed to a stop and raised his hands, checking his shoulder to see how much progress the boss had made.

James started to run, his goal was to get behind the Russian and have a clear shot at Mukhtaar. Conan sensed this and quickly realized James would be putting himself in Conan's line of fire.

"James, slow down. Just let this breathe for a minute. You can't step into my line of fire if I need to take this motherfucker down."

"Then take him down! He's not the one we want, Conan!"

The man from Belfast trained his iron sights on the Russian's chest, giving him room for error but likely taking him down either way. "Hold up there," he called to the Russian. "Down on your knees."

The Russian smiled. No way was he going alive.

"Last chance, mate. On your knees."

The smile left the Russian's face, and he put his hands in his pockets, pulling them out quickly. Conan assumed gun—the only assumption he could safely draw—and squeezed the trigger three times, sending a leaden parade of death on a linear course for the Russian's heart. As the big man stumbled and crumpled to the ground, his hands were free of weapons. It didn't matter. The Russian committed suicide by cop.

Conan left his Sig Sauer trained on the dying man as James sprinted forward with one objective in mind. Aadan turned and saw his pursuer, probably at fifty yards now, and liked his chances. Still in the tactical position but now at a full run, James put the target on Aadan's back and pulled the trigger. The Remington's kick rocked his shoulder and the barrel jumped high. Down range, it was a miss. James reacquired the back of the man who helped murder his parents, pumped another round into the chamber and fired.

Aadan stumbled but didn't fall. In the darkness, there was no telling if James hit the terrorist or not.

James slowed and took long, deliberate strides. He pumped the action once more, loading another shell of death into the smoking chamber. With every ounce of concentration he could muster, he aimed one last time, squeezed the trigger and felt the lead explode from the barrel, followed by a spark and a string of smoke. Ahead, at the end of the pier, he saw the figure of Aadan Mukhtaar leap off the side and into the water. He heard a splash, and a man yell.

He turned to check on Conan, who was searching the Russian's pockets. James shouted for him.

"Could use some help up here! He's in the water!"

Conan stood from his kneeled position and barreled down the pier, James well in front of him. Below, a marine engine sputtered to a start, and James ran to the wall, searching in the darkness for signs of Mukhtaar. He couldn't locate a man in the water, but he saw the Zodiac pull a U-turn and accelerate toward the open sea. A flash of light came from the back of the craft, followed by the familiar crack of an assault rifle.

Conan and James were taking fire and returned it with a vengeance. James unloaded the shotgun before emptying his Glock; Conan with two hands on his Sig pulled it empty and, popping another magazine, squeezed it dry.

The Zodiac's wake spilled a white glow in a sea of darkness, carving a path toward open waters, and Mathieu James and Conan MacGregor stood on the pier, panting with exhaustion, minds racing, ears ringing, searching for the answer to the most important question:

What happened to Aadan Mukhtaar?

EPILOGUE

Eight hours later, as the light of day illuminated the North Sea amidst rolling waves colored by gunmetal skies, the British Navy stopped and boarded the Norwegian vessel on its return voyage to Bergen, Norway. It had one goal: Capture or kill Aadan Mukhtaar, now wanted in the United Kingdom for the terror bombings in 2005 and 2023.

Following a thorough search and seizure of the ship, Mukhtaar was nowhere to be found. The Navy initiated a complete takeover of the vessel, detaining the crew. They denied any involvement.

Following their firefight on the pier, Mathieu James and Conan MacGregor returned to the Jameson family cottage near Newtonhill, relieving a bottle of whiskey of its burden before passing out—James on the sofa and Conan snuggled into a rocking chair.

In the morning, they made coffee and departed for Edinburgh, where James awaited travel plans from Alyssa Stevens. Conan returned to work at MI5, feeling the weight of the question the entire kingdom was asking: Was the mastermind of these terror attacks alive or dead?

Knowing the British Navy secured the ship bound for Bergen was helpful, but it left so many more questions. The Zodiac craft wasn't onboard or secured to the ship. Mukhtaar wasn't found. In the gun battle the previous night, as the Zodiac escaped the harbor and disappeared into the North Sea, did they kill those on board? Did the craft itself take rounds, eventually sinking? Mukhtaar jumped off the pier...he wouldn't survive long in the water this time of year. Did he die from a shotgun blast? Did he drown? Did the Zodiac crew pick him up?

His Majesty's Coast Guard assisted in a search for the craft. Time would tell a story that may not have an ending.

Ana-Marie Poulin had the primary byline in the *International Herald Tribune,* reporting from Paris on the attacks in Edinburgh. James had a secondary byline, offering color from the scene. Ever the journalist, he was prodding Conan for information and pulling whatever he could.

There would be many follow-up stories over the coming days, and James was happy to let Ana-Marie take the lead. He was exhausted and consumed by the unknown. Each hour that passed without news was one spent in agony and suffering.

In Los Angeles, Taylor Hendrix had just hung up with her beau, Mathieu James. She was relieved to hear from him and learn he was safe. James had told her he'd arrive the following day at LAX around 21:30, which made her laugh. She always had to subtract twelve and do the math. Some parts of the military stay with vets forever.

With the investigation in high gear, Alyssa Stevens put James on a flight to JFK from Edinburgh and granted his wish to head straight for California to decompress. She would meet him there in a few days to debrief.

Now handcuffed to a hospital bed in London, Andrey Morozov had recovered enough to tell the local detective constables everything he knew, which actually put him under the microscope in ways he hadn't intended. He thought he was helping, and before long he was meeting with officers from MI5 as well.

He shared his history with the deceased Igor Kozlov, including watching him go off the rails and become radicalized as the Russian assault on Ukraine continued, and the West's sanctions put pressure on working families at home in Belarus.

Andrey's future was undetermined. If Aadan Mukhtaar was alive, perhaps they could use Andrey as bait. MI5 believed Mukhtaar was too smart for such a ruse. After all, the mastermind of at least three terror attacks in Europe had evaded capture—and kept his identity hidden—for more than twenty years.

Francois Thies opened the door to his Zurich home and was greeted by Swiss authorities who had a lot of questions about his banking practices and his clients. He refused to answer anything and was led away in handcuffs as his wife and two children watched in tears, unaware the man in their life had been helping criminals fund their enterprises for decades.

Authorities believed Thies was soft, too attached to his lifestyle, and they would eventually break him. As he sat in a cold room on a metal chair, his hands chained to an iron bar bolted onto a steel table shiny enough to reflect his image, he stared into the one-way mirror on the wall, angry at himself for talking too much. His love for gab had likely put him here, and he wondered if Frank Murphy or Mathieu James of the *International Herald Tribune* were behind it.

Three days later, under a canopy of blue skies and a wicked arctic breeze greeting it head on, a 45-foot Beneteau Oceanis motored without sail into the Inner Oslofjord. Its deck railings were caked in ice, and its crew was topside, bundled but pleased to reach port after a treacherous journey.

Ports accessible to the North Sea were being watched by intelligence agencies, military and local law enforcement. Otherwise, the $400,000 sailing yacht would be just another ship in the water.

Aboard a small vessel patrolling the waters, a Norwegian Maritime Authority officer assigned to the Port of Oslo noted the arrival of the Beneteau Oceanis, entered it into the database tied to a cloud server, and added this note:

Vessel is towing a black Zodiac. Departure point unknown. Will monitor.

ACKNOWLEDGMENTS

It's hard to imagine any writer not having an early foundation built on reading. My late grandmother was a huge influence in my love for reading. She would tell stories of me reading the newspaper at age four, which might explain why I later became a journalist.

Grandma Sue would also introduce me to poetry. I didn't care for it, but she could recite just about anything from memory. She was always with a verse at the ready. Along with my grandfather Raphael, she served in World War II. He was in the Army (Pacific Theater) and she was a nurse in the Navy. Their generation read the tales of Ernie Pyle, the famed correspondent who brought the war to the doorsteps of millions of Americans.

She gifted several of his books to me which I have to this day. Coincidentally, I would follow Ernie's path and study at Indiana University.

My uncle, William Florence, was a newspaper editor. I loved visiting his family because he would take me into the newsroom and dump me with some poor reporter and let me shadow for the day. He always made me wear a tie. Today, I don't own a single one. One reporter, Mark Curnutte, mentored me for years. Mark remains one of the most gifted writers I know.

My parents, Barbara and Edward, encouraged me to explore my writing and photography passions. They let a 15-year-old me take an assignment from my hometown paper to cover the Pan American Games in Indianapolis—five hours away. I traveled alone by train and had the time of my early life. I was hooked. Unfortunately my father passed nineteen years ago. He wasn't much of a reader, but if this book was a movie I think he'd like it.

During and after college, I worked my way through the newspaper business before becoming disenchanted. I started a documentary film production company to tell stories in a different way. That run lasted 20 years before I burned myself out. When that flame was extinguished the pandemic hit, and I thought that was the perfect time to try another novel.

I failed. Again.

Four years later, completing this book was actually easier than I expected. Easy being relative, of course. I say that as someone who was unable to finish three prior attempts since the early 1990s at writing a novel. The truth is, I was going to regret not doing this and needed to find a new path.

Countless hours were spent researching how other writers I admire approached their books, and I borrowed many ideas and leaned into some of my own strengths to draft a plan that had to work.

Thankfully it did. And now the taps are open. As I write this on a warm summer day in Southern California, my second novel is complete and the sequel to *The Scotland Project* is in the works.

Life is weird like that.

Others who deserve recognition include Kieran and Veronica, who both read early drafts and provided critical, honest feedback. They are founding members of The Circus. If you know, you know.

Patricia Graves, the final editor of this book, delivered everything needed to this undisciplined writer of words. I am grateful for her keen eye and expert feedback.

Finally, I am appreciative of the frank conversations with Andrew Watts at Severn River Publishing and its Ten Hut Media imprint along with my publisher Julia Barron and publishing director Amber Hudock. It truly takes a village.

ABOUT THE AUTHOR

Matthew Fults is an award-winning writer and documentary filmmaker. He is a former newspaper journalist and editor, an accomplished brand photographer, and his documentary work has been praised by *The New York Times*, *Wall Street Journal*, *Detroit Free Press*, *Boston Globe* and *TV Guide* among others.

He is known for possessing a cinematic writing style and crafting scenes so rich with sensory detail that readers feel transported into the story. His travel essays have been humorously described as "the love child of Hunter S. Thompson and Ernest Hemingway on LSD," and his long-form story-telling is known for its poignancy, exceptional realism and literary style of journalism. Matthew lives in Southern California.

matthewfults.com

Made in the USA
Las Vegas, NV
26 December 2024

15364902R10194